BLOOD OF THE INNOCENTS

When two teenagers go missing on the same day on Mariner's patch, it seems to be nothing more than a coincidence. Yasmin Akram is the talented grammar-school educated daughter of devout Muslim professionals. Ricky Skeet disappears after storming out of his council house following a row with his mother's latest boyfriend. Mariner is not happy when – following media pressure – he is taken off the Skeet case and reassigned to the more politically sensitive investigation, but he soon finds that the picture of Yasmin her schoolfriends paint is far from her parents' description of her as a total innocent...

BLOOD OF THE INNOCENTS

BLOOD OF THE INNOCENTS

by

Chris Collett

Magna Large Print Books
Long Preston, North Yorkshire,
BD23 4ND, England.

British Library Cataloguing in Publication Data.

Collett, Chris
    Blood of the innocents.

    A catalogue record of this book is
    available from the British Library

    ISBN   0-7505-2396-4

First published in Great Britain in 2005 by Piatkus Books Ltd.

Copyright © Chris Collett 2005

Cover illustration © Adam Randolph by arrangement with
Piatkus Books Ltd.

The moral right of the author has been asserted

Published in Large Print 2005 by arrangement with
Piatkus Books Ltd.

Magna Large Print is an imprint of Library Magna Books Ltd.

Printed and bound in Great Britain by
T.J. (International) Ltd., Cornwall, PL28 8RW

To Richard for your love, support
and encouragement

Chapter One

Striding to the window, Tom Mariner pulled shut the metal frame with an irritable bang, before releasing the Venetian blind. It jerked down notch by notch, snagging on its tangled cords as if in the final throes of death. The immediate problem was solved, reducing the hammering and banging from the extension work in progress below to a series of muffled thuds, but neither action did much to reduce the heat or glare from the mid-morning sun that beat in relentlessly through the south-facing window. His was not an office designed for heat waves. It wasn't designed for cold snaps either, but right now the prospect of a biting frost or a raw wind was as distant as the Outer Hebrides and the sting of icy rain on his face would have been a refreshing relief. He needed a drink.

But the water cooler when he got there was empty and there were no replacement bottles, forcing him to sift through the loose change in his pockets and head for the soft drinks machine on the ground floor. He joined a long queue, then when his turn came the machine greedily swallowed his money then refused to cough the can. He was poised to give it a hefty kick when probationer DC Liam Grady intervened, calling down the stairs to him. 'There's a Ms Streep on the phone, sir. Claims she has some new information on a city-centre armed robbery you dealt with back in March. I did ask if she could come to the station, but she insisted that you'd want to go out to talk to her. To be honest, she sounded a bit of a fruitcake. Do you want me to deal with it?'

Mariner slammed his open hand into the side of the machine in frustration. 'No, it's OK. I could do with a break. I can get a drink while I'm OUT!' He glared at the machine. 'And if she is some kind of head case it won't take me long.'

'Right, sir,' said Grady uncertainly.

In fact it took Mariner less than ten minutes to get from the station to the address given: a house on a small but exclusive, newly built estate in leafy Bournville. Four-and five-bedroom executive homes set in several immaculately landscaped acres, their combinations of red-brick and mock-Tudor fascias rendering each one marginally unique. Number 18 stood towards the end of the winding cul-de-sac. Mariner walked up a block-paved drive, past a gleaming new MG soft top and pressed the doorbell. After a moment the door cracked open a couple of inches and behind it, out of sight of the street, Mariner saw Ms Streep.

Young and pretty, her thigh-length, burnt orange silk shirt complemented the colour of her eyes. As he watched she let it fall open at the front, revealing that underneath she was wearing very little. 'Please, come in, Inspector,' she smiled.

Mariner swallowed hard, his professionalism on the line. No contest really. With a furtive glance around to check that he was unobserved, he stepped into the hallway and as the door closed on him, she took hold of his tie, pulling his face down to her level and kissing him full on the mouth, while her other hand grabbed at his already expanding crotch.

'You have to stop doing this, Anna,' Mariner said, some time later, lying back on the pillows, his pale skin glistening with perspiration, while she sat astride his abdomen, now wearing only the silk shirt. 'Someone at the station is going to catch on to these women all specifically asking for me to make house calls when I'm meant to be working. I can't always just drop everything on a whim.'

Anna was pragmatic. 'This is only the second time, and you're entitled to some kind of lunch break, aren't you?'

'In theory, but you know how that plays out.'

'It's the only time during the week when I can guarantee that Jamie's out of the way. It seems a shame to waste the opportunity. Besides,' she added, artfully, 'you do always have the option of turning me down.' She slid down over his thighs and started work again.

Mariner's gaze swept over her exquisite body as he felt the blood flowing back to his groin. She'd put on a little weight since he'd first known her, rounded out a little, but all that had done was add to the perfection. 'Oh, yes,' he said, as if she'd pointed out something new.

In truth he was a little afraid of what might happen if he did decline these invitations. Anna had saved his life, well, his sex life anyway. Single-handedly, as it were, she had resuscitated his seriously ailing libido and now, to paraphrase Harold Macmillan, he'd never had it so good. Added to which, she was bright, she was great company and he ... well, he liked her ... a lot. It was too much to risk. Except at times like this, when he felt guilty knowing that he should be somewhere else, with his mind on other things. Fighting his natural urges, he raised himself reluctantly up on his elbows. 'I really should go.'

'OK.' Anna stopped what she was doing and climbed off him, eliciting another sigh. Her casual acceptance of the demands of his job disconcerted him. His ego would have liked the occasional protest, except that wouldn't have worked either. It never had with previous girl-friends. And Anna didn't have time to get hung up on what else may or may not be commanding his attention. Since assuming sole responsibility for Jamie, her autistic younger brother, she'd been presented with a whole raft of needs and demands that had to take precedence. Mariner understood that – most of the time.

Before dressing, he ducked under the shower for a few minutes, putting on Anna's lacy shower cap to keep his hair dry. He didn't want the other detectives on the squad thinking he'd developed a sudden fetish for showering in the middle of the day, even during a heat wave.

'Lovely,' said Anna when he reappeared still wearing the cap. 'And there's a pair of French knickers in the drawer–' Mariner snatched off the hat and threw it at her, spraying her liberally with water, making her wriggle and shriek and giving him the overwhelming urge to re-join her on the bed. 'What shall we do on Friday night?' he asked instead, reaching for his boxer shorts.

The hesitation was answer enough. She wrinkled her nose. 'Actually I fancy a quiet night to myself. I've got stuff to do.'

Mariner curbed his disappointment. 'Saturday then?'

'If you fancy coming begging with me.'

'Begging,' Mariner repeated, checking that he hadn't misheard.

'Look in the back bedroom.'

Mariner walked through, buttoning his shirt as he went. He pushed open the door, or tried to. After a few inches it jammed and when he poked his head through the gap, his eyes lit on an Aladdin's cave piled high with consumer booty: a wine cellar, electrical store and toy emporium all crammed into the tiny, confined space.

Letting the door close, he went back to Anna. 'If you've started shoplifting I'll have to turn you in, you know that.'

She ignored him. 'It's for the tombola stall at Bournville festival next month, to raise funds for Manor Park,' she said, proudly. 'Don't you think I've done well?'

'Manor Park's nowhere near Bournville,' said Mariner. The festival was a local event held in the grounds of the Cadbury factory, not two miles away, whereas Jamie's respite care facility was located a good six miles out of town, deep in the Worcestershire countryside.

'It doesn't matter, apparently. We're a registered charity, so they're happy to accommodate us. All we have to do is find a day's worth of prizes.'

'We?'

'Simon's helping me.'

'Oh, great.' A stab of irritation provoked by the mention of Jamie's care-worker forced out the response with more sarcasm than he'd intended.

Anna chattered on, oblivious. 'That might look like loads in there, but it'll be nowhere near enough to keep us going for a whole day. This Saturday we're targeting Harborne and Bearwood, asking all the shops if they've got anything to donate.'

'I'm not sure if that's legal.'

'We're only asking them. They're at liberty to say no.' She smiled one of her most persuasive smiles.

'Same as me then; Hobson's choice.' Mariner sat on the edge of the bed to tie his laces.

'You could donate something,' she said suddenly as the thought occurred. 'Granville Lane, I mean.'

'What, like a CS canister signed by the chief superintendent? That would be a coup for an adventurous five-year-old.'

'A weekend for two in the cell block? Or a set of handcuffs. I can think of a few couples who'd go for that.' Her smile was pure mischief. 'There must be something. What about a tour of the nick?'

'I'll give it some thought,' said Mariner. 'In all the spare time I'll have on Saturday.'

'Poor old you. Look, this is the least I can do. Manor Park has been a lifeline for me.'

'I know.' God, she was gorgeous, even with a face like that on her. And she was right. Manor

16

Park had made a huge difference to her life, and his.

'Shall I give you a call when we've finished?' she said. 'We could go out somewhere to eat.'

He sighed. 'I suppose it'll have to do.' Fully dressed, he leaned over and gave her a slow parting kiss. 'I'll talk to you soon.'

But driving back to the station Mariner couldn't shake off the creeping sense of dissatisfaction. He hadn't meant to sound so aggrieved. His reaction was especially ironic given that Anna's independence had been, for him, one of the big attractions in the first place. It had been liberating to be with a woman who had more obligations than he did, and who wasn't constantly checking up on him. But somewhere recently the balance had shifted and increasingly the relationship seemed to be only on her terms.

In the beginning her commitment to Jamie had made it inevitable, and Mariner had waited patiently while Anna did what she felt was right by her younger brother. But now with regular respite care Jamie was becoming more independent, and Mariner had always assumed that in consequence they'd get more time together. Instead, she just seemed to find other things to occupy her, such as this round of frenetic fundraising. The fact that she was completely open and honest about her intentions, giving him absolutely no reason to feel threatened, nor casting him as the selfish one, only salted the wound. This was a new experience. Having always been used to being more needed than needy, he found that the reversal wasn't a comfortable one.

17

The air conditioning had made his car just about tolerable by the time he pulled into the station car park, and he'd have liked to have languished a while in the relative cool. But, glancing up, he caught sight of a familiar figure pacing the pavement outside the main doors, dragging anxiously on a cigarette. He got out and walked over to her.

'Colleen?'

The young woman turned to flick ash on to the pavement. 'You took your time.'

'I was out on a call.' Shagging my girlfriend, but we won't go into that. 'What's up?'

'It's my Ricky,' she said. 'He didn't come home last night.'

Here we go again, thought Mariner, but he said nothing and hoped that his face had stayed in neutral. Mariner had known Colleen Skeet for more than ten years, back when he was in uniform and her husband used her as a punch bag on a regular basis. She must be in her mid-thirties now, though she still looked little more than a kid herself, small and painfully thin, her mousy hair pulled back from a pale, freckled face into a tight ponytail. Today, only the dark circles beneath her eyes betrayed her age and the degree of her anxiety.

'Have you reported it in there?' Mariner nodded towards the station.

'They said I could talk to someone. But I wanted to wait for you.'

'Well, here I am. Let's go inside. It's cooler.'

'I can't smoke in there.'

'You can smoke in an interview room.'

'You don't like it though.'

'Christ, Colleen, when did you start considering my sensibilities?' It raised a weak smile and Mariner pushed open the door. 'Come on.'

'So tell me what's happened.' The interview room was eight feet square, with a tiny window, no air and Colleen was putting a flame to her third Marlboro Light. She was right. Mariner didn't like it. But for her sake he put up with it. Doing his public duty.

'Ronnie turned up,' she said, blowing out smoke. She was sitting back in her seat, one hand cupped beneath an elbow. 'He was there Saturday afternoon when I got home from work.'

Mariner shook his head in despair. 'Why do you let him in?'

'He's the father of my kids.' Her eye contact was fleeting, defensive. 'Whatever he might have done, he's still their dad. He'd brought Ricky the new Man U shirt, when I'd already said he couldn't have another one.'

'All the options round here and he still supports Man U?' Mariner shook his head sadly. 'That lad's got no sense of loyalty.'

'Ronnie was spinning all sorts of yarns, you know, all the usual crap about how he'd sort things out and one day he'd come home and we could be a real family.'

'I hope you didn't fall for it.'

'What do you think? He'd already had a drink. Ricky knows it's all rubbish too, but underneath it all he really wants to believe him. Ronnie might not have been the best husband but he was good

19

with Ricky; taking him fishing and to the foot-ball. Ricky would love to have his dad back and us be a happy family again.'

'Wasn't all that happy as I remember it,' said Mariner.

'You know what I mean. Anyway, Ronnie stayed all day Sunday, took Ricky down the social club with him, stopped the night. On the sofa.' She emphasised those words. 'When we got up Monday morning, Ronnie had done his disappearing act. Ricky was disappointed but I thought he'd get over it. I mean, it's not the first time, is it? When he was little it didn't seem to matter so much; he had me. But now he's growing up. He sees his mates going off to the match or down the pub with their dads and he knows he's missing out.'

'How old is he now?'

'Fifteen, the kind of age where he needs a man about.' She looked up at Mariner, catching him off guard. 'You must remember that.'

Mariner had forgotten how well Colleen knew him. A moment of indiscretion in the dead of night, when she was going through a bad patch; her second beating within a fortnight. 'My dad used to hit me too,' she'd blurted out, through swollen lips, as they'd sat beside each other in A&E. 'I must deserve it.'

'That's rubbish,' he said. 'Nobody deserves this.'

She'd laughed, a short bitter laugh. 'Yeah, I don't suppose your old man ever laid a finger on you.'

'No,' he admitted. 'But that's only because I've no idea who or where he is.'

She'd looked at him differently after that.

'It's too long ago,' he lied now. 'I've forgotten.' And in his case there had never been any question of his dad turning up. He wondered if having a dad who comes and goes was worse than having one who's non-existent.

'Anyway,' Colleen went on, 'Ricky went off to school as usual Monday morning, a bit quiet but I never thought anything of it. He wasn't there when I got home from work that night. He must have come in after I'd gone to bed. Then last night, he didn't come in at all. His bed hasn't been slept in.'

'Ricky has done this before,' Mariner reminded her gently. 'Gone off.'

'Not like this. A couple of times he's stayed out all day at the weekend, and sometimes late after school, too.' She leaned in towards Mariner, urgency written all over her features. 'But he's never been out all night. First thing, I got a call from the school asking where he was because he hadn't turned up. When they talked to his friends – and that didn't take long – they hadn't seen him since yesterday afternoon. They got let out early because of the heat. Ricky hasn't stayed out this long since before Ronnie left us.'

'No.' The times Ricky had disappeared before were the occasions when he'd been an unwilling witness to his dad laying into his mum. As gentle as his dad was violent, Ricky hadn't stood a chance. The last time he'd run away it had been in shame because he hadn't been able to protect his mother when she'd needed it. He'd been ten years old. Afterwards, Mariner had spent a lot of

21

time with the boy, trying to reassure him that it wasn't his fault. They'd got to know each other pretty well, too.

'When Ricky stays out all day, have you any idea where it is he "goes off" to?' Mariner asked.

Colleen shrugged. 'It's not with his mates. And when I ask him he just says "around". Typical teenager.'

'How's Kelly?' In the past it was Colleen's older daughter who'd been the real headache, disappearing for days at a time.

'Kelly's settled down now. She's got a baby of her own and a nice fella.'

'Are you sure Ricky hasn't taken a leaf out of her book?'

'Ricky's different: he's quiet, sensitive. He's never stayed away all night. And he never misses school. Something's happened to him.'

No, that was another thing: Ricky didn't miss school. The boy's genetic make-up was a mystery. Against the odds, he was a studious kid with big ambitions and the common sense to know what he had to do to achieve them.

'Is everything all right at school? Nobody's giving him a hard time?'

'No.'

'He hasn't fallen out with his mates?'

She snorted. 'He hasn't got many to fall out with. You know Ricky, he keeps himself to himself.'

'Any girlfriends on the scene?'

'No.'

'What about you?' Mariner asked. 'Are you seeing anyone?'

'A guy called Steve. He's a friend.' A touch of

defiance crept in. 'A good friend. We've been together nearly a year.'

'Does Steve get on all right with the kids?'

'Yes. No. He finds Ricky hard because he's always got an answer for everything, always coming out with these long words. But he wouldn't be enough to make Ricky stay out all night. I know it.' She stubbed out her cigarette in a final gesture of defiance.

'All right, we'll ask around and see what we can dig up,' said Mariner. 'I'm sure Ricky will turn up with a good explanation for all this. I want you to go home. Let me know if you hear anything and we'll keep you posted. And try not to worry, eh?'

She snapped the Zippo and sucked the weak flame into her fifth cigarette. 'Easy for you to say.'

Showing Colleen out, Mariner stood for a few moments breathing deeply, taking advantage of the relatively clean air while he was outside. Ricky Skeet was a puzzle. The disappearing act was out of character, but then he was fifteen: a difficult age even without the unsettled home life. Colleen was right to be worried, but the chances were that seeing his dad again had provoked emotions that he couldn't handle and that in the fullness of time, when he'd got over the turmoil, Ricky would turn up. The kid probably just needed some space. Mariner heard the door behind him swing open. It was Delrose, the civilian receptionist.

'DCI's looking for you,' she called. 'And he seems to be getting a bit impatient.' Well, wasn't this developing into a perfect day? What a shame Anna's pitch at the festival wasn't the wet sponge

23

stall. Suddenly he had in mind a prime target. His mood deteriorating with every pace, Mariner went straight to the DCI's office and knocked on the door.

'Come.' The request was barely audible but Mariner went in anyway. As Acting Detective Chief Inspector Gavin Fiske looked up from his desk, Mariner was reminded of a tortoise emerging from its shell, blinking slowly with a smile that didn't hang around long enough to reach his eyes. His movements were slow and calculated, like those of a reptile conserving energy in the heat. A fly buzzed around the room and it would have been no surprise to Mariner to see the DCI flick out a long tongue to catch it.

As smooth as Jack Coleman was rough, Fiske was a good ten years younger than Mariner; all designer suits and Samsonite briefcase, with just the right amount of gel styling his hair and doubtless a bathroom cabinet full of 'male grooming products' at home. His bag for the gym sat conspicuously on the floor of his office, the habit reflected in the toned physique but not the unhealthy, pallid complexion. Mariner could never understand the logic of paying hundreds of pounds for the privilege of walking on a machine in a room full of sweaty bodies when the same effect could be achieved in the fresh air and changing landscape of the countryside. How could MTV ever seriously compete with the stunning view over the vale of Evesham from the top of Breedon?

In the three weeks that Fiske had been in the station covering while Jack Coleman was

24

seconded to Complaints Investigation Bureau on an internal investigation, he'd already acquired a nickname. The first time Mariner had heard him referred to as 'Fido' he didn't get it.

'Thinks he's the big I Am,' a staff sergeant enlightened him. 'Like the dog food.'

'Ah,' Mariner had said. 'And I'd assumed it was because he thinks he's the dog's bollocks.'

'Glad you could find a window,' Fiske said. It took a couple of seconds for Mariner to work out what he meant. The consensus was that Fiske had risen so quickly through the ranks partly due to his snappy vocabulary. He could ring-fence like no other and he was the first man Mariner had come across who regularly diarised, something that sounded to him like a complex medical procedure. What Fiske didn't yet appreciate was that though the buzz words might impress interview panels, in the real world they had the potential to make him a laughing stock. He'd walked into his first briefing at Granville Lane deporting a shield of ignorant self-confidence that had temporarily protected him from the sniggers that greeted his lexical repertoire, but that wouldn't hold for long. Mariner couldn't wait.

'Interesting afternoon, Inspector?' Fiske asked now, his unfortunate nasal inflection adding value to the patronising tone.

'Yes sir, I've been following up on a missing juvenile.'

'And prior to that? I've been trying to raise you on your mobile.'

'I'm sorry. The battery must be flat, sir.' Mariner hedged, suppressing the slightest twinge of guilt.

'Do I look like a complete prat, Mariner?'

What a question, thought Mariner, wondering if there was any way he could get away with the truth. Luckily the DCI saved him from himself. 'Where were you?' he demanded.

'I was responding to a call sir, PC Grady can conf–'

'Oh yes, from a "Miss Streep". Would that be Meryl by any chance? Fitting you in between filming, was she?' Guilty as charged, Mariner was annoyed to find himself colouring in response. How the hell did Fiske know where he'd been, unless he was checking up on him? Fiske didn't wait for a reply. 'Not exactly the example we want to set for junior officers, is it?' he said mildly. 'If you've ambitions to become Granville Lane's very own Peter Stringfellow, I suggest you wait until the end of the working day like the rest of us.'

'Thanks for the analogy, sir.'

But for all that, Fiske's irritation was carefully controlled. I'm on your side, said the knowing smile. We're all lads in this together. Failing to realise that Mariner wasn't together with anyone nor had he ever been.

The dressing-down complete, Mariner started towards the door. 'I'll take more care in future, sir.' In more ways than one.

But Fiske hadn't finished. 'Talk me through this missing juvenile.'

Stupidly, Mariner mistook the command for interest. 'Ricky Skeet, aged fifteen, went out yesterday morning but didn't come home.'

'Where's home?'

'Nansen Road. It's on the–'

'Oh, I know where that is.'

Mariner wasn't surprised. Long and winding, Nansen Road took its name from the grim council housing estate through which it ran, and whose reputation was notorious. Built in the 60s when housing was cheap and shoddy, the development comprised rows of boxy white stucco houses, interspersed with more space-efficient low-rise flats and maisonettes. During the 70s, the local authority had made it their policy to rehouse 'problem families' on these estates, in the hope that they would learn from their more socially conscientious neighbours. Of course that wasn't the direction in which the osmosis occurred. Instead, what had subsequently developed was a ghetto of problem families living alongside those like Colleen Skeet who couldn't afford to move on. It was also one of the crime hot spots of the locality and it was clear that Fiske had already passed judgement.

'Why wasn't this just reported to the duty sergeant and passed to uniform?' he asked.

'I have a history with this family.'

'Oh? Would that be personal or professional?'

Mariner hardened his voice. 'Colleen Skeet's former partner was violent. Over the years I got called to the house a number of times–' Where he'd spent hours trying to persuade Colleen to go into a refuge. On one occasion he'd succeeded, but she hadn't stayed long.

'Was?'

'Ronnie Skeet did everyone a favour and

27

cleared off a couple of years ago, with another woman.'

'And is that the sole basis for your relationship with this family?' Mariner hesitated. 'I can look up the case notes,' Fiske reminded him.

'The older girl has been in trouble: truanting, shoplifting, that kind of thing. She's run away before, too.'

'So. Not what you'd call a model family.'

'Colleen's had her share of problems over the years, yes, sir. She's a woman on her own trying to raise her kids and keep them from being poisoned by the influences around them. It doesn't make her a bad person. And I thought that was what we were here for, sir. To help people who are in trouble.'

'Don't lecture me, Mariner. Are we sure that this is a genuine disappearance?'

'I'm sorry, sir?'

'Are we sure that this boy wants to be found?'

'His mother wants him found. That's why she came to me.' Mariner made to leave. 'And if there's nothing else, sir, I need to get started on the risk assessment paperwork.'

'Someone else can do that. I need your expertise on something else.' *Expertise.* Good choice of word. Mariner should have been flattered. He wasn't.

'With respect, sir, this mother has approached me directly. I know the family and I think I'm the person best placed to–'

'And as your superior officer I think *I'm* the person best placed to determine your priorities, don't you think, Inspector?'

'And they are?'

'Another missing teenager.' His face said that the irony wasn't lost even on him. Christ. The OCU covered only one small area of the south of the city. What were the chances of two kids disappearing on their patch in the same day? 'In this case it's a seventeen-year-old girl,' said Fiske. 'I want you to handle it.'

Mariner had a premonition of a poisoned chalice heading his way. 'But I'm already–'

'Charlie Glover can take that on.'

'So that I can look for another missing kid? That makes sense.'

'Don't play the smart arse with me, Mariner. It won't do you any favours.' Fiske's voice was icy. 'This case is not the same as Ricky Skeet.'

'Oh, really,' said Mariner, unconvinced.

'I want you to follow it up. Consider it an order.' The pulse at his temple throbbed dangerously.

'Yes, sir.' And fuck you, too.

Fiske handed Mariner a picture of a young Asian girl who smiled happily from a standard school portrait. She looked younger than seventeen and wore the uniform of the girls' high school located in a middle-class residential area, several miles from Kings Rise Comprehensive where Ricky was a pupil. Middleham Road ran between the two, parallel to the Birmingham to Bristol railway line. The two kids were quite literally from opposite sides of the track. 'Yasmin Akram,' Fiske announced, importantly. 'Last seen by her friends getting her train at Kingsmead Station yesterday afternoon to go home. It's worth bearing in mind that her parents have some influence within the Asian community. I think you'll find the risk assessment profile on this one rather more urgent.'

So that was how this one was different. Yasmin Akram had hit the jackpot. She was young, female and respectable middle class. At one time, being Asian might have counted against her, but not any more, not in the wake of the Macpherson report; the enquiry into police racism that had followed the bungled investigation into the murder of black student Stephen Lawrence. These days, being from a minority ethnic group could be a positive bonus. Mariner bit back his objections. On that score Fiske was right, it wouldn't do him any good. The pretty teenager smiling up at him had to be found. She was young, vulnerable and at risk. It just didn't meant that Ricky Skeet wasn't.

'Her parents, Shanila and Mohammed Raheem Akram, run an independent Islamic prep school, Allah T'ala, in Sparkhill,' said Fiske. 'And until we've established that this is a simple missing persons, we need to keep our options open.'

Mariner picked up the inference immediately. For months now, right-wing nationalist groups had been taking advantage of the public fears of Islamic fundamentalist terrorist incidents to stir up unrest, and in recent weeks a number of Islamic institutions had themselves been under attack – from the eighty-six mosques in the city to countless businesses, large and small. Muslim schools in the city were amongst the obvious targets, mainly because of the threat posed by their academic success.

'If this does turn out to be politically sensitive,'

Fiske went on, 'I need someone on it who knows what they're doing and will cover all the angles right from the beginning.'

Coming from Jack Coleman, that would have been a compliment, but Mariner wasn't naive enough to take it as such from Fiske. The DCI was simply covering his own back. Mariner had the distinct impression that Fiske was out of his depth already. His previous posting in rural East Anglia had been poor preparation for a city as huge and socially complex as Birmingham. And while he'd probably read a few textbooks and attended a couple of seminars on equalities, Mariner doubted that Fiske would have any real grasp of the issues involved.

At the turn of the millennium, Birmingham had become the first European city to no longer have a single ethnic majority and Mariner had lost count of the number of minority groups that made up the million plus population. The whole spectrum of racial integration was represented, from communities that remained closed and self-sufficient, to those individuals whose physical characteristics were the only indication that their ancestors weren't of Anglo-Saxon origin. Over the years, Mariner had worked with colleagues and members of the public from every back-ground imaginable, but he still wouldn't presume to understand all the subtle implications of living inside a different coloured skin.

Added to that were the infinite configurations of family life, regardless of culture or class. He also wondered how much the DCI understood about handling the press on a case as potentially

31

high profile as this. If Yasmin's disappearance should turn out to be racially motivated, then they would be eager to join the dots and draw their own conclusions.

Fiske buzzed through to his PA. 'Is WPC Khatoon here yet?' In response, the door opened and a young Asian woman came in. Almost matching Mariner for height she was generously proportioned, and Mariner was reminded of how unflattering the police uniform could sometimes be.

'This is Jamilla Khatoon, a family liaison officer who's going to be on loan to us from Operational Command Unit 2,' said Fiske. 'She'll be working with you on this for obvious reasons. Jamilla, this is DI Mariner.'

He didn't hang about, did he? As they shook hands, Jamilla's expression was guarded and Mariner was left wondering how Fiske had prepared her for this introduction. Mariner forced a smile. 'Nice to meet you, Jamilla.'

Her tentative smile stretched to one that was broad and white. 'It's Millie, sir.'

'OK.'

'I want you to keep this low key,' Fiske intervened. 'Just the two of you on the preliminaries until we know what's going on. Talk to the family, friends, the usual. If this does develop into anything, we're going to have the media and the politicians crawling all over us. So let's get it cleared up quickly and cleanly, whatever it takes.' Then if I do screw up, at least not too many people will know about it, Mariner tacked on, in his head. It was Fiske's dismissing remark.

Chapter Two

Mariner seethed with resentment on the walk down to his office. For the second time that day he was leaving an encounter feeling manipulated. First Anna and now Fiske, working him like a puppet on a string.

Although there was a strong possibility that Fiske could be right, he resented the dismissal of Ricky Skeet's disappearance as routine, and entirely down to the kind of home life the kid had. Never mind that he was bright. He didn't stand a chance. Colleen wasn't going to like this one little bit. Added to that was the clumsy assumption that as a white, male officer, Mariner needed help to handle the Akrams. He'd be the first to admit that he was far from being an expert on Asian conventions, but the initial interviews would be standard stuff, establishing the facts. This was far too much too soon.

'Congratulations on being hand-picked by Mr Fiske,' he said to Millie, not without sarcasm. 'The press would have a field day with this: prejudicial use of resources so early on. We haven't even filled out the risk assessment yet.'

'With respect, I'm not sure that it's–'

'How long have you been in the job, Millie?' Mariner ploughed on.

'Just over a year, sir.'

'Something you might want to remember. If

you want the police and media to sit up and take notice when you disappear, you'd better be female and from a "good" family. Don't ever be male and from a broken home, with a dodgy dad, like Ricky Skeet, because then the media aren't interested and the police won't give a fuck.'

'Girls are more vulnerable,' Millie pointed out.

'Which doesn't means that boys aren't,' Mariner replied, with feeling.

'No, sir. Who's Ricky Skeet?' Millie asked.

'He's another kid who disappeared yesterday. I know the family so his mum contacted me. I've just been pulled off it. Not a good use of an inspector's time, as he's probably only a runaway. No fanfare of trumpets or special resources for Ricky Skeet, but then he's the wrong kind of MisPer.'

'I'm sure the officer it goes to will give it his best shot.'

'The officer it's gone to doesn't know the family and is up to his neck in other unsolveds.'

'And you're not? Sir?'

Said so innocently, Mariner couldn't help but smile. 'Let's get a drink, Millie. And then we'll see who knows anything.'

Fresh-faced PC Robbie Thorne knew more than anyone, having been the uniformed constable who responded to the initial missing persons call for Yasmin Akram. Summoned to Mariner's airless office, he sat down to form the apex of a human triangle with Mariner and Millie, and read from his notebook.

'Yasmin was last seen yesterday afternoon at

around four thirty, when she left the girls' school with a group of friends to go home,' Thorne said. 'She took her usual route: travelling three stops on the train to the university station where she gets off and walks several streets to her house. She was last seen by the friends, running for the train at Kingsmead.'

'And no one's heard from her since?'

Thorne shook his head. 'She carries a mobile, which as far as we know is working, but she hasn't used it. That's partly why nobody was panicking at first. She wasn't even reported missing until this morning.'

'After she'd been gone all night?' said Mariner.

'The father is away and the mother thought she'd gone to stay with a friend. It wasn't until the school called her this morning to say that Yasmin hadn't turned up that she realised that wasn't the case. That's when she contacted us.'

'Since when did schools start ringing up parents to ask where their kids are?' Mariner asked, remembering that Ricky had been subject to the same checks.

Millie supplied the response. 'Since the truancy rates went through the roof and school attendance became a government issue,' she said.

'Christ, when I was at school if you wanted to bunk off, you just did it. The teachers were grateful to have fewer kids in the class.'

'That was before results and league tables got to be so important.'

'Shanila Akram seemed concerned about her husband's reaction to involving the police, too,' Thorne added.

'Where is he?'

'Away on business, she said. He's due back later this afternoon.'

'Do we know if Yasmin's ever done this kind of thing before?' asked Millie.

'Only the usual. Once when she was smaller, she threatened to run away to her auntie's, but only got as far as the end of the street.'

'This auntie has been contacted?'

'Yes, sir. Mrs Akram has been in touch with all other relevant family members.' Thorne glanced at his meticulously taken notes. 'The only thing Yasmin had with her was her school bag. She didn't even have dinner money.' He glanced up. 'The school operates some kind of credit card system so no cash is exchanged. All that we know she had on her was her travel card that covers West Midlands buses and trains.'

'So theoretically she can't have gone very far.'

'Tell us about the family set-up,' said Millie.

'The family is Pakistani Muslim. Yasmin's the second of three children. There's a sister in her twenties who now lives abroad, and a ten-year-old brother. Paternal grandmother also lives with them. The home language is a mix of Urdu and English but the mother speaks English fluently.'

'How did she seem?' asked Mariner.

'About what you'd expect: pretty distraught.'

Mariner looked over at Millie. 'So, let's go and see for ourselves.'

Yasmin may have disappeared on their patch, but both the family home and her parents' school were some distance away. The foundation grammar school system in the city meant that hundreds of kids travelled such journeys every day.

The drive over to the inner city suburb of Sparkhill was about as uncomfortable as it could be. In the mid-afternoon sun Birmingham smouldered, heat shimmering up from the road, melting and splitting the tarmac and condensing the air to a stinking, exhaust-laden smog. In the last few weeks the city had got noisy and over-crowded, too small and cramped for its one million inhabitants, causing more than the usual friction and conflict. There had been a sharp increase in the number of domestic and common assaults and the number of road-rage incidents had risen by a quarter.

Even the trees looked as if they'd had enough, their leaves limp and lacklustre. Traffic on the outer circle route this afternoon had virtually ground to a halt, leaving drivers to stew impatiently in their vehicles. Despite the full-on air conditioning, Mariner could feel his shoulders beginning to prickle and itch and he glanced up in despair at the cloudless blue sky. After five weeks the heat showed no sign of abating. News reports were full of dire warnings about hosepipe bans and forest fires. Ironic, given that spring had been one of the wettest on record, submerging whole areas of the country beneath flood water for days at a time. Impossible to imagine now.

'What does it mean, Allah T'ala?' Mariner asked Millie, as they idled at yet another congested junction.

'Literally it means "God Most High".'

'So this is the school of God Most High.'

'That's right.'

'What do you think of segregated schools?'

Millie's answer was measured. 'Lots of parents, white and black, choose to send their children to private schools for many different reasons.'

'But these are primarily religious reasons. What kind of precedent are we setting for these kids? Already in this city we have Catholic schools, Jewish schools and Muslim schools, all telling these children that their religion makes them special and different from others. Then they leave school and we expect them to forget all that and take their place in a multicultural society.'

'The good schools also teach tolerance and respect for the religious beliefs and customs of others, whatever they may be. I don't think you'll find bigotry anywhere on the curriculum.'

As if to illustrate this crossover, the Allah T'ala turned out to be housed in an imposing ironstone building with white twin spires and a high arched window; a former Anglican parish church that dominated a meandering street of Edwardian townhouses. As they drove up they saw a man scrubbing at an illegible slogan that had been sprayed in red paint along one wall. Approaching from the same direction but on foot were two women in full *burkha*, the black robes leaving only their eyes exposed. A less common sight in the southern suburbs, Mariner was well aware of the connection between the mode of dress and the perceived oppression of women, and was surprised to find himself mildly unsettled by the sight. As the women neared the door marked 'Entrance', it swung open as if by magic, just wide enough to admit them, and they were gone.

Mariner hoped that, as a man, he wouldn't have a problem gaining access. As much as he was prepared to trust Millie he wanted to be there himself to talk to the Akrams. But the school was co-educational, which presumably meant there were male teachers. Vehicles on the forecourt outside the school were of mixed vintage and power.

Despite finding a patch of shade cast by an ancient spreading beech, they stepped out of the car into what felt like a fan-assisted oven and it was with reluctance that Mariner retrieved his jacket from the hook behind the driver's seat and slipped it on. Millie rapped the door-knocker, simultaneously holding her warrant card up to the peep-hole below. Again, the door opened marginally, sucking them into a dim reception room before closing softly again behind them.

Once Mariner's eyes had adjusted from the brightness outside he could see that this was the main administration office, crowded with phones, computers and filing cabinets. The walls were decorated with childlike powder-paint creations annotated with quotations, most probably from the Koran. A small, brown-eyed child fidgeted on a chair beneath the proclamation that: 'In the remembrance of God do hearts find satisfaction.'

Millie offered a greeting *salaam* to the young girl behind the desk. 'I'm Liaison Officer Millie Khatoon, and this is Detective Inspector Tom Mariner,' she said. 'We have come to speak to Mr and Mrs Akram.'

The girl flashed a brief sympathetic smile. 'Of course. I'll tell Mrs Akram you're here.' Picking up the phone she spoke briefly in what Mariner surmised to be Urdu, before rising from her chair. 'Please come with me.'

She led them through into a small lobby and up two narrow flights of stairs, gliding with the kind of feminine grace that her flowing robes seemed to induce. Behind closed doors they could hear the insistent chatter of children's voices. Shanila Akram's was a more orderly office and lighter, thanks to the broad window that overlooked the street. As they entered, she got to her feet and came towards them, extending a hand. Mariner took it. It was delicate and as cool as marble. Small and slight, she was also dressed all in black, her *hijab* head scarf, wrapped about her face like a nun's wimple. In ordinary circumstances she would be stunningly beautiful, with flawless olive skin, mahogany eyes and a full mouth, but today those features were clouded with tension and Mariner wondered how she was managing to work.

'Our school must continue for the children,' she explained apologetically when introductions had been made, as if she was party to his thoughts. 'And I felt it better to keep busy.' Busy was the word. Outwardly in command, she was a bundle of nervous energy, struggling to maintain eye contact for more than a few seconds at a time. As the conversation progressed she continually rearranged her robes, moved papers from one side of her desk to the other and then back again. She straightened a stack of books, opened and closed a drawer for no apparent reason, and her eyes rarely settled on anything for long.

The office girl had brought in chairs behind them and Shanila Akram asked them to sit. 'Would you like tea?' she asked.

'Yes, thank you.' This Mariner had expected from past experience. He was no great fan of the traditional sweet Masala tea, but knew that the atmosphere would be more conducive if the hospitality was accepted. However, when refreshment came, it was served Western style, for which he was grateful.

'My husband should be back very soon,' Shanila Akram told them. 'I haven't yet been able to contact him.'

Good, thought Mariner, we may be here when the news is broken. We'll be able to judge the reaction.

'Perhaps you could start by telling us about yesterday evening,' Millie began.

'Of course. I arrived home at a little after seven. It's a busy time of year, there is much to do here at the school. Preparations for the end of term. The children's *Amma*, my husband's mother, is at home all day so is there to welcome Yasmin and her brother. Sanjit was at home at the usual time. I had allowed Yasmin to go and stay with her friend–' She broke off uncertainly, as if she was going to say more of that but then changed her mind.

'And the friend's name?' Mariner prompted.

'Suzanne. Suzanne Perry. The arrangement was that Yasmin would phone from Suzanne's house to let me know that she was safe, but when I got home she hadn't yet phoned.'

'Did that concern you?'

41

Almost immediately Mariner regretted the insinuation. Shanila Akram's eyes filled with tears. 'Not unduly. I thought that perhaps Yasmin had forgotten, that she was having a good time. I tried to phone her friend's parents but that's when I discovered that their number isn't listed. By this time it was getting late and I just thought... Of course I know now that I should have persisted, but at the time I had no reason to think that anything was wrong.' She was on the verge of tears, but with effort of will she looked Mariner in the eye. 'It was a mistake. Of course I realise that now. I was ready to scold Yasmin for not keeping in touch, but I was shocked when the school contacted me this morning to say that she had not arrived and that her friends had not seen her since yesterday afternoon.'

'She didn't go to stay with Suzanne?'

'No. At the last minute she changed her mind and told her friends that she was coming home instead.'

'But she didn't.'

'No.' The woman's voice had dropped to a whisper. Through the open window they heard a car pulling up on to the forecourt below. Shanila Akram turned to look out. 'My husband,' she said. But her body language conveyed anything but relief.

They heard voices below and moments later Mohammed Akram burst into the room, his face a mixture of anxiousness and bewilderment. In his mid to late forties he was unexpectedly dressed in a dark business suit with a crisp white shirt and striped tie.

Shanila Akram jumped to her feet. 'Moshi, this is Inspector Mariner and Constable Khatoon. They are from the police.'

Akram shook their hands. 'Fakhra told me you were here. What's happened now? Have there been more letters?' As he spoke Akram pulled up a seat beside his wife and they both sat.

'It's Yasmin,' Shanila said, a tremor in her voice.

'What about her?'

'She has disappeared.'

'What?'

Something subtly changed in the atmosphere. Something Mariner couldn't identify. Shanila Akram's fragile confidence had deserted her altogether and she seemed to shrink back from her husband, as if he might be angry with her. Perhaps he would. She had been left in charge of the family.

'It appears your daughter changed her mind about going to stay with her friend yesterday evening, but didn't return home either,' Mariner said. Now Akram seemed confused.

'Yasmin was to go and stay with Suzanne last night,' his wife reminded him.

'She—'

'They had to finish their project, the presentation they were doing together. Yasmin was desperate to go,' Shanila pressed on. 'But she must have decided against it after all.'

'I don't understand.'

'The school telephoned me this morning to say that Yasmin hadn't arrived there. That's when I called the police.'

Akram's full attention was on his wife, Mariner

43

noticed. He seemed to have forgotten that they were there. 'Why didn't you wait– Never mind.' Mohammed Akram's eyes narrowed as he tried to make sense of what his wife had told him, and Mariner tried to read the emotion. Shanila Akram's demeanour had completely transformed. No mistaking who was the dominant person in this partnership. Only, it seemed, when he had swallowed his anger did Akram think to ask, 'Where has she gone? Have you spoken to her friends, to the rest of the family?' He reeled off a list of names.

His wife shook her head. 'I've tried them all. No one knows where she is.'

'It seems the last people to see her were her friends, yesterday afternoon,' said Mariner.

'So I'm to understand that she's been out all night?' Akram's anxiety was beginning to gain momentum, but again Mariner felt that there was more to it than that. 'How has this happened?' The demand was made of Shanila, who visibly flinched.

'I understand your concern, Mr Akram,' Mariner said, in an attempt to diffuse the tension. 'But the fact remains that it has happened, so we need to ask you some questions about Yasmin so that we can find her as quickly as possible.'

At that, Akram seemed to get a grip. 'Yes. Yes of course,' he shook his head slowly. 'It's just so hard to take in. I can't believe it. What is it that you need to know?'

'Your wife was talking us through the events of yesterday evening.'

'Well, as I'm sure she has told you, I have been

44

away on business since yesterday afternoon.'

'May I ask where you've been, sir?'

'We are opening a school in Bradford. I went to meet with some of our staff up there for a planning meeting.'

'And you left Birmingham at what time?'

Akram thought for a moment. 'It was around four thirty in the afternoon. I had an appointment with the printer and went on from there.'

'This friend, Suzanne. Has Yasmin stayed with her before?'

'No.' It was Mohammed Akram who answered, sharply, with a look to his wife that was clear disapproval and a frisson of conflict thickened the air again. They'd need to return to that.

'She has been to Suzanne's house for tea, but always came home later in the evening,' Shanila said, softly.

'And what did Yasmin take with her?'

'As far as I know the usual things: a change of underclothes, toiletries. Other than that it's hard to tell.'

'And you have no idea where else Yasmin may have gone. Are there any friends or relatives she might have gone to stay with instead?'

'I've contacted everyone I can think of. We have family in London, Bradford.'

'What about your cousin Ameenah?' Mohammed Akram asked of his wife.

'I've called them.'

'I understand Yasmin's sister lives abroad.'

'In Lahore,' said Shanila Akram.

'Is there any chance that Yasmin would try to go there?'

45

'She doesn't have a passport yet. We are in the process of applying.'

'And she wouldn't have money for a ticket,' added Mohammed Akram.

'Mrs Akram, I'd like you to think back to Monday night; Yasmin's last evening at home. How did she seem then?'

'She was fine.'

'And nothing unusual occurred?'

'Nothing. Except ... she was late home. There had been a problem with the trains, but it's not uncommon.'

'Does Yasmin enjoy school?'

This was safer ground, easier to elaborate. 'Yes, she's a clever girl. Her teachers are pleased with her.'

'It was a big decision to allow Yasmin to go to a school outside our own religion,' Mohammed Akram added. 'But the high school has an excellent reputation and we felt it would benefit Yasmin's career prospects to go there, even though it involved extensive travelling.'

'And there was nothing bothering Yasmin that you can think of.'

A glance between them that Mariner tried in vain to read. Could have simply been a clumsy and belated attempt at mutual reassurance.

'Nothing.' It was Shanila who spoke.

'Yasmin hadn't fallen out with any of her friends?' Millie asked. 'It happens all the time with girls that age.'

Mohammed Akram spoke up. 'If there is anything on Yasmin's mind she would tell us. She's a sensible girl, and we are very close. The family is important to us and we always encourage our children to be open and honest with us, so that we can support them.' Recited like a mantra.

'Anything could have happened to her. She's so young–' Shanila Akram's voice cracked with emotion.

Millie leaned over and put a hand on the woman's arm, demonstrating the value of her presence. 'The vast majority of missing persons turn up alive and well within seventy-two hours, Mrs Akram,' she said. 'We'll do everything we can to find Yasmin.'

'We'll need to look at her room,' Mariner said, offering something practical to focus on. 'It's just routine, but the sooner we can do that the better.'

'I'll come with you,' Akram volunteered.

'That may not be necessary. You said that Yasmin's grandmother is at home? If she can let us in–'

'Yes, of course, I'll let her know you're coming.'

'Then we won't keep you any longer,' said Mariner. He took a business card from his inside pocket and handed it to Mohammed Akram. 'If Yasmin does contact you, or you think of anything, however small, that might help, give me a call at any time. And of course we, in turn, will keep you informed.'

'I'll keep in touch,' Millie reassured Shanila Akram.

'Thank you.'

It was Mohammed Akram who stood to show them out. Signalling for Millie to go on ahead, Mariner waited until he and Akram had descended the stairs and were alone in the lobby

47

before saying, 'Mr Akram, when you first came in you seemed to think that we might be here about something else. You asked your wife about some letters. Do these relate to the graffiti outside?'

Akram rubbed a hand over his face. 'And the rest. It's become a way of life for us: graffiti, bricks through the windows, dog excrement through the letterbox. Recently my car was damaged.' His eyes lit up as he seized on an idea. 'Do you think Yasmin's disappearance is connected with these incidents? There are some sick people out there, Inspector,' he said, with growing fervour. 'After September eleventh we went through a bad time.'

'We can't jump to any conclusions at this stage,' Mariner said. The incidents would have been looked into, but it seemed a little premature to be making those kinds of assumptions, unless Akram knew something they didn't. 'Do you have any thoughts about who might be behind these attacks, Mr Akram? Or anyone who might have a specific motive to harm your family?'

'Apart from the usual?' Akram glanced up at Mariner. 'My wife and I built up this school from nothing. When we both left college as trained teachers we could see that the British education system was failing the children in our communities. Many of the children around here have little English when they enter the school system, so they are already at a disadvantage. We founded this school in an attempt to give them a better start. Now every year we are inundated with applications. We have expanded several times but

48

still we don't have enough space to take all the children who want to come here.'

'And plenty of people resent success,' said Mariner.

'While others feel very threatened by Islam, as I'm sure you are aware, Inspector. Bad enough having the country overrun with Asians, let alone *educated* Asians.' He took a pamphlet from his pocket. 'We get these all the time.'

The red, white and blue flyer was being published by an organisation calling itself 'The Right Way'. Mariner had encountered it before: a right-wing organisation led by Peter Cox, a known racist and white supremacist based in the city. 'When was the last time?'

'It comes and goes.' Akram was suddenly uncomfortable. 'It's been worse since the letter.'

'What letter?'

He shifted uncomfortably. 'I belong to an Asian business consortium. We have all been targets and we were sick of the constant harassment. We wrote a letter to the local press denouncing the cowards who instigate race crimes and in particular The Right Way.'

'So you could have inflamed the situation.'

'It was impulsive, something I now regret. It seemed like the right thing to do at the time, but it probably hasn't helped.'

To put it mildly, thought Mariner.

'This came through the post at the end of last week.' Akram took from his pocket another sheet, this time of A4, word-processed on a computer, which he handed to Mariner.

49

al-Fath (The Victory)
Punish the hypocritical men and the hypocritical women. For them is the evil turn of fortune, and Allah is wroth against them and hath cursed them, and hath made ready for them hell...

'It's from the Koran,' Akram said. 'My wife hasn't seen it. I didn't want to upset her, especially now–'

'It's powerful stuff. Do you know if anyone else has received anything similar?'

'I don't know. I haven't told anyone.'

'Not even the police?'

'What would be the point? It's completely anonymous. What could you do? It could have come from anywhere.'

'And the envelope?' Mariner asked, without hope.

'It was printed anyway, but I threw it away.'

'I'll need to take this to get it checked for fingerprints.'

Akram shrugged. 'As you wish.' But they both knew that as it stood it was a long shot.

'If you get *any* further communication like this from anyone, please let me know immediately.'

'Is it possible that Yasmin could have been abducted?' Akram had clearly begun to give the idea some thought.

'I think in the circumstances it's a possibility we shouldn't discount.'

'Please help us to find her, Inspector.'

'We'll do everything we can. You said you were away from yesterday afternoon? Where did you stay last night?'

'We have family in Bradford.' As he spoke, Akram pushed open the door to the reception area, where Millie was chatting to the girl behind the desk. Seeing them, she drew the conversation to a close. Akram showed them out.

Outside on the forecourt another car had been added to the collection: Akram's top of the range black Mercedes with the registration MOH 1. It had a vicious scratch along one side. 'Yours is the Mercedes?'

Akram nodded.

'It's a distinctive car,' said Mariner.

A glint of irritation flashed in Akram's eyes and Mariner began to recognise him as a man with a short fuse. 'I work hard. I should be allowed to drive the car I choose.'

'Naturally,' said Mariner, calmly. 'I only meant that it makes it an easy target. We'll be in touch, Mr Akram.'

Chapter Three

While they'd been inside, the sun had moved round and their own vehicle was no longer shielded from its burning rays. The heat inside gusted out when they opened the doors. It wasn't until Mariner pulled out on to Highgate Middleway, where the traffic and the air moved more freely, that he asked, 'So what have we got here, simple absconder or something more sinister?'

'I thought it was interesting that Mr Akram

51

made the point about his wife reporting Yasmin missing.'

'Implying that perhaps he wouldn't have? That she's over-reacting?'

'Could be. I thought his response was unusual. To begin with, he seemed angry, then once he'd calmed down he was almost businesslike.' Millie was perceptive.

'Maybe he's just a pragmatist: OK, this is the problem, so what can we do about it?'

'So far I can't see a clear reason why Yasmin would have run away.'

'Not one that they're telling us about. But does there have to be one? It could be that even Yasmin herself doesn't know. Perhaps she just needed some time away. Sometimes it happens.'

Millie turned to face him. 'Does it? That sounds like experience talking.'

Mariner shifted in his seat. Now wasn't the time. 'Think about it,' he said. 'Yasmin's parents are both high achievers, which makes me wonder what sort of pressure they put on their children.'

'Without playing a particularly active part in their lives. They're "busy people". Sounds as if most of the parenting gets left to grandma.'

'Even worse then: at seventeen, having an elderly woman breathing down your neck.'

'Yasmin might have a great relationship with her grandmother,' Millie said.

'Yes, she might.' But the ensuing silence signalled that they both had doubts.

'Have a look in the inside pocket of my jacket.'

Reaching round to the back seat, Millie fished out the plastic wallet containing the sheet of A4.

'What's this?'

'It's the latest of a series.' Mariner took her briefly through his conversation with Mohammed Akram.

'So he was pretty quick off the mark to finger Cox's organisation.'

Mariner shrugged. 'If you've been subjected to that kind of campaign it would be only natural. Though I did wonder about their knowledge of the Koran.'

'It would be a clever tactic though: turning someone's religious beliefs back on them.'

'Maybe.'

'Alternatively, this could have come from inside the community. Sometimes the in-fighting can be worse than anything from the outside.'

Mariner turned to her. 'You've got a reason for saying that?'

'Fakhra in the office was less than discreet. Competition to get into Allah T'ala is fierce. There are forty-six places available for the new term, and they've already had a hundred and thirty-eight applications.'

'Mm, Akram said as much to me.'

'Did he also tell you that one family in particular was upset that their child didn't get a place for September.'

'Not specifically. But forty-six vacancies for a hundred and thirty-eight kids doesn't make for great odds. Not getting a place is pure bad luck, no worse than losing on the lottery. Why take it personally?'

'This child is very disabled. The father is bitter about this anyway and has turned his frustration

53

on the school. According to Fakhra he's also religious fanatic and "a bit of a nutter". The consensus is that he was the one who damaged Akram' s car.'

'Did you get a name and address?'

'Fakhra was reluctant. She said she'd want to speak to Mrs Akram first. They don't want to make more trouble for this man's family. I think she already felt she'd said too much.'

'All we'd want to do is eliminate him from the enquiry.'

Millie wafted the letter in mid-air. 'In the meantime, how seriously do we take this?'

'It's hard to say. After the quote, it all gets a bit vague, so I wouldn't want to automatically jump to any conclusions. And it's not much of a lead. It could have been written by anyone with access to a PC.'

'Even Mr Akram.'

'That had crossed my mind.'

'You didn't immediately warm to him, did you?' Millie said.

'That obvious? I agree with you that his reactions weren't quite right, anger seemed to outweigh anxiety.'

'It's not always an indicator. People can be very good at covering their feelings, can't they? His wife is clearly not coping, so he may feel it's important to try and appear in control, even though he's not.'

'I felt it was more than that. I thought he seemed annoyed with her.'

'She'd been left in charge.'

'But that shouldn't make her wholly responsible. There seemed to be some blaming going on.'

Millie didn't seem convinced. She turned her attention back to the letter. 'But if this is a genuine threat we might be looking at abduction.'

'Could be. Akram was quick to suggest that too.'

'Wouldn't we expect a ransom demand?'

'Not necessarily right away. The timing would have to be right.'

'And in the meantime?'

'We continue to treat this as a missing persons and talk to the people who really know what Yasmin is thinking.'

In terms of location there could hardly have been a greater contrast between the small Islamic school and the girls' high school that Yasmin attended. On the Granville Lane patch, it was more familiar to Mariner. Purpose built in the mid 1930s the red-brick building nestled snugly in leafy suburbia, surrounded by acres of what at any other time of year would have been lush green grass, but which had by now been scorched to a crusty, brownish yellow by the relentless sun.

Here Mariner really was glad of Millie's presence. Pre-adolescent girls had ceased to be one of his areas of expertise for going on for thirty years. In addition, these were likely to be worried adolescent girls, given that one of their friends had disappeared. The meeting with Yasmin's closest friends was to be supervised by the head of pastoral care but, even so, Mariner felt a certain apprehension as, in the middle of the afternoon, he and Millie drove slowly along the winding, tree-lined drive.

They were a little early, so were invited to take a seat in the reception area to wait.

With its coffee-table reading and lush green pot plants it was more like the lobby of a private corporation, though it lacked the comfort of air conditioning. The power of the connection between aroma and memory never failed to amaze Mariner, and the combined old-school smell of cleaning fluids and cooked food was one of the most potent of all. His lightweight suit felt suddenly constrictive as he made a conscious effort not to let his own experiences affect his perceptions. His own schooldays had been far from the happiest of his life when he'd been a square peg in a round hole at the boys' grammar school he'd attended.

Nearly six feet tall by the age of thirteen, he'd stood out, literally at first, and then socially too, when people had gradually discovered that his was a single-parent family. Lone parents back then were still a relative rarity, and amongst his particular strand of lower-middle-class popula- tion were virtually unheard of. Throw into the equation his mother's eccentric mode of dress and outspoken views and any attempts of his to blend in hadn't stood a chance. He and Anna had recently watched the video *About a Boy* and in the central character Mariner had seen shades of himself, from the bizarre dress code to the gross social ineptitude. He too had been a victim of hand-knitted pullovers and oversized home- made PE shorts. Even his lunches had been outside the norm, with sandwiches made from home-baked wholemeal bread at a time when white sliced Mother's Pride was all the rage. It was during those years, at the age when conforming meant everything, that his relationship with his mother had begun to deteriorate.

Mariner wondered how Yasmin fitted in here. Looking at the most recent school photo, displayed on the wall ahead of them, there weren't many other brown faces. Did it mean that Yasmin had a point to prove, or was she made to feel like an outsider? The staff line-up was interesting too: the proportion of men to women more evenly balanced than he might have expected and Mariner wondered not for the first time what would make any man want to work in a school full of young girls, exposing himself to unattainable temptation.

Unlike the displays at the Islamic school, here around the main photograph were displayed sketched portraits, drawn, the label announced, by members of the Year 12 A level art group: pencil sketches of body parts. The most striking one was of a male torso, from the waist to just below the chin, displaying a series of intricate tattoos on the biceps and shoulders. It was expertly drawn, the proportions just right.

'Robbie Williams,' said Millie, knowledgeably, at the same moment as the deputy head appeared. Small and trim, her powder-blue suit and bright turquoise and yellow blouse, offset by shoulder-length blond hair, Mrs Darrow stood out like an exotic bird amid the drab navy blues of the school uniforms. She apologised for keeping them

57

waiting before setting off at a brisk, high-heeled pace along endless corridors, leading them through what seemed to be an impossible number of left turns. Occasionally, confident young women clomped by in heavy shoes and perilously short skirts, surreptitiously eyeing them up, perhaps thinking that they were parents, although Millie was way too young. Mariner took the opportunity of the lengthy trek to draw out Mrs Darrow's opinion of Yasmin.

'She's a popular girl,' was the somewhat trite reply. 'She came to us from her parents' Islamic school, which is a big leap, especially socially, but she seemed to take it absolutely in her stride.'

'Her parents implied that she's had a sheltered upbringing.'

'Relatively perhaps, but she's had the opportunity to spread her wings here. In many ways Yasmin's background is very different to some of the other girls, but because she's friendly and outgoing, she gets along with people. She's also not afraid to express her own opinions. Don't be misled into thinking of Yasmin as some "poor little black girl", Inspector.'

'Would anyone particularly resent that, an Asian girl being clever and popular?'

Mrs Darrow stopped and turned to face him. 'We don't tolerate racism or bullying in this school, if that's what you're implying.'

'That's not to say that it doesn't go on.' Mariner held her gaze. 'I can't imagine that there's any school that doesn't have a problem with bullying; some establishments are just more aware of it than others.'

Mrs Darrow's colour deepened before she walked on. 'You're right of course, Inspector, realistically it happens, but I've never known it to be an issue with Yasmin.'

'You have a high reputation in the area,' commented Millie.

Had she been a bird, Mrs Darrow would at that point have preened her feathers. 'Mm. We had an eighty-four per cent pass rate at A–C and a ninety-three per cent pass rate at A level last year. It put us into the top ten in the national league tables and this year we're on stream to do even better.' The numbers, largely meaningless to Mariner, fairly tripped off her tongue.

'And is Yasmin keeping up?'

'Her GCSE grades were excellent: six A stars, three As, one B.' She frowned. 'Although as with most of the girls, she's finding sixth form a little more of a challenge.'

'Why's that?' asked Mariner.

'The work is harder,' she said simply. 'Added to which these are adolescent girls, Inspector, at the mercy of their hormones. They get distracted. It's not an uncommon thing to happen. They're under an enormous amount of pressure, to be clever, pretty and popular. Some girls cope better than others. For Yasmin there's the additional conflict that what her parents want for her isn't necessarily what she wants.'

'And what does she want?'

'At present, just to keep her options open.'

'And her parents don't?'

'Like many of our parents, Mr and Mrs Akram have fairly fixed ideas about what constitutes a worthwhile career. Often those views can be quite traditional.'

'Medicine or law,' Millie chipped in.

Mrs Darrow smiled. 'Exactly.'

'What would be her teachers' response to a drop in standard?'

'We'd encourage her to put in that little bit more effort.'

'Would that worry Yasmin?'

'It's hard to tell, but I'd guess that it might unsettle her a bit. Yasmin's a bright girl, and I know her parents have high hopes for her.'

'Are they adding to the pressure?'

'No more than any other parents who want their child to do well,' Mrs Darrow responded quickly.

'What's your relationship with Yasmin's parents like?'

'They're very supportive. Many of the resources we acquire these days are accessed through specific government initiatives, often through matched funding.' Seeing the blank expressions she continued. 'We put up half and the DfES matches it.'

'Ah.'

'Yasmin's father has been very generous in our endeavour to acquire language college status.'

'What about friends? You said Yasmin is popular.'

'She's part of an established group.'

'And Suzanne Perry, the friend her mother thought she was staying with?'

'I was quite surprised about that, I must say. Their friendship has always been rather an

60

unlikely alliance.'

'Why do you say that?'

'I'll let you find out for yourselves. Here we are.'

They had reached their destination and Mrs Darrow pushed open the door of what seemed to be some kind of recreational room. Low, comfortable chairs were grouped around a couple of square wood-effect utilitarian coffee tables. At least she'd taken on board Mariner's request to keep this informal. There were five girls present. They had been talking, but quietened politely when Mrs Darrow appeared. They weren't cocky and street-wise like the girls Mariner was used to dealing with. Even at this age, they seemed cool and sophisticated and more than a little intimidating as they appraised their visitors and Mariner wished he'd checked his flies before coming in. Each girl had put her individual stamp on the school uniform, but one in particular stood out. She looked older than the others, not just because of her spiky red hair or the heavy black eyeliner that circled her eyes. There was something about her demeanour. She was the only girl in the room to return Mariner's gaze, and some.

There were three vacant seats. Mrs Darrow offered one each to Mariner and Millie, before making introductions and taking the other herself.

As Mariner had agreed with her beforehand, Millie took the lead in the hope that the girls might be more relaxed with a woman nearer their age and therefore more inclined to open up. Mariner was impressed with the way she handled

61

it, too: just the right proportion of friendly to professional.

'Hi. We're really glad that you agreed to meet with us today. If any of you has any idea where Yasmin might have gone, it's really important that you tell us now. It goes without saying that everyone's very concerned about her, and she may be in danger.' Silence. Time to be more specific.

'Yasmin told her mum that she was going for a sleepover with Suzanne. Is that right?' Millie scanned the room, inviting a response from Suzanne. When none came Mrs Darrow offered a gentle prompt. 'Suzanne?'

'That's right.' The sullen reply came from the spiky-haired girl, who addressed her answer to Mariner, at the same time shifting in her seat and conspicuously adjusting her tiny skirt.

'So what happened?' Millie asked.

'She changed her mind.' Her green eyes remained disconcertingly fixed on Mariner's, but Millie persevered.

'Why was that?'

'She said she wasn't feeling too well. And she felt bad about coming.'

'What about the project?'

Finally, Suzanne turned to face Millie. 'What project?'

'The project you and Yasmin were working on, that you had to finish?'

Suzanne frowned. 'First I've heard of it.'

'OK. Why do you think Yasmin changed her mind about coming?'

'Because of the row with her dad,' she said with exaggerated patience, finally switching eye

62

contact to Millie.

'What row was that?'

'About the sleepover.' Mariner could imagine her tapping the side of her head in despair. What kind of thicko was she dealing with here? 'Her dad wouldn't let her come.'

Understandably, Millie was puzzled. 'I don't understand. I thought she'd had her parents' permission.'

'Her mum's,' Suzanne corrected. 'Her dad had said absolutely no, but when she knew he was going away, Yasmin talked her mum round. That's the whole point. That's why she changed her mind. She felt bad about going against her dad.'

So the Akrams were in conflict about Yasmin's sleepover with Suzanne. That explained a lot.

'So the two of you hadn't fallen out?'

'No. Yasmin just succumbed to emotional blackmail, as she was expected to do.' Her voice was heavy with contempt.

'And as far as you're aware, Yasmin went straight home from school?'

'Yes. She said it would keep.'

'What would?' Mariner asked. Suddenly he was interested and Suzanne knew it.

'She had something important to tell me, but that by the next day it would be better, there would be more to tell.'

'Have you any idea what this was all about?'

'No. But Yasmin was pretty wound up about it.' She was playing him like a violin.

'Wound up how? Excited or worried?'

Suzanne took her time. 'I'd say excited.'

'But she didn't give any hints about what it was?'

'No.'

'Who travels home with Yasmin regularly?' Millie asked. A couple of hands went up tentatively. Mariner had forgotten what a programmed response that was. 'Could you tell us about that journey, yesterday?'

At last a shrug from the girl called Emma, with dark hair tied back and an uneven, lumpy complexion. 'It was just the same as any other. We had graffiti club after school so we were late leaving.'

'Graffiti club?'

Mrs Darrow smiled. 'No, we're not encouraging vandalism, Constable. It's just the trendy name for our art club.' A couple of the girls rolled their eyes, smirking at her use of the word 'trendy'.

'What time was that?'

'About quarter to five,' the girl whose frizzy red hair was escaping from her ponytail spoke up. 'We had to go back into school because Yaz couldn't find her travel card. We had to retrace our steps, everywhere we'd been that day.'

'And did you find it?'

'It was on the floor in the art room. The last place we'd been. Typical.'

'Go on, Emma,' Millie encouraged.

'It was the same as usual. We all walked down the road together. Some of us carried on along the main road to get the bus, while Yaz went down the side road towards the station for her train. We could see it coming in as she got there,

64

so she had to run.'

'Is Yasmin the only one to get the train?'

Another girl spoke up as confidence began to grow. 'Some other girls in the school do, but none of our crowd.'

'At that time in the afternoon, most of the girls would have already gone,' added Mrs Darrow. 'The only ones left are those who stay for after-school activities. We've asked for anyone who might have seen Yasmin on the train to come forward, but they haven't as yet. It's quite possible that no one did.'

'And no one else lives near Yasmin?'

Shakes of the head, but it didn't come as any surprise. They already knew that.

'And Yasmin didn't say anything about doing anything different or going anywhere yesterday evening? Could she have gone into the city, for example?'

'Suzanne?' Mrs Darrow prompted.

Suzanne merely shrugged and it was Emma who supplied the answer. 'We had a piece of English homework that was going to be hard. Yaz was going to phone me later when she got home.'

'And Yasmin was excited rather than worried about anything. Other than the disagreement about the sleepover, nothing recently upset her?' Mariner asked Suzanne directly.

'She was pissed off with her parents, but what's new?' She glanced at Mrs Darrow to see if her language would be censured and was satisfied by a disapproving glare. Mariner could imagine Suzanne being pissed off with just about anyone. She behaved like a girl who was used to

65

controlling adults for her own ends, and it was becoming glaringly obvious why Yasmin's parents didn't want to encourage the friendship between their daughter and this girl. He wondered what it was that made her so angry. But then he remembered that most teenagers were like that at some point – for no reason at all. He was just out of touch. 'Yasmin's old man doesn't give her an inch. She's always in trouble with him about something lately. He's a psycho.'

'Suzanne, that's going too far!' Mrs Darrow was looking not at all happy about the way this was going.

Shooting her a look that would fell an elephant at nine paces, Suzanne's 'what would you know?' remained unspoken, but it reverberated around the room nonetheless. 'Look at the fuss they made about her staying late for graffiti club.' It was quoted as evidence, making Mariner wonder if this girl might have a career in law ahead of her.

'They were unhappy about that?' said Millie.

'Her dad was unhappy about anything that wasn't work. "Go to school, go home, do your homework." Yaz is expected to be a good little Asian girl.'

'Does she resent that?'

'Sure she does, but not enough to do anything about it. She's not allowed to wear make-up, but instead of standing up to her parents she just puts it on while she's on the train coming into school and washes it off afterwards. She just gives in to them all the time.'

'But she comes to graffiti club.'

'Only because Sir stuck up for her.'

66

'Has anyone got anything else to add?' asked Millie after a respectable pause. More shakes of the head.

'Well, if there's anything else you think of, we'll be giving Mrs Darrow a contact number for us. And please remember, it's vital that you tell us anything you know, however small or unimportant it may seem.'

The teacher nodded in agreement. 'I'll put the number on the common room bulletin board.' And as there seemed nothing else forthcoming, she dismissed the girls back to their lessons.

'I'm sorry that wasn't more helpful,' said Mrs Darrow when they'd gone. 'And I would take Suzanne's last comments with a pinch of salt. Some of the girls at this age do have this "the whole world's against me" mentality, usually with parents and school at the top of the list. Added to that, their imaginations are fuelled by the constant confrontations they see on TV soaps. Suzanne in particular can be something of a drama queen.'

'Who runs this graffiti club?' Mariner wanted to know.

'The "Sir" Suzanne mentioned: Mr Goodway. He's the head of D & T.'

Mariner turned to Millie for clarification. 'Design and Technology,' she grinned, shaking her head sadly. 'I expect it was plain old woodwork in your day.'

'We could do with talking to him. It looks as if he may have been one of the last adults to see Yasmin yesterday afternoon.'

'We can see if he's free.'

Chapter Four

Brian Goodway blinked rapidly at them through dense wire-framed glasses. Although school was in session, he had what Mrs Darrow referred to as a 'non-contact' period, and they found him pottering about in the technology room, which Mariner discovered to be the home of wood- and metalwork, textiles and art. Picking him out on the school photo, Mariner wouldn't have attributed anything artistic to Brian Goodway. He was too tidy, more maths or geography, with his neatly knotted tie and one of those ubiquitous tweed jackets that had gone out of fashion years ago with everyone except a certain generation of teachers, although this one didn't extend quite as far as leather elbow patches.

The classroom was a different matter entirely: a chaotic arrangement of workbenches topped by the skeletal wire forms of half-finished sculptures and interspersed with spindly easels displaying adolescent creations in various stages of completion. Goodway himself seemed surprisingly unmarked by the fallout; several pairs of overalls hanging on the back of the door took the strain.

Mariner's eye was caught by a particularly ghoulish design, not unlike those on display in the entrance hall. 'Body art,' Goodway volunteered, seeing Mariner's interest. 'If you're going to motivate the kids you have to operate on their level. The days of sketching a vase of flowers or bowls of fruit are long gone. That particular effort was drawn by a young lady in class 9G. She's been working on it for three weeks now, mainly because of the problems she's had with the proportions of the eagle's head just here, getting those feathers to sit properly.' He ran a finger along the offending area, and Mariner had the impression that whichever of the creations he had picked on, Goodway would have been able to supply exactly the same amount of detail.

Goodway showed them some still life drawings that Yasmin had been working on. One was a pencil drawing of a hand, the veins and skin texture perfect. 'Yasmin is a very talented young girl,' he told them. 'Art is a discipline like any other. Along with creativity you must have an eye for precision.' He smoothed his sparse sandy hair over his scalp and took his glasses off to wipe them on a tissue. 'Occupational hazard,' he explained.

'I understand that you fought Yasmin's corner for her when her parents were reluctant to let her stay for the club.'

'It would have been a criminal waste if she hadn't been given the opportunity to develop her talents. As it is, she's been persuaded to give up art in favour of more academic subjects at A level. Graffiti club means that she can pursue both.'

'Would she make a living at it?' Mariner asked, wondering if this was the conflict of interests with what her parents had in mind for her.

Flattening his hair again, Goodway let out a

sigh. 'As a freelance artist? Not necessarily. Art is a competitive world.' He gestured towards a photograph of three teenage children, two boys and a girl, that was pinned to the wall above the corner desk. 'That's my daughter Chloe,' he said. 'She's in her twenties now and was gifted enough to get a place at the Slade Art College in London, but she still struggles to make a living as an artist. I try to ensure that the girls here have a realistic view of what they can achieve. Encourage them to get their academic qualifications too, looking at a more structured career within the art world, perhaps within graphic design or illustration.'

'How did Yasmin seem at your class yesterday afternoon?'

'Fine. The girls seem to like the club. It's a chance to relax and shake off the shackles of prescribed coursework.' A twinkle gleamed in his eye. Despite appearances, maybe there was a rebellious streak in there after all.

'She hadn't fallen out with anyone?'

Goodway shook his head. 'You know what youngsters are like. Even if she had I doubt that I would know. It may be a more relaxed class, but I don't fool myself that any of the girls would share much with an old fogey like me.'

Mariner wasn't so sure. 'Why do you think Yasmin's parents weren't keen on her staying for the graffiti club?'

'They're naturally protective of her. The club runs throughout the year and in the winter months it can mean the girls getting home well after dark. Yasmin had a longer journey than most.'

70

'What changed their minds?'

Goodway shrugged as if it was no big deal. 'I had a chat with them and they're reasonable people.'

Not what Suzanne seemed to be saying, but then the adult perspective would be a different one. 'Thanks, Mr Goodway.'

They were nearly out of the door when Goodway called after them, uncertainly. 'Yasmin's a good kid. I hope she turns up soon.'

Mariner turned back. 'So do we, Mr Goodway. So do we.'

'He seems like a very committed teacher,' Mariner remarked, as Mrs Darrow walked them back through the school.

'He's inspirational, a real Mr Chips. We don't get many of those any more. I think having had his own teenage children helps him to stay in tune with the girls.' She was full of admiration. 'We'll be sorry when he goes.'

'Goes? He seems a little young for retirement.'

'Mr Goodway wants to spend more time with his family,' was all Mrs Darrow would say.

From the art department Mrs Darrow took them to Yasmin's locker, opening it with a master key. It revealed little. The inside of the door was lined with the ubiquitous teen posters of pop stars and TV presenters, none of whom Mariner recognised. A wad of drawings or a sketchpad fell out and scattered on the floor. The drawings were good. Some of the same 'body art' that they had seen in the classroom. On the face of it they'd learned little to progress their search, except

71

perhaps to learn that Mr and Mrs Akram hadn't been entirely candid with them.

They were standing directly underneath the bell when it rang deafeningly, signalling the end of the day. Through the open door of the classroom opposite, they watched girls filing out, dipping into a bright red plastic crate on the way.

'Retrieving their mobile phones,' Mrs Darrow explained. 'The things are a nightmare. We tried banning them completely at first, but it was hopeless as practically all the girls have them. Parents complained too that they needed to know that their daughters were safe. Ironic, given this current situation. So, instead, most teachers collect them in at the beginning of each lesson, to remove any temptation to use them.'

'Couldn't the girls just switch them off?'

'Not with text messaging. The girls can be holding lengthy conversations without staff even knowing. It's a distraction we can do without.'

'Do any ever get left behind?'

Mrs Darrow knew what he was getting at. She shook her head. 'Very rarely. It's amazing. These girls might lose everything else: clothing, books, jewellery, you name it, but their phones seem to be surgically attached. The few that are get put in lost property. You're welcome to have a look.'

They did, but of the couple of outdated units that were there, neither could be identified as Yasmin's.

'Well, thank you for your time.'

'Not at all, Inspector. Whatever we can do to help.'

'I don't get it,' said Millie as they drove from the school. 'How can someone just disappear?'

'If she wants to, it's easy.' Millie had guessed right. Mariner spoke from personal experience. He'd done it himself when he couldn't face another night of coming home to the Spanish Inquisition. His mother had taken his popularity with girls particularly hard. Although he had vague memories of the occasional short-term 'uncle' early on, latterly it had just been the two of them and, as Mariner grew, the dynamics of dependency had shifted as his mother had discarded the other facets of her life to concentrate on him. Her whole life became dedicated to her only child and, at the time when other parents were letting go, Mariner's mother clutched on with increasing desperation, until finally he had to take the initiative and break away completely. So instead of getting the bus to school one day, on an impulse he'd caught the train to Birmingham and gone to look for a job. Except for brief visits he'd never gone back.

'If what Suzanne told us is right though, it sounds as if everything wasn't as rosy in the Akram household as we were led to believe,' he said now.

'You think she was telling us the truth?'

'It would account for the tension between Mr and Mrs Akram, wouldn't it? I thought he was just annoyed that his wife had contacted us before telling him. And having left her in charge it may be natural to hold her responsible. But if she'd gone against his wishes as well... Let's go and see what we can pick up at home.'

73

The two uniformed officers who were to help with the preliminary search met them at the Akrams' house, which turned out to be a detached red-brick, large and imposing, built at around the turn of the last century. It was the home of successful people. With the shrinking of the nuclear family, these houses were normally too big to fulfil a useful purpose as a family home and several of the properties on this street displayed boards to indicate their conversion to business hotels and retirement residences. The Akrams' property was set back from the road behind a five-foot high decorative wall; the entire front of the house shaded by a dark umbrella of chestnut trees, creating a cool oasis of relief from the heat. Grandma, an elderly woman in white *mengha*, came to the door, her eyes watery, whether from age or from weeping it was hard to say.

'*Salaam Allah Kouom*,' Millie smiled, knowing that she spoke little English.

The old lady nodded. '*Walaik um-asalaam.*'

Millie explained in Urdu the reason for their visit. Scrutinising Mariner's ID, the old woman nodded wordlessly and indicated that they should follow her. Akram had phoned ahead to let her know they were coming. She led them through the house. Cool and dark with high ceilings, it was neat and tidy and deathly quiet in the absence of anyone else.

Leaving the rest of the house to the uniforms, Mariner and Millie focused their efforts on Yasmin's bedroom on the first floor. It was comfortably furnished, the décor in feminine pastels, but

74

without extravagance. The giant desk that took up most of the room was clutter-free beneath a solid shelf of reference books, and there was no CD player, TV nor any of the other usual electronic paraphernalia that most kids were reported to have these days. Half a dozen cuddly toys were neatly arranged on the bed and a further shelf displayed a number of photographs, including a formal family group, presumably taken at her older sister's wedding. Millie picked up the photograph to verify this with Grandma. The two women embarked on an animated conversation, during which Millie successfully shepherded Grandma back downstairs, leaving Mariner to continue the search unobserved.

Yasmin's hair brushes were neatly aligned on the dressing table. If they were going to need DNA ... Mariner refused to let his mind move along that track. A small jewellery box contained a few simple gold chains and bracelets. Checking in the drawers, her clothes were neatly folded. The only hidden treasure Mariner found was a small pouch of eye shadows and mascara hidden under some T-shirts at the back of a drawer. Apart from the schoolwork there were no personal items: no diaries or letters that were going to help them out.

Mariner heard the front door slam and, moments later, a small figure appeared in the doorway. Yasmin's younger brother.

Mariner smiled. 'Hello. It's Sanjit, right?'

A nod. 'You're a policeman?'

'That's right.'

'Are you looking for Yaz?'

'Yes. Have you got any idea where she might

have gone?'

The boy shrugged. 'She doesn't talk to me, except for a bit of verbal abuse.' He made a quacking gesture with his fingers and thumb and Mariner curbed a smile.

'What are you looking for?' Sanjit asked.

'Anything that might give us clues about where Yasmin is.'

'Have you found her secret box?'

'No.'

Without another word the boy dropped to the floor and wriggled on his belly under the bed, emerging minutes later with a small, cardboard shoebox. 'She doesn't think I know about it.' He handed it to Mariner. Inside were an ornately carved rubberwood chest and a ceramic money-box in the shape of a teddy bear. Mariner lifted the lid of the first. It contained more make-up, a leaflet for the Tate Modern, illustrated with a Lucien Freud nude, and a couple of tickets for the London Underground dated March of that year. 'Did you go down to London too?' Mariner asked.

'No, she went with her school.'

Euston to Embankment. Must have been a special trip if she'd preserved the tickets. And why two tickets? Yasmin and Suzanne?

The moneybox, when he prised off the stopper in its base, contained three ten-pound notes and some loose change.

'It's her pocket money,' said Sanjit. And surely the sort of money Yasmin would have taken with her if the disappearance had been planned.

'Anything unusual happen lately?' Mariner

76

asked, replacing the items. 'Yasmin fall out with anyone?'

Sanjit rolled his eyes. 'She's always arguing with Dad, stomping around and slamming doors. We have to walk on egg boxes all the time,' he said, in an approximation of the phrase.

The woodentops had given the house a good going-over but found no sign of Yasmin nor anything else unusual, and nearly an hour after their arrival, Mariner pulled out of the drive hardly any the wiser.

'Not much to help us then,' he said. 'All we know is that Yasmin had a row with her dad about staying at Suzanne's, then apparently Mum gives in while Dad's away and says she can go. Did you ask Grandma about that?'

'Yes, and she has views all right although she was coy about expressing them. Naturally she sides with her son and sees this as a direct consequence of Yasmin's mother flouting his wishes.'

'So she blames Shanila rather than Yasmin.'

'Not exactly. She just implied that Yasmin is no different from your average teenager, and that it's her parents' duty to give her strict boundaries. *Righteous women shall be obedient. And those you fear may be rebellious admonish.* It's what the Koran says.'

'Then perversely, when her mother lets her go beyond those boundaries, Yasmin decides not to go to Suzanne's after all, but for some reason doesn't make it home either.'

'Because she'd had enough of rules and wants out completely?'

'She didn't take any money with her.'

'It's not necessarily long term. It could just be a gesture. Giving her old man the finger because of the hard time he's been giving her?'

'Anything's possible.' And that was the whole problem. There was nothing to narrow the scope of the search.

Back at Granville Lane DS Tony Knox had requisitioned the CCTV footage from Kingsmead Station, where Yasmin boarded her train.

'What's it like?' Mariner asked as they settled down to watch.

Knox shrugged indifferently. 'See for yourself.'

The black and white image was crude and snowy. Knox perched on a desk behind Mariner and Millie as they watched a train draw into the station. A number of people alighted while a couple further down the platform climbed on. Then, at the last minute, to the bottom right-hand corner of the screen a figure could be seen running for and jumping on the train. A split second before the doors closed on her she turned and gave them a full facial shot. No question it was Yasmin.

Knox snapped off the film. 'The footage from the university station isn't quite so helpful.' This was the station at which Yasmin would have alighted. 'It's harder to see Yasmin: there's a lot of movement.' It was the understatement of the year. The platform was crowded and although several people left the train, they had to strain their eyes to pick Yasmin out as any of them.

'There,' said Millie, eventually. Reaching out,

she pointed to a figure moving across the bottom of the screen.

'Right height and build,' Knox agreed. 'Same colour clothing from what you can see, and a bag over her shoulder.'

'Like just about everyone else,' said Mariner.

'She's walking pretty casually, too. In no particular hurry.'

'That's Yasmin Akram?' They all turned. They hadn't heard Fiske come into the room.

'We think it might be.' Mariner remained cautious.

'Good, so we know that she followed her normal route.'

'We're not—'

But Fiske didn't want uncertainty. 'Which means that she must have disappeared somewhere between the station and her house,' he cut in. 'I understand that from there she walks through part of the university campus to get home?'

'Yes, sir.'

'In that case let's do a search of the area between the station and her home. If that turns up nothing we'll do the railway track.'

'But—'

'You'll need to talk to the university security, too. Are we absolutely certain there's no one she could be staying with?'

'Her parents have spoken to anyone they can think of. Robbie Thorne is double-checking that. And we'll do the usual phone round of hospital emergency departments. I think we should—'

'So let's just get on with it, shall we? Organise the search for first thing in the morning. I'll make

79

sure that there are uniformed officers at your disposal and we can bring in an additional search team if necessary.' He was halfway out of the door before he turned and added, 'That's good work all of you. Well done.'

'He's easily impressed,' remarked Millie when Fiske had gone.

'He's just hoping that he might be able to stop shitting himself sometime soon,' said Knox.

'That's what I'm afraid of,' said Mariner, getting up from his seat. He caught up with Fiske just outside the DCI's office. 'Arranging a search at this stage is a bit premature, sir,' he said.

'Nonsense,' said Fiske. 'We've got the CCTV footage. What more do you need?'

'It's not entirely clear. I'd like to get it enhanced to be sure.'

'But I saw it with my own eyes and your colleagues seemed pretty certain. What reason is there to delay? Superintendent Bourne is due to meet with community leaders later this afternoon and it would be beneficial to have something substantial to give them. Get it done, Mariner, first thing tomorrow.'

'I'll need to widen the investigation team,' said Mariner. 'Millie and I can't do this alone. And Charlie Glover's in the same boat.'

'Use whoever you need,' said Fiske. 'Charlie Glover's on a different enquiry. For the moment our priority is to find Yasmin Akram. If Charlie Glover doesn't like it he can come and talk to me.'

And giving Mariner no further opportunity to argue, he turned and went into his office, resolutely closing the door.

So that's what the hurry was all about: Fiske's desperation to impress Superintendent Bourne with the efficiency of his leadership. Mariner hoped that Yasmin Akram would turn up soon, alive and well. He also hoped that somewhere along the way Fiske would shoot himself comprehensively in the foot.

When he got back to the office Knox had gone.

'Isn't he a jolly soul?' said Millie. 'Not one word to me after you'd gone out.'

At the time Mariner had barely noticed but now he thought about it, Knox had seemed unusually subdued, and he hadn't been particularly welcoming to Millie. 'Promotion back to CID must be losing its novelty value,' he concluded, hoping he was right. After all, it had been a couple of months since Knox had returned to the fold following his digression, so the initial elation must be wearing off.

'Anything else?' he asked.

Picking up the phone, Millie shook her head. 'I'll start on the calls.' She'd be checking the usual: hospitals, hostels, and women's refuges, within a ten-mile radius. If that yielded nothing, they'd spread the net.

Meanwhile, Mariner ensured that the photograph of Yasmin was being circulated citywide, including to the press, and fixed a TV bulletin for the nine o'clock local news.

It was close to eleven when they both resurfaced. Now they had to sit back and wait for the results. 'We've done everything we can for now.

81

We might as well knock it on the head for tonight,' said Mariner.

'I'll see you in the morning, sir.'

It being mid-week Anna would have her hands full with Jamie, so there was little point in Mariner calling round to see her tonight. Despite the heat, the aromas of Sparkhill had lingered with Mariner and were tweaking at his appetite, so when he drove past Yasser's, his local Balti house, and saw that it was still open, it was impossible to resist stopping.

Only when he was inside did he see that Tony Knox had fallen on the same idea. Nodding a greeting, Mariner placed his order and sat down beside Knox on the bench.

'Dinner's in the dog, eh?' he joked.

Knox looked momentarily blank. 'Oh yeah,' he said, eventually catching on.

'Tell Theresa it's my fault,' Mariner went on. 'Keeping you out all hours.'

'Sure.' But unusually for the otherwise gregarious Knox, he wasn't inclined to talk. Not that Mariner minded. He was tired himself, and there had been enough talking today. So they sat in companionable silence until Knox's order was called and he got wearily to his feet.

'See you in the morning,' said Mariner.

'Right, boss.'

But ten minutes later, as he left the restaurant himself, Mariner was surprised to see Knox with his carrier bag: standing, waiting at the bus stop. He pulled over and lowered a window. 'Want a lift?'

'Nah, you're all right, boss.' Knox glanced up the road hopefully, though it was late and Mariner could see in his rear-view mirror that there was no sign of any red, white and blue double decker.

Both men knew that Mariner would have to virtually drive past Knox's doorstep on his way home and by now Mariner was curious to know what was going on. 'This is ridiculous, Tony,' he said. 'Get in.'

Knox wouldn't meet his eye, but this time he concurred.

'I didn't know your car was off the road,' said Mariner conversationally as his own vehicle began to fill with the warm smell of cumin and coriander.

'The bus is fine.'

Drawing up outside Knox's house Mariner noted the complete darkness. Knox's kids were grown up now, his daughter living with her own child and partner and his son away at university. 'Theresa not home, then,' Mariner said.

'She's up in Liverpool, has been the last few weekends. Her mother's not well.'

'I'm sorry. How old is she?'

'Seventy-two.'

'Well, I hope she pulls through.'

'Thanks.' Knox pushed open the car door. 'I won't ask you in, boss, the place is a bit of a tip. But cheers for the lift.'

Chapter Five

Closing his front door on the world, Tony Knox bent to pick up the mail from the mat. He'd recovered from that first plunging disappointment he'd felt on seeing the empty driveway, but now anticipation rose again as he embarked on the emotional bungee jump that had become his end-of-the-day ritual. He sifted through the post, each letter stabbing at him anew as he passed over bills and junk mail and found none bearing her handwriting. Disgusted, he tossed them on to the growing stack. She hardly ever wrote to anyone so why would she suddenly take to writing him letters? Especially now.

For a moment he hovered over the phone, wondering whether to check call minder now, or to wait, in the superstitious hope that patience would be rewarded with a positive outcome. Superstition lost out. Leaving his supper on the kitchen table, he returned to the phone and keyed in the number of the answering service. Two new messages. His hopes soared again. 'Come on, come on!' he urged the recorded voice. But call one was from a call centre in Delhi, asking him to reconsider his mortgage arrangements and message two was a hang-up. Cresting the wave of optimism, he came tumbling down on the other side and the searing emptiness that had taken temporary residence somewhere above his dia-

84

phragm returned: the same black hole he'd woken up with every morning for the last two weeks.

Walking back into the kitchen, Knox stared at the plastic carrier bag, smelled the rich spices, and they made him want to gag. Instead, in the lounge he picked up the next in the neat row of Glenfiddichs that he'd stockpiled over the last few Christmases. For years they'd stood untouched in the cupboard. He didn't really even like Scotch, but the in-laws had got it into their heads years ago that he did. Now, after less than a fortnight, the shelf was nearly empty. Still, it needed using up and if it got him to sleep at night and helped him to face the day, that couldn't be a bad thing. The phone rang as he was swallowing the last dregs in the glass. He raced to pick it up.

'Dad? It's Sinead.' Knocked back again. 'Mum told me. Are you OK?' Asked out of concern or sense of duty?

'I'm fine.'

'Will you be able to sort this one out?'

'I don't know, love.'

'You have before.'

'This is different.'

'Well, if you need anything, you know where we are.' The offer was cool, the onus on him. The sub-text: this is your fault, you stupid old git. Well, he didn't need his daughter to tell him that.

'Dave and the kids OK?' he asked.

'We're all good; just worried about you.' Christ, when did that about face happen? So suddenly he hadn't even noticed it. 'See you, Dad.'

'Bye, love.' Cradling the phone, he looked

85

around the room at the depressing mess: the accumulation of soiled mugs and glasses, items of clothing discarded from the nights when he couldn't face the bed they'd shared and had opted instead to sleep on the sofa. He'd clean it up later. But first he'd have another drink. He couldn't find his glass so he swigged straight from the bottle, the first mouthful burning a path to sweet oblivion.

Mariner, likewise, returned home to an un-characteristically empty house. His lodgers, Nat and Jenny, students at the university, were away backpacking in Eastern Europe for their summer vacation. After years of contentedly living alone, he was surprised to find how much he missed them. The top floor of the canal-side house was almost a self-contained unit, so it wasn't as if they were under each other's feet all the time. In fact, Mariner had seen more of them since he'd invested in a DVD player – they used it more than he did. But they'd given him an insight into the student life he'd missed out on, and he liked having them around.

Snug in the winter, in the summer the house could get stuffy, so he threw open all the windows in an attempt to entice in some stagnant air.

The light on his answer phone was flashing, so he pressed the play button. Two hang-ups and his mother: 'How are you, dear? It's so long since you've been to see me. Give me a call soon, would you? There's something I want to talk to you about.'

Mariner sighed. What scheme was she hatching

now? Something, no doubt, that would involve him in endless discussion and research on her behalf, which would come to nothing when she changed her mind, like her idea of selling up and moving to a retirement property in Weston-super-Mare. That one had kept him busy for weeks. Three times inside a month he'd even taken her down there to get a feel for different areas. Then, on a whim, she'd dropped the idea and that was when he first developed the suspicion that she'd concocted the whole thing just to keep his attention focused on her.

When he'd left home as a teenager, he'd hurt her. He knew that and had come to regret the fact, even though at the time his leaving had been pure self-preservation. It was only a matter of three or four years before their relationship was re-established, but she'd never let him forget the digression. Since that time, she'd demanded assurances that though they had their separate lives, as long as he was able, he would be there to support her. And she'd held him to his word, making sure that at regular intervals some project or minor ailment would occur that required his attention. Projects that invariably failed to come to fruition, but were enough to keep him dangling. Over the last few years her demands had increased in frequency so that she seemed to be developing classic 'cry wolf' syndrome. With a stab of guilt, Mariner thought of Theresa Knox ploughing up and down the motorway to visit her mother on Merseyside. Funny, Tony hadn't mentioned that before. How long had it been going on?

Cracking open a bottle of home-brewed Woodford's Wherry, kept cool by storing it in the lowest depths of the old-fashioned scullery, Mariner took his dinner out on to the canal-side. The water was silent and still, with hardly any sound from the surrounding city and no breeze to sway the birches on the opposite bank. With the cooling of the air the smell of vegetation was strong: Mariner even caught a hint of perfume from the single strand of wild honeysuckle a few feet away. Screaming swallows had given way to bats and crane flies, but even now the air was mild and sultry. If Ricky or Yasmin were sleeping rough tonight, at least they'd be warm.

Usually at this time of the year there would be a couple of narrow boats parked a few hundred yards up river where the two canals joined, but the low water level was discouraging most, forcing them to steer a central line or risk being grounded in the mud. In some areas of the country stretches of the waterway had even been closed. It being the close season, fishermen, too, had given up on the dark, stagnant waters and even the ducks seemed lethargic in their quacking.

In the twilight he could just make out the perfect symmetry of the guillotine lock beyond the junction with the Stratford-on-Avon canal, put there years ago for just such circumstances as these. The two canals were on different levels and it was to prevent the water running from one into the other: one of the remnants from the city's industrial past as a contest was created between the canals and the river that ran alongside.

His meal finished, Mariner took a long shower

to wash off the grime of the day, before tuning in to watch the late news report on TV.

'There are growing concerns for the safety of schoolgirl Yasmin Akram, who disappeared on her way home from school yesterday afternoon,' the anchorman said. The same smiling photograph that Mariner carried in his pocket was flashed up on the screen. 'She was last seen boarding a train for the university station, and police are appealing for anyone who may have any information about the schoolgirl's whereabouts to get in touch.' The bulletin ended with the Granville Lane telephone number. It would prompt the usual flurry of crank calls. Some anorak was bound to have seen Yasmin abducted on to a spacecraft by aliens, at the very least. An incident information centre had been set up at Granville Lane to weed out the genuine stuff.

Mariner wondered if Colleen Skeet was watching. If so, she'd want to know why there was no mention of Ricky. He'd deal with that one tomorrow.

He tried Anna's number a couple of times but strangely her line was engaged. A bit late to be canvassing for donations, he thought, but he didn't like to consider any other possibilities. And now he'd left it too long to think about calling his mother. That one would have to wait, too. Checking that his mobile was charged and switched on, Mariner went to bed.

It was an undisturbed night and Mariner woke early to another blistering morning: the sun pushing up over the skyline, already dazzlingly bright. He got to the office to find, among other things, a call from Colleen Skeet waiting to be returned. Millie was already at her desk, deep in a phone conversation; trawling the hospitals once again, just in case. Mariner gestured 'drink' and got a thumbs up in reply.

On his way to the water cooler he had to pass DS Charlie Glover's desk. Glover too was on the phone, shirtsleeves up, tie hanging loose and a thin sheen of sweat coating his pale features. He looked as if he'd been up for hours. Without breaking the conversation, he looked on warily as Mariner sorted through his in-tray, finding the file he wanted two thirds of the way down the pile.

'That's great. I'll look forward to hearing from you soon,' said Glover, concluding the call. He replaced the receiver. 'Can I help you, sir?' he asked mildly.

Mariner was reading the top sheet of the chosen file. 'Not much progress,' he observed.

Glover leaned back in his chair. 'I'm doing the best I can with just the one pair of hands, one pair of legs and a desk full of other crap.' He wasn't being insubordinate, merely stating the facts.

It's not enough though, is it? Mariner wanted to retort, even now picturing Colleen sitting at home, poised by the phone, longing for it to ring. But he kept quiet, because Glover was right. It was just one case among dozens. And it wasn't Charlie's fault that it had been pulled from Mariner and given to him.

'I've talked to the lad's friends,' Glover went

90

on. 'Not that he's got too many of those. He seems to be a bit of a loner. According to the school, he's a bright kid with a promising future. Nobody saw him beyond Tuesday afternoon when he left school. He went off on his bike. And we've checked the places his mum says he usually hangs out.'

'Fido thinks he's a runner.'

Glover shrugged. 'Could be. He's taken his life savings with him.'

'Has he?'

'All seven quid of it. Did you know he'd been talking to his mum about joining the army?'

'The army?'

'Apparently she didn't take him too seriously.'

'I'm not surprised. He's not that sort of kid.'

'Maybe he wants to be that sort of kid: a hero.' To make up for the times he hadn't quite managed it before.

'Colleen has phoned me. OK with you if I return it?'

'Sure.'

Back at his desk, Mariner made the call. Colleen picked up before the phone had even rung.

'Why have they taken you off it?' she demanded immediately.

'Something else came up.'

'Something more important than Ricky?'

'Something different.'

But she wasn't listening. 'Is it that girl? She went missing round here, too. I saw it on the telly last night.'

'Charlie Glover's a good bloke,' said Mariner,

sidestepping the question. 'He'll do a thorough job. He's talking to Ricky's friends–'

'Huh. That won't take long. Why can't they put Ricky's picture on the telly?'

'They still might. They're doing a search of the places you suggested first. Plus, we've issued a description of Ricky and his bike. We're doing all we can, Colleen.' But it wasn't enough, and it wouldn't be enough until Colleen had her son back safe and sound. That twinge of guilt returned, remembering what he'd put his own mother through all those years ago.

The knock on the door preceded Fiske. Mariner groaned inwardly.

'Anything?' Fiske demanded. 'Any results from last night's appeal?'

'It's still too early.'

'But there's nothing? I thought not, which is why we need to push on.'

Tony Knox appeared.

'The search volunteers are awaiting your briefing, boss,' he told Mariner.

'What search volunteers?'

Fiske smiled knowingly. 'I've enlisted the help of the Operational Support Unit and their team of specialist "search-trained" officers. We need to up the ante,' he said. 'Yasmin's been missing for two nights now. As you so rightly said, you need to widen the investigation team, so I thought it would be helpful if I put in a word on your behalf. Uniform have rounded up some volunteers to help do the search, too. It seems they're awaiting your instructions.'

'But as I said yesterday, sir, we still don't know

for certain where Yasmin got off the train. The last people with a definite sighting of her were the friends who saw her running for the train at Kingsmead. We don't have–'

'You have the CCTV footage.'

'I don't think it's conclusive.'

'It's enough.' Fiske's abrupt departure said the debate was over.

'They're all waiting for the party to start,' prompted Knox.

Mariner glared at him. 'Well, we'd better get on with it then.' He didn't like this one little bit. 'Either he lets me run this or he doesn't,' he muttered, on the walk to the briefing room. 'We don't have enough clear evidence that Yasmin even got as far as the university. Next thing, we'll have finance on our backs telling us we've run out of money.'

'He has to be seen to be doing something,' Jamilla said, trailing behind.

'Even if that something could be a complete waste of fucking time?'

'Look on the bright side, boss,' said Knox. 'There's an outside chance it might not be.'

Because the main search area was on the university campus, as a courtesy they had to get permission from the Dean to go ahead. Before going to see her, taking Millie and Tony Knox, Mariner parked by the university railway station and walked the route that Yasmin would have taken, to give them an idea of the general lie of the land. Emerging from the station, a tarmac footpath took them through well-groomed park

93

land that ran for several hundred yards alongside a piece of rougher, untamed ground before climbing a slight incline towards the central cluster of mock-Elizabethan buildings that was dominated by the clock tower pushing up into the cornflower sky. Outward from the core, buildings encompassing every architectural era of the twentieth century had grown up. The path emerged on to a network of roads, just along from the stripy arm of a security barrier. Some of the roads were public thoroughfares: connecting the main routes that ran either side of the campus, and linking the different faculties of the university.

From there, Yasmin would have walked past the main student union building and out on to a well-populated public highway. Looking back, it was plain that the most vulnerable section of Yasmin's journey would be between leaving the railway station and getting to the main body of the campus. And that would be where they would concentrate their search.

Dean Angela Woolley's office was situated on the first floor of one of the original university buildings that surrounded the impressive Chancellor's court, and was overlooked by the three-hundred-foot tall Chamberlain clock tower; affectionately known as Old Joe. An information board outside told them that they were on the site of one of the original red-brick universities, built at the turn of the twentieth century with the intention of educating those who would manage the Midlands' burgeoning manufacturing industries. Not much call for that any more, thought Mariner. But its reputation had lived on and now

94

the university seemed to serve as many students from overseas as it did local youngsters. The main building reeked of academia, an atmosphere that Mariner found at once comfortable and intimidating.

'You ever wish you'd gone to university?' he asked Knox, as they stood cooling their heels outside Woolley's office.

The vacant response said that the thought had never entered Knox's mind. 'You?' he asked. Mariner wasn't so certain. Sometimes he wondered how different his career path might have been had he taken that route. How different his whole life might have been. People like Fiske met their life partners at university, or emerged with a core group of friends. It was certainly an opportunity that would have been open to him. 'No,' he said. 'I don't.'

Angela Woolley was sturdily into middle age, her hair set in a rigid perm, the colour of honey. They didn't need to explain their purpose in being there: she was fully abreast of current events.

'Anything we can do to help, Inspector. Though I'm sure nothing untoward could have happened here in the university without someone noticing. There aren't many students on campus now because of summer recess, but there are some and I'll make sure that word gets round to the relevant departments to cooperate with your officers.'

Along with all the search team from the operational command unit, a handful of students had also come forward to help, mostly postgraduates. The summer exams were over and many of the students had gone down, but a straggling line of about forty strong swept across the ground like an ill-disciplined advancing army.

After issuing instructions, Mariner left Sergeant Pete Welford to supervise the search, while he and Knox walked along to the hut at the barrier to talk to the security guards who had been on duty on Tuesday afternoon. Not that Knox was much help. He seemed to be having problems focusing on anything today. One of the security guards thought he remembered having seen Yasmin on occasions but not every day, and he couldn't recall seeing her on Tuesday.

The problem was that this wasn't unusual. The guards didn't stay in their hut all afternoon, especially in this sort of weather, when the flimsy structure offered little relief from the heat. And at this time of year, when there were fewer students, most people coming in and out would have their own passes. The rules were more relaxed and it was not unusual for them to leave the barrier raised for lengthy periods of time. Neither man had noticed anything out of the ordinary on Tuesday afternoon. And this was not an area covered by CCTV so the police were entirely reliant on the vigilance of the security personnel. Leaving the booth, Mariner was immediately accosted by a young woman.

'Are you here about the girl who's gone missing?' Speaking with the upward inflection at the end of the sentence that placed her as a native of the antipodes. She was in full Bondi beach ensemble: low cut denim shorts that were a good

96

eight inches off joining company with the cropped T-shirt that strained over an ample bosom; all off-set by a rich, caramel tan. Instinctively, Mariner glanced across at Knox for signs of awakening interest. On any other day his tongue would have been practically hanging out. But for once there were none.

Mariner nodded. 'We're the investigating officers.'

'They've told you about the flasher, right?'

Mariner looked towards the security guard who squirmed uncomfortably.

She shook her head knowingly. 'I thought as much. A couple of months ago, back in May, one of my roommates, Lizzie, got flashed at.'

'Do you know exactly what happened?'

'Oh yeah. I mean it was a bit of a giggle, but it shook her up.'

'What time of day was this?'

'Early evening; about five, half five. She was coming back over the meadow.'

'The meadow?'

'It's what we call that rough ground down there.' She pointed down the hill from where they stood to the area that the search party had just left – the area that Yasmin would have crossed immediately after leaving the station.

'Go on.'

'Well, the way she told it, Lizzie was just walking along the path minding her own when this guy jogged past her. She thought nothing of it but then as she rounded the corner and into the trees there he was again, standing with his back to the path like he was taking a leak. But as

97

she approached he turned around and it was all sticking out there. He grinned this nasty little grin and mumbled something about getting "caught short".'

'Did Lizzie think that could have been genuine?'

She shook her head. 'Not a bit. She said, "No guy I know pees with a stiffy like that."'

'So what did Lizzie do?'

'She said something like, "Get a life, saddo," and got past him as fast as she could. She came straight home and told me all about it.'

'Did she report it to the police?'

'She didn't think it was necessary. Just some perve getting his kicks. And I think she felt pretty stupid too, you know? It upset her more than she thought it would and she just wanted to forget it. I think she was kind of ashamed that it had got to her.'

'It's nothing to be ashamed of.'

'I know but I guess you always think if you're in that situation you'd be cool and just laugh it off, because it's so pathetic. But I think it shocked her, and she knew that this guy could see that. So she'd given him what he wanted, hadn't she?'

'Did Lizzie feel physically threatened in any way?'

'No. It was like her reaction was enough. That's why she felt so stupid.'

'There's nothing stupid about flashing.' It was always the same story. Even with the progress made in forensic psychology, flashing had never lost its reputation as one step down from an old music hall joke. 'Did Lizzie tell you what he looked like?'

'Not really. I don't think she got a good look. It was turning to dusk and she said he was facing sort of sideways, with a baseball cap pulled low.' She gave a wry smile. 'And I guess she wasn't exactly focused on his face, you know?'

'Did she tell anyone else about it?'

'She didn't want to. But I made her write it all down, just in case, and she was going to think about it. In the end she chickened out and mentioned it to one of her tutors, who said she'd pass it on. They told her security would deal with it – issue a warning to students and let the Dean know and to be honest, I think that suited Lizzie.'

'And?'

'We heard nothing more. Than a couple of weeks ago there was this rumour going round that it had happened again to a couple of other girls, in practically the same spot. I wondered if it could be the same guy. I know Lizzie did too.'

'Where's Lizzie now? We may want to talk to her.'

She pulled a face. 'I can't be very specific. She's hitching in France with her boyfriend.'

Mariner was sure none of this had got as far as the police. Incidents like these would show up on the monthly Intranet bulletin. There had been a spate of indecent exposures, as there often was when the weather got warmer, but nothing that he could remember having been reported on or around the university. He turned to the guard. 'You knew about this?'

He shrugged. 'I'd heard something, but we were told not to make an issue of it.'

'It already is an issue. What makes it worse is that we weren't told.' Angela Woolley would have to be confronted about that.

'Do you know the names of any of the other girls?'

She shook her head. 'Sorry.'

Mariner knocked and walked into Angela Woolley's office, leaving the Dean little opportunity to protest. She was packing things into a briefcase. 'I'm sorry, Inspector, I'm due at a–'

'I think that might have to wait.' Now he had her attention. 'Do you understand why we're here today?' he demanded. 'That we're here searching for a seventeen-year-old girl who may well have vanished less than a mile from this office? Why didn't you tell us about the indecent exposures that have been occurring next to this campus for the last two months and more? Of course, that's not counting any incidents that haven't been reported because the victim is completely unaware that it's happened to anyone else but her. Ms Woolley, you seem to have a sexual deviant operating on your campus. I think you'd better tell me everything you know.'

In effect, they'd had the better account from the student and Angela Woolley's version demonstrated that she'd barely attended to the facts. At least now though, she had the grace to be embarrassed.

'I'd really like to know whose idea it was to suppress this information,' Mariner said.

'It wasn't a question of suppressing it. We just felt it was better that only a limited number of people should know. What we didn't want to do was cause panic among the students, or deter any prospective students. Miss Greenwood was offered counselling, as were the other three young women–'

'You mean there are at least four?'

'Really, Inspector, this all happened weeks ago and I'm sure it was just a harmless student prank. There haven't been any incidents since the end of–'

'You mean, there haven't been any *reported* incidents. And why would students report it when none of this information is acted on? These incidents are never just "harmless pranks". Have you ever met any sexual deviants, Ms Woolley? Any convicted rapists among your acquaintances?'

'I don't know what–'

'Let me tell you something about rapists then, because in my line of work I've met one or two. And guess what? They don't wake up one morning and decide that today they are going to rape. Rape is just one stage in a progressive pattern of sexually deviant behaviour. And that pattern starts, more often than not, with flashing: indecent exposure; an unsolicited demonstration of naked sexual power to an unsuspecting victim. Then, when the buzz begins to wear off from that relatively harmless little pursuit, and believe me, it nearly always does, that's when things start to turn nasty. If you're so concerned about adverse publicity, I wonder what prospective students would make of the fact that for the last few months failure to disclose information to the police has exposed existing female students at this university to the risk of being attacked by a potential rapist.'

Angela Woolley did not have a reply.

'Christ. Since when did education become an exercise in PR?' Mariner boiled as they left the building. Short of any response from Knox, he answered his own question. 'Since it became a commercial enterprise, that's when. It's all about reputation and money.' He took a deep breath. 'We'll need to track down all the girls who've been victims to this flasher and take statements from them. It might not have anything to do with Yasmin, but they need to be investigated just the same.'

They had been given one other name. Helen Greenwood was a library assistant who fortunately remained on campus throughout the holidays.

'Go and get a detailed statement from her,' Mariner said to Knox. 'Then I want you to go back to the station to follow up on any other similar incidents there have been locally and see if there are any links.'

'Yes, boss,' said Knox, with about as much enthusiasm as a bloodhound on valium.

Librarian Helen Greenwood was thirty-three, so she said, but to Knox she could have been anything up to fifty. Her mousy brown hair was held off her face by an old-fashioned Alice band and her blouse and skirt could only be described as 'sensible'. All that was missing Knox thought were the horn-rimmed glasses. He really didn't want to do this. He'd other things on his mind. Greenwood was already behaving as if she was afraid of him, but then, he was a man so she probably was. He couldn't imagine her having had much experience of the opposite sex.

She was about to take her lunch break. 'I've brought sandwiches and I usually go out for a bit of fresh air,' she told Knox apologetically.

'Well, perhaps you could walk me to where it happened,' Knox suggested. 'Then you can tell me about it.'

'Oh, I don't know...'

'We'll take it slowly. You can stop any time you like.'

'All right,' she said, sounding as if it was anything but.

It was going to be a waste of time, thought Knox. She was scared of her own shadow. She led him down the footpath, back towards the railway station until it almost reached the meadow, where the path went briefly through an area of shrubs and there was plenty of scope for concealment. She stopped abruptly. 'It was about here.'

'So he could easily have been waiting over there on the rough ground until you came along, then hopped over the wire. Was there anyone else about?'

'Not here. I mean, the campus wasn't deserted, but there was no one down here at the time.'

'Do you take the same route every day at the same time?'

'I did then, yes, but not any more. If it's quiet I walk all the way round on the road now.'

'Can you describe exactly what happened?' Knox took out his notebook, partly because his memory didn't seem to be all that reliable at present, but also so that she wouldn't have to look at him while she talked.

'I was just walking down to the station to catch the train, along here. It was one of the first nice warm days we had. He just stepped out from the bushes in that way that everyone says they do. I didn't notice at first, then he smiled at me so I smiled back but his smile was sort of ... lewd, and then we were almost level when I happened to glance down. I don't know what made me do it, and I saw that he had his, his ... thing out'

'His pri– His penis?'

'Yes. He was holding it. And it was huge, and horrible. I just felt sick.' Glancing up, Knox saw that she'd flushed scarlet. He looked back at his notebook.

'What did you do?' he asked.

'I just got past him, around him, as fast as I could and hurried down towards the station.'

'Did he follow you?'

'I don't know. I didn't dare to look back, but I don't think so.'

'So what was he like?'

'That's the silly thing. I don't really know. I didn't notice. I only glanced at him for a second.'

Great. 'Was he white or black?'

'White.'

'You're sure?'

'Yes, he seemed to have a very high colour, from the little I could see. He had this cap pulled down low so I couldn't really see his eyes, but his cheeks and his chin were–'

'What?'

'Sunburnt, I think. His chin was very red.'

104

'What colour was the cap?'

'Dark. Blue or green, I think. One of those that most young men seem to wear these days.'

A baseball cap. 'How tall was he? Same as me?'

She looked Knox up and down. 'Taller, I think. And thinner.'

Knox pulled in his stomach. This was better than he'd expected. 'You're doing well,' he told her. The other overriding image, she said, was the powerful smell of his cologne. 'It smelled sort of cheap and nasty. It was much too strong.'

Taking the statement and getting back to the car took Knox around an hour. A couple of times he'd had to ask Helen Greenwood to repeat what she'd said because he'd missed it. Now, back in the office, be was finding it difficult to concentrate on what was on the screen in front of him. He'd some detective work of his own to do and wouldn't be able to settle until he'd done it. The office was quiet, everyone taken up with the two investigations. Knox reached for the thermos he'd brought with him. He needed a bit of Dutch courage for this.

Minimising the program he was in, he connected to the Internet.

'It's someone I've known for years,' Theresa had told him during that painfully brief conversation on the phone.

'Do I know him?' he'd asked. She hadn't answered, which meant that maybe he did.

'Where did you meet?'

'It's not important.' But Knox had already worked it out. The only someone she could have known a long time who they both knew could be someone from school. Theresa used the computer all the time. She'd been on courses and could find her way round it better than he could. He also knew that she visited the various school reunion sites that were springing up. Once she'd urged him to have a look.

'It's fun,' she'd said. 'You get to find out what's happened to all those spotty oiks.' But Knox had declined. He didn't have the same enthusiasm for the past as Theresa did. It must be a woman thing.

There were half a dozen sites offering to put people in contact with old acquaintances. Knox logged on to the first and typed in the name of the secondary school they'd gone to and the year they'd both left. By the time he clicked to proceed, his palms were sweating and his heart pounding. Would he know who it was? Would he recognise the name?

'Anything?' Mariner's voice behind him sent the mouse skidding across the desk. He hadn't heard anyone come in.

'No. Nothing yet, boss.' Knox minimised the screen but Mariner was already looking over his shoulder.

'Are we sure we're looking in the right place?' But it was curiosity more than anything else.

Knox fumbled for the notes he'd made. 'Checking back over the indecent exposure incidents in the south of the city during the last six months, there have been two others as well as the unreported ones at the university, bringing the total to six,' he said. 'All occurred at different times of the day, and on the surface there seems little to connect them.' He'd plotted the incidents on a map, which they now pored over. 'As you can see, boss, they all happened in secluded areas, but then the flasher is hardly likely to strike in the middle of a busy shopping centre, is he?'

'It would be a first.'

'One common thread seems to be that a lot of them take place fairly near railway stations.'

'Like Kingsmead. OK. How did you get on with Helen Greenwood?'

Knox reported what she'd told him.

'Sunburnt, eh,' said Mariner. 'That might be helpful.'

Calling in at the incident centre revealed that the news bulletin had been less fruitful. Although there were a handful of possible sightings of Yasmin to follow up, the descriptions were vague and there didn't appear to be anything that held any great significance. Mariner could safely leave Knox to follow those up. As the search of the university campus had turned up nothing either, apart from a handful of spent spliffs, the logical thing to do was to widen the search to the stretch of railway track between Kingsmead Station and the point at which Yasmin left the train. That would be a much bigger operation requiring far more manpower, which Mariner didn't like to think about just yet. As far as he was concerned, they were already jumping the gun. Instead, he wanted to concentrate on the information they had got. On an investigation like this it was important to be systematic, starting at the core

107

and working gradually outwards, making sure not to miss anything.

DCI Fiske, however, was like a dog with a bone and any decision on how to prioritise this was all but taken out of Mariner's hands. Now that Yasmin's disappearance had been on TV, the press were on to it, presenting exactly the sort of case that would capture the public's imagination. Always on the lookout for an 'angle', the media were playing up the possibility of a racially moti-vated abduction and, ever helpful, Fiske was equally taken with the idea and was making noises about a press conference for the parents.

'What about this letter?' he demanded at the daily update he'd insisted on. 'If it's genuine, it was a pretty open threat.'

'Forensics have found nothing on it,' said Mariner. 'And it's hard to tell how genuine it is, given that it's such an indistinguishable note. The Akrams have had similar stuff in the past.'

'But this follows the consortium letter to the press: a provocative act if ever there was one. If the initial campaign has failed to subdue them – which it patently has – then the perpetrators might feel that it's time to do something more dramatic. And so far, you don't seem to have come up with any other logical reason why Yasmin should have gone missing.'

'We're still exploring all the possibilities.'

'Like what?'

'Well, for one thing we've learned that every-thing in the Akram household wasn't as rosy as we'd been led to believe. Mr Akram and his daughter had disagreed.'

'I'm not saying you shouldn't keep the family under scrutiny, but you can do that while following up other avenues. The racist incidents have to be examined. Mohammed Akram has sent us a list of dates and occurrences going back over three years.'

'I haven't seen that.'

'It was passed directly to the superintendent. This is a copy.'

Mariner took the sheet. The incidents were as Akram had described them to him yesterday, fairly low level: excreta through the letterbox, windows broken, graffiti sprayed, sometimes as often as weekly and usually at night. Up until now the school had always been the target. Attached to the list was a copy of the letter written to the local press, by Akram and several other business owners in the area, denouncing what they called 'terrorism by stealth' perpetrated by 'those too weak to reveal themselves'. It described The Right Way as a club for cowards who indulged in covert, petty crime instead of openly confronting the issues. The question was whether it was enough to prompt such drastic action from The Right Way and, if so, could they expect a ransom note at any time?

'And that, Inspector, should be your next line of enquiry.'

Mariner opened his mouth to complain, but stopped himself. It was a valid route that would have to be pursued at some time. They may as well do it now and with any luck, his deference would keep Fiske off his back for a few hours.

But before entering the lion's den, Mariner wanted a bit more information about the man they might be dealing with. Detective Sergeant Bev Jordan came over from the Racial Crimes Unit at Lloyd House to talk to him and Millie.

'What do you need to know?' she asked when they were installed in Mariner's office.

'Everything there is to know about Peter Cox.'

Jordan grimaced. 'He's a nasty piece of work in every respect. He runs a very active cell of The Right Way who hold extreme views on repatriation, birth control programmes and all the rest of it. He's denounced the BNP for being too moderate.'

'What a charmer.'

'You said it.'

Mariner handed Jordan the leaflet Mohammed Akram had given him. 'Is this one of his?'

Jordan nodded. 'This is exactly the sort of stuff he writes. In the past there have been various threats against groups and individuals. And he has his own little band of fanatically loyal followers in the south of the city and beyond, mainly recruited via the Internet, though not exclusively. He spreads the word in local pubs, particularly those on white, working class housing estates: areas of high social deprivation where white kids are pretty frustrated with their lot, but generally powerless to do anything about it. One of his main themes is the threat of Islamic fundamentalism. Muslims taking over jobs, local businesses–'

'And schools.'

'Particularly schools, because that's where it's all seen to be taught. He'd be encouraged by the

110

current climate, too. Since September eleventh there's been a huge rise in the membership of these types of organisation.'

'And beyond the leafleting and general incitement?'

'Oh, the usual petty harassment: damage to property, disgusting things sent through the post. We have a couple of informants on the inside, but Cox is clever, he's very careful not to be directly involved. He relies mainly on the mental instability of his recruits. He provides the ideas, they carry them out. So far we've only ever been able to charge a few individuals with criminal damage. There's one in particular, David Waldron, who's a real fall guy for Cox.'

'Are you aware of the antagonism with the Asian business consortium?'

'Oh yes. That's been brewing for a couple of years and the letter to the press won't have helped the situation, but again, Cox is too smart to let something like that get to him. It was only a letter, after all. It's his followers who would be more upset by it.'

'Do you think any of them would go as far as abduction?'

'Up until recently I'd have said no, but there has been a worrying trend lately, which is that – thanks to the Internet – these groups are developing international links and are being increasingly influenced by their counterparts across the pond.'

'In what way?'

'A spate of letter bomb attacks in the South of the US was followed, weeks later, by the letter

111

bomb attacks here, in Manchester and Leeds last month, remember?'

'And?'

'Three weeks ago there was a high profile abduction of a black senator's daughter by right-wing activists in Savannah, Georgia. The senator was proposing legislation to curb the distribution of certain right-wing propaganda.'

'And has the girl been found?' asked Knox.

'Oh yes. Strangled and dumped in a garbage skip. It's believed that there was no intention to release her alive.'

'Christ Almighty. Do you think there's anyone in The Right Way who would go that far?'

'It only takes one. We know that the case has been discussed among them and Cox likes his followers to "prove themselves" by using their initiative, so it would only take one of them with a particular bent for this kind of activity, and we have our abduction.'

'And Waldron?'

'He's on remand at present, so effectively out of the picture. It might be worth a chat with Peter Cox, though. Find out if he's hired any new recruits lately. Yasmin was last seen at four forty-five on Tuesday afternoon, wasn't she? It would be interesting to know what Cox was doing then, too.'

'I can't wait to meet the animal who causes so much misery.'

'He's not what you'd expect,' said Jordan. 'He might not put it to any great use by working for a living, but he's bright; a graduate. He just prefers to utilise his talents for stirring up trouble.'

112

The other surprise was that Peter Cox lived in a smart neighbourhood in a homely 1930s semi with bay windows and a porch. Given what Jordan had told them, Mariner guessed that it was his parents' house, the one he'd been born and raised in. What set it apart from its neighbours was the jungle of a garden and the limp, discoloured curtains hanging behind grimy windows. It was a neighbourhood for young families. As there were no garages, Mariner drove the length of the street, looking in vain for a parking place, and was eventually compelled to settle for a neighbouring street.

He craned his neck to concentrate on a reverse park, which he executed smoothly.

'Very neat,' said Knox. It was the only time he'd spoken on the entire journey. His words seemed to sweeten the air somehow, but Mariner dismissed the sensation as his own over-active imagination. They climbed out of the car and walked back to number forty-eight, where the warm smell of decaying refuse became stronger.

The doorbell showed little indication of being connected to anything, but Mariner pressed it anyway and beside them at the bay window the faded velvet drape was pulled aside and a round, white face peered at them.

'Mr Cox?' Mariner called out, politely, holding up his warrant card. 'Could you spare us a few minutes?'

The face regarded them with distaste, but the curtain dropped back and moments later the door was opened.

'Can we come in?' Mariner asked. It was obviously the last thing Peter Cox wanted, but he nevertheless stepped back to allow them in.

What sprang out first at Mariner from the gloomy hallway were the framed posters on the walls. From his limited knowledge of the Third Reich, Mariner thought one of them might have been Rudolf Hess. The other was unmistakable: Adolf Hitler's eyes focused purposefully on something in the middle distance, one hand on his hip in a pose which, in Mariner's opinion, made the Führer look rather camp. He thought it best not to mention this. The atmosphere inside the house was acrid: stale cigarette smoke with an underlying feral smell. Cox took them into a small, front living room that was piled high with books and papers, in the centre of which was an old battered sofa. A computer monitor hummed gently from the corner of the room.

Cox himself was small and weedy, as unhealthy as a plant starved of natural light, as if he never ventured out of his dark and dingy lair. Balding slightly, he was pale as uncooked pastry and the amber-coloured stain on the index finger of his right hand tallied with the pile of home-rolled dog-ends in the makeshift ashtray. 'How can I help you, Officers?' he asked politely, with what sounded more than anything like bored resignation.

'Just a simple question,' said Mariner. 'Where were you on Tuesday afternoon at around four forty-five?'

'Now, why would you want to know that?' But before they could answer, he laughed out loud.

'This is about that little Paki, isn't it?' He shook his head sadly. 'Dear me, you must be desperate if you've come to me about that.'

'Her family seems to be on the mailing list for your enlightening pamphlets.'

'I hardly think that's significant. We have an extensive target audience.'

'And David Waldron, one of your party members, was caught inflicting damage on property in the area.'

'As I said at the time, I can't be responsible for the actions of all our members. All I do is provide a forum for like-minded people to share their views and concerns.'

'In the same way that the National Socialist Party of Germany provided a forum?'

'I repeat, Waldron was acting independently. I had nothing to do with any of that.'

'Until Mohammed Akram brought your name into it. He said some not very nice things about you publicly, some highly provocative things.'

'Do you seriously think a bit of name-calling's going to bother me? It's what you get when you're prepared to stand up for what you believe in. Goes with the territory. Our territory.' He noticed Knox looking around. 'Want to search the house, do you?'

'It would help us to–'

'Well, you'll need a warrant and a fucking good reason,' Cox said, mildly.

'So maybe you could answer the question, just for the record.'

But disappointingly, Cox did have an alibi, and a fairly unassailable one at that: at the crucial time he'd been speaking at a meeting of 'like-minded people' in Walsall. He travelled on the train. And if, as he said, the meeting didn't end until four thirty, it would have been practically impossible for him to have been anywhere near Yasmin Akram when she disappeared. It would be easy enough to verify.

'It still doesn't mean that he hasn't put someone else up to it,' Mariner said to Knox, as they traipsed back along the street.

'Mm.' Knox grunted.

Back at the car Mariner saw he had a message on his mobile. He rang back. It was Millie. 'I've got a name for you. Fakhra has coughed up the identity of that disgruntled parent: a guy called Abdul Sheron. Oh and another thing–' Suddenly she sounded uncomfortable. 'DCI Fiske is organising a press conference.'

Chapter Six

'Police Constable Khatoon should get her facts straight before she comes bleating to you.' Pacing the floor of his office, DCI Fiske was angry. Very angry, if the colour of his face was anything to go by. Even so he seemed keen to defend his actions, Mariner thought with some satisfaction. 'I am not organising a press conference, I have merely indicated to the press that one is imminent, and asked the TV station to be on standby.'

'Which, with respect, sir, is as good as declaring

it where the media are concerned,' said Mariner, seriously wondering if Fiske was beginning to lose it already. More than accustomed to keeping the press at bay, he'd never had to fend off an over-zealous commanding officer before. 'The timing of press conferences is crucial and I'd have preferred to hold it when I was ready. If you want me to continue as SIO then I need to be able to do things my way.' His powers of diplomacy were being stretched to the limit.

'That seems to involve doing very little, as far as I can make out. This case is developing a high profile–'

Yes, and who have we to thank for that? thought Mariner.

'We need to be seen to be acting. We should be looking at running a reconstruction, too. People expect it.'

That was the problem with having all these bloody crime programmes on TV. The public thought they knew better how to do the job. 'It's much too soon. We're following up outside leads, and after a week, we'll get someone to walk the route to encourage any new witnesses to come forward, but we can't discount Yasmin's family and immediate friends yet. We already know that the parents aren't telling us everything.'

'So having them in for a press conference would provide you with an opportunity. TV cameras are an excellent way of stripping away any pretence.'

'Yes, sir.' Mariner turned to go, thinking that in some cases just the opposite was true. 'And maybe, sometime, you could go over that egg sucking thing with me again, sir,' he murmured under his breath.

'Let's bring them in,' Mariner said to Jamilla on his return to the office.

'Any particular way you want me to steer things, sir?'

'No, save that for afterwards. Keep it all light and conversational on the journey in. That way, Akram's guard won't be up – if it needs to be.'

As the Senior Investigating Officer, Mariner had no choice but to accompany Fiske at the appeal, which passed in a blur of flash-bulbs and quick-fire questions. Afterwards, he, Knox and Millie watched the playback. Mohammed Akram was calm and dignified while even his wife, clinging to her husband for support, remained composed, despite the obvious strain. She seemed smaller than she'd looked two days ago, as if she'd lost about half a stone, and all of it from around her face, where the skin was pale and sagging. Mohammed Akram did all the talking, reading from the prepared statement he'd been given by the press officer, appealing to Yasmin to come home, or to anyone who may be holding her to please let her go. Throughout, his voice was clear and steady, his gaze straight into the camera.

'He's a cool one,' Mariner conceded.

'Don't be fooled,' said Millie. She was right to be cautious. Even when parents had made an emotional public appeal for the return of their offspring, they couldn't be eliminated from the enquiry. Distress and guilt had the habit of manifesting themselves in very similar ways and

118

in recent years, increasing numbers of murderers had successfully, at least for a while, concealed one with the other.

Before being returned home, the Akrams were taken into a side room and offered refreshments. Having fielded the inevitable questions from reporters, Mariner went to talk to them. Two sets of eyes turned hopefully on him as he went into the room. He shook his head. 'I'm sorry, there's nothing new. But I do need to clarify a couple of things with you.'

'Anything,' said Akram, looking shaken now that the ordeal was over.

'We've spoken to Yasmin's friends and I understand that you were not entirely happy about Yasmin staying the night with Suzanne.'

Mohammed Akram responded instantly. 'It was nothing. It was the kind of thing every parent and child goes through.'

'Is that why it didn't seem important enough to mention?' asked Mariner. 'I must impress on you that anything out of the ordinary, however small, could be of help. Tell me what happened exactly.'

'Yasmin asked to go and stay with her friend, overnight. I said no.'

'Why was that?'

'It was a school night and she would have homework. It was inappropriate.' More to it than that, but Mariner wouldn't push it now. Was Akram just trying to be diplomatic about his dislike of Suzanne, or was it power games between Mum and Dad?

He looked from one to the other parent. 'So am I to understand that Yasmin was defying you by

119

going to Suzanne's?'

'She was defying me, not her mother.' Akram glanced at his wife. 'After I had left the house on Tuesday morning, Shanila allowed Yasmin to go.' The accusation was there along with the obvious source of that additional tension.

Shanila Akram made a weak show of sticking up for herself. 'Yasmin was threatening to go to Suzanne's anyway. I thought it much better that she should go with our blessing than deceive us. I thought if she was allowed to go once she would get it out of her system.'

'So you encouraged her to collude with you in deception.' Mohammed Akram's anger was building.

But his wife was equal to it. 'I would have told you when you returned.'

'Do you approve of Suzanne, Mr Akram?' Mariner asked. There followed enough of a hesitation to confirm the antagonism that existed there.

'It's not a question of approval.'

'Then what is it?'

'You went to see Yasmin's friends. You've met Suzanne?'

'Yes.'

'Then you'll know that she is very different from Yasmin.' Full marks for tact.

'And does that bother you?'

'As we've already told you, Yasmin is relatively inexperienced at life. It would be easy for her to be influenced by a stronger, more ... worldly personality, someone who has different values.'

'So you've discouraged the friendship.'

120

'We have been realistic. We can't prevent Yasmin from mixing with whoever she wants to at school. Let's just say that we haven't done anything to encourage it.'

'How does Yasmin feel about that?'

'Kids get angry, you know, especially if they can't get their way.'

'She said–' Shanila Akram stopped abruptly.

'What did she say, Mrs Akram?'

'She said we might regret it if we tried to prevent her from doing things.'

'Like staying with her friends. So then, Mrs Akram, you decided to allow Yasmin to go and stay with Suzanne.'

'Yes.' She addressed her husband. 'I was concerned that we were being too strict on Yasmin and that she might rebel. I thought that once it had happened, when my husband saw no harm had been done and that Yasmin appreciated the gesture, it would be for the best.'

'For the best? How can you possibly say that now? Look at what has happened. Now we have no idea where Yasmin has gone.'

'Of course I can see that now, but at the time–' Mrs Akram's eyes filled with tears. Her husband reacted with a contemptuous snort.

'How did Yasmin react when you told her she *could* go to stay with Suzanne after all?' Mariner pushed on, keen to maintain the momentum.

'She was excited, happy. She hugged me. But I know she was mindful of her dad's feelings, too.'

'Mindful how? Do you think Yasmin really intended to stay with Suzanne, or could she have decided to get back at you for making life difficult

121

for her? Could she have run away?'

Akram was unequivocal. 'Yasmin isn't like that. Even if she was still angry she wouldn't take it this far. If she decided to punish us it would be a gesture, that's all. She would go somewhere safe; to someone within our family. I believe Yasmin thought of her duty to me, and was intending to come home. Something prevented her from doing so. Something has happened to her, Inspector, and I really think your time would be better spent out there looking for her instead of dissecting our family life. I don't understand why you are persisting with this. I told you about the trouble we've been having. Why aren't you talking to Peter Cox?'

'We are following that line of enquiry, but we have to ensure that all possibilities are covered. Tell me about Abdul Sheron.'

'How did you know about him?'

'That doesn't really matter. Just tell me.'

'Abdul is an old friend. Things have been a little strained because we felt that we couldn't meet the needs of his youngest child in our school. It can be hard to accept but it is for the good of the child.'

'I understand he was angry about that.'

'At first he was, yes, and that was to be expected. His daughter has lots of problems and it is hard. But our families have known each other for years. Abdul would not do anything to hurt us. It's out of the question.'

And on that note, Mariner allowed Millie to take them home.

'What do you think?' Mariner asked Knox after

122

they'd gone.

'He's working very hard at trying to steer us towards the racist angle,' said Knox with rare lucidity.

'And away from anything else? My thoughts exactly.'

As a follow up, Mariner had suggested a few directions for Millie to take with the 'informal conversation' on the way back, and was waiting for a debrief when she returned to the station.

'What else did you find out?'

'About as much as I would if I'd been making a social call. But I do think Shanila is beginning to open up and talk to me more as if I was a friend of the family than a police officer.'

'Surely that can be far more productive.'

'Sometimes. Depends on how much they decide to patronise me and how much they disapprove of my role.'

'What do you think?'

'They still hold a fairly traditional view of the female role. Not outright disapproval, but probably not what they'd want for their girls.'

'Yasmin's older sister lives abroad?'

'Yes, we talked about her; she was married earlier this year, apparently.'

'Fairly recently then. And how often does she see Yasmin?'

'Quite often, according to Mum and Dad. Her husband is a successful lawyer and travels extensively. They were over here just a few weeks ago.'

'Was it an arranged marriage?'

123

'Sounds like it, in that the two families already knew each other and the match was obviously approved by both sets of parents.'

'Might Yasmin have wanted to escape from that scenario?'

'It depends on how strictly they follow it through. Arranged marriage is not always a bad thing. Usually these days, the son or daughter has the right of veto. This couple are a mix, like their dress: her in traditional, him in Western. On the one hand, Shanila Akram seems very Western and liberal, but at the same time I get the impression that Mohammed likes to keep Yasmin on a tight rein.'

'By not allowing her to stay overnight with her friend,' said Mariner. 'Although I can see why Suzanne would be a less than ideal playmate.'

'It's not that uncommon, of course. Yasmin's parents want her to have all the advantages of growing up in Western society, as they so successfully have, but within the confines of their religious rules. Problem is, the two are not always compatible and it's hard to find a balance. It can present quite a tension. To Yasmin, at her age, it probably seems as if she gets the worst of both worlds. She gets to work hard to achieve what her parents want her to, but without the social life enjoyed by her friends.'

'So they limit her.'

'They'd say they're protecting her. Family life is important to them.'

'Doesn't make it any easier for Yasmin.'

Millie shook her head. 'You have no idea.' She spoke with feeling, and Mariner realised for the first time how little he knew about his colleague's own background.

'I asked them again about Abdul Sheron too,' Millie said. 'Neither of them believes he'd be involved but they have at least agreed that we can go and talk to him.'

'No time like the present.'

Millie pulled a face. 'Sorry, sir, I've a few calls to make.'

'That's OK. Knox!'

Chapter Seven

Sheron's address turned out to be a hardware store down the Stratford Road from Allah T'ala, between a shop selling wedding sarees, and an Indian sweet shop. At ground-floor level was a family-run hardware business that flowed on to the pavement outside, with stacks of plastic buckets and storage boxes arranged in neat rows alongside mops, brooms, cleaning cloths and tubs of cheap batteries. The family lived in the flat above the shop. Mariner's opening words established that Sheron didn't speak English, so one of his brothers agreed to interpret for him. Mariner kicked himself that he hadn't waited for Millie instead of bringing Knox, who was chewing grimly on some menthol-smelling gum.

They followed the two men through the shop and up a flight of dark, narrow stairs. The flat at the top was grubby and dismal, the floor

125

uncarpeted and strewn with piles of newspaper and a few broken toys. From one corner, a huge wide-screen TV dominated the room, the sound turned down so as to be virtually inaudible. A long sofa was arranged directly opposite and beside the sofa, on the bare floorboards, sat a child of about three or four: pretty, with dark curls framing a delicate face. Her head wobbled as she balanced uncertainly and her limbs occasionally twitched violently. As they went in, their footsteps echoing on the wooden floor, she seemed to look up at them and smile, but Mariner could tell that her eyes were unfocused. Transparent tubes were taped under her nose, the other end connected to a tank that leaned against the wall. Sheron and his brother completely ignored both the child and the elderly matriarch who sat at the end of the sofa, her eyes fixed on the giant screen, and the conversation was conducted with all four men standing in the corner of the room. Most of the communication was with the man who introduced himself as Hasan, Sheron's brother.

'I'd like Mr Sheron to tell us about his involvement with the school, Allah T'ala,' said Mariner.

The brother spoke and for a few minutes, they jabbered an exchange in their native language. Then for the first time Hasan acknowledged the child. 'This is his daughter, Shebana,' he said. 'He put her name down for the school two years ago. His other children went there and he has given them money. Now it's time for Shebana to go they are saying that they can't help her. It's because she has problems, but they say they haven't got enough teachers or enough room for her oxygen. All her siblings and cousins have gone to the school, but not Shebana. Now you see she is here, she will have no school to go to and it's the fault of the Akrams. They have been unfair and it made him angry.'

Still muttering, Sheron walked across the room and retrieved something from a drawer. It was a glossy magazine, a prospectus. He thrust it in front of Mariner, rapping a forefinger angrily down on the page.

'He's saying, "Look at this. See what it says here," Hasan told them. 'It's written in this fancy book but the words don't mean anything.' Sheron was becoming angry and more agitated as his brother spoke.

Mariner looked. The brochure talked about welcoming all children of all different abilities. He turned the booklet over in his hand. At the bottom of the last page was the name of the printer, presumably the one Akram had been to see on the day when Yasmin disappeared.

'It is an insult to his whole family. That's why he's so angry.'

'Angry enough to damage Mohammed Akram's car?' Mariner asked.

'He knows nothing about that,' said Hasan immediately, and Mariner suddenly wondered if the deed had been carried out on Abdul's behalf. It was pointless to pursue it further, though. It would be impossible to prove. The significant thing was that this was clearly still an open wound, the situation unresolved. The question was: how far would Sheron's demonstrable anger drive him? The Akrams had made a victim of his daughter, would he want to do the same to the Akrams?

'Does Mr Sheron know Yasmin Akram?'

'Of course we do. She was friends with my daughter,' said Hasan.

'Was?' Mariner picked it up straight away.

'Going to that school has corrupted her. Now she thinks she is better than her old friends.'

'Does he know anything about her disappearance?'

Hasan spoke to his brother. The response came back immediately: more anger.

'How would he know that? He doesn't really care. Now they can know what it feels like to fear for their child.'

Hardly the same thing, but Mariner hadn't really expected anything different. 'Where was he on Tuesday afternoon at around four forty-five?'

'Abdul was here in the shop. You can see we have a business to run.'

Thanking Sheron and his brother for their time, they walked back out on to the busy street to the sound of voices raised in Urdu; the discussion continuing beyond their departure.

'Akram certainly seems to have got up his nose,' said Knox.

'Yasmin herself doesn't seem that popular with them, either. I thought "corrupted" was an interesting choice of word.'

'He just meant she's got too big for her boots. Yasmin goes to a posh school. Maybe she flaunts it.'

'Another reason to wipe the smirk off Akram's

face,' Mariner pointed out.

'But if they've abducted her, where is she and where are the demands?'

'There might not be any. The Akrams' distress might be enough.'

'But Yasmin disappeared a good six or seven miles away from here, near the university.'

'That's what I was thinking. Sheron would have had to be highly organised to operate in a part of the city that he's not familiar with. Where would he get the means?'

'That's where,' said Knox. His eyes were on the opposite side of the street as they watched Hasan Sheron emerge from the shop and climb in behind the wheel of the private hire vehicle that was parked on the kerb outside. 'How convenient is that?'

Impulsively, on their way back, Mariner asked Knox to wait in the car while he called in on Colleen. The house had had a sparkling new coat of white emulsion since his last visit, and the rotten windows had been replaced with uPVC, ill-disguising the fact that the house was basically structurally unsound and riddled with damp and should have been condemned years ago.

The front door was open so he called out, 'Hello. Anyone about?' She came to the door, her hair hanging lank and unwashed, the inevitable cigarette on the go. Her face, when she saw him, was a mixture of hope and fear. It was a mistake to have come.

'I've no news,' he said straight away.

'So why are you here?' She was dressed

unflatteringly in a loose white T-shirt over faded black leggings, her bare feet in cheap velour slippers, worn through at the toe. 'To tell me that you've found that missing girl?'

'I can't talk to you about other cases that we're handling.'

'How come her parents get to go on the telly? All they've done for my Ricky is put up a few posters. Why can't I go on to ask him to come home?' The belligerence in her voice belied the desperation.

'It's not always appropriate. It depends on the circumstances.' How could Mariner tell her that she just wasn't TV material? That the success of a press conference depended on the public identifying and sympathising with the parents, and that neither of those was likely for a single mother on her third partner in as many years. They would make the same assumptions that his DCI had.

'You think that girl's more important than my Ricky.'

'I think nothing of the sort, Colleen, and you know it.'

'Maybe not you, but the others. Just because she comes from a rich, Asian family. I'm not stupid, you know. I get what's going on here.'

'We're doing what we can, Colleen,' Mariner said. It was true, to a degree.

'So where is he?' She took a step back. 'Where's my Ricky? Come and see me when you've found him.' And then she carefully closed the door in his face.

If it did transpire that Ricky had simply run away, Mariner would personally lynch the boy

130

when he turned up, for having put his mother through hell.

The blatant hypocrisy of such thoughts was spelled out immediately he got home, with yet another message from his own mother on the answering machine.

'There's something I want to talk to you about,' she said again. 'I suppose it will have to keep until next time I see you.' Implying that it ought to be soon. He wondered if this 'something' was what he'd been waiting all his life to find out, but then that's what she'd be hoping he'd think. She was playing games with him again; one of the things she did for fun to get back at him for what he did all those years ago. Not that he could really blame her. He'd once asked her how she felt when, as a fifteen-year-old, he'd run away from home.

'I just wanted you back, unconditionally,' she'd replied. Only then did Mariner fully realise how much he must have hurt her. It had taken him weeks before he'd contacted her to tell her he was safe. What kind of torture had he inflicted on her in the meantime? It was something else on the list of things that they never talked about. Instead, she had other ways of making him pay. Well, he didn't have time for her games right now, or time to comply with what would be her excessive demands. He couldn't face that tonight, but at the same time, he couldn't help wondering how Shanila Akram would be holding up right now. Had Yasmin run away, for the same reasons he had: because she'd felt stifled by her family, or because she didn't like what they had planned for her?

He got through to Anna first time.

'How's the fund raising going?' he asked, out of politeness.

His restraint didn't wilt her enthusiasm. 'It's great. People are being so generous, though we're still waiting for some contributions.' It was a blatant hint.

'I'm thinking about it.'

'Yeah, well don't think too long, eh? How are things going with the missing girl?'

'Don't count on my company for the weekend, will you?'

'Interestingly enough, I never count on much where you're concerned, but that's OK,' Anna said, cheerfully. 'Good thing we both know the score, isn't it?'

'Sure.' Mariner's chest tightened.

'I know you're not allowed to say, but how's it going?'

'Even if I could say there'd be nothing to tell. It's frustrating, to say the least.'

'Mm, well,' she said slowly, her voice dropping half an octave. 'We can't have you frustrated, can we? There ought to be something I can do about that. What you need is a few soothing words to help you relax.'

'How's Jamie?'

'Jamie's fine. Glued to the TV as we speak. Want to know what I'm wearing?'

'Go on, then.'

'Is that better?' she asked him afterwards.

'Infinitely,' he said, although he didn't like to dwell too much on the fact that this was what

132

their relationship had come to.

The next morning, Mariner gathered the team to review what they'd got so far. It wasn't much. The incident board displayed a blown-up version of Yasmin's photograph; an enlarged section of the street map covering the area where she'd disappeared; and a time line, leading nowhere. Colleen's complaint about the absence of a press conference for Ricky seemed unfounded. Yasmin's had yielded little in the way of new leads. Only one call received had produced anything of substance to follow up, and then that had turned out to be a dud too.

'What are the options?' Since he looked more like his usual lively self this morning, Mariner addressed the question to Tony Knox.

'If we rule out accidents, basically there appear to be three possibilities at this stage, boss: first possibility – Yasmin has gone off of her own accord.'

'Why would she do that?'

'She'd had a row with her parents,' said Millie.

'Not her mother. Her mother has given in to her,' Mariner reminded them.

'She'd rowed with her dad though, and he seems to be the one who wields the power.'

'And maybe she's just had enough,' offered Knox. 'From what we've heard, it's not the first time the old man's been down on her.'

'OK. But if that is the case, would Yasmin let things go this far? She's an intelligent and, so we're told, considerate girl. Surely wherever she was she'd eventually let her parents know that

133

she's safe. We're three days in now and nothing. And she doesn't appear to have taken any money with her, so how is she living?'

'All right then. Second possibility: she's been abducted and is being held against her will.'

'Who by?'

'Peter Cox and his mates?'

Mariner was doubtful. 'Having talked to him, I don't quite see it. It's not really Cox's style, and if it was one of his followers, I'm not convinced that they'd be well organised enough. Cox may be clever, but according to DS Jordan most of his honchos are pretty inadequate people.'

'Could be just a random pick-up,' offered Knox. 'Someone offering her a lift home from the station.'

'But we keep being told that she's a bright, sensible kid,' countered Millie. 'She wouldn't have gone off with a complete stranger.'

'And why would she need a lift? It's a short walk to her house from there, and it's a warm sunny evening. What reason would she have to get into a car with just anyone?'

'Might not have been a stranger. Yasmin would know the Sheron family. We haven't ruled them out yet and Hasan drives a minicab. It would be the most natural thing in the world for him to offer her a lift.'

'It's risky, though, in broad daylight. Chances are that someone would remember seeing him.'

'Except that it's exactly the kind of common-place occurrence that most people don't notice. The alternative leaves us looking at a total unknown, perhaps connected to the earlier attacks on the university campus, which would be even more noticeable.'

'There are no reports of anyone in the area seeing or hearing anything out of the ordinary on Tuesday afternoon, implying that Yasmin did nothing to draw attention. Even though term has ended there are still quite a few students around.'

In the silence that followed, Mariner held an internal mental debate about whether he should voice his thoughts. Eventually, he had to come out with it. 'What we haven't yet given any thought to is the possibility that Yasmin could have stayed on the train and got off at a different stop.' No one had thought about it because they didn't want to and because Fiske had effectively put them off that particular scent.

'Jesus,' said Knox. 'If Yasmin had stayed on the train she could have gone into the city. That would open up a whole new set of possibilities.'

'But we saw her on the CCTV,' Millie reminded them. 'We watched her get off the train at the university.'

'I'm not so sure about that,' confessed Mariner. 'I'd like to see it again.'

To humour him they loaded the video and watched once more, comparing the two clips.

'See, to me it doesn't look like the same person. The gait is different.'

'How can you tell? She's running on the first, walking on the second.'

'I know, but it still doesn't look right to me. The second one has a slightly bigger build.'

'There's not much in it.'

'No, that's true.'

'So it could just be camera angle.'

Mariner was getting the distinct impression that he was alone on this. Everyone else wanted, understandably, to believe that Yasmin had alighted from the train as usual at the university. It would make their lives so very much simpler.

'If she went into the city she could have gone anywhere.' Knox put their thoughts into words. It opened up the possibilities of London, Glasgow, anywhere in Britain, in fact. And it didn't bear thinking about that Birmingham International Airport could have been on the agenda.

'But she had no money and as far as we know wasn't planning to meet anyone.'

'As far as we know.' But Mariner was increasingly beginning to feel that where Yasmin Akram was concerned they'd barely even scratched the surface.

'It still brings us back to the *likelihood* of it being someone she knew,' said Knox. Making for safer ground.

'Sure, statistically we have to consider the immediate family,' conceded Mariner. 'Mum and Dad were cagey about the row they'd had. In fact, they've been less than forthcoming all the way along, which makes me wonder what else they haven't told us. But it's a long way off any kind of motive. We need to do some more digging, folks.'

Mariner's phone rang and Millie picked it up. Her face broke into a smile. 'I think we might have something,' she said.

Chapter Eight

The call nearly hadn't made it past the incident room, due to the perceived reticence of the caller, who'd had a change of heart halfway through. One of the less experienced civilian staff had fielded it, and almost logged it as a time-waster. It was only the quick thinking of a more experienced girl named Tanya that recognised its importance. She played back the recording of the initial contact.

'Hello, is that the police?' It was the voice of a young woman, timid and hesitant. It didn't sound to Mariner like any of Yasmin's school-friends. His heart rate quickened. Was it Yasmin?

'You're through to the incident room, yes.' A pause. 'How can I help? Do you have some information?'

'Yes. No. I don't know.'

'Who's speaking please?'

'I can't tell you that.'

'That's OK. Is it about Yasmin Akram?'

'There's something you should know.' Another long pause, broken only by the uneven rasp of shallow breathing; someone poised on the brink of a decision.

'What did you want to tell me?'

'Nothing. No, it's nothing–' A click and then the empty line hummed.

Mariner exhaled, suddenly aware that he'd been holding his breath throughout the exchange.

137

'You said you'd traced it?' he asked Tanya.

'It's a doctor's surgery in Edgbaston.' She gave them the address. So probably not Yasmin.

'It's a couple of streets away from the Akrams,' remarked Millie. 'The family GP?'

'I bet the doctor didn't make that call. The voice was young, lacking in confidence.'

Praising Tanya for her vigilance, Mariner verified the number and checked the surgery's opening hours. He didn't want to scare anyone off so he'd do this alone. By ten-thirty he had parked outside the converted bungalow and was watching the last of the patients leave. When he'd seen no one enter or exit for ten minutes, he locked the car and walked up the footpath. The waiting room was empty and behind the desk only a receptionist remained, her faced creased with concentration as she entered data into a computer. She was young and of mixed race, with a smooth complexion the colour of milky coffee.

Taking a gamble, Mariner walked up to the desk and showed her his warrant card along with what he hoped was a friendly smile. 'Hi. Did you make a telephone call at eight fifty-four this morning?'

Wide brown eyes looked up into his and her lower lip began to twitch and tremble. 'How did you...?' Her voice was just a whisper but Mariner recognised it at once. He heard a door open behind him.

'Is everything all right, Nadine?' The woman who spoke was in her mid-forties with dark, penetrating eyes; she barely reached Mariner's shoulder. More Middle Eastern than Asian

138

continent, her short, greying hair was swept back off her forehead. She was casually but immaculately dressed in slacks and a sleeveless blouse. 'I'm Dr Shah. This is my practice,' she said.

'DI Mariner. I'm the senior officer investigating the disappearance of Yasmin Akram,' Mariner explained. 'I have reason to think Nadine contacted our incident room this morning with some information, but, unfortunately, the call was terminated before she was able to pass it on.'

'Nadine?'

The girl's eyes flicked from one to the other of them until her face crumpled and she finally succumbed to tears.

'Come into the consulting room,' said Dr Shah. 'I'll make some tea.' She turned to Mariner. 'I don't know what's going on here but I'd like to talk to Nadine alone first. Yasmin is a patient here, so I have to ensure that anything Nadine has to tell you is not likely to be a breach of confidentiality.'

Mariner fought down his frustration. 'If Yasmin is in some kind of danger then patient confidentiality may be an irrelevance,' he said. 'It's important that we have access to any information that will help us to find her.'

'I appreciate that, Inspector, but I would ask you to respect my professional judgement. Yasmin is my patient and needs to know that she can trust me. Any decision about what to tell you is mine and mine alone. I will listen to what Nadine has to say. If I consider that there is anything that will help in your investigation without compromising my relationship with Yasmin Akram, then I will allow her to pass it on.'

Mariner had no option other than to wait and hope. While the two women were closeted in the doctor's consulting room, he placed the waiting room outside like an expectant father. He was flicking through a leaflet on heart disease when the door abruptly opened. Dr Shah appeared, looking grim-faced. 'Inspector, I think you need to come in.'

In the tiny room Mariner pulled up a chair, so that his knees were almost touching Dr Shah's.

'It is with reluctance that I tell you this,' said Dr Shah. 'But if it does, as you say, put Yasmin in danger then I would be unable to forgive myself for not passing on this information. I would just ask that you use it judiciously.'

'You have my word.'

'I've been the GP for Yasmin and her family for nearly ten years, so I know Yasmin very well. Just over a month ago Yasmin came to see me because she wanted to begin taking the contraceptive pill.'

'The pill?' Mariner could barely contain his surprise. It flew in the face of everything they'd been told so far about the girl.

'You understand that, ordinarily, I would not be telling you this.' It was obvious that the doctor was still wrestling with the dilemma.

'Of course. You're doing the right thing.'

Dr Shah seemed less convinced, but she continued. 'At seventeen Yasmin is of course above the age of consent, but knowing her family's traditional views I was more than a little surprised by her request. She openly told me that she had not discussed this with either of her parents and felt unable to do so. But, as we talked it over, it became clear that Yasmin was already seeing someone and intended to proceed with or without my help.'

'I see,' was all that Mariner could muster. So much for honesty and openness with her parents, he thought.

'She seemed a little apprehensive,' Dr Shah continued. 'But made it clear that she was going ahead with the physical relationship and wanted to have some control over protecting herself. Yasmin is a bright girl and had clearly thought this through. The logical thing for me to do was at least prevent her from getting into trouble. I also agreed that I would respect her privacy in this matter.'

'So her parents don't know.'

'That's right.'

'And you're sure that Yasmin is in a relationship?'

'Of course I can't be absolutely certain, but that's what she told me. I had no reason to disbelieve her.'

'Did she mention any names?'

'That side of it really isn't my business, but no, she didn't.'

'Well, thank you, Dr Shah. That certainly adds a new dimension to our investigation.'

Dr Shah looked over at Nadine, who had dried her tears and sat silent throughout. 'There's more to it than that,' she said. 'Contraceptive pills affect women differently and I wanted to ensure that Yasmin would have no side effects with the one I prescribed, so initially, she had only a month's course as a kind of trial. The plan was that if she was happy with it she would come back for a full six months' prescription, which she did, at the beginning of last week.

'On the day Yasmin came in for her repeat prescription our computer system was down so I wasn't issuing any non-urgent prescriptions. I feel that those printed are preferable as there can be no query about the interpretation of hand-writing. Yasmin didn't need the pills immediately so we agreed that as soon as it was ready the prescription would be left at reception for Yasmin to collect when she could. The following day our computer was working again, so I prepared the prescription and it was put in the envelope marked with Yasmin's name to await collection.' She turned to the receptionist. 'Tell the inspector what happened, Nadine.'

The girl cast Mariner an anxious look. 'Mr Akram has also been having ongoing treatment for high blood pressure.' Somehow that didn't come as any surprise to Mariner.

'He came into the surgery to collect a repeat prescription and saw the envelope with Yasmin's name alongside his. He asked if it was for his daughter. He gave me her address and date of birth and I checked and found that it was hers, so I gave it to him to pass on to her.'

'Isn't that against the rules?'

Nadine's face told him that it was. Her tears had subsided, but weren't far away. 'I'm really sorry.'

'She is new to the job,' Dr Shah said. 'We had talked about this, but clearly I didn't place

142

enough emphasis. I must take full responsibility.'

'So you handed Mr Akram a prescription for his daughter for the contraceptive pill that he had no idea she was taking? Did he look at it?'

'No, he left the surgery. But he must have opened it outside. He came back in and wanted to know why Yasmin had been to the doctor and what was wrong. I said I didn't know and he started to get angry. He took out the prescription and demanded to know what it was.'

'And you told him.'

'I recognised it and I didn't think. I said I thought it was for a contraceptive pill.' The girl was dying inside and Mariner almost felt sorry for her.

The doctor rushed to her defence. 'To be fair, that is almost irrelevant. Mr Akram could have walked into any pharmacy or accessed any Internet site to find out what the drug was for. The damage had already been done.'

'What was Mr Akram's reaction when you told him what the prescription was?'

'He was furious. He didn't say much but I could see from his face. I told him that the pills could be to help regulate Yasmin's menstrual cycle and help with period pain. I had to do the same thing once. But he didn't listen. He wanted to speak to Dr Shah, and when I said she was out on her rounds, he stormed out.'

'Did he come back?'

'No.' Dr Shah provided the answer.

'Who did you think he was angry with, Nadine?'

'Me; Dr Shah; Yasmin maybe? I don't know.'

143

Being forced to face the implications of what had happened for the first time, Nadine's voice cracked and again she dissolved into tears. Dr Shah put a protective arm around her.

'Thank you,' Mariner said to the doctor. 'I appreciate your sharing this with me. I understand what a difficult decision it has been.'

When Nadine was calm again, Dr Shah walked him out. 'I may never know if I've done the right thing, but that's something I'll have to live with.'

'I feel sure that you have,' said Mariner. 'If it helps us to find Yasmin...'

'When I saw the news of her disappearance I recognised her, of course, but the talk has been of racially motivated abduction, and I thought you would naturally find out about any boyfriend through Yasmin's friends. Nadine didn't even tell me about her mistake because she was afraid she would lose her job.'

'And will she?'

'I think everyone should be allowed to get things wrong at least once, don't you?'

Given the number of times he'd fouled up over the years, Mariner felt he was hardly in a position to argue.

Back at Granville Lane, Mariner was keen to have Millie's take on this news, and asked the key question: 'How do you think Akram would have reacted to this?'

'He'd have gone ballistic,' she said, bluntly.

'Hm, that's what I thought.'

'Several things would have upset him: the fact that Yasmin was in a relationship–'

'The receptionist didn't tell him that. He might have accepted her explanation that Yasmin was taking the pill for other reasons.'

'But he'd be annoyed that Yasmin had gone behind his or his wife's back to arrange contraception and that the surgery had complied.'

'So as Nadine said, his anger could have been directed at the doctor's practice?'

'He didn't get back to Dr Shah to complain though, did he? I think he'd have been far more upset about the fact that Yasmin might be seeing someone. If he didn't buy Nadine's explanation for the pill then there's probably little worse that Yasmin can have done to anger him. He's already told us how "innocent" she is and now he's suddenly being told he might be wrong about that. There's a lot of pressure on girls in our communities to keep themselves pure for their future husbands, and we know that arranged marriage is one aspect of Muslim life that the Akrams subscribe to. If it became public knowledge that Yasmin was sleeping around it would make it harder for her parents to find her a husband of any standing. And that would be important to a family like the Akrams. They value their reputation in the community and made a good match for their older daughter. They'd want the same for Yasmin. Previous relationships would limit the possibilities. She would be soiled goods.'

'And this is more information they've chosen not to share with us.'

'This would be quite a blow to the family pride and reputation. They wouldn't be keen to share it with anyone. It wouldn't be great publicity for

145

their school either, to have their own daughter flouting fundamental Islamic beliefs. Part of the reason many parents choose Islamic schools is to protect their children from exactly this kind of thing: the corruption of the outside world.'

'Hasan Sheron wasn't so very far off the mark after all. How strongly do you think Akram would react to this knowledge?'

'Well, we already know that Mohammed Akram doesn't take things lying down,' said Millie. 'That would be especially true where his daughter's concerned. And we know that he has a short temper.'

'So now, suddenly, we're presented with a fat, juicy motive. No wonder he's been trying to divert our attention elsewhere. Do you think this would give Akram enough reason to harm Yasmin?'

'You've heard of so-called honour killings?' Millie asked.

'Like Abdullah Yones?'

'He stabbed his sixteen-year-old daughter eleven times in a frenzied attack because she had started to wear make-up and had a boyfriend and others in the community began referring to her as a prostitute. He saw her behaviour as an affront to his honour.'

'But Yones was Kurdish, wasn't he?'

'There are plenty of examples of similar situations across other cultures. In Pakistan, Samia Sarwar was shot dead with a gun disguised as her mother's walking stick, right in front of her lawyer. Islam doesn't condone such violence, but like any religion, honour can be used as a justification.'

'You think Mohammed Akram is capable of that?'

146

'I'm saying it happens, that's all. Perhaps Akram wouldn't need to go that far.'

'What do you mean?' Mariner asked.

'Well, on that Tuesday afternoon Akram travelled up to the school in Bradford. He's got contacts up there. Maybe it would be enough to get Yasmin away for a time. It may even be that he's planning to spirit her away abroad into an arranged marriage before her reputation becomes public knowledge. Remember, it was the school who reported Yasmin missing, and when we first went to talk to the Akrams he seemed almost irritated with his wife that the alarm had been raised. He said, "You should have waited?" We took it as being a control thing, but perhaps he had planned to let Mum in on it.'

'So why doesn't he just come clean about it now? Christ, he knows what we're putting into this investigation.'

'Because the timing's wrong. If it hasn't been followed through he can't afford to yet. And he wouldn't tell his wife because she might give the game away or she may not approve of or support such actions. By reporting Yasmin missing and involving us straight away, Shanila could have provided her husband with the perfect smoke screen, but one he'd have to keep in place until the job is done.'

'If Akram knows that Yasmin is safe, he's a hell of an actor. Remember the appeal? Where does all that angst come from?'

'It has different roots. In any other circum-stances Akram is a law-abiding man. What he's doing is the best thing for his daughter and family,

147

and he wouldn't hesitate to bend the rules, but he'd also know that at the very least, it's a gross act of deception. He wouldn't be comfortable with that.'

'But family come first.' Mariner couldn't deny that there was a certain logic to what Millie was saying. 'So Dad plays along with the general view that Yasmin has gone missing until she is married off and it's too late to do anything about it. Forcing Yasmin into a marriage against her will is hardly likely to be what she wants.'

Millie agreed. 'And it's a major human rights issue. There are all kinds of pressure groups who'd have a field day if he was exposed. None of which would enhance Akram's image as a liberal, Westernised Muslim.'

'The other alternative is that Akram genuinely doesn't know where Yasmin is because she has run away. From what we're finding out about her, Yasmin doesn't sound like the kind of girl who's going to sit around and let herself be coerced into a marriage she doesn't want, however necessary her parents might think it is.'

'Either way we need to get Akram's side of the story on this,' said Millie.

'One thing we haven't found out yet.'

'What?'

'If Yasmin is on the pill because she's in a relationship – who the hell is it with? Someone's keeping a low profile.'

'The relationship was obviously a secret one. Probably the boyfriend knows the way Akram would react too.'

148

Chapter Nine

Mariner was put straight through to Mohammed Akram. 'You have some news, Inspector?' His hope was palpable. If he was covering up he was doing a brilliant acting job.

'No, I'm sorry, Mr Akram. But I do need to speak to you again. I wondered if I could meet you at your home. You may prefer to speak to us without your wife.'

'Why would I want to do that?'

'I'd like to talk to you about an incident that occurred at your doctor's surgery last week.'

Silence, then: 'I see. I'll meet you at the house.'

Akram's Mercedes was already parked on the looped tarmac drive when Mariner pulled in behind it. He was surprised when the door was answered by a pretty young woman in purple and black salwaar kameez. 'I'm Amira,' she said. 'Yasmin's older sister. I flew in this morning to give some support to my parents until Yasmin is found.' So the tired eyes in such a young face could have been jet-lag or worry. If this was some kind of scam, Mariner doubted that Amira was in on it. 'My father is in the garden. I'll take you to him.'

Mohammed Akram was sitting on a wooden bench in a shaded patch at the bottom of an expanse of lawn that was crowded on all sides with bulging shrubs. He was tie-less and the sleeves of his dress shirt were rolled up. A variety of garden chairs was scattered around him and Mariner took his chance on a flimsy, white plastic affair. Amira did the same.

Mariner glanced up at the elder daughter. 'Mr Akram, what we have to talk about may be a little sensitive–' he began, but Akram stopped him.

'I want Amira to hear it. At some time I have to tell my wife, so I would like Amira to know.' He seemed fidgety and unrelaxed, but then he already knew that this was going to be a difficult conversation.

'All right then. As I indicated on the phone, I have some questions regarding your visit to Dr Shah's surgery. I understand that you had an appointment there last Friday?'

Akram's eyes narrowed. 'How did you find out about this?'

'We have been in touch with Dr Shah.' No need to tell him who initiated the contact.

'She had no right–'

'Mr Akram, how we came by this information at this stage is irrelevant. We would have got to it eventually through routine checks on Yasmin's medical history. For Dr Shah it was a difficult decision to make. Like the rest of us, she is worried about Yasmin's whereabouts, but she only found out today what had happened. Would you like to tell me now, in your own words, what occurred, and then after that, you may want to explain why you kept this from me.'

Akram looked suddenly exhausted. 'That one's easy,' he said. 'I didn't tell you because this is our family business. I'm not proud of how I reacted – over-reacted – at the surgery and it really has nothing to do with Yasmin's disappearance. We had discussed the situation and resolved it.'

Just like that, thought Mariner. 'I'd still like you to tell me.'

Akram sighed. 'It's only what I expect you already know. On Friday afternoon I went to Dr Shah's surgery to collect my repeat prescription. I was making a further appointment when I noticed an envelope with Yasmin's name on it. I asked if it was for my daughter. I had no idea that it contained a prescription. Girls, women, they have regular health checks and I thought that perhaps it was some kind of reminder. The receptionist asked my address and Yasmin's date of birth. When the details corresponded with those on the prescription she let me have it.'

'And you opened the envelope.'

To his credit, Akram didn't looked pleased with himself, but then he'd had ample time to concoct this little charade. 'There was nothing on the envelope to say that it was confidential and I thought if it was an appointment, Shanila and I would need to think about how we would get Yasmin to it.'

'And when you saw that it was a prescription?'

'I was surprised. I wasn't aware that there was anything wrong with Yasmin or that she had been to see the doctor. Normally, Shanila would tell me about anything like that.'

'Did you know what the prescription was for?'

'Not right away. I went back into the surgery and asked the receptionist. She said she thought it was for a type of contraceptive pill.'

151

'And you were surprised?'

'Inspector, I was everything you would expect me to be: shocked, horrified, angry and disappointed. Do you have children, Inspector? A daughter?'

'No.'

'I couldn't understand why Yasmin would need this and I was angry with our GP for having written such a prescription without telling me or my wife. She's just a child.'

'You were certain your wife didn't know?'

'Shanila and I don't have secrets, especially about our children.'

Yet Shanila allowed Yasmin to go to her friend's against your wishes, thought Mariner. He tried to catch Amira's eye but she was gazing intently towards the house, her face troubled. Instead he said, 'Doctors have certain rules of confidentiality they must–'

Again the anger flared up. 'Yasmin is only seventeen. She doesn't mix with boys. What would she want with the contraceptive pill? What sort of country is this where professionals can make decisions about a child's life without the knowledge of her parents?'

'So you were angry, Mr Akram.'

'At first, yes.'

'Who were you angry with?'

'The receptionist, the doctor, for writing this prescription without my knowledge and, I felt sure, without my wife's knowledge too.'

'And Yasmin?'

'Yes.'

'You said you were angry "at first"?'

'The girl told me that the pills could have been prescribed to control Yasmin's menstrual cycle, that it could be perfectly innocent.'

'And did you believe that?'

'When I took some time to consider it, thought rationally about the facts, it seemed the only logical explanation.'

'So you accepted it.'

'It was obviously something I needed to discuss with Yasmin.'

'And when did you do that?'

'I went to meet her from school. I thought we would be able to talk about it in the car on the way home.'

'And did you?'

'When I arrived outside the school Yasmin came out with her friends: Suzanne and some other girls. She wasn't pleased to see me. She didn't want a lift, she wanted to walk with her friends. Yasmin doesn't like to show how much she cares about her family in front of her friends. I told her I wanted to talk to her about something, but she said we had the whole weekend. Suzanne said something to her.'

'Did you speak to Suzanne?'

'She is an interfering b–' He stopped himself. 'She had probably put Yasmin up to it.'

'What made you think that?'

'The girl has a reputation.'

'For what?'

'For being easy with the boys. You only have to look at her clothing; it's indecent. She was encouraging Yasmin to behave the same way.'

'Is that the real reason you wouldn't let Yasmin

go to Suzanne's house?'

'That girl is a bad influence.'

'So did you give Yasmin a lift?'

'Only from the university station. I went and waited for her there when she got off the train. I drove her home and we talked about it then. I didn't want that conversation brought into the house.'

'And what did Yasmin tell you?'

'She told me the same thing as the receptionist, that she was on the pill to control her periods. They had been irregular and uncomfortable and that the doctor thought the pill would alleviate those symptoms. She hadn't thought it necessary to tell her mother or me.'

'Did you believe her?'

'I wanted to. Yasmin is growing up. There are certain ways in which we must respect her privacy.'

'That doesn't answer my question. Mr Akram, what would you say if I told you that Yasmin had given the doctor a different story?'

'What do you mean?'

'Yasmin told Dr Shah that she needed to go on the pill to protect herself. That she was in a relationship that was already physical.' He was deliberately testing out Akram to measure the reaction, but to his credit Akram looked genuinely shocked.

'Yasmin denied it and I believed her.'

'So you believed that she was taking the pill for medical reasons and your anger with Yasmin passed, and yet you didn't confront Dr Shah about this.'

'It was the weekend. The doctor wouldn't be available.'

'Did you give Yasmin the impression that you were angry with her? Did you, say, raise your voice to her?'

'I might have. I was upset.'

'Is it possible that your behaviour could have prompted Yasmin to run away?'

'Yes, of course it's possible. Do you think I haven't already thought of that?'

'If Yasmin was seeing someone, a boy, have you any idea who that might be?'

'When I asked her outright Yasmin denied it, and she wouldn't lie to me. As far as I'm concerned she has no contact with any boys.'

'Thank you, Mr Akram.'

Amira got to her feet. 'I'll show you out.' She took Mariner back up the garden and round the side of the house to his car. When they were out of earshot of her father she said, 'Inspector, it might be helpful for you to know that I can't be as sure as my father that Yasmin wasn't in a relationship. I know that for some months she had been coming under pressure from her friends to have some fun. She couldn't talk to my parents about it, but she often rang me for my advice.'

'And what did you advise her to do?'

'I told her to relax. That virginity isn't as important as our parents seem to think, and that if an opportunity comes along that she wants to take, then she should take it.'

'And did an opportunity come along?'

She flashed an apologetic smile. 'That's what I don't know.'

155

Millie met Mariner as he came back into the building.

'How did it go?'

'He certainly seemed upset by it all.'

'Guilt.'

'Trouble is, what kind of guilt? Is he feeling guilty because he knows what's happened to Yasmin and he's stringing us along, or feeling guilty because he may have caused his daughter to run away?' Mariner fed back what Amira had told him, too.

'It would be interesting to get Suzanne's perspective on that story,' said Millie. 'If Yasmin has been seeing someone, she'll be the one to know.'

'We'll talk to her on Monday.'

'Yes, sir.' Jamilla hesitated, about to say something else.

'And?' prompted Mariner.

'Tony Knox,' she said. 'Is he all right?'

'In what way?' asked Mariner, regretting the hint of defensiveness that he knew had crept into his voice. It was enough to put her off.

'It's OK. Nothing, I'm sure.'

'His mother-in-law's ill and his wife's away. He's distracted, that's all.' Mariner hoped it was true. He wasn't oblivious to the fact that Knox and Millie didn't seem to have established much of a working relationship when he wasn't there. He'd never seen Tony Knox as a racist, but then the situation had never previously arisen.

Millie shrugged. 'Like I said, it's nothing.'

Nonetheless, Mariner took the next opportunity

to quiz Knox. 'How are you getting on with Millie?'

Knox seemed surprised by the question. 'Fine,' he said.

'She's a good officer. I think she's brought an added dimension to the investigation.'

'Yeah.'

Mariner had successfully backed himself into a corner. The next question was: And do you have a problem with her being Asian? Instead he took the easy way out. 'How's Theresa's mother?' he asked.

'What?'

'Theresa's mother. I take it she's still up there, looking after her?'

'Oh. She's up and down, you know, but Theresa just wants to be there.' Knox stared into space, lost for a moment in his own thoughts, before turning his attention back to the database he was working on. That was definitely it, Mariner thought. It was Theresa's mother that was the problem. Touching that a bloke could be so concerned about the mother-in-law.

A walk-through was scheduled for late Tuesday afternoon, one week after Yasmin's disappearance, and would provide an opportunity for the press and media to assemble and publicise the event to anyone who may have been in the area on the day that Yasmin vanished. Local newspapers, radio and TV were well represented and now that the case was gathering momentum there would be national coverage too. To maximise the potential for witnesses to come forward, they had to take the most likely option, based on Yasmin getting off the train at the university station as she would normally have done, and walking home. The length and complexity of the journey turned everything into a major production, with three different camera crews on the train and at either end of the walk.

Mariner was pleased with the turn-out, though. Even considering that many of the onlookers were simply there to rubber-neck, the more people there were, the greater the chance that Yasmin would continue to be the topic of every-day conversation and the greater the chance that someone, somewhere, would recall seeing something of relevance last Tuesday afternoon. Posters of the seventeen-year-old peppered the walls of the station and officers distributed more of the flyers among the small crowd that had gathered, though Mariner couldn't imagine anyone who hadn't just jetted in from Mars being unfamiliar with that smiling snapshot.

The group of young girls from a neighbouring school, including the one who was to be Yasmin's double, had been carefully primed and taken several times through each step of the journey as Yasmin would have made it. Miraculously, at the appointed time everything was ready and Mariner was able to give the instruction to begin. On cue, the girls left the high school and began the walk down towards the railway station. A small crowd followed them, supervised by uniformed constables, but despite the numbers an unnatural hush had descended, interrupted only by the staccato snapping of camera shutters.

On instruction the girls waited at the top of the road leading down to the station until the train was seen approaching so that 'Yasmin' could run for the train in the way that 'she' had done on Tuesday. Today, the train was several minutes late, causing tense moments while everyone stood about waiting for it. They'd been able to arrange for the original driver of the train to be back on duty, in the hope that his memory would be jogged, but as there was no routine ticket check on board they were relying on other passengers to have seen Yasmin. This was likely to prove difficult as, at this time of the afternoon, the trains going into the city were almost deserted; all the passenger traffic going in the opposite direction, at the beginning of the rush hour.

An additional carriage had been laid on for press only – based on the assumption that Yasmin had got on the train and continued her journey home, they followed her to the university station from where she would have walked home. The route took them along the walkway through the university grounds and past the meadow where Helen Greenwood had encountered the flasher, confirming that it would have been all too easy for Yasmin to draw attention to herself and solicit an unwelcome approach from a stranger. It seemed more implausible than ever that anyone with a gramme of common sense would attempt a random abduction in these surroundings, and in broad daylight.

A film crew from the regional TV station was there to film this part of the journey and a clip would be broadcast the following evening on the regular 'Crimestoppers' slot. Before long, the story would be national news, too. That would really open the floodgates to the cranks.

Mariner watched the beginning of the reconstruction before he and Knox drove across to the university to pick up the end. Despite his reservations, Mariner felt that it was going well, and that they would have done enough to stir the memories of anyone who was around that Tuesday afternoon. What they really needed was one good, solid lead.

Mariner's wish was granted, but not from the expected source. The walk-through successfully concluded, he and Knox were on their way back to Granville Lane when the radio crackled into life.

'The manager at Comet electrical superstore has just phoned. He's got something you might be interested in.'

'Like what?'

'Yasmin Akram's mobile phone.'

In a move worthy of Starsky and Hutch, Knox made an illegal U-turn at the next traffic lights and they drove to the retail park where the store was based. Even at this time on a weekday there was a steady stream of traffic in and out of the park. The garden centre next door was displaying everything to enhance the summer experience and they had to pick their way through barbecues, garden furniture and pot plants.

Inside the store, Mariner showed his warrant card and asked to speak to the manager. Mark Williams looked about fifteen, clean cut in a dazzling white shirt with the company logo on the pocket. With a dramatic flourish, he put a plastic bag down on the counter. Mariner opened the bag and removed the only item: a purple mobile phone. 'A Nokia 3100 with a mauve oil and water removable cover,' said Williams, though whether the pride was in the phone itself or his own professional knowledge, was hard to tell. 'The bloke who brought it in had found it. He came in to check the registration, so that he could return it.'

'He couldn't get that from the phone?'

William shook his head. 'It's "pay as you go" so we had to track the owner on the system. Every time one of these is bought, it's logged with the company: in this case, Nokia. You can check it out with anyone who sells the brand of phones. This one is registered to Miss Yasmin Akram,' he said. 'As soon as I saw that I knew whose it was, so I thought we should call you.'

'You thought right,' Mariner said. He looked around at the customers browsing the displays. 'Where's the guy who brought it in?'

'Mr Hewitt? He couldn't wait, but he left his address and his mobile number.'

'You let him go?'

Williams's face fell. 'He had to get back to work. I'm pretty sure he's kosher.'

'He'd better be, for your sake.'

Mariner called the mobile number. When it was picked up, after several rings, there was noise and disturbance in the background: animals yelping.

'Mr Hewitt?' Mariner enquired, over the din.
'Yes.'
'You handed in a phone belonging to Yasmin Akram.'

161

'That's right.'

'We need to speak to you urgently. Where are you?'

'The animal rescue centre on Barnes Hill.' It explained the soundtrack.

'We'll be with you right away. Don't go anywhere.'

'I wasn't planning to.'

Meanwhile, Knox had bagged up the phone so that they could drop it in at Granville Lane to be sent on to forensics without delay. That tiny device could prove invaluable in the search for Yasmin Akram.

In this heat you could navigate the city with your eyes shut, from the acrid Longbridge paint shop to the sickly-sweet halo surrounding the Cadbury factory. The aroma that lingered over Barnes Hill was a not entirely pleasant antiseptic with a hint of dog crap. The pound was quiet, but for the persistent yapping of some kind of small breed dog. It was getting on Mariner's nerves before they even reached the office, but he guessed the staff working there must be immune to it.

'Be with you in a sec.' Paul Hewitt was processing paperwork in a tiny office just behind the reception desk. As they waited, a lethargic Labrador wandered in out of the heat and plopped itself down in a basket in a corner of the room.

When Hewitt finally appeared, Mariner had a visual impression of a kind of understated Friar Tuck: medium height and rotund, his shiny bald scalp circled by a fringe that resembled a monk's tonsure. Large, square-framed glasses rested on the bridge of his nose and his cheery smile

162

completed the image. 'We'll go in the training room,' he said. 'It'll be cooler in there.'

The room was indeed airier and had a table large enough to spread out the map that Mariner and Knox had brought with them.

'So, where did you find it?'

'Kingsmead Reservoir,' Hewitt said. 'Right here.' Hewitt jabbed a finger at a spot right on the edge of the map, just beside the blue blob that symbolised water.

Although he'd heard of it, Mariner's knowledge of Kingsmead Reservoir extended no further than a label on the incident room map: an uninhabited wilderness on the other side of the railway track to the station, between the main Birmingham to Bristol line and Birchill Lane. The reservoir itself, though once functional, had ceased to be useful after Birmingham began drawing water from the Elan Valley, storing it in the much larger Bartley Green reservoir. 'But that's in the middle of nowhere,' he said.

'I know,' agreed Hewitt.

'So what were you doing there?' asked Knox, more than a little pointedly.

Hewitt was unruffled. 'We got a call from St Clare's, the old folk's home that backs on to it, just here.' He put an index finger on the map. 'One of the old biddies had got it into her head that she'd seen a man there beating a dog. She thought he might have killed it.'

Hairs stood up on the back of Mariner's neck. 'When was this?'

'She mentioned it to the staff a few days ago, apparently, but nobody took her seriously at first.

The old girl has her "senior" days, if you know what I mean. But she wouldn't let it drop. I think she must have driven them mad over the weekend with it, so to humour her, they gave us a call, first thing this morning. I drove over with Sue, my partner, and had a look at the place she described. It took some finding, I can tell you. Even though Lily, that's Lily Cooper, showed us from her window where she saw it happen, it was still difficult to find a way in. We had to use the *A–Z*.'

'I'm not surprised,' said Mariner, looking again at the map. There was no obvious access to the site.

'When we got to it, there was no sign of any dog where the old dear said, but just to make sure we had a good hunt around, as far as we could – most of it's like untamed jungle – and that was when we found the phone, lying there in the grass. We brought it back to the office, charged it up then keyed in to find the user identity. But because it's one of those "pay as you go" phones I had to take it to a dealer so they could look up the name and address of the person who bought it. The Comet store's not far away. We've all seen the news bulletins so once they'd looked it up, it didn't take long to put two and two together.'

'Well, I'm very glad that you did,' said Mariner. 'This could be quite a breakthrough.' Suddenly he sensed that there was more. 'Was there anything else you wanted to tell us?'

Hewitt lowered his voice. 'I wouldn't want to be alarmist, but near where we found it there was brown stuff, sort of staining on the grass. I didn't

164

say anything to Sue, but it looked to me like blood.'

'We'll need you to take us to the exact spot, Mr Hewitt.'

Hewitt slapped his thighs, a little nervously Mariner thought. 'Whenever you like.'

Chapter Ten

They followed the same route that Hewitt had taken to get to the reservoir, past the railway station, over the line, past a pub called the Bridge and on to Birchill Lane, flanked on one side by a public park and on the other by wild woodland, broken only by a tall and rambling building that looked as if it had once been a country residence of some kind.

'That's the nursing home.' Hewitt said, just as the sign for 'St Clare's' came into view. Just along from the home they passed the entrance road to a small industrial park, which was followed by another half a mile or so of sparse, unhealthy look-ing woodland, to a row of four derelict cottages. The houses were fenced in by heavy-duty spike-topped railings, with a huge pair of steel-framed, chain-link gates padlocked against trespassers. A board in the entrance announced that the en-closed land was on the market for development.

To the side, a narrow, unmetalled service road curled round to the back of the cottages into what once might have been their gardens, with perhaps an orchard, but was now an open piece of rough ground of about a quarter of an acre. And it was here that Hewitt took them, Knox easing the car cautiously over the uneven terrain to avoid damaging the suspension. They drew to a halt in a small grassy clearing, pock-marked with litter and the sort of detritus left behind by glue sniffers. Here and there were areas of blackened grass where fires had been lit and an old, filthy mattress lay on its side, springs spilling out of it like guts from a dead animal. Even in daylight any vehicle parking here would have been shielded from the view of houses on the opposite side of Birchill Lane by the cottages themselves, the trees and the rampant, overgrown shrubs.

'This was the nearest place I could find to park,' Hewitt said. 'I was hoping to find a way through somehow. I was encouraged by the fact that other people obviously use it.' He was referring to the tyre tracks carved out of the hard earth and the little heaps of dog-ends. 'When I looked around I saw that opening, there in the trees.'

He'd done well to spot that, thought Mariner. It was nothing more than a small gap in the undergrowth. 'Lead the way,' he said.

By now it was well after seven, but time had drawn none of the heat or humidity out of the day and even in shirtsleeves they sweltered. Knox and Mariner followed Hewitt through the wasteland, along the only clear path that cut a swathe through the low undergrowth, and straggling birches that had undoubtedly provided the adjacent road with its name. The dirt underfoot had been dried solid by the long, hot summer, but at one point, Mariner stopped at a small patch where water drained across its width, throwing up a couple of distinct footprints and a narrow tyre track, possibly belonging to a bike.

They smelled it before they saw it: a thick, peaty methane smell. Then, as the path meandered from one side to another, the trees began to thin to low shrubbery, then long grasses, and finally the path broke out again into the glare of the evening sun, at the edge of the reservoir, if that's what you could call it. Today it was simply an expanse of black mud, shrunken and dried by the drought, with a single broad channel flowing sluggishly across the centre from the far side, maybe five hundred yards away, towards where they were standing now. 'Kingsmead Reservoir,' Hewitt announced.

Mariner marvelled at how such an expanse could exist on their patch without any of them really knowing about it. The size of three football fields, it was a vast and untamed open space, the water's edge crowded with willows and reeds and shoulder-high grass. The land was bordered along the far side by the Birmingham to Bristol railway line and beyond that, a high bank of distant houses; the 'cottages on the ridge' from which the community of Cotteridge had taken its name. The factory site took up much of the near side, almost as far as the trees they'd walked through, though it finished four hundred yards away, behind substantial wood-panelled fencing. The only building that had any kind of direct view of the area was St Clare's.

'How could we not know about this?' Knox said.

167

'I'd heard about it.' Mariner admitted. 'It's part of the River Rea that runs down from the Waseley Hills right though the city and to Spaghetti Junction at the other end. It's been neglected for years but there has been a conservation group, Birmingham Riverside Trust, working on areas further up stream to try and clear it and create more of a leisure area: footpaths and cycle tracks, that kind of thing. I've seen posters around advertising for volunteers.'

As they surveyed the scene, a train thundered by on the opposite side of the water; not the local train that Yasmin would have caught, but the Birmingham to Bristol express. They heard rather than saw it, the wooden fence hiding it from view, and equally preventing any passengers from seeing anything on the reservoir. Anyone operating down here would know that they had almost complete privacy from prying eyes. The thought made Mariner shiver, despite the heat. Alongside the railway were the long production hangars of a glass manufacturer, separated from the track by a fifteen-foot wall topped with broken glass and razor wire. Anything along that stretch could be discounted as means of access.

They had come to a junction of sorts in the footpath: to the right was the rickety bridge that crossed the out-flow stream at the back of St Clare's, but going round to the left, skirting the edge of the reservoir, there were also clear signs that other feet had trodden.

'Lily had mentioned the bridge, so we went this way,' said Hewitt, leading them round to the rotting structure. Constructed from wooden

168

planks, it was in a state of disrepair, the boards mottled with holes, though still sound enough to take their combined weight. On one side the railings were snapped in two. Underneath the structure the water moved reluctantly on to a square plate of deeply rusted metal, accumulating at a pair of wooden gates. Though firmly shut, there were enough rotten crevices to allow the pathetic dribble of water to slowly insinuate itself through them to where it barrelled and cascaded limply over a concrete shelf and down into a narrow tunnel.

'So what's all this about?' Knox asked, peering over the edge.

'It looks like some kind of slow-release mechanism to make sure the reservoir doesn't go completely dry or flood,' Mariner said. 'They have them on some canals. As the reservoir fills, the pressure builds on that plate until it eventually gets unlocked by the weight and volume of water, the gates open and the water surges down the spill-way into the tunnel.' But he was talking to himself. Knox had already lost interest.

Hewitt crossed the bridge to where the path broadened out slightly on the other side. 'This is where Lily said she saw the action, and that was where we found the phone, lying just there,' he said, pointing to an area of longish grass just to the side of what would have been a path. 'And that's what I thought might be blood.' Initially camouflaged, on closer inspection there was no missing the brownish stains, some of which were as dark as creosote on the yellowing grass. Mariner's first thought was how Sue, Hewitt's

169

partner, could have overlooked them.

'But where's our dog?' he murmured to himself. 'Is there a way down here from the station?' he asked, looking up at the chain-link fence that separated them from the platforms and car park, two hundred or so yards away.

'I think there used to be,' said Hewitt. 'But I wouldn't know where exactly it comes out. I can't imagine that anybody uses it any more because, since the factory was demolished, it wouldn't go anywhere. The industrial units block off the other side. If you wanted to get to Birchill Lane it would be much simpler to walk along the road instead.'

But longer, thought Mariner, making a visual sweep through 360 degrees. As a walker, he was accustomed to scouring overgrown tracts of land for signs of a thoroughfare. Many times he'd come to a so-called public footpath across a field that some uncooperative farmer had planted over in the hope of discouraging ramblers. Only a few weekends ago, he'd had to battle his way through a field of maize that had grown taller than him, completely obscuring the right of way.

Generally speaking, he wasn't alone in his determination and there were others who wouldn't be deterred, which meant that usually, as in this case, a soft line marking out the faintest traces of human disturbance could be seen. Nettles and cow parsley stems that elsewhere were waist high had been snapped and crushed, the long grass swept over. He struck out along it a little way and was proved right: though not well-used and with hardly a break in the solid foliage, it was a definite path; recently forged down from the back of the

170

station to where they now stood, and passed through, perhaps three or four times, since the early summer. The logical destination would be the cluster of low-level pre-fabricated units a quarter of a mile away, but the greenery in that direction looked untouched. 'What have we got there?' Mariner asked.

'Small businesses, that sort of thing,' Hewitt replied. 'There's a sign on up the road.'

'We should have a closer look,' Mariner told Knox. 'Meanwhile, I don't want everyone tramping around here like a herd of elephants just yet. We need to cordon off the area and get a team down here ASAP to do a thorough search.' He scanned the area. It wasn't going to be easy. The surrounding ground had been left to go wild for years and the grass was dense and impenetrable, with some vicious-looking brambles and nettles. Added to which they'd need to cover the disused cottages. It was all going to take valuable time and manpower. Meanwhile, forensics could get down here and verify that the staining was indeed blood, though Mariner, from experience, was pretty sure that it was.

He looked at his watch. Gone eight o'clock. By the time they could get anything organised it would be going on for nine and even at this time of year the light would start going. In this hostile terrain it would be a nightmare. Despite the urgency it would be better to have the light on their side to avoid missing anything. In only a few hours the sun would be coming up again.

'OK, let's get off here. We'll need to get the area sealed off and do a thorough search first thing

171

tomorrow.' They trekked back along the narrow path to where the car was parked and Knox could call through to Granville Lane to organise securing the site. They were just about to leave when a distant roar greeted their ears and another vehicle appeared in the mouth of the clearing, with a lone driver. Seeing the assembled group he applied his brakes, clearly considering whether to continue or to turn and retreat. Before he could, Mariner approached, arm outstretched, holding out his warrant card, Knox at his heels. When he was near enough to be clearly identified, the car driver reacted with a resigned movement of the head and put on the handbrake.

'DI Mariner, Mr–?'

'Pryce, Shaun Pryce,' the man obliged, indicating a degree of familiarity with this routine. 'It's all right. I'll come back another time.' He glanced up into the rear-view mirror as if to go, but Mariner was close enough to place both hands on the sill of the door.

'Would you mind getting out of the car a minute, Mr Pryce?'

Standing alongside Mariner, Shaun Pryce was considerably shorter than him, a wiry young man of about thirty, his platinum hair edged with lethal-looking ginger sideburns. Testosterone oozed from every pore, his stylishly crumpled combats and a faded black tank top displaying his muscular arms and shoulders to their fullest advantage, including a couple of elaborate tattoos. He saw Mariner looking at them.

'My personal *hommage* to the Robster,' he said, pronouncing the word with an exaggerated

French accent. 'That's where you've seen them before. So what's going on then?' He grinned, exposing perfect, gleaming white teeth, his eyes roving from one to another of the policemen, distinctly cagey despite the outward charm. Leaning back on the car door, he was a picture of relaxation but, folding his arms, he kept a wary eye on Knox who was prowling around the battered VW Golf. Old and scruffy, the vehicle had bits of electrical equipment lying on the parcel shelf, including several coils of plastic sheathed wire. A St George's flag sticker decorated the rear window.

Mariner ignored the question. 'What brings you here?' he asked.

'I saw the car and came to see what's going on. I wanted to make sure it wasn't kids messing about. One day they'll set fire to the trees and the whole lot will go up.'

No kids Mariner knew had access to a top of the range Vauxhall Vectra, he thought, but he didn't pursue it.

'So you've been here before,' he said instead.

Pryce shrugged. 'A couple of times. It's peaceful. Somewhere to come and unwind a bit.' As if to sanction the rustic image, an evening blackbird chose that moment to begin its repetitive song. For many people, Mariner included, it might have been a credible response, but Shaun Pryce just didn't look the type to derive his relaxation from a patch of scrubby, rubbish-strewn grass.

Knox leaned in through the car's passenger window and retrieved something from the back seat. 'Come being the operative word, eh, Mr Pryce?' The magazine he'd retrieved displayed a

173

full montage of photographs of naked women striking far from modest poses. That was more like it.

Unembarrassed by the find, Pryce smirked. 'You know how it is. I have a high sex drive,' he said. 'I'm sure you can be a bit of a wanker sometimes, Officer.' He was deliberately baiting Knox. He was playing with fire. Muscles bunched around Knox's jaw, but he kept control.

'Where exactly do you do this unwinding?' Mariner asked. 'It must be a bit stuffy in the car in this weather.'

'Just around.' Pryce glanced around the general area, none of which looked the least bit inviting.

'Ever go on to the reservoir itself?' Mariner nodded towards the path they'd found.

Pryce shook his head. 'No.'

'Never? Why not?'

'No point. Why walk half a mile through the jungle when everything I need is here.'

'When was the last time you were here?'

'I couldn't really say. Like I told you, it's only occasionally.'

'Try to think.'

'Couple of weeks ago, maybe.'

'Can you be a bit more precise?'

'I can't honestly remember.' He glanced at his watch, a hint that he'd like to go now.

'What time of day was it?'

'After work.'

'And what sort of work is it that you do, Mr Pryce?'

'Actually, I'm an actor.' So that was why he was enjoying this so much. Kid thought he was in an episode of *The Bill*. 'I'm resting at the moment, except for a bit of modelling but–'

'Been in anything I'd have seen?' challenged Knox.

'As I said, mostly modelling work, although I've been up for an audition for Jimmy Porter at the Rep.'

'I thought you said you came down here after work.'

'When I'm resting I do electrics. I'm working on an extension.'

'Nearby?'

'Just up the road.'

'Ever seen anyone else down here?'

Pryce laughed. 'That's the whole fucking point. It's *private*.'

'Have you ever owned a dog, Mr Pryce?' Understandably perhaps, the question took Pryce by surprise. 'No.'

Knox opened the driver's door for Pryce to get in.

'Aren't you going to tell me what's going on?' he asked.

'No.'

But Knox did take details of where he was working before they allowed him to get into his car and watch him reverse skilfully out of the clearing, right hand down at precisely the right point.

'Thinks he's God's gift,' said Knox, bitterly.

'Were you thinking what I was thinking?'

'That flag of St George was conspicuous in the back window of his car.'

'He might not have put it there of course,' said Mariner. 'It's a pretty old car. He seemed more

175

New Age than National Front to me.'

'That hair, though. Would have made any Aryan proud.'

'Even though it was dyed. What do you think?'

'He admitted himself, he's a little tosser. He didn't come down to check us out, he was surprised to see us. He braked as he came into the clearing.'

'And he's been here more than a few times,' Mariner agreed. 'That space isn't an easy one to reverse out of, avoiding the potholes, and he did it like a pro. Nor would I rule out him going on to the reservoir itself. How else would he know it's a half a mile of jungle unless he's been through it? No. Shaun Pryce wasn't telling us anything like the truth. The question is, is it because he knows something or is he hiding something? Just for the record, check whether we've got him on our books.'

'What for?'

'I don't know, but I think Shaun Pryce might be the kind of cocky little bugger who likes to play games.'

They took a last look around, but there was nothing more to be gained here. 'OK, let's knock it on the head for tonight and get some sleep while we still can,' said Mariner. 'We'll start the search first thing in the morning.' Knox didn't offer any resistance.

It was nearly ten when Mariner was ready to leave Granville Lane. He tried to phone Anna to let her know what was going on, but was wasting his time: all he got was her answering machine. It

176

irritated him disproportionately. He looked up to see Tony Knox doing nothing more useful than staring into space. 'Do you want a lift home?' he asked. Mariner half expected a rebuttal, but for once Knox took the sensible option.

'Fancy a drink?' Mariner added, when they got to the car.

'All right.'

'Spoken like a man who has nothing better to do,' said Mariner. 'How could I fail to be flattered?'

They stopped off at the Boat, Mariner's local, where tonight the garden seemed the most comfortable option. Even with a pint in front of him, Knox's reticence continued and ten minutes in, Mariner half-wished they hadn't bothered. 'We've been married too long,' he said, in an attempt at levity. 'Nothing to say to each other any more.'

Knox grimaced, before draining his glass. 'One more before the bell?'

Mariner had hardly started his. 'OK,' he said, and gulped it down. What a waste. Minutes later, Knox was back with two pints and a whisky chaser for himself. 'It's been a long day,' he said.

Mariner wasn't about to disagree. 'Cheers,' he said, before the silence set in again.

'So how do you think it got there?' said Knox suddenly.

'What?' Mariner was startled by the unprecedented verbosity.

'Yasmin Akram's phone,' Knox went on. 'It's on the other side of the track from where she would catch the Birmingham train.'

Mariner pounced on the interest. 'I've been

177

thinking about that. She must have dropped it,' he said. 'Someone else picked it up and took it there. If we're certain that she got on the train it's the only possibility.'

At last Knox appeared to engage. 'Well, we are certain, aren't we? The CCTV footage at this end is pretty clear. We all saw her getting on the train. You can't argue with that.'

'I wouldn't mind looking at it again.'

'What for? We've no reason to think that she didn't board that train. Why the hell would she have been going down to the reservoir? There's nothing there.'

'Bearing in mind what Dr Shah has now told us, there already seems to be plenty we don't know about Yasmin. And what did you think about Paul Hewitt? Is he straight?'

'It was just a chance discovery. He and his partner were led to it and there must be plenty of other people involved who'll be able to corroborate that.'

Mariner was inclined to agree. 'It will be easy enough to check with the nursing home and with his partner, Sue.'

'Your version's much more likely. Someone else picked up Yasmin's phone and took it to the bridge.'

'So how does that fit with what Lily saw?'

'If she saw anything. Hewitt implied that the old girl might not have all her marbles.'

'The bloodstains are there all right.'

'Except that we don't know for certain that they are blood.'

Knox was right. They'd need forensic confirmation that it was blood. If it was human blood, the next step would be to get a DNA sample from the Akrams to make a comparison. He didn't relish that prospect one little bit.

'It could just be that whoever picked up Yasmin's phone was the guy who Lily saw beating the dog,' Knox said, now fully engaged in the discussion.

'And I wouldn't rule out Shaun Pryce from all this, either.'

'Do you think he's the mystery man? We now know that Yasmin could have been seeing someone. She could have arranged to meet him anywhere between here and the station.'

But Knox picked on the obvious flaw. 'Except how would Pryce have known Yasmin? She's a schoolkid, he's an out of work actor and part time leckie.'

Mariner sighed. 'And we don't know for certain that there is any mystery man. Yasmin could have invented him in an attempt to be more sophisticated than she really is. We haven't talked to Suzanne yet and I got the impression of some pretty fierce competition going on between the two of them.'

'I do love a simple, straightforward case,' said Knox, wryly.

Mariner frowned. 'Ever had one?'

The thought was enough to render Knox sullen and morose all over again, and by the time Mariner dropped him off outside his house he was back to his monosyllabic self. Mariner offered a silent plea for Theresa to come back soon.

Mariner himself took the briefing at six the next morning at the entrance to what had become, overnight, the official reservoir car park. As much manpower as was possible had been mustered to conduct the second search, packing the areas with bodies. A new buzz in the air had been created by the discovery of the phone: introducing, thank God, a point of focus at last. As DCI Fiske was quick to point out, if didn't negate the possibility of Yasmin getting on the train as usual, but suddenly the options had opened up again. The relevant portion of the map showing the reservoir had been enlarged, circulated and apportioned, and Mariner split the group into teams of three to ensure that every square metre would be covered. 'We'll start with the more accessible areas: the land around, then if we need to, the water itself.'

Protective overalls, scythes and secateurs had been provided to assist with the mammoth task of hacking back the undergrowth, making the search party took like *Ground Force* on the rampage. The sun was already climbing steadily and Mariner had arranged for bottled water to be delivered: he didn't want anyone collapsing with dehydration.

Yasmin's phone was already at the lab where it would be checked for fingerprints and any messages analysed. Fortunately, on a case like this, it would take priority and could be rushed through in twenty-four hours. Mariner sincerely hoped they wouldn't come across anything more sinister or conclusive first.

With the search begun under the supervisory eye of DS Mark 'Jack' Russell, Mariner took Knox and went to the nursing home to talk to Lily, the woman who had witnessed the attack. St Clare's retirement home had exactly the kind of stale hint-of-urine aroma that seemed to go with the territory. 'God, I hate these places,' Knox said.

'One of our fastest growing industries,' remarked Mariner.

'But what's the point of festering away for years in a place like this. What kind of life is it? We're all living too long.'

His supporting argument was right in front of them. The office they'd been asked to wait in overlooked a kind of sun lounge, where high-backed easy chairs were clustered, most accommodating an elderly resident, even at this early hour. It was probably the same as hospitals, Mariner thought, everyone roused at the crack of dawn whether they liked it or not. Close to the TV, two elderly ladies stared fixedly at some kind of morning chat show, although whether either of them was actually watching it was impossible to tell. A uniformed nurse came and spoke to one of them. Painfully slowly, she helped the old woman to her feet and they shuffled out of the room, arm in arm. The girl looked about sixteen. What age was that to be carrying out intimate tasks for people old enough to be her grandparents? Mariner tried to envisage his mother in a place like this, but he couldn't. She'd be the world's worst resident. 'They're all white,' he said, suddenly noticing the fact. 'Mohammed Akram's mother won't end up in one of these.'

'Mr Mariner? I'm Nora.' The woman who breezed in was the member of staff Lily had confided in. A solid woman of around fifty, Norah's substantial bulk and bosom were held in by the starched blue nurse's uniform apparently worn by all the staff. 'Do you mind if we go outside? I'm gasping for a fag.' Gasping was the word. As they walked, she wheezed in rhythm with her stride, leaving Mariner wondering how she could cope with such a physically demanding job. They stood outside the front door, under a dripping lime, as traffic roared by on Birchill Road just a few yards away.

'Can you tell us what happened last Tuesday afternoon?'

Nora tapped half an inch of ash on to the path. 'It was tea-time. Lily was in the dining room, along with all the other residents when she said she didn't feel well. As she's still fairly independent we suggested that she should go back to her room and have a lie down. When I went up a little later to check on her, she was standing transfixed, in the middle of the room, staring out of the window. She was in some distress. I thought she'd had a funny turn or something, but when I asked if she was all right she grabbed my arm and said we mustn't under any circumstances let Casper out because she'd just seen a wicked man beating a dog to death down by the reservoir. I got her to show me, but of course, when we looked out of the window there was nothing to see.

'I didn't think any more of it then because although, generally speaking, Lily's one of our more lucid clients, she does have her moments.

182

Casper was the cat she left behind when she moved in here four years ago, so she was clearly getting a bit confused. When I reminded her of this she realised her mistake, but I could see that something had upset her. I thought it was over and forgotten but a few days later, Lily said she hadn't been able to sleep for thinking about it, so I asked her to show me again where she'd seen it.

'She told me exactly the same story and the description of what she saw didn't change. She insisted that she'd seen this man and that the poor dog could only be dead. As it was bothering her so much, I thought the least I could do was humour her and call the RSPCA. They'd be able to go and have a look and confirm that there was no dead dog. And Lily would be reassured to know that she'd been mistaken. There was nothing to lose.' She looked from one to the other of them and her voice dropped to a whisper. 'The man I spoke to said they found blood.'

'Well, we haven't established what it is just yet, but it would be helpful if we could speak to Lily herself, in case there's anything else she remembers. Would she be up to that?'

'I think so.'

'Would any other of the residents or staff have seen anything?'

'No, everyone else was in the dining room on the ground floor, which looks out over the side garden.'

'You said this happened at tea-time. What time would that have been?'

'About quarter to five.'

Twenty minutes after Yasmin had said goodbye

to her friends and disappeared off the face of the earth. Mariner didn't like that timing one little bit.

Back inside, they trooped up a winding staircase to Lily's room, a twelve by twelve box of floral wallpaper and chintzy fabrics. The bed was covered with the kind of peach-coloured candle-wick bedspread Mariner hadn't seen for years. On top of the mahogany chest of drawers were the assorted remnants of Lily's life: a few photographs and a couple of pieces of cheap porcelain; a varnished seashell purporting to be a gift from Bridlington. Not much left to show for more than seventy years on the planet.

The view from the window wasn't much to speak of either, overlooking as it did the jungle of yellowing scrubland that encircled the reservoir. Naturally, Lily had her windows open and even up here you could smell the sour, stagnant water. Mariner feared another setback when Lily turned out to be a frail old woman with whiskers sprouting from a face that was as lined and furrowed as the dry ground outside. Her sparse silvery hair had been permed into tight curls, exposing patches of scalp as pink and smooth as a baby's flesh, and the cotton frock she wore hung loosely on her withered frame. She was perched on an armchair, her eyes closed, but she opened them as they arrived, huge blue irises staring at them through the magnifying lenses of her glasses.

'Lily, these are the policemen I told you about. They just want to ask you some questions,' Nora said gently.

'Anything you like,' said Lily, encouragingly alert, once she'd come round. 'I know what I saw.' Perhaps she would turn out to be a decent witness, after all.

'I'll get some chairs,' said Nora, returning moments later with a couple of the moulded plastic variety, which she arranged beside the old lady. Mariner sat, but Knox maintained a disinterested distance, staring out of the window.

'Can you tell us exactly what you did see?' Mariner asked.

'It was tea-time, but I didn't feel like eating, especially the rubbish that they give us here; ratty-twee or some such foreign muck.' Mariner waited for Nora to contradict her, but then saw the game glint in Lily's eye. Why had he assumed that because she was old there would be no sense of mischief? 'Anyway, I came into my room and I could see someone down there on the bridge. He caught my attention because there's never anyone down there and the movement was ... well ... violent. He was swinging his arm up and down, up and down, hitting something on the ground.'

'Can you show me exactly where?' Mariner asked.

Using the armrests for support, Lily pushed herself up from the chair shakily and they joined Knox at the window, looking out at where the yellowing field with its dark kernel swarmed with police officers, moving laboriously through the undergrowth, heads bowed as if performing some ancient religious ritual.

'He was right next to that little wooden bridge, the one with the broken railings, to the left of it where the long grass starts again.' Nothing wrong

185

with her eyesight, then.

'Was he standing or kneeling?' Mariner asked.

'He was standing, his legs apart, but he was bent over, low.'

'Could you see his face?'

'No, because he had his back turned to me. He just kept swinging his arm up and down, up and down.' Her eyes filled with tears. 'That poor little defenceless creature.'

'The dog.'

'Yes.'

'Could you see what colour the dog was?' Mariner peered out. It was unlikely that she could have. If what she said was right, the creature would have been hidden by the tall grass.

Lily shook her head. 'Not very well, the grass was too long.'

'But you're sure it was a dog?'

'What else–?'

'Could it have been that he was say, banging his shoe on the ground to dislodge something that was in it?'

Lily gave him a withering look. 'I know what I saw. The way he was hunched over, you could see the hate in him. He sort of stood back to look at what he'd done. The creature was moving, then it stopped moving.' She looked out at the search. 'I must say, it's very good of you to have all those people looking for a dog.'

'Is there anything else you can tell us about this man?' Mariner asked. 'The colour of his hair, say? What he was wearing perhaps?'

'I think his hair was brown and he was wearing a suit, like yours.' She looked at Mariner. 'A nice

186

summer suit, except yours is lighter. The one he wore was darker, more of a light brown. I remember thinking that he would spoil it, and how warm he must be, too.'

Gazing out of the window, Mariner tried to establish whether Lily would have seen the comings and goings of Shaun Pryce.

'You said you never see anyone down there, Lily. Do you mean that? Never?'

'Never.' She was adamant.

'Have you ever seen a young girl down there? Or a young man, over on the other side?'

'No.' On that point she stood firm.

'Up until about a week ago she wouldn't have been able to see much at all from up here,' put in Nora. 'That row of cypress trees was so tall it used to completely block the view.'

It was only then that Mariner noticed the line of tree stumps at the bottom of the garden, the timber inside freshly exposed.

'They were lovely trees,' said Lily. 'I was sad to see them go.'

'Lucky for us that they did,' said Mariner. 'Thank you very much, Mrs Cooper,' he said, absently. 'You've been very helpful.'

He turned to Nora. 'We'll need to come and take a written statement.'

'Of–'

Suddenly, as they watched, a shout went up and the figures working below began converging on an area a couple of hundred yards away from the bridge, where the foliage was at its most dense. Seconds later, Knox's mobile rang and Mariner felt a sudden weight in the pit of his stomach.

187

Knox took the call out in the corridor, returning moments later, his face grim. 'We're needed down there, boss.'

Chapter Eleven

It was only a few hundred yards away as the crow flies, but the drive around to the reservoir was nearly a mile in the car and seemed to take them an adrenaline-fuelled eternity. By the time they got there, the reservoir itself had been cleared of all but the essential personnel, the search parties had retreated to avoid contaminating the area and were congregating in the parking area to await further instructions. As Mariner and Knox bumped towards them over the uneven ground the mood was sombre, voices low. Russell greeted them at the edge of the wood. Beneath his tan he was white faced, his eyes dull with shock.

'We didn't find it until we were almost on it, despite the smell,' he said. 'The stink of the reservoir masked it.'

'Is it her?' Mariner asked, but Russell had already set off, eager to get this over with and pass on the find to a more senior officer.

This time they followed the initial path over the bridge, continuing around on the other side of the water. On their last visit this had been uncharted territory, where the searchers before them had been forced to slash away the grass and brambles to create a narrow passage. Even now, the thorns clawed at their trousers, their feet tripped on loops of tangled grass. It was heavy going, speed impossible and the hike around the edge of the water seemed interminable. The heat beat sickeningly down on Mariner's skull, while his imagination conjured up every possible variation on the horror he was about to see, the psyche's desperate effort to prepare and defend. Even then, it came nowhere close.

As Russell had warned, rounding a clump of burgeoning shrubs, it was the smell that hit first, the cloying stench that smelled like nothing else on earth, the unmistakable odour of human decay. After the smell came the noise: the high-pitched, triumphant buzzing of busy insects. Finally, the grotesque discovery came into view.

'Jesus Christ.' Bile rose in Mariner's throat and behind him he heard the glug of Tony Knox's involuntary retch.

Bizarrely, what first held Mariner's attention were the many different shades and shapes of grass that had moulded themselves around the body, as if his brain was forcing him to focus on the peripheral detail to avoid the unspeakable. To begin with, it was hard to make sense of, obscured as it was by the dense foliage, where an attempt seemed to have had been made to bury it under the thick strands of grass.

The soles of the shoes were visible first of all. They were the easy part: normal, like any pair of shoes on any pair of feet. Pulling away the grassy coverage, Mariner forced himself to work his way visually up the battered, bloody and decaying form, and by the time his eyes reached the insect-infested skull he already knew. 'Turn it over,' he instructed Russell. Russell did so. 'Christ.' Although the face and side of the head had been half eaten away, it didn't matter. The Nike track-suit and Manchester United football shirt were unmistakable from the description he'd been given only days earlier. 'It's Ricky Skeet,' he said, dully, while inside he wanted to bellow all the breath from his lungs. Why hadn't he listened to Colleen? Why had he let Fiske bully him into believing that Ricky had just run away? He'd never be able to live with himself over this.

'Call Charlie Glover and get SOCO–'

'They're on their way, sir.'

Mariner forced himself to take another look. SOCO would confirm it but the state of Ricky's body would indicate that he was the 'dog' Lily had seen being beaten to death.

'We haven't found his bike yet,' said Russell. 'It must be around here somewhere and it might give us a clue about how he got in here in the first place.'

'It might lead us to a witness, as well.'

'There's something else interesting the lads came across, sir.' Russell walked them back over the bridge, towards where they'd left their cars. This time though, he passed by their entry point and kept right, skirting under the trees to around the edge of what, at wetter times, would have been the lake's edge. The flattened area was perfectly concealed by the high grasses around it, like a small arena. They were standing now on the oppo-site side of the water to the side where Ricky's body lay, and the reason for the location was

190

obvious. Unlike the other side of the reservoir, this area would have been bathed in sunshine for most of the afternoon. 'The guys have found a couple of used condoms too,' Russell said. 'We've bagged them up. But there's no other sign of activity.' Like blood, he might have added.

It was the side nearest to the clearing where they had met Shaun Pryce. Knox stooped to retrieve something from the ground. 'Good place to relax, eh?' He held up a home-rolled dog-end, putting it to his nose. 'Most animals don't shit in their own back yard,' said Knox, grimly. 'Shaun Pryce doesn't come down here on his own and he doesn't settle for the clearing, either.'

Even as Mariner saw Charlie Glover approaching from twenty yards away, leading a procession of white-boiler-suited SOCOs, he could read the expression on his face. It told Mariner that he was racked with the same guilt. He waited on the bridge while Charlie went to look at the body.

Five minutes later Glover returned, a man in a daze. 'Christ, it's like the arsehole of hell,' he said, numbly. 'What in God's name was Ricky Skeet doing down here? It must be what, three or four miles from his house? And how did he get in?'

'God knows. Good place to hide out, though. No one would think to look here for him.'

'Well, we didn't, did we? But how would he even know it existed?'

Mariner gazed out over the dark, cracked mud. 'Ricky's dad used to take him fishing. Maybe there were fish in here once.' They were back on the bridge, close to where Yasmin's phone had been found. 'This whole thing makes no sense. Yasmin's phone here and Ricky's body way over there.'

Glover looked around, saw the brown stains on the grass. 'If it's his blood then Ricky was killed here. He could have somehow come by Yasmin's phone.'

'That's the only plausible explanation. There's the possibility that Yasmin was seeing someone, a boy, or man. Do you think there's any chance it could have been Ricky?'

Glover thought about that. 'I don't see how. How would they have met? They're at different schools, from different parts of the city. He's two years younger.'

'That's what I thought. Unless it was a chance meeting. They could have met down here, or at the station,' Mariner offered.

'What would have taken Ricky to the station?'

Mariner shared his scepticism. 'All we found was Yasmin's phone. I think a more likely explanation would be that she dropped it and someone – Ricky perhaps – found it and brought it here.'

'Or he stole it.'

'Ricky doesn't do that. And anyway, when would he have had the opportunity? It's much more likely that Yasmin dropped it. The afternoon she disappeared, she had to run for the train. It could have happened then.'

'Haven't you got CCTV on that? It may have picked it up and might also show us if Ricky was at the station.'

'Sure,' Mariner said, absently, his mind not really on it. He knew he should be focusing on

Yasmin but now all he could think about was Colleen waiting at home in hopeful ignorance. He didn't want to leave all that to Charlie Glover.

Tony Knox was hovering. 'Shall we bring in Pryce?'

'Who?' Glover's ears pricked up.

'A guy called Shaun Pryce turned up while we were here yesterday, back in the clearing, but claims that he doesn't come on to the reservoir itself.' Mariner filled Glover in on the main points of the conversation with Pryce.

'But I think he's a more regular visitor there than he told us. That flattened area of grass looks tailor-made for him. He wasn't telling us the truth about that, and he doesn't come here alone, either.'

'Judging everyone by your own standards, Tony?' said Glover.

Mariner cringed on Knox's behalf at the reference to his colourful past, but he took it well enough. Would have been something of a double standard not to. 'There were a hell of a lot of fresh dog-ends for one person,' he said.

'The weather's been dry for weeks. They could have built up over a period of time. And if he's down here screwing some girl, why didn't he just say so? It's no big deal. In fact I'd have thought it was something he'd want to brag about.'

'She'll be married, won't she? Didn't you ever see *Confessions of an Electrician?* He'll be having it away with someone else's missus.' There was a bitter edge to Knox's voice. 'Maybe Ricky saw Pryce knocking off some woman and threatened to let it out, so Pryce had to shut him up.'

'How would Ricky know that what he saw was

illicit? For all Ricky knew it could have been Pryce and his wife having a bit of open-air fun.'

'Maybe Pryce didn't like having an audience.'

Mariner shook his head. 'Oh no, Shaun Pryce would love it. He's an actor,' he added, for Glover's benefit.

'He might not be so keen on being watched if things aren't going his way,' Glover said.

'Can't imagine that,' said Knox, sourly.

'Perhaps Ricky was a regular visitor down here, too. Had seen what Pryce was up to and been blackmailing him?'

'Well, right now Pryce is the only other person we can place down here, so we at least need to talk to him.'

'Yes, we do,' Mariner agreed. 'We need to know *exactly* what he did down here, when he was here and for how long – going back for the last couple of months. But I don't think there's any urgency. I get the feeling that Shaun Pryce might be in a more talkative mood once news leaks out about where we've found Yasmin's phone.'

'You're sure he won't disappear?'

'Oh no, judging by yesterday's performance, if he is involved, he'll want to be around for his bit of the limelight.'

'I'd better go and tell Ricky's mother. Do you want to come?'

Mariner winced. Running the scene in his head, he could hear Colleen's screaming and sobbing as if it was real, and see her beating her fists against Glover. 'Not yet. She needs to know that you're in charge. And we've got things to do.' Or was he taking the coward's way out, unable to face

Colleen after letting her down so badly, afraid of the hysteria that would ensue? Later, Charlie told him it hadn't run like that at all. She'd taken the news in a stunned silence. Somehow that had been even worse.

As they left the site, a low loader bearing a Portakabin was driving on. The incident room would be set up here to maximise the use of local intelligence and deepen the search. One of the first tasks would be a door to door to try and establish when and where Ricky was last seen. The Murder Investigation Unit would support Charlie Glover's OCU investigation and a team would be put on to searching the reservoir area for the murder weapon. The diving team would have to be contracted in from a neighbouring force, since their own divers had gone the way of the mounted division and fallen victim to budget cuts. Trawling the reservoir would be a mammoth task in all that thick black mud. Close behind the truck was a couple of unmarked vehicles, one of them a grey Transit.

'The vultures moving in,' observed Knox. Inevitably, the press would have picked up news of the discovery from the morning's activities over the air waves. 'Want me to get rid of them, boss?'

'Be as unpleasant as you like,' said Mariner.

What Mariner was less prepared for was the mob of reporters already assembled outside the entrance to Granville Lane. News had travelled fast and they were not a happy throng. Knox and Mariner got out of the car just as Fiske appeared at the main doors to read a prepared statement.

'We will do everything within our power to bring the killer of Ricky Skeet to justice,' he concluded.

'Is that the same kind of everything you did to find him when he went missing?' someone called out.

'We followed all possible lines of enquiry. I have no doubt that my officers did all they possibly could to prevent this situation from occurring.'

'Mrs Skeet doesn't seem to agree with you on that.'

Fiske was getting hot under the collar. 'Any complaints about the way this enquiry has been handled will be dealt with through the usual channels.'

'Whitewashed, you mean.'

Mariner signalled to Knox and they slipped round the building and into a side door. Along the corridor they ran into Fiske, making his escape. 'Bloody press,' he grumbled.

'Perhaps they've got a point this time,' said Mariner.

'And what the hell's that supposed to mean?'

'We didn't exactly pull out all the stops for Ricky, did we?' Mariner reminded him.

'Given his profile we followed the correct procedures.'

'I'll tell his mum that. I'm sure she'll feel greatly reassured. "Your son's dead, but given his profile, we did everything by the book, Colleen."' Deep down, Mariner recognised that he was more angry with himself than he was with Fiske. If he'd made more of a stand against the arrogant bastard instead of caving in at the beginning this might not have happened. 'We've got a kid we hardly looked for dead and another we've wasted energy on looking for who might have eloped with her lover.'

'We got it wrong. Sometimes it happens.'

'You can say that again.'

Millie was up in the office. 'You heard?' Mariner asked.

Her face said it. 'I'm sorry.'

'Yeah. But we have to turn our attention back to Yasmin. There's always the chance that the two cases aren't linked. I know the probability has slumped a bit, but still the only two people we can definitely place down at the reservoir at any time are Shaun Pryce and Ricky Skeet. Yasmin's phone was there but that's all. We still don't know for sure that she was too: let's deal with the reality first, before we go off speculating about other things.' She'd been gone more than a week now and their one breakthrough had led them nowhere.

'Let's see the CCTV footage again. We might be able to establish if Yasmin dropped her phone, and I want to be absolutely sure that it's her getting on that train.'

'But we've been over that, boss,' Knox groused.

Brushing aside his complaints they played the tape yet again. They watched as Yasmin boarded the train and the door closed behind her, as on every previous occasion. As the train began to draw away, Knox switched the tape off.

'That's definitely Yasmin,' said Millie, swivelling on her chair to face Mariner. 'She looks right into the camera.'

'And no sign of her dropping her phone,' said Mariner.

197

'But she started running from the top of the road. She could have dropped it anywhere before she comes into view.' Her disappointment was tangible.

'Well, we may soon find out about that, anyway. Her phone should be back from—'

'Look, boss.' Tony Knox had suddenly become animated. While Mariner and Millie were talking he'd turned the tape on again, watching it with half an eye.

Mariner turned his attention back to the screen as Knox wound back the film at speed. 'But we've already seen—'

'Look, for Christ sake!' At the point at which Yasmin boarded the train, Knox pressed the play button again. The train began to move off, and as it did so, a door further down the carriage reopened, a figure appeared and after a second's hesitation, leaped from the moving train on to the platform. It stumbled and almost fell before regaining its feet and, when it straightened, was unmistakable.

'She got off the train,' said Knox, with a degree of satisfaction.

'Nearly killing herself in the process,' observed Mariner. 'Christ. Why didn't we think of that?'

'Think of what?' They were so caught up in their find that Fiske's voice startled them. Sneaking up on them was becoming a speciality.

'Yasmin Akram had us all fooled,' said Mariner. 'Play it back, Tony.'

'What ag—?' Mariner glared at him and dutifully Knox reran the tape yet again. As they watched, Mariner provided the commentary. 'She runs for the train, giving her friends – and us – the impression that she was going as usual, but gets off again before the train pulls out. He looked up at Fiske, calculating how far he could go. 'She never even got as far as the university.'

A muscle bulged in Fiske's jaw. 'Are you trying to make some kind of point, Mariner?'

'Only that perhaps we could have saved ourselves considerable time and resources if we'd been a bit less hasty with the search, sir,' said Mariner calmly.

But Fiske wasn't so easily beaten. 'We did the right thing based on the information available at the time,' he replied, icily. 'Not forgetting that in the course of those actions, we've exposed a sex attacker operating in that area.'

'Oh, very good, sir.' Knox grinned inanely, before realising, along with everyone else, that the pun had been unintentional.

'Given that new information has come to light, I'd have thought your time would more usefully be spent following it up rather than playing games of "I told you so".' And with that, Fiske turned and walked out.

'Fucking moron,' muttered Knox. Mariner should really have reminded him about respect for senior officers, but it was good to have Tony Knox back on the planet again, however fleetingly. Instead, he brought them back to task. 'So why does Yasmin get off the train?'

'Because she has other plans?'

Having recovered from her leap from the moving train, they watched as Yasmin walked along the platform, towards the footbridge and off the screen. 'What it doesn't tell us is where she went next.'

'Except that there's a camera positioned at the back of the station too,' Knox remembered. 'It would be worth checking out the tape from that now. She's going towards the footbridge. She could be crossing the line.'

'In more ways than one.'

'Yasmin's just full of surprises, isn't she?'

'Let's get the tape.'

Yasmin did indeed appear on the footage from the back of the station, descending the pedestrian bridge and moving across the screen towards the station car park, but that was the extent of the camera's coverage.

'So where's she off to?'

'Suddenly, it's not beyond the realms of possibility that Yasmin dropped her phone at the reservoir.'

But as Knox went to switch off the TV, Mariner spotted something else on the screen. 'Look at that; bottom right-hand corner.' Next to the kerb was the offside wing and part of the bonnet of a dark vehicle.

'A Merc,' said Knox. 'You can tell from that radiator grille.'

'Is there anyone in it?' asked Millie, as they all squinted at the screen.

'Hard to see; it's from the wrong angle. Can we home in on that licence plate?'

They could, but it was still too blurry to be of any use.

'Mohammed Akram drives a black Mercedes,' Mariner reminded them.

'That's neat. Maybe Yasmin got off the train again because she saw someone she knew.'

The time on the corner of the screen said: 16.29. 'How accurate is that?'

'According to Akram, he'd been to the printer and by half past four was on the motorway on his way up to Bradford by that time,' said Mariner.

'Is the printer in the city?' asked Knox.

'I assumed it was in Sparkhill, near the school. TMR Printers, it's called. It was on the prospectus Hasan Sheron showed us.'

Knox reached for the *Yellow Pages* and flicked through until he found 'printers'.

'Here we are: TMR Reprographics. Two branches, one in the city and another–' He looked up for dramatic effect. 'On Birch Close.'

'Shit,' said Millie.

'Thanks for that valuable contribution,' Knox said. But he did seem to be joking.

'And from there it's just a short drive up to the station where the CCTV picks up his car,' said Mariner. 'If it is his car.'

'And it would be no problem to get on to the motorway from here. There's nothing stopping him from going back out through the city centre and up to Spaghetti Junction, or even up the Wolverhampton Road to the M5. then M6. The fact that Yasmin stayed for the art club and left school late would have helped him out. He'd also probably have known that she was on her own so it would have been the ideal place if he didn't want to confront Yasmin in front of her friends, or back at home.'

'So he could easily have picked her up from the

201

station and taken her with him.'

'What time did he check in with the family in Bradford?' Knox wanted to know.

'Not until nearly eight. But he says he stopped off at Sandbach Services for something to eat on his way and that there were roadworks on the M62, which there are.'

'It doesn't rule him out, though. It's still a bloody big coincidence if he was in the area at all at around that time.'

'An appeal for the driver on local news can rule out anyone else.'

'When did he say he'd confronted Yasmin about the pills?' Millie asked.

'On Friday. He said they'd sorted it out. But there might have been unfinished business.'

'What if Akram had talked Yasmin into going up to Bradford with him?'

Mariner was dubious. 'Without telling her mother what was going on?'

'They probably wouldn't have wanted her to know about the contraception.'

'But that doesn't tie in with Akram forbidding Yasmin to go to Suzanne's. He couldn't have known that his wife would give in and let her go.'

'He might know his wife better than she thinks.'

'The receipt from the service station only indicates a meal for one.'

Mariner sighed. 'OK, folks, we're wandering into the realms of speculation again. Let's get back to the facts.' *Just the facts, Jack.*

'We have Ricky, Yasmin and Akram all in the same area at the same time,' said Knox. 'That's fact.'

'Only if it is Akram's car.'

'And I still don't get where Ricky comes into this,' Millie said.

'He might not,' said Mariner. 'We could still be looking at two entirely unconnected events. Maybe all Ricky did was to find Yasmin's phone at the station and take it with him to the reservoir, where he was attacked and he dropped it, simple as that. Meanwhile, Yasmin, unaware that she's even lost her phone, meets her dad at the station.'

'Are we absolutely certain that Yasmin and Ricky didn't know each other?' Knox asked.

'I just don't see how they would,' said Millie.

'But we don't know for sure that they didn't,' Knox insisted, the tension in the room thickening.

'They don't need to have done. If Ricky was in the wrong place at the wrong time, Akram could have just jumped to the wrong conclusion.'

'What are you talking about?'

'Maybe the phone does provide the link. How about if Ricky found the phone, as we thought. Yasmin's home number must be on it. Ricky phones that number to establish its owner, gets Akram who arranges to meet him to collect it. Akram's at the printer, Ricky knows the reservoir, so they arrange to meet at a mutually convenient spot. Akram is still wound up about Yasmin being on the pill, jumps to the wrong conclusion about Ricky having her phone and loses it.'

Knox's facial expression fell just short of contempt. 'That's a hell of a conclusion to jump

203

to. A kid finds his daughter's phone so he assumes he's having sex with her?'

'We don't know what's on that phone.' Millie stood her ground. 'There might be some interesting messages. Could be that Ricky tried blackmailing Akram: perhaps he demanded money before giving it up. Akram's already pissed off about all the hassle he's been getting. This could've been the final straw.'

Seeing Knox's colour rising, Mariner spoke up. 'It's an interesting idea, but knowing Ricky, I'm not sure that he'd have done that kind of thing,' he said, calmly.

Millie shrugged. 'He'd run away from home. I didn't think that was his kind of thing, either. And if he wasn't planning on going back he was going to need more money.'

'So why did Paul Hewitt find the phone still lying there?' Knox almost sneered. 'Akram would have taken it with him.'

'Ricky was in a bad way, wasn't he? The attack must have been violent, impulsive even. Maybe he just lost it and in the heat of the moment he dropped the phone and it got forgotten. He'd have been pretty caught up in what he was doing. Or somebody disturbed him.'

'Down there?'

'OK. He looked up and saw Lily watching him.'

'I doubt that he'd see her from that distance,' said Mariner. 'And even so, if the phone was what this was all about, he'd hardly leave it behind, would he?'

'Or go in bloodstained clothing back to the station to meet his daughter.'

'He was going away overnight. He would have had a change of clothing in the car.'

'That's crazy. If that *is* what happened, Ricky would have had hardly any time to find the phone, alert Akram and arrange to meet him. I'd say it was virtually impossible.' Knox glared at Millie, who refused to be intimidated. It was a stand-off.

'And I think we're getting a bit carried away here, folks,' Mariner intervened, quietly. 'We need to look at it from every angle, but this isn't getting us any nearer to knowing where Yasmin's gone.'

'I think we need to check her dad's movements up in Bradford,' Millie insisted. 'If she has simply been spirited away, it would explain why he didn't seem so anxious at the start.'

'Look into that, will you?' said Mariner. 'It remains a possibility, but one of many. At the moment all we have is Yasmin's phone, Ricky dead and Yasmin vanished.'

'Like one of those lateral thinking problems,' said Knox.

Millie pulled a face. 'I was always rubbish at them.'

'I need some fresh air,' said Knox.

When he'd left the room, Millie asked the question Mariner had been dreading. 'Are you sure it's not me?'

'Tony just takes the job seriously,' said Mariner, brushing it off.

'Implying that we don't?' She had a point.

Mariner was saved from making any further crass remarks by the news that Charlie Glover was back from the Pathologist's office with the preliminary findings.

Chapter Twelve

Glover cut to the chase. 'Everything so far says the blood on the grass is definitely Ricky's,' he said. 'It was a frenzied attack involving repeated blows to the skull with a blunt instrument. It would have been messy.'

'So the clothing the killer was wearing—'

'—would be pretty well covered in blood.'

'According to Lily, it was some kind of brown suit.'

'Yeah, I've spoken to her. Her eyesight seems pretty sharp and what she's told us seems accurate so I think we can go with that. So the brown suit would have needed to go to the cleaner's or even more likely to have been destroyed. Hard to explain to Sketchley's why your suit is covered in someone else's blood.'

'Have we got a time of death?'

'Thanks to the weather the body was pretty ripe, as you saw. But they're saying it's been there about seven days. That would put it at sometime late on Tuesday afternoon.'

Lining it up nicely with the last time that Yasmin was seen alive. 'Anything else?'

'Only what Lily's already said: she's pretty certain that the man she saw had dark hair.' Like Mohammed Akram, thought Mariner. Did he own a brown suit? 'It could, of course, depend on the angle of the sun at that time,' Glover went on.

'If the sun was behind or overhead it could be the one detail that she's mistaken on.'

'It's possible,' agreed Mariner. 'What about Colleen's boyfriend, Steve?'

'We're checking him out, but so far his alibi looks sound. He was still at work.'

'That's a pity.'

'Yeah, isn't it? And so that you know, Ronnie Skeet was in Wolverhampton.'

'Any thoughts on how it played out?' Mariner asked.

'Well, we've got blood on the grass by the bridge, but around that, nothing, and no sign of disturbance. However, working back from where the body was found is a kind of tunnel through the grass, leading almost back to the bridge, and also smeared with blood. It makes it look as if Ricky was killed at the bridge, then his killer, probably thinking he was dead, carried him into the long grass and dumped him, coming back to the path to cover his tracks. It looks as if Ricky could have dragged himself further through the grass, creating a kind of tunnel, to the point where we found him.'

'Christ, so he wasn't dead.'

'And crawling even further from the path did his killer a favour by delaying the discovery of his body. We're continuing the search in the direction he was going: to see if he was making for anything in particular. But he may just have been trying to get away. And you were right about the reason for Ricky being there,' Glover added. 'I asked Colleen. His dad did used to take him fishing on the reservoir, but not for years. We

207

still haven't found his bike, but did they tell you about the Anderson?'

'I didn't get time to check in yesterday.'

'Further round still from where Ricky's body was found we came across an old Anderson shelter. From all the empty cans and crisp packets it looks as if Ricky had been there before.'

'He used to go off for the day at weekends,' Mariner said, recalling the conversation with Colleen. 'Is this all going to the press?'

'It might have to. Fiske is desperate to get them off his back. How does a berk like him get to be in his position?'

'Gift of the gab,' said Mariner. 'Did you ask Colleen about Yasmin?'

'Yeah, and nearly got a black eye for it.' Glover recounted the conversation conducted under the beady gaze of Steven Marsh. 'He didn't seem to appreciate the timing.'

Mariner grimaced.

'And Colleen, of course, took it as further proof that we were more concerned with Yasmin than with Ricky, but basically the answer was no. She couldn't see how Ricky would have known that "posh little Asian kid", even when I told her about the phone.' Glover paused. 'Question is, though: would Colleen have even known?'

Mariner reported back on what Glover had said as he and Knox drove over to Allah T'ala. For once, Knox seemed unnaturally chipper, his jaws working hard on a gobbet of chewing gum, which he'd lately taken to chewing almost constantly. They were shown up to the same office where

Mariner and Millie had first gone, and where Mohammed Akram, in shirtsleeves, his tie hanging loose, was poring over some architect's drawings. He jumped up as they went in, his face a turmoil of emotions. 'You've found something?'

'Nothing more. I'm sorry,' said Mariner, wishing that he could read that face. 'PC Khatoon has kept you up to date?'

'She told us about the boy, and that Yasmin's phone was nearby. Do you think–?'

'We're trying to establish the facts,' said Mariner, 'which is why we need to clarify a couple of things with you.'

'My wife is teaching a class.'

'That's fine, I think you should be able to help us. The printer you were at in Kingsmead on Tuesday afternoon,' said Mariner. 'It's some distance from your school. Why there?'

'My last supplier closed about a year ago. I happened to mention this to Yasmin's teacher one parents' evening. Yasmin had been awarded a certificate and I asked where they had got it printed. She recommended the place. I decided to try them.'

'And tell me again, what time were you there on that Tuesday afternoon?'

'Around four o'clock. I left twenty or thirty minutes later. The meeting didn't take long. I just needed to look at some proofs. But you know all this. I already told you.'

'Will the printer be able to confirm that timing?'

'I'm sure that he will.'

'And from there you drove up to Bradford.'

'As I've already told you,' said Akram, irritably.

'Did you go anywhere near Kingsmead Station?'

'No. I had no reason to do that.'

'Yasmin would have just been leaving school at that time.'

'I suppose she was. I didn't really think about it.'

'You weren't tempted to meet her to discuss your recent disagreement?'

'As I said before, that matter had been resolved.'

'Mr Akram, do you own a brown suit?'

A slight pause. Surprised about the question or thinking about an answer? 'Yes, I do. As a matter of fact I have it here. It's due to be dry-cleaned.'

That was a piece of luck. 'Could we see it?'

'Er, yes.' Akram left the room and after several minutes returned with the suit, protected in a plastic cover. It was a shade of mid-brown. For a suit that was going to the cleaner's it seemed spotlessly clean.

'Mr Akram, I'm going to ask you again. Do you have any idea about the whereabouts of your daughter?'

Akram looked him straight in the eye. 'And I will tell you again, Inspector. No, I have not.'

'That suit looked OK to me,' said Knox as they cooked again in the car.

'We didn't ask him if he owns more than one.'

Knox gave him a sidelong look. 'Just because all your suits are exactly the same colour–'

'Two colours, actually,' Mariner corrected him.

'All I'm saying is: most of us have a bit more imagination.'

'Thanks.'

'Any time.'

'Akram is consistent about the timing, though,' conceded Mariner. 'Did the printer verify it?'

'Over the phone, yes.'

Mariner sighed. 'Even with the techies' enhancements on the CCTV footage, I'm not sure that we'll be able to determine the licence plates or the driver of that car.'

'And if he's telling the truth, he'd have left the city before that was filmed.'

'Did you believe him, that he didn't realise that Yasmin would be at the station at that time?'

'Yeah.' Knox nodded. 'You're not thinking about your kids all day long, especially when they get to that age. You're starting to lead separate lives.'

'Some more than others,' said Mariner. 'It just would be nice to know for sure.'

As it turned out, they soon did. The appeal the night before had brought forward a young woman.

'A Miss Devreaux called in just after you left,' Millie told them. 'Her fiancé met her from the station in his midnight-blue Mercedes. He parked exactly where the camera is pointed. They even had a row because she was late.'

'Shit.'

'Does it rule Akram out?' Millie asked.

'It confirms that he wasn't at the station then.' Mariner sighed. 'But Yasmin's phone was found *between* the station and the printer. I want to go and talk to the printer.'

'Nothing like going over old ground,' muttered Knox.

'It's called being thorough,' said Mariner.

'Yes, boss.'

Printer Tim Randall was pretty certain about the timing of Akram's visit. On arrival, they'd walked through the warm and humid prefabricated hangar, where the dominant smell was of warm plastic. Stepping around an obstacle course of thrumming computers and boxy digital printers, they ducked under the spaghetti tangle of cables and wires tossed carelessly over the fragile steel beams and into the quieter design office, where a couple of graphic artists were laying out proofs on long tables. 'We were in the middle of a big print run,' Randall went on, 'and as he left, I remember looking at the clock to see how much time we'd got left to finish up. We were cutting it a bit fine.'

'And what time was it?'

'A couple of minutes off half past four, give or take. That clock probably isn't a hundred per cent accurate.'

So that was that.

'He didn't drive off straight away.' The young man who spoke up was leaning over the drawings, cornrows sprouting from his head.

'Are you sure?' asked Mariner.

'I went out for a fag about quarter to five and he was still there, his flashy Mercedes parked down at the end of the loop, by the bins.'

The lad wasn't wearing a watch, Mariner noticed. 'How can you be so sure of the timing?'

He grinned. 'I'm trying to quit, so I'm spacing them out. This week I'm out there at five o'clock, last week it was quarter to.'

'Did you see him drive off?'

'No. He was still out there when I came back

in. Doesn't take long to smoke a fag and I'm only allowed the one.'

'Was Mr Akram definitely in his car? Was there anyone with him?'

He swayed his head doubtfully. 'All I saw was the car.'

Outside, they looked down towards 'the loop' – the neck of the cul-de-sac – to the row of industrial-sized steel bins. They were backed up against the wood-panelled fence, on the other side of which was the reservoir.

'The kid saw Akram's car parked outside at quarter to five. It doesn't mean that he was in it. He could have easily been down there with Yasmin.'

'When we were on the bridge we didn't look to see if you could get on to the reservoir from this industrial estate.'

'If there was a way through, surely we'd have noticed it.'

'Not if we weren't looking for it. And it may only have been used once or twice. If Akram did have unfinished business with Yasmin, it would have been a much more private place to meet her.'

They found what they were looking for in minutes. Behind the giant bins a panel of fencing had split, creating an opening easily large enough for someone to squeeze through. Standing on the concrete plinth, Mariner could look down towards the bridge and the sludge beyond. Running through the long grass was the unmistakable pale line caused by a single passage through it.

213

'So what now? Back to Mr Akram?' Knox asked.

But Mariner shook his head. 'We need to keep on to everything else, too. I'd like to have a closer look at what you found on Shaun Pryce first.'

But the database had turned up little of interest. 'Only one minor offence in the past, boss: possession of cannabis.' Knox closed the record sheet. 'I thought this was more interesting.' He'd book-marked a site and when he double-clicked it, a whole web page appeared devoted to Shaun Pryce: actor and model. On it, Pryce was described as a 'talented and versatile' character actor who'd played a range of diverse and challenging roles, most notably as a romantic lead, and who was also available for modelling and voice-over work. 'I bet he wrote that himself,' said Knox. 'Shame we can't bring him in for blatant self-promotion.'

'I want to talk to him again, though,' said Mariner. 'He frequents the reservoir area and I'd like to know what he really does there. SOCO found spliffs and condoms. I want to see if there's anything else we can shake out of him. I wonder if Charlie Glover would like to come.'

'Sounds like fun,' was Glover's reaction.

The daytime contact Shaun Pryce had given them belonged to a property about three quarters of a mile from the reservoir; a collection of houses in what estate agents would refer to as a 'much sought after area'. Consequently, most had been extended in one way or another. The addition

214

Pryce was working on was huge, almost doubling the size of the property. Plenty of electrical work here to keep him busy. There was no sign of his VW Golf in the line of assorted vehicles parked outside, but when they asked Mrs Paleczcki, the owner of the house, she took them through to where Pryce was working alone, in what looked like a newly created ground-floor room.

'Shaun, there's someone to see you.'

Their footsteps echoed as they went in. Pryce turned from where he was kneeling on the bare floorboards, screwing a double socket to a freshly plastered wall. Raw wires sprouted from the walls elsewhere around the room, waiting for his attention, and the air was clouded with fine dust. A tinny radio blared some kind of phone-in programme that ricocheted around the emptiness. Elsewhere in the house were the sounds of other work progressing.

'Would you like a cup of tea, love?' Today Pryce was in T-shirt and shorts, his tattoos standing out vividly against his bronzed skin, and there was no mistaking the look on Mrs Paleczcki's face as she spoke to him. Knox had guessed right: it was *Confessions of an Electrician* all over again.

Pryce grinned at her. 'You know just what to say to a man.'

The hospitality wasn't extended to Mariner or Glover: Mrs Paleczcki not encouraging them to hang around any longer than was necessary.

'How can I help?' Pryce asked, his demeanour casual, but the voice guarded. He seemed to have lost some of the confidence he had a couple of days ago. But then a lot had happened since then, and he would know that they'd found Ricky.

'By stop pissing us around and telling us what you really get up to at the reservoir,' said Mariner, without ceremony.

'Is that where they found that kid?'

'You know that very well. We've found your little retreat, too.'

'Oh.'

'So? What is it you do there?'

'I go there to top up my tan.'

'Most people sunbathe in their own gardens or in the park.'

'I haven't got a garden. I live in a flat. And anyway, some of the modelling work I do, my tan needs to be comprehensive.'

'You sunbathe nude.'

'I'm not harming anyone.'

Mrs Paleczcki came back in with a mug of tea. Mariner wondered if she knew about Pryce's all-over tan. He decided that she probably did. When she'd gone he asked:

'When was the last time you were there? And this time we'd like the truth.'

Pryce hesitated. Debating what to say to avoid incriminating himself?

'The day I met you lot.'

'Don't be a smart arse, I mean before that.'

'The week before.'

'Day?'

'Tuesday.'

Bingo. 'What time?'

'About one o'clock.'

'Till when?'

'I don't know. Half one, two.'

'Is there anyone who can verify that?'

'The rest of the crew here can vouch for me.'

Mariner looked around him pointedly. 'And they are?'

'Upstairs right now. We started on the loft conversion this week.'

Mariner could only guess at the motley bunch that comprised Pryce's co-workers. He'd have laid bets that, like Pryce, they'd be mainly casual labourers with more than a couple of criminal records between them. He didn't have much confidence in any of them as a solid alibi. Nonetheless, Glover went up to check it out.

'So what were you doing for nearly an hour? And don't give me any bird-watching bullshit. We all know you wouldn't know a redshank from a shag.'

'I was chilling out. It may not look like it to you but this is bloody hard work, especially in the heat. Sometimes I have to help with the labouring too.'

'My heart bleeds. Take Mrs Paleczcki with you?'

'She's a married woman.'

'But you've taken women there before. Either that or you're the only man I know who practises safe sex with himself.'

'You sure they're mine? I'm a good Catholic boy, me.'

'When's the last time you took a woman there?' repeated Mariner.

'Not for a while.'

'Oh? What about your insatiable sexual appetite? Losing your touch?'

'The last one I took there didn't like the long grass. Said it scratched her. Got into all those un-

217

comfortable little places. So I haven't bothered since.'

'When was that?'

'Ages ago. Probably sometime back in May. It's hard to remember.'

'See a lot of women, do you?'

'I can't help it if they find me irresistible.'

'Anything else? Had a smoke, did you?'

He could see that they'd found the cannabis. No point in denying it. 'I might have smoked a couple of joints.'

'Does your employer know about your habit? It must improve your wiring skills no end.'

'I know what I'm doing. I'm careful.'

'Do you know a boy called Ricky Skeet?'

'Is that–?'

'–the boy whose body we found yesterday afternoon by the reservoir? Yes. He'd been bludgeoned to death. We have the time of death as sometime on Tuesday afternoon.'

Shaun Pryce looked as if he was about to throw up.

'Did you know him?'

Pryce's voice dropped to a whisper. 'No.'

'What do you wear when you're working?' Mariner asked suddenly.

'What?'

'What do you wear? Your clothes?'

Pryce splayed his arms. 'What you see. Jeans, T-shirt, shorts if it's a hot day.'

'Do you own a brown suit?'

Pryce sneered. 'Shit colour, you mean? No thanks.'

'What about overalls?'

218

'Too restrictive.'

Glover appeared in the doorway and gave the faintest nod.

'Right,' said Mariner. 'That's all for now. Thanks for your time.'

'What do you mean "for now"?' said Pryce, uneasily.

'You've admitted to being close to the scene of a murder at around the time it was committed. We may have some further questions. Don't worry, we'll see ourselves out.'

As they were leaving, Mariner turned back to Pryce. 'Where's the car today?'

'I left it at home. Came on my bike. I do, when I get up early enough. Helps keep me fit.'

'Is that what you did on Tuesday? Were you on your bike then?'

'I might have been. I don't honestly remember.'

Glover and Mariner got reluctantly back into their sweltering car.

'He seems pretty cool,' Glover observed.

'Meaning, he has nothing to do with this?' Mariner was disappointed.

'Or that he's good at covering up. He's an actor, after all.'

'He didn't hesitate about owning up to being at the reservoir on that Tuesday.'

'He must know we'd find that out, anyway. Yeah. As long as he sticks to the timing there's not much we can do about it. What about his alibi?'

'The other guys are saying that he was back after lunch and then they didn't knock off until nearly six,' Glover said.

'So we may have to accept that Pryce probably wasn't there when Ricky was killed.'

'If we choose to believe them. Or if they even know. The other three have been working on the loft all week while Pryce has been downstairs, more or less on his own. Would they even know if he disappeared on his bike for an hour? He could easily get down to the reservoir in that time. I can't shake off the feeling that he knows something, that there's something he's not telling us. Do you believe the nude sunbathing?'

'Yes, it fits in with the image.'

'But he denied having a brown suit. We could have pushed him on that.'

Mariner turned to face Glover. 'We've seen his suit already, most of it: a light brown suit? It's this famous allover tan he keeps bragging about. Wouldn't have to take that to the dry-cleaner's, would he?'

When Mariner got home late that night, he realised he still hadn't contacted his mother, but when he tried, the phone just rang on and she had no answering service. She'd probably got the TV on too loud to hear it. He thought about calling one of her neighbours but he wouldn't want to risk getting anyone out of bed, so he didn't bother.

Chapter Thirteen

Next morning, the lab report on Yasmin's phone had come back, along with the analysis of the calls made, and Mike Finlay, the technician who would be able to clarify anything that didn't make sense. Mariner asked Knox and Millie to sit in on it. Most of the fingerprints on the handset matched with those taken from Yasmin's room at home. A couple of larger, smeared prints were as yet unidentified. 'But could belong to the parents,' Finlay said. 'We're rechecking that.'

A transcript of all the saved messages was attached. Mariner had never signed up to the text message culture, continuing to use his own mobile like a traditional telephone, and to his unfamiliar eyes the calls read like the Enigma Code.

'These are all messages?' Mariner asked the technician, feeling ignorant.

'It's on a save cycle of about a month,' Finlay told him. 'But this is quite a sophisticated phone and works a bit like e-mail, automatically saving the messages sent, too.'

'So we've got everything she sent and received over the last month?'

'Not quite. Some messages have been deliberately deleted. I'm not surprised, either, given the content of some of the others.'

'Oh?'

'A bit on the racy side.' Confirming that Yasmin wasn't quite the innocent they'd first thought her to be. 'Where we can, we've linked the phone numbers to Yasmin's phone book, so most of the messages, though not all, can be attributed. Messages to and from her parents and sister were easy to identify, especially as there aren't that many. Some of them also have only an initial or what looks like a nickname to identify them.'

'And the hot ones?' Tony Knox asked.

'They all appear to be to or from someone known as Lee.'

Lee. So Amira was right. Yasmin could have been seeing someone after all. The contraceptive pill wasn't just trying to be grown up in front of her friends. She really needed it. But why had none of her friends mentioned Lee?

'The one you'll be most interested is this one. It's the last message sent, on Tuesday at around lunchtime.'

'CU @4 things 2 TL U'

'What does it mean?'

'It makes more sense if you read it out loud: "See you at four. Things to tell you."'

'That was what she said to Suzanne. I'd thought that Lee was the something. Maybe she was telling him that she was on the pill, so it was all systems go.'

Finlay nodded sagely. 'It looks as if Yasmin had arranged to meet this Lee at four o'clock on the day she disappeared. I think you need to speak to him.'

'Do you reckon?' Knox was straight faced.

'There's one other message received after that, in

222

the middle of the afternoon, but she's deleted it.'

'Christ, how can you tell that?'

'It leaves a trace, a bit like the imaging you get on a computer hard drive. Perhaps she deleted it because it was a bit strong for her parents' eyes again.'

'Thanks,' said Knox. 'We'll bear it in mind.'

'Can we be sure from this that Yasmin had her phone right up until Tuesday afternoon?' Mariner asked.

'Somebody did. The prints would indicate that it was probably her, because those are the clearest. The rest is for you to find out.'

'Thanks,' said Millie quickly, before Knox could get in. 'You've been very helpful.'

'OK,' said Mariner, when Finlay had gone. 'At least we now have the boy Yasmin was seeing, and we know it wasn't Ricky.'

'Unless he was using an alias.'

'Let's not complicate things for the sake of it. We should go and talk to her family about this.'

'I think we'd be better off talking to her friends, sir,' Millie suggested. 'They're more likely to know who she's been texting, especially given the content of some of these. It's not the kind of stuff she'd want to share with her mum and dad.'

On their return to the school, Mariner took with him photographs of Akram and Pryce. A cluster of girls was gathered outside the school gates. 'Isn't that Suzanne?' said Millie.

'Yes, let's get her on her own. She may be more inclined to talk.'

Millie was driving, so pulled over to the kerb to

let Mariner out of the car.

'Suzanne. Can I have a word?'

The girl turned and gave her friends a knowing smile before breaking away from them and sashaying over to Mariner, obviously pleased to have been singled out for special attention. 'What can I do for you, Inspector?' The suggestion in those few words made Mariner's skin crawl.

He pretended not to notice. 'You've probably heard, we've found Yasmin's phone. There are several text messages on it from someone calling himself Lee. Do you know who that might be?'

'I might.' Suzanne shrugged and raised her eyebrows at her friends, eliciting a bout of giggling. Another one playing hard to get. Mariner snapped. 'Suzanne, a boy has been murdered. And not far from where we found his body we also found Yasmin's phone. You need to tell us everything you know. Loyalty to friends is commendable but it's not going to help Yasmin. At the very least, she may be in serious trouble, so we need to find out where she is.'

His tone shocked her out of her complacency. 'Lee is a boy Yasmin knows,' she pouted. 'And it's not really Lee. That's just his tag.'

'What is his real name?'

'Lewis Everett. He just calls himself Lee.'

'Are you sure about that? Did Yasmin know a boy called Ricky Skeet?'

'Is that the boy who–' The veneer of confidence was all but gone now.

'Yes. Did Yasmin know him?'

'I don't think so. I've never heard that name before.'

'How well does Yasmin know this Lee?'

'They sort of went out for a while.'

Finlay had been close to the mark. 'Why didn't you tell us about him before?'

She wrinkled her nose. 'It's history. Yaz hasn't seen him for weeks.'

Except, thought Mariner, that he was still texting her as recently as the day she disappeared. And Yasmin had recently gone to the doctor's to go on the pill.

'He goes to the boys' school up the road. We met them on a school trip, to London.'

The tickets in Yasmin's treasure box.

'Them?'

'He's mates with my boyfriend, Sam. We all met up on the same trip. Yaz and Lee started it, really. We all went off to see the London Eye, then we couldn't find our way back to the bus. We got on the wrong Underground train. It was wicked. All the teachers were going crazy because me and Yasmin had gone off with *"boys"*. They were worried about what her parents would say.'

'What about your parents?'

'Mine don't give a toss. It was Yaz's they were worried about. Pretty rich coming from them.'

'What do you mean by that?'

'Darrow and Goodway. They were all over each other. It was disgusting. Mr Goodway's wife had only left him a couple of weeks before, but she couldn't keep her hands off him.'

Was this a further example of teenage fantasy? 'But surely Mrs Darrow is–'

'Ms, actually.' The self-satisfaction crept back. 'She's divorced.'

225

'How did Yasmin's parents react to what happened?'

'They never found out. In the end Yaz persuaded the teachers not to tell. She promised that she wouldn't see Lee again so she had to meet him in secret, after school.'

'But you said she isn't seeing him now.'

'She isn't. It's over.'

'Who finished it?'

'Lee did.'

'Why?'

'Yasmin hadn't got the guts.'

'For what?'

'What do you think? What do all boys want? You're all the same.' She looked Mariner up and down with eyes that were experienced beyond her years. 'Eventually, Lee got the message that it wasn't going anywhere.'

'That Yasmin wouldn't sleep with him.'

'Yeah. She was "saving herself" for the right man, the one her parents were going to choose for her. Silly cow.'

'When did all this happen?'

'Ages ago.'

'Was Yasmin upset about the split?'

'Yeah. She wanted me to come out in sympathy and finish with Sam, too.'

'And did you?'

'No. It was totally unreasonable.'

'So you're still seeing Sam?'

'Yeah. He rocks.'

'Do you think Yasmin could be jealous of you and Sam? Did she think she was missing out?'

'It was up to her, wasn't it? She'd made her

choice between her parents and Lee. She chose her parents.'

'Do you and Sam have a full relationship?'

'Do you mean sex? Of course we do.' Treating the question with the disdain it deserved. 'Sammy's hot. But I'm not stupid. I've been on the pill for months.'

'Did you ever suggest to Yasmin that she should go on the pill?'

'We talked about it, sure: we all know guys don't like skins, but it was too late for that. Yaz blew it.'

'What would you say if I told you that Yasmin was texting Lee as recently as the day she disappeared, and that she'd asked her GP to prescribe the pill?'

Suzanne's eyes widened. 'I'd say fucking good for you, Yaz. She finally decided to do it. That must have been what she was going to tell me.'

'That's what we think, too. But why would Yasmin suddenly change her mind about sleeping with Lee? Has anyone been putting her under pressure?'

'Yaz doesn't need anyone else to do that. She's well good at doing it for herself.'

'If Yasmin was going to meet Lee again, where would she have met him?'

'I don't know. When they were going out he sometimes used to meet Yaz from school, or they'd meet down near the station where she gets her train. Lee gets the train home too. He lives in this big posh house in Barnt Green with a pool and everything. There's a pub down by the station called the Bridge. Yaz used to talk about

227

seeing Lee at the Bridge.'

Except Yasmin could have meant another bridge. Maybe it was she who had dropped her mobile phone there. But was it before or after Ricky had been attacked? And did the two occurrences really have anything to do with each other? Millie had parked the car, so Mariner caught up with her outside reception, and reported back on the conversation. 'So perhaps that's what it's all about: Yasmin trying to keep up with her friends. The status of being on the contraceptive pill.'

'Better than the status symbol of being landed with a baby at seventeen,' said Millie. 'Like Finlay said: we need to go and talk to Lewis Everett.'

'I'd like to get the official take on what Suzanne told us too. Let's see if *Ms* Darrow is around.'

The deputy head was in her office, and they were shown in just as Mr Goodway was leaving. Mariner couldn't help but see them in a new light, though it was hard to tell if what Suzanne had said was true. As Ms Darrow herself had said, teenage girls could be prone to overactive imaginations.

'Can you tell us anything about the Year 12 trip to London in the spring?' Mariner asked, when they were settled.

'That was months ago,' said Ms Darrow. 'Some of the girls went on an art trip to the Tate Modern with students from the boys school. Mr Goodway and I took them, along with a teacher from the boys school. We run quite a few joint trips. It cuts down on the expense and also allows the youngsters to mix, which is an important part of their social development.'

'From what I understand, the trip certainly enhanced Yasmin's social development.'

'Ah. You know about the incident, then.'

'We've heard one version but would be interested in your account of events.'

'It's very simple. When the time came to leave, all the girls were accounted for except Yasmin and Suzanne, and two of the boys were also missing. They eventually turned up at the coach, almost two hours late. People were beginning to get worried.'

'Where had they been?'

'Sightseeing. It was all perfectly innocent. They simply got lost and had to get the Tube back to the meeting place. London's a big place, Inspector. I wouldn't be taken in by any embroidery that might have been added.'

'Why didn't you tell us about this before?'

'As I said, it was months ago. Why would it be relevant? It seemed unnecessary to drag it all up again.'

'Did you tell Yasmin's parents about what happened?'

The smile went and the defences went up. 'We didn't think it necessary.'

'Because you knew how they would react.'

'We didn't want to jeopardise Yasmin's education because of one foolish episode.'

'Or jeopardise the generous donations Yasmin's father was making to the school.'

'That's a very cynical view, Inspector. The truth is that it was just one of these passing crushes girls have: completely normal and harmless, and

229

over before it had begun. It had run its course so there seemed no need to rock the boat.'

'It wasn't quite over, though.'

'What do you mean?'

'Yasmin was still in contact with the boy in question, Lee, up until last Tuesday. And she had begun taking the contraceptive pill. Her father found all this out shortly before Yasmin disappeared. I wonder how he would feel if he knew that you had been responsible for introducing Yasmin to her lover and had let things "run their course"?'

The colour drained from Ms Darrow's face.

'Thanks, Ms Darrow. That's been helpful. We will naturally have to discuss this with Yasmin's parents. You may want to prepare for the fallout.'

Subdued by the revelations, Ms Darrow showed them out into reception again, where Mariner's attention was caught anew by the body art sketches. This time though, they triggered a recent memory. He'd seen some of those designs somewhere else, only yesterday afternoon.

Digging it from his inside pocket he held up the picture of Shaun Pryce in front of Ms Darrow. 'Has this young man been here, to the school?'

'Sorry? Oh, yes, he's an actor. He came and did some modelling for us about a year ago. We try and include life portraits in the syllabus where we can. It was a mistake though, really.'

'Why?' Millie was surprised. 'The pictures are very good.'

'The young man in question liked to flirt with the girls. He seemed to get them rather excited.'

'I'll bet he did,' murmured Mariner. 'Did he

model for Yasmin's class?'
'He might have.'
'Think!' barked Mariner. 'Did he?'
'Yes. I think so.'

'So Shaun Pryce has a link with the girls school and may have known Yasmin. Now why the hell didn't he tell us that?'
'Do you want to go and talk to him again?'
'Not yet. Let's get Lee out of the way first.'

Built during the same era, the boys' school was structurally a mirror image of the girls, but there the similarity ended. Less well cared for, soft greenery gave way to show cases full of competition trophies, and raw testosterone hung in the air. Mariner identified himself to the matronly receptionist. 'We need to speak to one of your students: Lewis Everett.'
'I'll just need to check with Mr Blyth. One moment, please.'
Head Teacher Gordon Blyth, a small man with thinning black hair and a voice from the valleys of South Wales, came out to speak to them in person. 'I'm afraid Lewis isn't here at the moment,' he said. 'He's doing work experience.'
'Where?'
Blyth had to go away and consult with the person responsible for organising these things. He was back moments later. 'At a place that makes kitchen units, on Birch Close. It's–'
'I know where it is,' said Mariner. He looked at Millie. 'Now we are going round in bloody circles.'

Within a few minutes they were back on the small industrial estate, four units down from TMR Reprographics. The manager of Dunhill's Kitchen Design was not a happy man.

'Work experience, is that what they call it? Little bugger hasn't turned in for work again today. He cleared off last Tuesday afternoon and I haven't seen him since.'

'What time on Tuesday afternoon?'

'About half one. The kid's a waste of space. He's hardly put in a full day's work since he started here. I ask you. What kind of a worker is he going to make?'

'Have you rung the school to find out where he is?'

'I haven't got time to go chasing round after him, I've got a business to run. It'll just go on his report at the end of the week. He wasn't much use, anyway. He's a spoilt little rich kid who doesn't like getting his hands dirty.'

Outside, just a few yards away were the refuse bins that concealed the gap in the fence.

Mariner put through a call on his mobile to the head of the boys school. 'We're at the kitchen workshop, but Lewis isn't. In fact, he hasn't been here since last Tuesday. I trust you didn't know that.' The pause at the other end of the line confirmed it. 'I'd like Lewis's home address, please.'

Lewis Everett's daily train journey home terminated at the exclusive hamlet of Barnt Green that nestled complacently at the foot of the Lickey Hills. The Everetts' house was 'big and posh' as Suzanne had described it, hemmed in on all sides by woodland on a private road that

232

wasn't even graced with a proper Street name. Hawthorns here had rather more to do with the shrub than it did the home of West Bromwich Albion. Mariner tried to picture the Akram family living round here. He couldn't. Number 5, Hawthorns, consisted of five room widths of 1950s mock-Georgian with a broad double garage, behind impressive wrought-iron gates and a paved drive. Burgeoning ten-foot leylandii divided the property from its neighbours. A side gate was unlocked and they pushed through and approached the building. Mariner stepped over a dark stain that marked the otherwise flawless drive, but closer inspection revealed only engine oil. Pushing the button on the studded oak front door prompted nothing more than the jangle of a bell deep inside the house. Millie peered in through the window to see a neat and tidy sitting room, plush carpeting, gleaming antique reproduction furniture, everything in its place.

'At work, I suppose,' Millie said. 'We'll have to come back later.'

'On holiday,' called a disembodied voice from behind the hedge. The rhythmic chopping in the background that they hadn't even noticed, abruptly ceased. Mariner followed Millie back out through the gates and round to the adjacent property, an equally imposing edifice with tall windows and curving bays, in the style of Rennie Mackintosh. A man, tall and white haired, with a weathered face and sinewy arms, stood mid-way up an aluminium stepladder, brandishing a pair of garden shears. 'I do their garden, too,' he said. 'And they've gone away. Mr and Mrs have,

233

anyway. Three weeks in the Bahamas. They do it every year at about this time. Due back early hours of Thursday morning.'

'It wasn't Mr or Mrs we were looking for,' Mariner said. 'It was Lee. Lewis.'

The man thought for a minute before slowly shaking his head. 'Haven't seen him for a few days, either.'

'You're here every day?' asked Millie.

'Look at the size of these gardens. This street is a full time job for me. This time of year I get here at seven in the morning and don't go home until at least six, sometimes later if I've a job to finish. And by the time I get to the end I have to start all over again.'

'So when was the last time you saw Lee Everett?'

He thought for a moment. 'Monday. He was around then, driving that car of his too fast up and down the road. Only a matter of time before he kills someone.'

Mariner and Millie exchanged a look. 'You didn't see him on Tuesday?'

'Let me think. Tuesday I was doing the back lawn at Number 8. I'd have been round there for most of the day. They've got more grass there than Wentworth.'

'And you definitely haven't seen him since?'

'No, but you might want to check with Margaret.'

'Margaret?'

'Margaret Ashworth, their daily help.'

'Do you have her phone number?'

'No.' He shook his head, before nodding an

234

acknowledgement towards a green Land Rover Discovery that had driven up and was pulling into the driveway opposite. 'But Mrs Goldman would.'

Dashing across the road, Mariner and Millie sneaked in before the electric gates could close. Mrs Goldman was stepping down from her Land Rover Discovery, stretching out long legs clad in gleaming white cotton jeans, her equally dazzling blouse highlighting the deep tanning on her arms. On seeing Mariner's warrant card, the friendly smile on her immaculately made-up face dissolved to a troubled frown. 'Not another burglary,' she said, opening up the boot of the vehicle to retrieve Waitrose carrier bags. 'Who this time?'

'It's nothing like that,' Mariner reassured her. 'We need to get in touch with your cleaner, Margaret Ashworth.'

'Margaret? Why? What's happened?'

'We're trying to track down Lewis Everett.'

'Oh. Do you have to?' she said with feeling, slamming shut the tailgate. 'It's been so peaceful these last few days.'

Mariner offered to carry one of the bags.

'Thanks.'

They followed her round to the side of the house where she let them into a kitchen the size of Mariner's entire ground floor. It was sparse and modern, with wall-to-wall limed oak cupboards, and a wide central station that held a butcher's block. Another wall was dominated by a huge green-enamelled Aga; otherwise the appliances were in clinical stainless steel, everything as spotless as Mrs Goldman herself.

235

Margaret was clearly a treasure.

'Can I offer you something to drink, something cold, perhaps?'

Mariner placed the bag alongside the others she'd deposited on the counter top. 'That would be very welcome. Thank you.'

Opening a fridge the size of a wardrobe, she dropped chunks from an ice dispenser into beautifully crafted crystal tumblers, topping them up with an orange-coloured fruit juice.

'You remarked on how quiet things have been over the last few days,' said Mariner. 'Implying that it's not always the case.'

'Lewis takes full advantage of his parents being away,' she said with feeling. 'We get treated to the latest rock bands at full volume most evenings. The warm weather encourages him to keep all the windows open too, of course, which makes it worse.'

'No one complains?'

'Oh, one or two of the neighbours have tried talking to him. It's a question of getting through, though. Lewis is a very intense young man. The sulky and broody type, a regular Liam Gallagher – or is it Noel? You never quite know what's going on inside his head. To be truthful, I think his parents may be a bit afraid of him, and they're lovely people, so nobody really wants to upset them. We just all put up with it. When you live in a little community like this one it's important to get along. And to be fair, Lewis isn't that much trouble when his parents are around.'

'When was the last time you saw him?'

She thought about that. 'I haven't seen him – or

heard him – for about a week. Last Monday or Tuesday, I think.'

'If we could just have Margaret Ashworth's number–'

'Yes, of course. I'll get it for you.' Mrs Goldman was also good enough to let Mariner use her phone, but Margaret Ashworth was out shopping. Her daughter was expecting her back in a couple of hours.

'We may as well go back to the shop,' Mariner said. 'Thanks for the drink, Mrs Goldman.'

'Not at all. Good luck with Lewis.'

On their way back to the station, they had to drive past the girls school. It was the end of the afternoon and they saw Suzanne Perry arguing with a man beside a big flashy car, as girls swarmed out past them.

'Look at that,' said Millie. 'What do you think's going on there?'

Mariner put a call through to Knox back at OCU 4. 'Could. you run a vehicle check on a Volvo estate, personalised plate SDP 2.'

Moments later Knox came back. 'The car is registered to a Mr Stephen Perry, 39 Silvermere Road, Kingsmead.'

'She's being shown up in front of her friends by an over-protective father,' Millie concluded. 'Now who's being paranoid?'

Charlie Glover was also checking in at Granville Lane, where they found him brooding over the incident room map.

'How's it going?'

'Slowly. There's still nothing to indicate that Ricky would have known Yasmin. It's looking more and more like sheer coincidence that they were around there at the same time.'

'So nothing new?'

Glover shook his head. 'We're still looking for a murder weapon. How about you?'

For the benefit of Knox, too, Mariner filled Glover in on the afternoon's developments. 'So now we have Yasmin and the boyfriend missing. The boyfriend works at the industrial units and Yasmin's phone is found between the station and there. It gives us a whole new scenario.'

'If Yasmin was trying to prove to Suzanne that she could cut it in the romance stakes, and if she wanted to get away from her parents, what better way to do both simultaneously than to elope with her boyfriend? She could have planned the whole thing, including the sleepover at Suzanne's, which she never had any intention of following through.'

'But Suzanne seemed certain that the relationship with Lee was finished,' Millie reminded him.

'That's what Yasmin told her. The bigger the surprise then, when her friend finds out what she's done. Suzanne said that Yasmin was excited, had something to tell her. Might have been rather more than we thought.'

'If Yasmin's eloped she hasn't taken much with her,' Millie said, quietly.

'She wouldn't need to. Boyfriend Lee isn't short of a bob or two.'

'Where does that leave us with Pryce?' asked Glover. 'Potentially, we now have four people on or around the reservoir that afternoon, three of whom know each other. Akram knows Yasmin, Yasmin knows Lee.'

'And as we found out this afternoon, Shaun Pryce probably knows Yasmin.'

'Pryce insists he was there much earlier. Surely we can rule him out now.'

'If we believe him.' Mariner was sceptical. 'I'm sure there's something going on with him.'

'And Akram's still in the picture, but only in the background.'

'Which leaves us with Yasmin, Lee and Ricky as the most likely – in that order. As far as we know, Ricky doesn't know Lee or Yasmin, but perhaps he saw something, tried to stop it and Lee turned on him.'

'Perhaps eloping wasn't on the agenda,' Millie put in. 'We know for sure that Yasmin had just gone on the pill, and that she was all set to lose her virginity. Maybe that's what they were meeting for. Shaun Pryce could have even suggested the location. We don't know how he gets his kicks. Perhaps he was planning to watch. So Yasmin gets there. Lee turns up with high expectations, but Yasmin then gets cold feet and won't play. Lee gets rough with her and Ricky, there by sheer coincidence, intervenes to help her–'

'And Lee turns on him.'

'Mrs Goldman said he's a bit of a sullen bastard.'

'And Randall called him a spoilt kid. Implying that he's used to getting what he wants.'

'Then Lee and Yasmin panic about what's happened and disappear together.'

239

'Or Lee panics and forces Yasmin to go with him.'

'And Pryce?'

'Pryce witnessed the whole thing, which is why he's playing silly buggers with us.'

'So why doesn't he just tell us?'

'Because he could be implicated on some level: especially if he just stood back and watched it all happen.'

'Or more than that, it turned him on.'

Mariner sighed. He couldn't ever remember standing on such fast-shifting sand. The phone rang.

'Margaret Ashworth,' said Millie. 'She'll meet us at the house.'

Chapter Fourteen

'Have you got a search warrant?' were Margaret Ashworth's first words to them when they arrived. Fortunately, Mariner was able to persuade her that it wasn't necessary since she was merely cooperating with the police enquiry. 'We don't want to search the premises,' he said, 'only see for ourselves that the place has been uninhabited for a few days.' They had to wait while she disarmed a complex security alarm and then carefully removed her shoes in favour of fluffy pink mules just in front of the door, glancing disapprovingly at their own heavy footwear.

'You wouldn't want me to take them off, love,

240

believe me,' said Knox.

Margaret took them up a sweeping staircase to Lee's room, just off the first landing at the back of the house. The curtains were drawn, rendering it almost pitch black inside.

'He likes them kept closed at all times,' Margaret Ashworth told them. Switching on the ceiling spotlights revealed a room that was a far cry from the single bed, nightstand and wardrobe that had furnished Mariner's room at the same age. There was a double bed, a bank of technology including PC, games console, TV, video recorder and DVD player, even a kettle, fridge and a microwave. It was virtually a self-contained flat with everything a young man could want. 'Christ, if I had a place like this and the folks were away I wouldn't do a disappearing act,' was Knox's comment.

Spaces on the purple-painted walls were covered with posters of surfers riding massive waves, along with some of Lee's own gruesome drawings. A battered skateboard leaned against the wardrobe. Mariner picked over the untidy desk, a jumble of papers, books, CDs and lad magazines. He was itching to rifle through the drawers too, but Margaret was keeping a beady eye on them from the doorway.

'How about a cup of tea, love?' Knox asked, summoning the best of his scouse charm. 'I'm parched. I'll bet you make a smashing cuppa.' But Margaret wasn't having any of it and her arms remained resolutely folded.

'You're losing your touch, mate,' murmured Mariner.

241

'Tell me about it,' Knox retorted. The rubbish bin had been emptied so there were no clues there, but tucked behind it, Knox found a small silver tin of the kind that normally holds travel sweets. This one didn't. Knox sniffed the dried green substance. 'He's got something in common with Shaun Pryce, then.'

Mariner wasn't that surprised. He walked over to inspect the computer that was switched off and his eye was caught by a glossy scrap of paper that had slid underneath the monitor. He edged it out with a fingernail. Dusty and slightly bent at one corner, it was a strip of photographs of the kind taken in an instant photo booth. 'Tony.' He held it up to show Knox. Lewis Everett and Yasmin Akram; grinning broadly, their faces squashed together to fit into the shot. 'At least it confirms that they've been an item.'

'Not much care taken with preserving it,' said Knox. 'A one sided relationship, d'you think?'

'Could be,' said Mariner. Another one, he thought, with feeling. Downstairs, a kitchen memo board bore postcards from various locations around the world, along with a number of business cards for local tradesmen and a couple of dental appointment cards. The answering machine might have been a source of additional information, but until they had permission it was off-limits.

'Have you any idea where Lewis might have gone?' Mariner asked Margaret, who was hovering, ever vigilant, watching over them. 'Did he say anything to you?'

She snorted. 'He doesn't even tell his parents

242

what he's up to. He's a law unto himself.'

They did, however, get from Margaret a good description of Lewis's car and its registration, and she even, if a little reluctantly, allowed them to borrow a more naturally posed recent photograph of the man himself from a display in the lounge. He was as Mrs Goldman described him, scruffy and staring defiantly into the camera, a frown where the smile should have been.

'It'll help us to eliminate him from our enquiries,' Mariner said, as a sop, though in reality Lewis was inching nearer by the minute to the main frame. It would have been good to be able to delve a little deeper but, until Mr and Mrs Everett returned, their hands were tied. Mr Everett was, apparently, a director of several small companies, so would certainly have some legal connections. He wouldn't be too pleased about coming home to find his house had been ransacked when there was no concrete evidence for doing so. They had little choice but to wait a day or so and hopefully do it with his blessing.

What they could do, meanwhile, was issue a nationwide description of Lee and his car, highlighting to colleagues in other forces the possible link with Yasmin. Mariner would go with Millie to talk to the Akrams as well. Their reaction to all this information would be educational.

Mariner wanted both parents together, so they went back to the house in the early evening. Amira was present too, giving her mother some much needed support. Shanila Akram was displaying increasing signs of strain. Her eyes seemed sunken in her pale face, and Mariner would have guessed that food and sleep had become irrelevancies. Mohammed Akram was faring better, because he knew that his daughter was safe, or was it just that he was able to put on a better show for them?

'We're fairly certain now that Yasmin may have been seeing a boy called Lee or Lewis,' Mariner said, when they were gathered in the garden. 'Has she ever mentioned him to you?'

'Yasmin doesn't know any boys, only her cousins.' Mohammed Akram was calm but firm.

Mariner had no choice but to hand over the photo booth snaps and watch shock and bewilderment creep over their faces once again. 'As you can see, there's no doubt that Yasmin knows this particular boy. She met him on a school trip when they spent some time together. We've also confirmed this with the school. It means that we have to consider the possibility that Yasmin could be with him now. They have both disappeared.'

In an unprecedented outburst, Shanila Akram turned on her husband. 'Do you see what we've done? We've pushed her into the arms of a boy. If we had let her do this out in the open, and if you hadn't–' She stopped herself, and for a moment the air was thick with the unspoken.

'Hadn't what, Mrs Akram?' Mariner prompted.

'I was going to say "argued with her",' Shanila Akram replied, weakly. Mariner didn't believe her, but the moment had passed and she was no longer prepared to say what she'd intended.

'It's my fault,' said Amira, shakily. 'I encouraged her.'

244

Her mother stared. 'But why? Yasmin is so young, and she should be pure for her husband.'

'Amma, that's ridiculous, antiquated nonsense,' said Amira, her voice strengthening. 'I had been with several men before Ravi and I married.'

'Amira!'

'It's true. But Ravi doesn't mind. In fact, he liked that I had some experience and knew what to do. Yasmin is the same. She needs some experience. She should get to know some boys.'

'So you told her to make a whore of herself?' Mohammed Akram was beside himself with fury.

'Of course not. I just said that if a chance presented itself she should take it. Virginity is overrated. And I know that Yasmin was under pressure from her friends. She felt excluded.'

'It takes a special kind of courage to stand by your principles,' said Akram coldly. 'And this is the price we pay for giving in to temptation.'

Amira dissolved into tears and this time it was her mother who moved across to offer comfort.

Mohammed Akram glanced at Mariner. 'We would like to be left alone now, Inspector.'

'Whatever other skills she has, Yasmin's pretty adept at keeping all the different facets of her life separate from one another,' said Millie as they drove away.

'It's something we all learn to do, some more efficiently than others,' said Mariner, thinking that he'd managed to get it down to a fine art: his work, mother and Anna all running on separate, parallel tracks.

Kings Rise was holding a memorial service for

245

Ricky the next morning at a local church, to assist pupils through the grieving process, though how many of them would genuinely be mourning the boy was open to debate. It was another unrelentingly hot and dry day, and it was obscene to Mariner that the sun could shine so cheerfully over such an event. Fiske had insisted on accompanying him and Charlie Glover, keeping the police presence to a minimum. The three of them slipped into the back of the church and had to stand in the unbearable heat: the place was so packed with family and schoolfriends. If this lot was anything to go by, Ricky had more mates than his mother knew. Half the church seemed to be filled with spotty adolescent kids. Mariner tried not to think that it might just be a sick excuse for a day off school. One of Ricky's uncles spoke nervously, and with hesitance, about the 'grand lad' Ricky had been, while Colleen's sobbing seemed to echo throughout the whole chapel. Mariner detested the indignity of these manufactured occasions and, as the congregation rose falteringly to its feet and began an uneasy rendition of the final hymn, he noticed one or two of the kids stifling giggles. When Fiske's pager went off, he wanted to punch his superior officer in the face.

Afterwards, they joined the long line that filed past the family to pay their respects.

'What the hell is he doing here?' demanded Colleen emotionally as Fiske appeared in front of her. 'You did nothing. Nothing!' Suddenly she lunged for him. Mariner heard camera shutters clunk behind them and knew that this would not be Fiske's finest hour. Turning his back on the debacle, Mariner walked over to where Charlie Glover stood, lighting up a cigarette. At least Colleen would appreciate that particular brand of camaraderie.

They drove in an uncomfortable silence back to Granville Lane, where Tony Knox had mixed news. 'Lewis Everett's parents are home. They flew in from the Bahamas in the early hours of this morning, boss. But they don't know where he is either. As far as they were concerned their precious son was looking after the house and doing his work experience. They admit that he can be a bit wild but they don't see him eloping with anyone. Too selfish for that, so they say.'

The vestibule they'd entered the previous day was, this afternoon, cluttered with matching Luis Vuitton luggage and a bulging sack of golf clubs. Mr and Mrs Everett were nicely tanned, but they no longer looked very relaxed.

'Thank you for seeing us so promptly,' Mariner said. 'I realise you must be tired and jet-lagged and have things to do.'

'This is not the kind of reception you expect or want on return from a peaceful holiday,' admitted Mr Everett, with slight irritation. 'But we'd like to sort it out as soon as we can.'

'You'll be aware by now that a young girl has gone missing in the area. We have reason to believe that she was having a relationship with your son.' Mariner produced the photo. 'This is Yasmin Akram. Did you know that Lewis was seeing her?'

Everett gave the picture a perfunctory glance

before passing it to his wife. 'Lewis has had various girlfriends. We don't always meet them.'

'And Yasmin?'

'I don't recall her, do you, darling?'

Mrs Everett was studying the snapshot more carefully. 'No.'

'And have you any idea where Lewis may have gone? We need to find him. He may be the last person to have seen Yasmin before she disappeared.'

'I've had a look round,' Everett said. 'Some of his camping gear has gone from the garage, but as to where he's gone, I wouldn't know.'

'We'd like to do a more thorough search of his room, if that's all right.'

Everett flattened a yawn. 'If you must.'

'Do you know if Lewis kept any kind of diary?' Mariner asked Mrs Everett.

'I don't think so.'

'Perhaps we could have a look on his computer.'

Even on the more thorough search, the only paperwork they could find was a school planner, but it contained nothing personal. On his PC they looked for traces of records on Outlook but there was nothing.

'What would Lewis do for money while he's away?'

'He has an allowance paid into his bank account and a debit card that he can use to withdraw cash from ATMs. He has a credit card too,' Everett told them.

'We'll need the details. The credit card company may be able to help us track his movements.'

Lewis's credit card records provided the break

248

they needed. A phone call to the company revealed that since the day of his disappearance, Lewis had been spending heavily at petrol stations, restaurants and surfing shops in the area around Newquay in Cornwall.

Knox contacted local police with the description of Lewis and his car, with a request to publicise it widely, especially around the campsites in the area.

'That could take some time,' he was told. 'There's hundreds of them and in this weather they're pretty full, too.'

'Do what you can, will you?' Then it was back to the waiting game.

When Mariner got home that evening, he found that his answering machine had been working overtime. An unexpected message from Anna told him that she had the chance of a night's respite from Jamie if he felt like calling round. It happened occasionally when Manor Park had an overnight vacancy. Mariner looked at his watch: it was ten fifteen. It didn't take long to make up his mind.

The house was dark: Anna making the most of the opportunity for an early night. So often was her sleep disturbed by Jamie's nocturnal wanderings that she took a full night when ever she could. Mariner let himself in and, after taking a long, cleansing shower, eventually slipped into bed beside Anna.

'Hello, you,' she murmured, sleepily.

'Hi.' In the heat of the night she'd thrown off the duvet and he could make out the luscious

249

curves of her body. He slid a hand round over her stomach and up towards her breasts, feeling his own body starting to respond.

But Anna wriggled away. 'Mm, I'm really tired.'

Pity. Sighing heavily, Mariner had to content himself with moulding his body to hers and breathing her scent. He lay there for a while, trying to drift off, but sleep just wouldn't come. Eventually, he got up and prowled the rooms, coming to rest at the bedroom window where he stared out at the eerie orange glow cast over the street by the sodium light, until at last it was faded out by the dawn. The next morning he felt like death warmed up while Anna was full of energy. 'I've got a meeting with Simon about the festival this evening,' she bubbled. 'Any chance you could sit with Jamie for me?' Suddenly, irrationally Mariner began to question the motives for that late night phone call.

'Sure,' he said, indifferently.

She picked up the undertone. 'Is that going to be a problem?'

'Of course not.' But he wasn't convincing.

She was still watching him carefully when the phone rang. 'It's the wife,' she said, handing it over.

In fact it was Tony Knox. 'Cornwall police have come back to us. They've found Lewis Everett. But he's not there with Yasmin. He's there with his mate Daniel who's also skiving off work experience.'

'Really gives you confidence in the future generation, doesn't it? Are they are on their way?'

'They're being escorted back this afternoon.'

250

'We'll talk to Lewis as soon as he gets here.' Which, he realised, might mean interviewing him through the evening. He gave Anna an apologetic look. 'I'm sorry, I won't be able to make it to-night after all, something's come up.'

She studied him for a moment. 'That's OK, I can take Jamie with me. Simon won't mind.'

Mariner picked up his jacket. 'I'll see you later, then.'

'Sure, have a good day.' No hint of disappoint-ment, not even the demand for further explan-ation, so why, as he walked out to his car, did Mariner feel so piqued? Because Simon *wouldn't mind*. He wouldn't, would he? Bastard. In all honesty, what Mariner had really wanted her to say was that she would cancel the appointment. Knowing that he was being unreasonable, he recognised the growing feeling inside him for what it was. He was jealous, of Simon Meadows, with whom Anna seemed to spend ever-increas-ing amounts of time.

It was essential to her autistic brother's well-being that Anna and Meadows should get on, so it came as a bit of a shock to Mariner that he should begin to resent their relationship. But it was turning into something he couldn't deny, even to himself. After all these years of bearing witness to the devastating impact of human jealousy, a tiny part of him was beginning to appreciate its power.

Lewis Everett arrived back in the city in the early afternoon and had legal representation right from the start. His father made sure of that, and insisted on being present, too.

Approaching six feet tall, Everett was lean and

251

lanky in that gangling, post-adolescent way, his hair fashionably mussed and with a few days' fuzzy growth on his chin. The first thing to draw Mariner's attention, as they faced each other across the interview room table, was the tattoo on his left forearm. Mariner wondered if he'd got it at the same tattoo parlour as Shaun Pryce.

'I understand you're seeing Yasmin Akram,' Mariner began.

'Was seeing, past tense. It was months ago.'

'How did it start?'

'We met on a school trip.'

'Oh yes, the trip to the Tate. You were late back to the bus.'

'We went sightseeing. Got carried away.'

'And lost. You continued to see Yasmin after that?'

'Not for long.'

'Who broke it off?'

'I did. She was a prick tease.'

'Lewis!'

'Please, Mr Everett. We agreed: no interruptions. What do you mean by that, Lewis?'

'She used to wind me up. All over me, hands going everywhere, then suddenly the parents and their religious beliefs would come into her head and she'd want me to stop. She'd say she couldn't go any further. I got fed up with it.'

'But you saw her again recently.'

'I see her sometimes across the platform at the station, waiting for her train. One day a couple of weeks ago, she sent me a text. Said she wanted to meet me again. She had something important to tell me. She asked me to meet her from school.'

'And?'

'I told her I wouldn't be at school the next week. I was doing work experience up at the factory centre.'

'Huh.' Lewis's father couldn't stop himself. Mariner silenced him with a glare.

'I told her she could come over to the centre on Monday after school. She'd be finished before me.'

'And did she come?'

'Eventually.'

'What do you mean?'

'She was late. She'd walked all the way round on the road. It's miles.'

'She didn't know about the short cut over the reservoir.'

'No.'

'Did you tell her about it?'

'Yeah, so she'd know next time. Anyway, by the time she got to Dung Heap's it was nearly time for her to catch her train.'

'But did she tell you?'

'What?'

'The "something important" she wanted to say.'

Lewis snorted. 'She said she really missed me and that she'd changed her mind.'

'About what?'

'About doing it – sleeping with me.'

'What had brought this on?'

Everett lifted his bony shoulders. 'Who knows? Her mate Suzanne had been giving her a hard time. And there was something about her sister, too.'

'So she was planning to go through with it this time.'

'I said, great, but what was she going to do about protection. I said it would be easier if she just went on the pill.'

'That's very considerate of you,' put in Tony Knox.

'If you must know, I thought when I said that she'd back down again.'

'But she didn't.'

'No. She'd already sorted it. I was pretty stunned. Her dad had even found out, but she'd fixed him too.'

'She told him she was on the pill for medical reasons.'

'Whatever.'

'So what did you do?'

'We arranged to meet again on the Tuesday afternoon, after school. I was going to get off work early and we'd go back to my place. She was going to tell her parents she was staying at her mate's house for the night.'

'So what happened?'

'Monday night, Dan called with this big plan about going down to Cornwall. But it was cool. I could meet Yasmin as planned then we'd go down afterwards, drop her off at the station or something on the way.'

'Have your cake and eat it.'

'Then, Tuesday morning, Dan called to say we'd have to go earlier or we wouldn't get a pitch at the camp-site. I texted Yasmin to let her know I wouldn't make it, and that I'd see her when I got back.'

'Just like that.'

Lewis shrugged again. 'I felt bad letting her down. She'd gone out on a limb for me but, well, you know–'

'Girls in Cornwall more of a certainty?'

'Less complicated. Yasmin had messed me around before, so she could easily do it again.'

'What time did you send the text?'

'Some time that morning.'

'What exactly did your message say?'

'I'm going to Cornwall with Dan, don't bother turning up at the reservoir. To be honest, I was pretty convinced she wouldn't come. I thought she'd bottle it at the last minute like before.'

'Is there any chance that Yasmin could have misunderstood your message?' The shrugged responses were beginning to get on Mariner's nerves. 'And what time did you leave to go to Cornwall?'

'I left the workshop at lunchtime, about one o'clock. I told them I didn't feel well–'

'Christ, Lewis, when are you ever going to do a decent day's work?'

'Mr Everett, please.' He turned back to Lewis. 'Then what did you do?'

'I went home and packed my stuff, and waited for Dan. But his car was leaking oil–'

'All over my drive, I notice,' Lewis's father interrupted.

Mariner lost patience. 'Mr Everett, if you can't remain silent I'll have to ask you to leave. Go on, Lewis.'

'We didn't get it fixed till nearly four.'

'And you went on the motorway?'

255

'Straight down the M5.' He sliced through the air with the edge of a hand.

'Did Yasmin ever talk to you about her parents?'

'Only to moan about how strict they are.'

'She ever talk about running away?'

'Not for real.'

'But she had mentioned it.' A nod. 'Did she say where she would go if she did?'

'No.'

'Did you think about taking her to Cornwall with you?'

'No way.'

'Will anyone be able to corroborate the time you left?'

A shrug. 'Dan?'

'Your best pal? Not much of a back-up,' said Knox.

'The traffic cameras might pick up the car.' Lewis was hopeful.

But Mariner kept pushing. 'I still don't understand why you turned down a perfectly good opportunity on your doorstep to drive all the way down to Cornwall. Especially given that Yasmin had started contraception for your benefit. Was she too tame for you?'

Lewis's face screwed up in a flash of irritation. 'She was using me too, man. All of a sudden she had this thing about losing her virginity. That's all she wanted me for. Listen, I really like Yasmin, but like I said, she's a mess. When we were going out she didn't really know what she wanted. And I've heard about her dad, too. He sounds seriously scary. Cornwall was just a laugh, a chance to get away from all that.'

'Without the responsibility,' put in Mr Everett.

His son stared back insolently. 'Yeah, that's right.'

'Ever heard of a boy called Ricky Skeet?' Mariner slid the photograph across the table. 'This is him.'

Lewis looked at the picture, at ease with the question. 'No.'

Knox produced the grass. 'We found this in your room.'

'It's for personal use. To be honest, it's been there ages. I'd forgotten all about it.'

'Where did you get it?'

'A friend got it for me.'

'What's his name?'

'John Smith.'

'You sure it wasn't Shaun Pryce?'

Again, it was a smooth response. No hint of recognition. 'No.'

Mariner put the second photograph on the table. 'This is him.' Lewis frowned.

'What?' said Mariner.

'It's just – weird. I'm pretty sure I don't know that guy, but it's like I've seen that picture before.'

'This picture? Or one like it?'

'Could be one like it.'

'Have you ever been into the girls' school?'

'No.'

'That is weird, then.'

They were able to let Lewis go home with his father in the late afternoon. His car was impounded for fingerprinting but Mariner was pretty sure they were wasting their time.

'Young lad like him, you'd have thought that

he'd jump at the chance of a girl offered to him on a plate,' Mariner said to Knox afterwards. 'Would he really forgo that opportunity?'

'He was hedging his bets. Yasmin had messed him around, hadn't she? Like I said, the girls in Cornwall must have seemed more of a cert.'

'He seems relaxed enough talking about Yasmin. On balance, I think he's telling the truth. And it will be easy enough to check out his story with this Dan.'

'They've had the whole drive back here to get their stories straight.'

Knox followed up by talking to Dan, who was able to confirm Lewis's version of events in every detail. And though the occupants were a blur, Lee's Grand Vitara could be picked out on motorway CCTV, passing Bromsgrove at 4.09 on that Tuesday afternoon.

In all probability they'd drawn another blank and Mariner could reasonably have taken the rest of the evening off to help out Anna. But he chose not to.

Instead, he went back to Finlay.

'Is there any way of knowing the content of Lee's last message, even if Yasmin deleted it afterwards?'

'There is one deleted message: the last one received, which would have been it. As I said before, the ghosting is there. But there's no way of knowing what that message said.' So they had Lee's word that the text was calling off the meeting. For all they knew he could have been calling to confirm it.

'If she got the message from Lee, why did she still go there?' Knox wanted to know.

'We still don't know for certain that she did,' said Mariner. 'All we know for sure is that she got off the train again.'

'And her phone found its way to the bridge,' said Millie.

'But supposing she did go to the bridge,' Mariner said. 'Say, somehow, she misunderstood what Lee had said. What would she do when he didn't turn up?'

'I'd expect her to wait around a bit, then when it's clear he's not coming, go back to the train station.'

'Unless she saw it was the opportunity she'd been waiting for,' said Mariner. 'She's getting grief at home and with her friends. Suddenly she's in a position where she's accountable to no one. Her mum thinks she's with Suzanne. Her dad's far enough away not to be giving her much thought. A window opens up of a few hours when no one's going to miss her: a chance to get away.'

'On a West Midlands travel card?' Knox was doubtful.

'Don't forget that this is all at about the same time Ricky is killed on that very spot. We've thought about Ricky witnessing something and being killed for it, but what about if Yasmin saw what happened to Ricky and it scared her into running away.'

'Which brings us back to where we came in last Wednesday: where has she gone?' Mariner got up from where he'd been sitting, massaging his temples to ease the headache he was developing.

'Potentially, we've got several people at the reservoir at that time and now we have photographs to go with them. Let's go and talk to Lily again, see if we can prompt her into remembering anything new.'

The air felt as if it was closing in on them as Knox drove them back to St Clare's, armed now with photographs of Yasmin, Lee, Mohammed Akram and Shaun Pryce. Dusk was a couple of hours away but the sky had dulled to a misty grey and, when they got out of the car, Mariner noticed his shirt speckled with tiny storm flies. He was hoping that Lily would recognise at least one of the photographs, but she simply shook her head at each of them.

'Are you saying you don't know?' Mariner asked.

'No. I'm saying it's not him.'

'None of them? You're sure?'

'Absolutely.'

'Well, thanks for looking.' It was not what he wanted to hear.

'Not at all.' Lily smiled. 'You were lucky to catch me again, Inspector. I shan't be here for much longer.'

'Oh?'

She beamed with pride. 'I've won a competition. Twenty-five thousand pounds.'

Mariner was impressed. 'That's fantastic. What competition was that?' Going over to the little table in her room, she handed him a letter. It was the sort of 'Congratulations! You have been selected to receive one of our stunning prizes' variety of junk mail that every household receives on a weekly basis. All it required in return was that the recipient sign up to a monthly magazine to be entered into a prize draw.

'Lily, this isn't–' Mariner began gently, but Nora caught his eye and gave a tiny, warning shake of the head.

'I'm going to buy a nice little flat,' Lily went on, enthusiastically. 'And I'm going to have a party for all my family and friends too. You must come, Inspector.'

'I'd love to,' said Mariner, with a sudden sinking feeling.

Nora showed them out of the building. 'I know what you're thinking and yes, it's true, she does have days when she's confused, but not every day. She still saw what she saw.'

'I know.' But now Mariner was beginning to wonder exactly what it was that Lily saw. On the way home, the pain that had been moving round his skull throughout most of the day began to tighten like a vice, as thoughts bounced around his head, seeking out connections. He considered again whether he should go to Anna's but something stopped him. What he needed was some time on his own to think. In the cottage, he washed back a couple of painkillers, sat back in the armchair and closed his eyes.

Mariner was woken at around midnight by what he at first thought were fireworks: these days, especially in summer, the universal way to celebrate any special event by waking all the neighbours. But the air had grown stickier still, and the next rumble he heard was preceded by the unmistakable flicker of lightning. The storm crept

261

slowly on to the city like a slothful beast, grumbling and complaining, building in strength until the thunder shook the house and lightning flashed with dazzling intensity. Then the rain came, pounding on the water and trees like no rain Mariner had heard before. He leaned on the sill of the open window to breathe it in. Mesmerised by the cool freshness after the weeks of intolerable heat, Mariner took his keys from the shelf and stepped outside into a puddle that covered his shoes, and just walked. Shining under the street-lights, the gutters had become rivers, gardens vast ornamental ponds, as the water sought to find an outlet through the hard, dry earth.

Within seconds, his clothes were soaked through and his hair plastered to his head, but the heavy drops beat soothingly on his head and shoulders as he walked the deserted streets, while the storm raged overhead, before finally admitting defeat and moving off to terrorise elsewhere. As the rain weakened to a light drizzle, Mariner let himself back into the house, where he stripped off his wet clothes in the hall, climbed the stairs and collapsed into a restless, dream-ridden sleep as dawn was beginning to prise open the sky.

He was woken from a deep, heavy sleep by the phone. It was Fiske. 'Yasmin Akram,' he said abruptly. 'There's been a development.'

Chapter Fifteen

Not 'breakthrough', Mariner noted, but 'development'. It didn't sound good. Fiske, playing the drama queen again, couldn't just come out and tell him. But it was serious, judging from the number of people who had been contacted and brought in on this Sunday morning. With everyone crammed into the small and stifling briefing room, Fiske broke it to them. 'The body of a young Asian girl has been found in the river that runs through Kingsmead Park,' he said. 'We think it's Yasmin Akram.'

Missing person to murder victim, in two simple sentences. Murmurs of disgust rippled round the room, an odious Mexican wave.

'She was discovered early this morning by a park ranger.'

'How close is that to where her phone was found?' someone asked.

'It's about a mile away, down from the station but on the other side of Birchill Road. We'll be setting up an incident room as soon as identity is confirmed.' He turned to Mariner. 'DI Mariner, who has been investigating her disappearance, will continue to lead on the ground.'

The flash storms had caused chaos across the whole of the Midlands area. Towns along the Severn, like Bewdley that had seemed to be almost

263

permanently under water last autumn and spring had fallen victim yet again. And in Birmingham itself, they drove through streets that were still several inches under water. But the freshness the rain brought was short-lived. It continued to be a sticky and stormy day; the sun a white smear against the grey-yellow sky, the peculiar half-light threatening more showers.

It was a slow drive down past the railway station and to the park, in a convoy of cars that inched its way through patches of deep flooding. In the car park, a small group had already gathered and uniform were having a nightmare task keeping kids away from what had become an instant water park. 'Who found the body?' Mariner asked the nearest officer.

'Andy Pritchard.' He pointed over to a young lad in khaki shirt, trousers and high waders, standing isolated from the pack. 'Park ranger. There's a couple of them cycle around all the local parks, dealing with vandalism, that kind of stuff. Today he's on his own.'

'The Lone Ranger,' observed Knox.

'He's pretty shaken up,' the officer added.

'Who wouldn't be?'

Andy Pritchard had one of the worst cases of acne Mariner had ever seen. He was virtually hiding under the peak of his green ranger's cap. Nearby, two more officers were transferring soggy books and papers into evidence bags. A saturated, dark-blue back-pack lay at their feet. Mariner recognised it from the description they'd had of Yasmin's. Putting on waders, he and Knox went with Pritchard to where he'd found the body, in a remote corner of the park.

'I saw the books first of all,' he told them as they sloshed through water eight inches deep, 'floating along on the surface. I couldn't work out where they would have come from. Then I saw the bag. So I went upstream to see if there was anything else, and that was when I noticed what I thought were clothes caught on the tree roots on the other bank. When I had a closer look–' he lifted the binoculars, '–I could see that it was something more.' They had come to the main channel of the river: although there was no distinguishing it from the pond they'd just waded through. Stopping abruptly, Pritchard pointed across to the opposite bank a couple of yards away, where they could now see a dark, sodden bundle of clothing, long black hair fanning out behind. 'Then I saw her face.'

'Now I'm a believer,' muttered Knox under his breath.

As if to confirm Pritchard's story, the water suddenly bulged, turning the body and for a split second they looked into what was unmistakably the pale, lifeless face of Yasmin Akram.

'What time was this?' asked Mariner.

'About seven o'clock. We work dawn till dusk in the summer months.'

'But you didn't call it in until nearly eight,' said Knox. 'Why was that?'

Pritchard flushed. 'I wasn't sure what to do. I thought about trying to get across to her but the water was too deep and too fast flowing. I thought I might lose my footing. It's gone down a bit since then. I thought the best thing was to

265

call you.'

'It was the best thing,' said Mariner, though preserving this scene was going to be a joke. 'Is there a way round on the other side?' He looked up at the steep embankment, knowing the answer already.

Pritchard shook his head. 'This is the closest we can get. You'll have to wade across.'

Here, the main course of the stream was six or seven feet wide. From where they stood, the level had risen to Mariner's knees, and now and again he had to lean into the powerful current.

'OK. Thanks, Andy, we'll take it from here,' said Mariner. 'If you go back up to the road someone will take a full statement from you.'

Pritchard on his way, Mariner turned to Knox. 'Want to try and get a bit nearer?'

'After you, boss,' said Knox.

They edged out towards the middle of the fast-flowing brown water, dodging the debris that rushed by, until the level was up to their thighs. The floor of the stream was soft and yielding and a sudden surge caught them unawares. Knox staggered, and almost fell, but found his footing again. 'The flow is uneven,' said Mariner, bracing himself. 'We just need to get the timing right to get across the deepest section.' He watched and waited. 'OK – now!'

Taking advantage of the next lull, they pushed across the mid-stream, grabbing at sodden vege-tation to steady themselves in the shallower water on the opposite bank. Now they were standing directly over the deceptively animated body as it danced and swayed on the water, the clothing

266

grasped firmly by the exposed roots of an over-hanging willow. Despite the bloating effects, there was no doubt about the identity. Several dark blemishes on Yasmin's face threw up the possibility that her death had been accompanied by violence. For Shanila and Mohammed Akram, the agonising wait was over, but about to be replaced by something infinitely worse. Millie would be dealing with that. She was probably there right now. Mariner forced himself to not think about it.

Straining to keep his feet in the surging water, Mariner looked around him. It was unlikely, as far as he could see, that Yasmin would have been put in here. He voiced the thought to Knox. 'To get to this point she'd have had to be carried the way we came through the park, which, in the sort of weather we've been having, would have been busy on into the late evening, and far too public. The only time to have done it would have been under cover of night.'

'Even then it would have been risky,' said Knox. 'People walk through this park to get from the main Pershore Road through to Birchill Road.'

'We need to look further up.'

They were hailed by a shout from the other side of the stream. SOCO had arrived in overalls and waders. Mariner talked them across the river.

'It's definitely her?' asked DC Chris Sharp.

'No question,' said Mariner.

Sharp shook his head sadly. 'Trouble is now, that after last night's rain, all your physical evidence will have been washed away.'

'No kidding?' said Mariner. 'Just do what you can, eh?'

Mariner and Knox left SOCO to do their work. Battling against the rushing torrent and clutching at the overhanging bushes, they staggered upstream as far as they could get, to where the stream emerged from a tunnel beneath the road.

Knox looked up towards the parapet: a brick wall topped with waist-high railings. 'She could have gone in here,' he said. 'It would only take a couple of minutes. Stop the car, open the boot and tip her over the edge, she then gets carried downstream.'

'It's a busy road,' said Mariner. 'Late at night would be easier, but you'd still run the risk of someone driving past and seeing.' Looking up on the other side of the road, he noticed they'd come out opposite St Clare's retirement home.

'This stream must connect to the reservoir,' he said.

Knox foraged in his pocket and produced the rather crumpled map. 'You're right, boss. It looks as if we're just further downstream from the wooden footbridge.' Where Ricky Skeet was killed and where Yasmin had arranged a rendezvous with Lewis Everett.

'How does the river progress down to here?'

Knox traced a finger down the map and Mariner couldn't help noticing how chewed his fingernail was. 'It looks as if it must be under the ground, through some kind of tunnel,' Knox said.

'And above the ground it's all green, so more of what we can see: rough woodland, and pretty impenetrable at that. And the river doesn't surface at all?'

They both studied the map. 'Doesn't look like it, boss. The next place it appears on the map is at the spillway next to the reservoir.' Knox looked up. 'You think she could have been put in there?'

'It's where we found her phone.'

'She travelled all this way underground?' Knox was doubtful.

'Let's go and have a look. And get hold of someone who knows more about the river.'

Millie had been adamant at the time. She could handle this on her own. The Akrams had got to know her, and Shanila, in particular, she felt, trusted her. But now she was here it was different. She'd spent the drive over going through all the different possible strategies for breaking the news; set pieces she'd previously rehearsed only during training. Prepare the way but don't prolong the agony, use their names and make it personal. She needed none of it. Taking one look at Millie's face, Shanila knew why she'd come. 'You've found her, haven't you? Oh God, you've found her!' Before she let out a horrible, gut-wrenching howl, that went on as long and as hard as her lungs would allow.

The reservoir had undergone subtle changes since their last visit: where it hadn't been cut down, the foliage had been beaten flat; there was a higher tide mark; and the rank, sulphurous smell had been replaced by a fresher one of damp plant life. Looking more closely they could see that the channel down the middle was moving faster and a torrent of water gushed noisily down the spillway. From the bridge the damage was clearer. The wooden gates, there to control the flow of water, had been cast aside and lay in a jumbled heap at the base of the concrete shelf, along with bricks that had broken loose from the mouth of the half collapsed tunnel.

'It's flowing pretty fast now, fast enough to take a pretty big object with it,' Mariner said.

'But you saw how it was on the day Hewitt brought us here. It was barely a trickle because we'd had no rain. It would hardly have carried a feather down with it.'

'But Hewitt also said something about the water collecting and releasing every so often. Maybe the day Yasmin was killed was one of those days. We need to find out more about this.'

'Mr Mariner?' The elderly gentleman who approached them looked as if he was almost ready to join Lily in St Clare's. He came unsteadily along the path, using a stick for support. When he got almost to them he proffered a hand. 'Eric Dwyer,' he said. 'One of your colleagues asked me to meet you here. I'm the chairman of the local river conservation group.' Dwyer's cheeks were weathered a rosy pink, but much of the rest of his face was obscured by glasses and a pair of extravagant mutton chop whiskers.

'So you know all about this reservoir,' said Mariner, shaking the bony hand.

'I dare say I know as much as anyone.' He looked out over the water. 'It was built at the turn of the century to top up the canal system in times of drought. It's what's known as a feeder lake: the water diverting away from and back into the

270

canal.' He peered over the bridge. 'My, my, that's taken a battering.'

'I understand that these gates were meant to open under pressure.'

'That's right.' He went on to describe what Mariner had already surmised.

'How big a release is it when it goes? Enough to carry something big with it, say seven or eight stone in weight?' Mariner wondered if Dwyer had any idea what kind of object they were talking about.

If he did he wasn't curious enough to ask. 'Given the gradient of the incline, I'd say easily. I've never seen this one in full spate, but I've seen other similar mechanisms and they usually flow at about ten cubic feet per second. That's quite a force.'

'How often does this release occur?'

'At this time of year, as you'd expect, not very often. The drier the weather the longer it takes for the pressure to build. It'd be once a day, if you're lucky.'

'And would there be any way of telling what time of day this was occurring recently?'

'Unfortunately not. It would depend entirely on the flow into the reservoir.'

'And after heavy rain, such as we had the other night?'

'After heavy rain the water would just flow straight through, much as it's doing now. The gates would be permanently open, almost as if the reservoir were just part of the river. The river flows to here from its source in the Waseley Hills right through to Spaghetti Junction. After last night's storms, by the time it got to this point it would be torrential, hence the damage. That will take some sorting out.'

'So what's down there?' Mariner pointed into the tunnel.

'At this end, a series of valves and valve vaults to control the flow.'

'Would they hinder anything passing through?'

'To a degree. The mechanisms are old, have been there for decades and under no particular pressure: but the sudden influx of last night's rain was clearly enough to break the sluice gates and could have equally damaged or destroyed the valves too.'

'But we've had rain like this before. Why would this happen now?'

'Probably because of the work we've been doing upstream, clearing all the rubbish and dredging out where the river has got clogged up.' He shook his head regretfully. 'We've been too thorough.' He looked back over the pool itself. 'The water hasn't had such a clear run for years.'

'Sounds like hard work.'

'It's not always. We're quite a sociable group, too.'

'Ever had a guy called Shaun Pryce in the group?'

'Shaun Pryce? I don't remember the name.' Mariner described Pryce to Dwyer.

'He doesn't fit our profile. We're mainly middle-aged, retired folk with too much time on our hands and a concern for the preservation of our city. But that said, people come and go. Occasionally we get more ecologically aware students who come and join us.'

'I wonder if you could let me have a list of your members some time.'

'Consider it done.'

Mariner looked out over the wasteland of the reservoir. 'So your work hadn't brought you as far as this, then?' Mariner asked.

'Not yet. We're running a bit behind schedule, dependent as we are on volunteers. But we did all the prep work some time ago.'

'What does that involve?'

'Myself and another member coming down here with someone from the rivers authority to look at what there is and what needs doing. That's how I know about the tunnel.'

'When did you come here?'

'It would have been in about March, I suppose. We were being somewhat optimistic, as it turns out.'

'And who came with you?'

'Sheila Carr was the other member. It's interesting because I'm sure that at that time the railings weren't broken. It's not something we put on our work list.'

'Well, thanks for coming down here, Mr Dwyer, it's been very helpful.'

Watching him go, Mariner took another look around, noticing anew the break in the timber railings. 'Lily mentioned that,' he recalled.

'It's not that recent,' Knox was examining them. 'The wood on the inside of the break is weathered too.'

'I think we do have to consider it a probability that Yasmin was put in the water here,' Mariner said.

273

Knox nodded agreement. 'But is this where she was killed?'

Arriving at the Newton Street mortuary later that afternoon, Mariner's stomach began to bubble gently. Outside, the temperature had soared again: a signal that the storms had been just a blip on the meteorological radar.

'Lucky for us that they happened at all,' remarked pathologist Stuart Croghan. 'Or Yasmin's body might have remained hidden.'

This wasn't the first child murder Mariner had worked on, but contrary to popular belief, the average detective rarely deals with murder cases, children or otherwise. The experience was always guaranteed to be traumatic, even though the meeting would be conducted in Croghan's office with reference to photographs, rather than walking around the cadaver itself, in the manner of all good TV detectives.

Croghan had been working non-stop since the body had been brought in a couple of hours ago and already the file on Yasmin Akram was thick with detailed notes. Much of this information would be saved for the inquest, so Croghan confined himself to the salient points, knowing exactly what would be of practical use to Mariner now.

'Death was by asphyxiation,' Croghan told him. 'She was strangled with some kind of ligature, probably some kind of wire. There's no apparent discolouration or abrasion in the ligature wound so it was a clean or treated wire.'

'Plastic coated?'

'Could be. It was quite soft, around a twenty-eight gauge – about three millimetres thick. You can tell that from the shape and depth of the groove.'

'Some kind of electrical wire, perhaps?' Mariner was hopeful.

'It's possible but I couldn't be certain.'

'But not an accident, then.'

'Absolutely not. She was already dead when she went into the water. There are diatoms in the throat area but not in the bloodstream, heart or lungs.' Meaning, she hadn't inhaled water. The microscopic algae were reliable indicators.

'Decomposition is patchy though, which is unusual, not in keeping with being totally submerged throughout. Different areas of the body seem to have decomposed at different rates.'

'Consistent with spending a few days in a drainage tunnel with an irregular through-flow?'

'That would probably do it, yes.'

'How long had she been exposed to the water?' he asked.

'I'd say several days. The decomposition pattern is going to make it hard to pinpoint the time of death very accurately. We'll analyse stomach contents but there's a limit to what that can tell us, too.'

'But we're looking at her being killed roughly when?'

'It's more than a week ago.'

Mariner gave Croghan a look that said, 'Thanks for nothing'.

'I did warn you,' the pathologist said.

'Anything else that would help?' asked Mariner.

275

'Quite a bit of post-mortem bruising that would imply that she had a rough journey after she was put in the water.' Yasmin progressing through that underground tunnel.

'Any sign of a sexual assault?' asked Mariner.

'No physical signs, as far as I can see. And from the internal I'd have said that she wasn't sexually active. However, she's not wearing any underwear. Curious.'

Croghan was right, that was curious.

'So Lee's message could have been confirming their meeting,' said Millie. She looked shattered after the visit to the Akrams, but had insisted on being present for the debrief. They'd gathered again in Mariner's office: it was becoming a regular club meeting. 'Yasmin disappeared at around the time Lee left. He could have done it before he went. Perhaps he wanted her to go with him and she refused.'

'And the missing underwear would mean some kind of sexual activity, or the start of it,' Knox added.

'But as Croghan said, this doesn't look like a spur of the moment thing. It smacks of premeditation. I can't imagine that Lee would set out to kill Yasmin.'

'No. It would have to be someone who just happened to have about their person a piece of electrical wire,' put in Knox. 'Like Shaun Pryce.'

'Maybe that's what Ricky saw,' said Millie. 'Someone assaulting and killing Yasmin.'

'So why didn't the killer tip him over the bridge too?'

There were still so many questions. 'I should go and talk to Yasmin's parents,' said Mariner. 'They'll want to know what comes next.'

'I'll come with you, sir.'

The smiling face of Yasmin Akram beamed at Mariner from where the photo sat at the centre of the shrine for family and friends to pay their respects in the sitting room, where Millie and Mariner had been shunted to wait. Bypassing the huddle of people on the pavement outside, they'd been shown directly into the cool, formal room that was lavishly furnished and spotlessly clean and, Mariner guessed, rarely used.

The house was busy, but in here an eerie silence reigned. If the body were not still being held at the mortuary, they would, Millie told him, be looking into an open coffin. A knock on the door preceded Amira, her dark mourning clothes emphasising the paleness of her skin. Millie got up and gave her a hug. 'How's your mother bearing up?'

'She's OK. My father's taking care of her.' Her face crumpled. 'All this is my fault,' Amira said. 'If I hadn't encouraged her–'

'That's not true, Amira,' said Millie firmly. 'Someone else did this. They are responsible. You only wanted what was best for Yasmin.'

'I've let them all down.' Overcome with grief, she began to weep, and while Millie attempted to console her, Mariner was suddenly struck by the inappropriateness of his presence here. This intrusion on the family's grief, bringing the constant reminder of unnatural death was one of the

277

most repulsive aspects of the job. He got up suddenly. 'I'll come back another time,' he said.

Millie chose to stay, and when Mariner drove away he found himself close to Anna's house. Suddenly he was aware that he'd been letting down a number of people too. The Akrams he could do little about for now, but he could make amends with Anna. He took a chance and stopped by her house, but was disconcerted to see an unfamiliar car on the drive. Laid across the parcel shelf was a green sweatshirt bearing the embroidered Manor Park logo. He parked and walked round to the side of the house, from where he could smell the charcoal fumes from a barbecue and hear the sound of music and laughing, as if a party was in full swing. The voices were predominantly male.

Mariner opened the side gate. The first person he saw was Jamie, typically detached from the group, pacing the edge of the lawn, head down, muttering to himself and wringing the hem of his polo shirt in his hands. He was wearing shorts: something that even a few months ago he wouldn't have countenanced. Good old Manor Park.

Clustered at the far end of the patio, nearest the kitchen door, Anna stood, leaning back against the picnic table, wine glass in hand and deep in conversation with a man lounging below her on a garden chair, his back to Mariner. Anna wore a scrap of a vest and a denim skirt short enough to offer the Kingsmead girls some strong competition. Her face was open and smiling and

278

attention focused one hundred per cent on her guest, whose gaze would have been at about the level of her smooth, lightly tanned thighs. No marks for guessing where his mind would be.

'Any more drinks out there?' called another man's voice from the kitchen; someone else clearly at home.

Sickened, Mariner turned to go, but he was too late. Without even seeming to glance in his direction, Jamie had seen him.

'Spectre Man,' he said loudly.

In those early days when Anna had addressed him as 'Inspector Mariner', Jamie had found it impossible to get his mouth around it, Spectre Man being the closest he could get. Highly appropriate today when Mariner felt exactly that: the spectre appearing at the feast.

'Hi, Jamie,' Mariner said.

Hearing Jamie speak Anna had immediately looked up and Mariner tried to read her face. Surprise certainly, but anything else? Hard to tell. She left her guest and came over. Big smile but no kiss: maybe he was giving off the wrong signals, or maybe not. 'Hi. We weren't expecting you. Coming in?'

We? 'You've got visitors.'

'That's OK. Come and join us. You can meet Simon and–'

'I'm not much in a party mood. We found Yasmin Akram.'

'Yes. I heard about it on the news. I'm sorry. Why don't you stay anyway and have a drink?'

He did consider it, but only for a split second. 'No. It's fine. There's a lot to do.'

'All right.'

It was one of those occasions when she disappointed him. It had been a tough day and Mariner wanted to share it with someone. He was restless, and for once his own company wasn't enough, so short of anything better to do, he went back to Granville Lane. After a while Millie returned from the Akrams' house, looking drained, and by nine thirty only the two of them remained in the incident room.

'Come on,' Mariner said, 'I'll buy you a curry.' Then he realised what he'd said.

Millie just laughed. 'I know a place where you can get the best,' she said. The place turned out to be her ground floor flat, in Acocks Green.

'This is fantastic,' said Mariner as he scooped up rogan josh with a spicy naan that was as light as a feather. He hadn't eaten all day, and until now hadn't realised how hungry he was.

'Don't get too excited,' Millie said. 'I didn't cook it myself. My mum sends it over now and again. I think it helps to salve her conscience when the rest of the family won't have anything to do with me. Dad doesn't know she does it.'

'Oh?'

'Long story,' Millie said.

'I've got time. If you want to, that is.'

'Why not?' She dropped her chunk of bread into her dish and sighed. 'My parents aren't quite so enlightened as Yasmin's. They always expected me to be a traditional Pakistani wife. I had to learn to cook and sew – all the usual. But when I got to about Yasmin's age, I started to realise that there could be more to life than that. I was doing

280

pretty well at school and decided I wanted to go to university. I fancied being a forensic scientist. But my dad has a rather more traditional view of the female role than the Akrams. Within our community the whole *raison d'être* of a woman is to look after her husband and produce lots of healthy children. I would have to do it the hard way. Over a number of years, I saved enough money to start paying my way through college, but a few weeks before I was due to go, Dad got hold of my building society book, confiscated my savings and that was the end of it.'

'Christ, I had no idea.'

'Naturally, this led to a massive row with my dad. I called him a lot of things that I shouldn't have and my family and the rest of the community shunned me. I left home and came to live with a sympathetic auntie in Alum Rock, and this job was the nearest I could get to what I really want to be.' Partly to conceal her emotion she got up and carried her plate to the kitchen.

Mariner followed her through. 'Do you still have ambitions for forensics?' he asked as they stacked dishes in the dishwasher.

'I don't know. I like what I do now.'

'You're bloody good at it,' he said.

'Thanks.'

'I mean it. You've built a great relationship with the family.'

'Today was horrible, having to tell them.'

'It was always going to be. It's one of the bits that doesn't get any easier.'

'I keep trying to imagine what they must be going through. Their own child. It must be–' Her

281

eyes watered and she wiped at them crossly.

Mariner put a hand on her shoulder. 'You made it as easy for them as you could,' he said. 'You supported them. It's all you can do. You can't bring her back.'

'No, but I still wish I could.'

Afterwards, Mariner couldn't really be sure how it happened. One minute he had his arm around Millie comforting her, the next her lips were fused to his, her tongue, sweet and spicy, probing his mouth. Maybe the curry had aphrodisiacal properties, or perhaps seeing Anna like that had left him gagging for it. Whatever it was it seemed like the most natural thing in the world that he should kiss her back, his hands roaming her shapely body. And by the time her hand slid down to unzip him he was already hard.

They made love urgently, only making it as far as the sofa, Mariner's trousers shoved down to his thighs. For him it was over in minutes, too soon for Millie, who continued her frenzied pumping on his softening member for what seemed like an eternity, until spasms rocked her and she finally allowed him to withdraw, deflated and sore.

'Sorry,' Mariner said. 'That wasn't up to much.'

'No.' She seemed not to mind. 'But probably about what you'd expect from a couple of drunks. I'll call you a cab.'

Thankfully, Mariner made it inside his own front door before his bowels decided to erupt. He awoke the next morning, still half-clothed, mind and body feeling lousy in equal measures. His system clearly wasn't accustomed to industrial-strength curry and Millie's mother's, good though it was at the time, had consigned him to the bathroom for much of the night. He'd a thumping hangover and his dick hurt about as much as his ego. He didn't think Millie was the type to broadcast details of their pathetic encounter around the station, but you could never really tell with women.

When the phone rang, he really hoped it wasn't Anna. It wasn't. It was Mark Russell. 'I thought you'd want to know, sir, we've got another body.'

Somehow Mariner dragged himself under the shower. Every time he moved his head, pain jangled round it like the vibrations in a bell. Forcing down coffee and painkillers, he put on his sunglasses against the agonising glare of sunlight and got a taxi to Granville Lane, where he saw that his own car had miraculously materialised in the station car park. The movement of the journey in had made him feel queasy again, but somehow he managed to stagger upstairs, roll down the blinds in his office and make it to his desk, where Mark Russell came to brief him on the latest discovery.

'She was found a little way downstream from where Yasmin was found.' Russell was saying, but Mariner was momentarily distracted by Millie walking into the bull pen. She smiled a brief 'good morning' to them both through the glass partition, but her face gave nothing away.

'Sir?' Russell said.

'I'm listening.'

'She was found by Ben: a liver and white

springer spaniel who's apparently a keen swimmer. His owner, a Mr Lovell, took him to the park this morning as usual, and Ben had what I s'pose you'd call a "swamp day". Mr Lovell had to go looking for him, and that was when he saw the woman's body, caught on an old bit of fencing that runs alongside the stream. Yesterday, that part of the park would have been completely under water but the flooding has subsided overnight.'

'And what do we know about her?' Mariner forced himself to concentrate.

'Not much yet. She's an older woman: late forties or fifties. The pathologist at the scene said she's been in the water a lot longer than Yasmin: could be weeks or even months. She's got similar kinds of bruising, though.'

'So she could have been released at the same time, when the mechanism disintegrated.'

'It's likely. They think there won't be much in the way of forensics, thanks to decomposition, but we've got a pair of earrings that may help in identification, and there was a large splinter of wood caught in her cardigan.'

'From the bridge?' Mariner thought of the railings.

'SOCO are down there now.'

'Do we know how she died?'

'Her skull has been smashed, but Croghan seemed to think that may have happened when she fell into the water.'

Mariner fought down a wave of nausea. 'Any ID?'

'Not yet. Tony Knox is going through the missing persons.'

'OK, let me know when you find anything.'

The best solution to avoid throwing up, Mariner found, was to remain as inactive as possible. There were things to do but, for once, he'd let the answers come to him. He got Russell to bring him some water, then began sifting through the messages that had accumulated on his desk. He didn't trust himself to return any of the three calls from Anna and consigned the yellow message slips to the bin. The next was from a Sahira Masud. Mariner couldn't place the name, not even in connection with Yasmin Akram, so began sifting through the thousands of names on file in his head, in an attempt to attach meaning to this one. In the end he had to pick up the telephone to find out.

'I live next door but one to your mother,' Mrs Masud reminded him, patiently. 'I'm afraid she's had a slight stroke.'

The words had more of an impact than Mariner could ever have imagined, temporarily displacing his own fragility. As the contact between himself and his mother had dwindled over a number of years, Mariner had always thought that he would be quite detached from any such news. He'd been wrong. Now he felt bad that he hadn't returned her calls. Was that what she'd been ringing about, to tell him she wasn't feeling well? 'Will she be all right?' he asked, with far more anxiety in his voice than he would have expected.

'She's fine.' Mrs Masud was instantly reassuring. 'But they've taken her into Warwick Hospital to keep an eye on her overnight. You might want to—'

'Yes. Thanks for letting me know.' Any decisions about visiting her he would make himself, after weighing up whether it was likely to make her worse or better.

'She's on ward eight.'

'Thanks.' Mariner looked up to see Millie standing in the doorway, swinging his car keys. She came and laid them on his desk, all the time studying his face, which Mariner guessed was probably an interesting shade of grey.

'Everything OK, sir?' she asked.

Mariner nodded and instantly regretted it. 'Look, about last night,' he said. 'I was pretty pissed.'

She returned a wan smile. 'You and me both, sir. To be honest I can't remember much about it. Probably best forgotten.'

'Yes, I'm sure you're right.' Mariner was weak with relief.

'In my job I move around a lot,' she went on. 'I try to bag an Inspector at every OCU I'm assigned to. You did enough.' Mariner gaped at her. 'Joke,' she said, deadpan, before walking away.

Tony Knox was next in line. The bacon sandwich in his fist nearly had Mariner reaching for the bin, but he was oblivious to Mariner's state. Then again, he didn't look all that hot himself. His shirt was creased and slightly grimy and he didn't appear to have had time for a shave today.

'We've got a possible match on the body, boss. Barbara Kincaid. IC 1 female, aged forty-four, reported missing back in March from an address on Banbury Road.'

'That's what? About half a mile from the reservoir?'

'The other side of the station. According to the husband's statement at the time, she'd been suffering mental health problems: depression. She left the house sometime late one night and didn't come back. The description of what she was wearing on the day she disappeared matches clothing on the body, and we've asked him to come in and identify some jewellery she was wearing.'

'Russell said something about a splinter of wood?'

'Yeah. It's a possible match with the wooden railings of the reservoir bridge.'

'So she went in at the same place Yasmin did.'

'It looks like it.'

'She could have been the one who leaned on them and broke them. It wouldn't have taken much. They were pretty well rotten through. What do you think?'

'Either that or she threw herself in, got tangled up in the drainage mechanism. It's a bit desperate though.'

'Desperate feelings lead you to do desperate things. Let me know when identity's confirmed.'

The final straw was Fiske, who hovered in the doorway, distinctly reticent, and Mariner was soon to find out why. 'The Skeet family have made a complaint,' he said.

'About what?'

'About the way the disappearance of their son

was handled, that it wasn't given enough of a priority. How far do you think they'd take it?'

'What do you mean?'

'Is Colleen Skeet the vindictive type?'

If it hadn't required the effort of standing up, Mariner would have been tempted to walk over and punch his smarmy face. 'Colleen Skeet isn't any "type", sir. As I seem to remember it was thinking of her family as a "type" that got us into trouble. Right now, she's a woman grieving for her son. I couldn't begin to understand what's going on in her head.'

'I thought you said you knew her.'

'I know Colleen, sir. I know very little about those who might have any influence over her, especially at a time like this.'

'Will you talk to her?'

'I'm not sure that that's a very good idea.'

'I do hope that as a fellow officer I will be able to count on your support, Inspector.'

Not a request, just a statement. That was a hard one. Mariner felt not a shred of fellowship for the man.

Chapter Sixteen

Fiske had given Mariner the nudge he needed though, and by mid-afternoon, having exhausted all the paperwork he could reasonably do at this time, and starting to feel halfway human again, he ran out of options. He hadn't had the guts to face Colleen directly since Ricky's death. Now was as good a time as any, and from there, he could go over to see his mother. Moving very carefully, Mariner picked up his jacket and keys and walked out to his car.

He went to pass through an exit door at the same moment as someone else, being escorted from the building by Mark Russell.

'I'm sorry.' To avoid a collision the other man stepped back, exactly mirroring Mariner's action.

'After you.' Mariner found himself looking into a vaguely familiar face, but there was no reciprocal recognition and he dismissed it. It happened all the time in this job, as a consequence of meeting so many people. Then, crossing the car park, it came to him. He went back to reception.

'That man who just left. What was he doing here with Russell?' he asked Ella.

'I think he's the guy who came in to identify his wife's jewellery. The second body that was found. Poor bloke.'

'Can I use the phone?' Mariner called up to Russell. 'The body found today, I thought her name was Kincaid.'

'Ms,' said Russell. 'She kept her maiden name when she got married.' He told Mariner her married name. Poor bloke indeed, thought Mariner.

He found Colleen sitting smoking on her front step in the yellow late afternoon sunshine, a grotesque pastiche of contentment. 'You've got a bloody nerve,' was all she said as he walked up the path.

'I'm sorry, Colleen: really sorry.' Was there ever

a way of instilling those words with adequate feeling? Mariner doubted it.

'I bet you are,' she said. 'Sorry that you're all in the shit.'

She was wrong about that, but there was no point in arguing. 'Are you really going through with it?'

'Yes she fucking is,' snarled a voice from behind her. It belonged to a giant of a man with thick muscles and apparently no neck. Steve, Mariner guessed. 'So why don't you piss off out of here and stop harassing her?'

Yeah, why didn't he? 'I'm sorry, Colleen,' Mariner said again. 'Ricky was a great kid.' And he turned and walked back to his car.

'Tom?' she called after him, her voice smaller than before. He looked back. 'I know it wasn't your fault.'

Mariner nodded briefly and walked on.

Back in the car, Mariner thought again about the connection he'd learned about from Russell. The reservoir, Yasmin Akram, Barbara Kincaid and, through her husband, the link between them all: Shaun Pryce, with his predilection for middle-aged housewives. Mariner wondered if there was any way Barbara Kincaid could have known Shaun Pryce too. He must know her husband. He'd have to drive along Banbury Road on his way out to Leamington to visit his mother. That was fortuitous.

There was a considerably delayed response when he rang the doorbell of the three-floor terrace, but eventually the door opened on Brian Goodway. His shoulders were hunched, and even on this warm afternoon he wore a thick cardigan over his open-collared shirt, his body temperature thrown off balance by delayed shock. He was apologetic. 'I was upstairs. The kids are at home but they never answer the door, even though it's usually for them. Teenagers, eh?' He shook his head despairingly but his heart wasn't in it, he hadn't got the energy.

Mariner felt another flush of sympathy for the man. 'Mr Goodway, I know this is a difficult time for you, but I understand you identified your wife's jewellery this afternoon.'

'That's right.'

'As you know, I'm investigating Yasmin Akram's death. This may be important. I wonder if you could spare a few minutes.'

'Um, yes, of course.' He seemed disorientated and vague and Mariner almost changed his mind. But he was here now and followed Goodway past bikes propped in the hallway into an untidy lounge with a high ceiling and a wide bay with sash windows. Like the Akrams' sitting room, it felt cool and unlived in, probably because most of the space was taken up by a polished walnut baby grand piano.

'Barbara's,' Brian Goodway said, although Mariner hadn't asked. 'She used to teach piano part-time. The number of pupils had dwindled over the years but she liked to do it. It was something for herself.' Already used to speaking about his wife in the past tense, but then she'd been missing from his life for months.

'Is that why she kept her maiden name?'

'It was like a stage name. Barbara was a

291

performer: music, amateur theatre, that kind of thing.'

For the first time, Mariner saw the black and white portrait photograph. The subject was stunningly glamorous. 'Is that her?'

'Yes, taken a few years ago now.' Not the woman Mariner would have identified as the natural partner for Goodway.

'The teaching was supplementary,' he was saying. 'At the time we married she had quite a reputation locally, so understandably didn't want to lose that. Inevitably though, once the children came along, the family became more of a priority and she had to put her other ambitions on hold.'

'That can't have been easy.'

'No. I know she found it frustrating at times. She was very artistic. But she continued to provide accompaniment for a local drama group from time to time. Please sit down, Inspector. Can I get you anything? A cup of tea?'

'That would be good, thank you.' It was the last thing Mariner wanted, but it would give Brian Goodway something else to focus on while they talked. He sat down on a lumpy sofa, draped with an Indian print throw. Somewhere in the house, a low bass throbbed a steady beat. Looking around it was clear that this room wasn't a priority for decoration, being papered with ivory-coloured anaglypta that had gone out of fashion ten years ago. There was a vertical strip from the light switch to the ceiling that had been torn away, and fresh pink plasterwork inserted. It was precisely what Mariner had been hoping for.

Goodway returned with two mugs, handing

one awkwardly to Mariner, before perching on the piano stool opposite.

'They said they found her downstream from the reservoir,' he said, talking into his tea mug. 'Near to where Yasmin was found.'

'So I gather,' said Mariner.

'Oh God.' Dropping his gaze, Goodway fumbled in his pockets, coming out with a handkerchief, which he used to noisily blow his nose and conceal the fact that he was weeping. 'I'm sorry.'

'No, I'm sorry, Mr Goodway. I realise how hard this must be for you. But I won't keep you any longer than necessary.' Mariner turned his attention to his tea, to give Goodway time to compose himself. The dark green mug had seen better days and Mariner could barely pick out what was left of the design: the row of cartoonish trees that had succumbed to the regular abrasion of a dishwasher. He took a scalding mouthful.

Goodway sighed. 'It wasn't a huge surprise when Barbara went missing, you know,' he said. 'She'd been depressed on and off for years, and since Christmas it had got much worse. We've got the children, of course, and for the last five years we've been looking after my mother, too. Sometimes it got on top of her. It was exhausting. Barbara said more than once that she could fully sympathise with these women who just walked away from it all and never came back. But I never thought she'd really–'

'Did your wife often walk near the reservoir?'

Goodway shook his head. 'I don't know. I didn't even know there was a reservoir there until

293

the body of that boy was found there and I saw it on the news.'

Just like the rest of us then, thought Mariner.

'Barbara went out walking a lot, particularly in the evenings. She needed to, to get a break from everything. But I didn't really know where she went. There are parks around, and I suppose I just thought that she walked around the streets.'

'Did your wife ever talk about meeting anyone?'

'No,' said Goodway instantly, then he seemed to reconsider. 'It did cross my mind once or twice. Barbara had been an attractive woman, but I'm sure—'

'I'm sorry,' said Mariner. 'I'm just exploring the possibilities.'

Goodway frowned into his mug. 'The thing I don't understand is that the reservoir is miles from here.'

'There's a quicker way down to it from behind the station,' said Mariner. 'Your wife must have known about it.'

'She lived in this area all her life,' said Goodway, as if that explained it. He looked up at Mariner hopefully. 'I keep wondering if perhaps it could have been an accident,' he said. 'The children ... it would be so much easier...'

Mariner thought of the broken railings but he didn't want to give the man false hope. 'There will have to be an inquest of course. But it's possible, Mr Goodway. The coroner will consider all the evidence.'

'Barbara was taking anti-depressants at the time. She wasn't always thinking clearly.'

'I understand,' said Mariner. 'Thanks for your

294

time, Mr Goodway.' He got up to go, pausing by the strip of fresh plasterwork. 'You've had some electrical work done.'

'Actually, it was months ago. I'm not very practical around the house and rewiring was long overdue. I haven't quite got round to decorating again.'

'Looks like quite a job. Did you do it yourself'?'

'Heavens no. I'm hopeless, I'm afraid. We had a proper electrician come in to do it.'

'Was it by any chance Shaun Pryce?'

For a moment Goodway looked startled. 'Yes, it was. How–?'

'He modelled for students at your school.'

Then Goodway remembered. 'Ah, of course, you've seen the art work on the walls.' He hesitated. 'It was Barbara who discovered him, you know, at one of her drama productions. I got home from school one day and here he was. We got talking and he said that really he was an actor. I thought he was so striking that I asked him to come and model for the girls at school.'

'Did Shaun Pryce model for Yasmin's class?' Mariner asked.

'Not her class, but I think he sat for the art club on one occasion.'

'Your head said he was quite friendly with the girls.'

'Yes. In fact it became a bit of a problem. He was a bit too friendly.'

And what about your wife? Mariner wanted to ask. How friendly was Shaun Pryce with her? But now was not the time. The man had more than enough to contend with.

Mariner would have liked to report this latest news back to the team and get on to Shaun Pryce right away, but he had put off seeing his mother for long enough.

He decided to drive over, taking the M42. Even though the rush hour was officially over, it was still heaving with traffic. Hard to believe that just a few years ago this was the open, green country-side of the North Worcestershire way. On one of his frequent Sunday walks, he'd had the dubious pleasure of peeing on the foundations, right where the services were now.

His mother had rarely been ill. Not enough to be hospitalised, anyway. She wouldn't make a good patient. Maybe this episode would make her consider her own mortality and think about tying up any loose ends. His gut tingled with an edge of anticipation. Maybe now she would finally give in and tell him.

He'd been seven years old when he'd first confronted his mother with the question that had been increasingly bothering him, and that he was being asked by some of his schoolfriends. 'How come everyone else has got a mum and a dad, but I've only got a mum?' Over time, of course, he'd come to realise that somewhere on the planet he must have a dad like everyone else, but that for some unknown reason, the man had failed to take any active part in Mariner's life. Nor did his mother ever talk about him. When he was a kid, it had opened the way for all kinds of romantic notions, but with adulthood came the realisation that the truth was likely to be far more mundane: that his father had simply been married to another woman.

It had crossed his mind on occasions that his mother could have been bluffing all these years, and that in reality she didn't have any idea who his father was, but in the midst of her vagueness there had always been consistency. And once, when she'd thought he was too young to notice, he remembered overhearing her say to a friend how much like his father he looked.

It took him just over half an hour to get to Warwick. The hospital was a little way out of the town, sandwiched between a housing estate and a business park: the hybrid collection of buildings a reflection of the town itself. He could have been driving into the car park of a supermarket with its brash Pizza Hut style building squatting alongside its darker Victorian predecessors. Ward eight, Coronary Care, was on the second floor of the old hospital and he'd arrived with a cluster of friends and relatives just at the start of visiting hours. He spotted his mother right away. A nurse was at her bedside, checking her blood pressure.

'This is a turn-up,' Rose said, when she saw him approaching. 'West Midlands police having a quiet spell, are they?' The whiplash sarcasm reminded Mariner of where he'd developed a taste for it.

'Hello, son, how nice to see you,' he countered.

She was unyielding. 'I don't have to spell it out, do I?'

'If you did I'd really think something was wrong.'

'This is my son,' she told the nurse. 'He's a policeman.' Most mothers would have instilled the statement with some degree of pride, but Mariner's managed to imbue it with savoured distaste. Mariner could recall with great clarity the look on her face the first time he'd turned up unannounced at her house, in uniform. It had been his intention to shock her, of course, and he'd succeeded. 'You've done this to spite me, haven't you?' she'd said.

'Don't flatter yourself. Why does everything have to be about you? Perhaps I've actually done this because it's what I want.' How could he begin to explain that after the unlimited freedoms of his unruly childhood he craved discipline, order and routine. Only after he'd had that grounding was he ready to flex his individuality again, when CID had offered him the chance.

'So how are you?' he asked now. 'What happened?'

'I went a bit dizzy and my arm went numb, that's all. But now it's passed and I'm ready to go home. Except, of course, they won't let me until the man from del Monte says "yes". So I'm stuck here until the morning.' Any speculation about the origins of his own belligerent nature was always instantly dispelled by any conversation with his mother.

'What were you doing?' he asked.

'I was up a stepladder, decorating the hall.' Said so casually, it was easy to forget that she was a woman fast approaching seventy. Once she'd got used to the fact that he'd left home for good, she'd reverted to her youthful independence.

'Was that what you were ringing me about?'

'There was something I wanted to tell you.'

'What?'

'Well, obviously it's nothing important enough for you to call me back. So it'll keep.'

Which probably meant it was nothing at all. She was punishing him for the time it had taken him to respond. Mariner was tired of his mother's games, and he could be as stubborn as she was. He wasn't going to give her the satisfaction of begging her to tell him. Or reveal the extent of the guilt he felt because he hadn't returned her calls. She seemed about to tell him anyway but changed her mind. Sod it. She'd do it when she was ready.

'I have been busy,' he said.

'I know. I saw you on the local news. But even a phone call would have been nice.'

'Yes.'

'Anyway, now you're here you may as well make yourself useful.' She leaned over and opened the cabinet by the bed. 'Mrs Masud has brought me all these things that I don't really need. It was kind of her but will you take some of it back to the house?'

'Yes, of course.'

She sorted out a plastic carrier bag of things that were surplus to requirement.

'I'll come and see you tomorrow.'

'Twice in two days, eh? Must be a record. My cup runneth over.'

Outwardly, the tiny, neat cul-de-sac in Leamington where his mother still lived had barely

299

changed since he was resident there too. The two of them had moved suddenly from their London home when Mariner was about three and it was the only place he could remember living as a child. Built between the wars, it originally belonged to his grandparents and they'd shared it right up until Granny and Grandpa had retired to a bungalow in Pembrokeshire, where he'd then spent some summer holidays. Tonight, he could hardly get down the road, which like many was coping badly with the increase in car usage. Even with all of them parked half on the pavement, a practice of which Mariner strongly disapproved, there was barely enough room for another to pass.

The street rang to the shouts of the usual motley gang of neighbourhood kids playing and getting along, or not, regardless of shape, size or skin colour. One or two adults were out too, tending their gardens as dusk fell on the balmy summer evening. Mariner pushed open the iron gate, which sported a recent coat of paint, as did the glossy white windowsills of his mother's house. Guilt nibbled at him again. Rose had given up waiting for him and got on with it herself, which had put her where she was. It surprised him. His mother had always eschewed the trappings of constant acquisition and modernisation, so it was unusual that she'd have bothered with decorating at all.

Walking up the drive, he saw Mrs Masud and thanked her for ringing him.

'I wasn't sure if anyone else would have contacted you.' Mariner wondered what she meant by 'anyone else'. Who else was there?

His mother was one of the few remaining white residents in the street. During the late 60s and early 70s Asian families had begun moving in, prompting a mass exodus of whites, and leaving his mother in the minority. She'd barely even noticed. He let himself in the front door. The house smelled overwhelmingly of emulsion and white spirit and it took him a couple of minutes to work out what it was that looked different. The hall stairs and landing were coated in fresh paint, but then he'd known about that already. Then he realised: it was the tidiness.

Following his grandparents' departure, the house that he'd grown up in had always been awash with clutter. Treasures collected along the way from every conceivable source, saved for a rainy day, or in case they came in useful; mementoes and keepsakes, all randomly arranged on shelves and furniture, with barely a space between them. The genes responsible for orderliness were something else he'd inherited from his father.

Now, many of the shelves and surfaces were bare in preparation for more decorating. She was blitzing the place. He walked through the downstairs rooms and each one was the same. It was not before time. The place hadn't been touched in years, but even so, he couldn't help wondering what had prompted the sudden burst of activity. It crossed his mind that there could be more to the hospital admission than he'd thought, but rejected the idea almost immediately. Everything had been too relaxed.

Upstairs in her bedroom was a more familiar

scene, the dressing table crowded with trinkets. He put away the things that he'd brought home for her and, out of habit, checked each of the other rooms. In the spare room he found a stack of black bin liners stuffed full to bursting, with what had once taken up shelf space downstairs; there were old clothes and bric a brac; artefacts that stirred memories of Mariner's childhood. Some of it was from the second large bedroom, the one that nobody had used since he left home. It too had been decorated. It was still a far cry from Lewis Everett's room. His mother was putting things in order for something, but right now he had little capacity for another mystery. Mariner returned the rest of the items he'd brought with him to what he deemed to be the most appropriate places, and left.

On the way home he had to drive very near to Tony Knox's house. Following the visit to Brian Goodway, Mariner wanted to sound him out. The ground floor lights were encouraging, but the look on Knox's face when he came to the door was not. The fumes nearly knocked Mariner off his feet.

'All right, boss?' Knox was surly and suspicious to an identical degree.

'I wanted to talk to you about something. Can I come in?'

With great reluctance, Knox stepped aside to let Mariner pass. Mariner almost wished he hadn't bothered. The living room looked just that. A lot of living had been going on in here and some clean air wouldn't go amiss. Knox repositioned himself in the dent in the sofa opposite the TV that had been permanently created by a lot of sitting. Around him was the detritus that could only have accrued over considerable time: a handful of mugs, several squat, green beer bottles, a plate bearing the remains of an unappetising looking sandwich. Even Knox himself looked lived in, wearing a stained T-shirt over scruffy, faded jeans. And Mariner noticed that the trademark buzz-cut was beginning to grow into a crew.

'Theresa not back yet?' Mariner asked, unnecessarily.

Knox grunted. 'She's not coming back.'

'Her mum's taken a turn for the worse?' Mariner asked, struck by what a strange coincidence that was.

But Knox blew that one out of the water. 'It's our marriage that's taken a turn for the worse,' he said. 'Theresa's left me.'

'Christ. Are you sure?'

Knox gave him the withering look the question deserved.

'I mean, are you sure this isn't just another temporary thing?'

'I'm sure. It hasn't happened overnight.'

'So what have you been up to this time?' Mariner had already had personal experience of Knox's extra-marital activities over a year ago, when Knox had hooked up with Jenny. When Theresa had kicked him out, he and Jenny had ended up staying at Mariner's place. It wasn't the first time Knox had strayed and, although at the time it had seemed like their marriage was over, happily it was only a matter of weeks until Knox

303

saw sense, and Theresa found it somewhere within herself to forgive him.

Mariner wasn't aware that Knox had been dipping his wick again but it didn't mean that he hadn't. He'd never really understood what made Tony Knox tick. But surely, even he was bright enough to grasp the obvious truth: that a woman will only put up with so much. 'I thought you were meant to have given all that up,' he said.

'Not guilty, boss.' Knox held up his hands in defence. 'I haven't played away from home since Jenny. Then, just as the halo was polishing up to a nice shine, Theresa told me she was leaving.'

'Maybe she just needs some space,' Mariner said, cringing inwardly at his choice of words.

'She's moved in with another bloke. Does that sound to you like she needs space?'

'Bloody hell,' was the best response Mariner could come up with. 'Why didn't you say?'

'It's not something I'm that proud of. She met him over the Internet. It makes it worse, somehow. It's so bloody tacky.'

'Only because of what you and I both know. I'm sure there are plenty of responsible people who use the Internet as a legitimate means of communication.'

'Is this what you'd call legitimate? They've been at it for months, years even, for all I know. All the while I thought she was going back up to Liverpool to visit her sick mum she was really busy rekindling an old flame. Romantic, isn't it? All she was waiting for was for Gary to leave home before she followed suit. She doesn't need me any more. She said that her job with the kids was done so there was no other reason to stick around.' He faltered. 'When I asked her what about us, she said, "What us?".'

Mariner thought the word was ironic but all he could muster was: 'Christ. I mean: Christ.'

Knox grimaced. 'That the best you can do? No "poetic justice" lecture?'

'You know me better than that. And I'm not about to feed the gossip mill either.'

'Doesn't matter, does it? It won't be long before it's all round the canteen. There'll be a few sides splitting over this. The sad old fart's got what he deserved.'

'I'm sorry, mate.'

'Not half as fuckin' sorry as I am,' Knox retorted, bitterly. 'It's like there was this whole other little parallel world going on that I never even knew existed, but suddenly, hindsight opened the door and there it was. Suddenly, I can see what a total shit I've been. I thought I had it all under control and meanwhile, Theresa's the one pulling all the strings. This must be the first time in my life when I've looked forward to the prospect of overtime. And do you know what the biggest fuckin' irony of all is? Now that I'm free to go out with any woman I like, I'm just not interested.'

'Do you know who this other bloke is?'

'Oh yes.'

'She told you?'

'She didn't have to. Come and look at this.'

Mariner followed Knox up the stairs to a small back bedroom where a PC sat on a small desk. He logged on to the Internet and typed in a web address. 'Old Friends' said the banner that unfurled before them.

'What's this?' asked Mariner.

'It's one of these school reunion websites. Watch.'

Mariner watched as Knox typed in the name of a school and a date and a list of names appeared on the screen. Theresa Fitzpatrick (Knox) was among them. But he ignored it, instead clicking on Stephen Lamb. Up came the details for Stephen Lamb. A brief paragraph revealing that Lamb, now forty-nine, had built up a successful construction business and, after a recent divorce, was single again. The end of the message asked if anyone knew the whereabouts of Theresa Fitzpatrick. It was followed by an e-mail address and a crystal clear invitation.

'Do you think somebody told her?' Mariner surmised.

'She was well capable of finding it herself. She's been e-mailing him for months. And all that time, not a hint of what was going on.'

'When did you find out?'

'Thirteen days ago. She went up to her mother's, so I thought. But then she sent me the letter saying that she isn't coming back.'

'Christ.' The silence that followed seemed to stretch for hours.

'Want a drink?' Knox asked. He'd clearly already had more than enough, but now wasn't the time to point that out.

'All right.'

Knox poured him a generous measure of Scotch and the silence resumed. 'How long have you been together?' asked Mariner eventually.

306

'Since we were fifteen. We met at the Coconut Grove in nineteen seventy-nine.'

'The what?'

'It was a nightclub in Tuebrook. There she was, dancing round the handbags with her mates. She was the most gorgeous thing I'd ever seen. But she was a good Catholic girl. She made me wait.'

'What, until you got married?'

'Till she knew I was serious. Jesus, the number of nights I went home with my nuts on fire.'

'How many times were you unfaithful?'

Knox visibly flinched. 'You mean the number of other women? Four in total. The first one was the hardest. I felt really bad about it. But after I'd done it that once it got easier, easier to convince myself that I wasn't doing any harm. Theresa was busy with the kids. She was shattered all the time. I convinced myself I was doing her a favour, taking the pressure off.'

'Did you ever do it out of spite?'

'No. Why?' He looked up at Mariner.

'Nothing. Forget it.'

But Knox couldn't. The cogs were turning. 'Christ, you haven't–' he said at last, having figured it out.

Mariner's silence said it all.

Knox raised an eyebrow. 'You've cheated on the gorgeous Anna? What the hell would you want to do that for? I thought she was hot.'

'She is, when she's available.'

'You knew about Jamie before you started it.'

'That's the thing. It's not Jamie. His respite hours are increasing all the time. And anyway, just because he's there doesn't mean I can't see her. Jamie's OK with me. He always has been. It's all the other stuff.'

'Like?'

'Well, right now we're organising a stall for the Bournville Festival.'

'What's that when it's at home?'

'It's like a fair: home-grown leeks and maypole dancing.'

'Nothing wrong with a bit of pole dancing.'

'*Maypole* dancing; this is sweet little girls in pretty dresses skipping around waving bits of ribbon.' They both thought about that. Then Mariner said, 'They probably attract the same kind of spectator, of course.'

'And this is what you're jealous of. Sounds to me like you're getting serious about our Anna.'

'Not really.'

'But you don't like it when she plays hard to get.'

'I don't know if she really is. It's just as if what we've got isn't that important to her. It's just one small aspect of her life.'

'Does she know how important it is to you?'

'What do you mean?'

'I mean, have you told her?'

Mariner had to think for a minute. 'Not in so many words.'

Knox laughed. 'You really don't get it, you pathetic loser, do you? I can tell you've never read a woman's magazine.'

'I haven't.'

'Not even in the dentist's waiting room?'

'My dentist gets the *Great Outdoors*.'

'Talk to Anna! Tell her what you've told me.

308

How else is she supposed to know that you want more of a commitment?'

'I'm not sure that I do.'

'Oh, you do.'

'What is this? Your new career as Mary Knox: Agony Aunt?'

'Oh yeah. I'm a real expert, me. I bet you've never told her that you love her, either.'

Mariner couldn't answer him.

Knox shook his head in disbelief. 'Christ, what does she see in you?'

'I'm dynamite between the sheets,' said Mariner, looking on sheepishly as finally, combined with the whisky, he reduced Knox to uncontrollable mirth.

'So who is it?' asked Knox, when he'd wiped his eyes.

'What does it matter? It was only once. An aberration.'

'Who?'

'Millie.'

'With respect, sir, you're a fucking moron.'

'Millie's a great—'

'I didn't mean that.'

'No.' Mariner turned his attention back to the monitor. 'So this is your old school?'

'For its sins. The entries go back for years. There are people who were at my old school in nineteen forty-three. Can you believe that?'

'Are you on here?'

'You have to be joking. I wouldn't want to own up to my career choice. There's a few people I recognise though, kids and teachers. Some of the stuff about the teachers gets pretty libellous. You

309

should have a go. Look up your old school.'

'No thanks.' Mariner could think of nothing worse. There wasn't a single person from his time at school that he would have the slightest desire to make contact with again. And he had other, more pressing, things on his mind. When they'd had strong coffee and Knox seemed almost human again, Mariner expounded his theory.

'It all just keeps coming back to Shaun Pryce,' he said. 'I don't think it was only electrical work that he did. I think he was offering Barbara Goodway another kind of service.'

'He really fancies himself. I wouldn't be surprised,' Knox agreed. 'He was very keen to tell us about his high sex drive, and from what we see he doesn't have a steady girlfriend, so how else does he get by?'

'Do you think Yasmin would have gone for a bloke like Shaun Pryce?'

'Yasmin?'

'I was just thinking: Pryce might have been useful to her. If Yasmin was still in love with Lee, Shaun would have come in useful for winding him up. She knew Lee was working at the industrial units and they used to meet on the bridge. Perhaps she arranged to meet Lee to show him what she was getting up to with Shaun. Maybe she wasn't going on the pill for Lee at all, but for Shaun Pryce.'

'Except that Lee's insisting that he didn't show that afternoon. I don't really buy that.'

'OK. Let's try the pure coincidence theory. Maybe Lee confirmed their date but had decided to stand Yasmin up. He told us he thought she was leading him on. Yasmin turns up at the bridge but no Lee. However, the guy who is there, lurking in the grass, getting his rocks off, is Shaun Pryce. Pryce recognises Yasmin from the school art classes and he's horny anyway, so he decides to try it on. But Yasmin isn't interested, so Pryce loses it. The river, or at least the spillway, is in full spate so he dumps her over the edge.'

'Lucky with the timing.'

'Pryce could have known about the water release, though. He goes there regularly. He could have easily concealed her in the short term before coming back at the right time to dispose of her properly.'

'But Pryce wasn't there that late in the afternoon.'

'So he says. That day we met him in the clearing, he was saying he went there after work. Then suddenly it's one o'clock? You saw him at the reservoir. He was loving it. And at that time he must have thought he was safe. Yasmin's body was well concealed. Barbara Goodway's had been there for months, and this time there was Lee in the background to deflect our attention too. Yasmin probably told him that she was meant to be meeting Lee.'

'The PM indicated a degree of premeditation.'

'Not if he just happened to have a length of wire in his pocket. Whichever way you look at this, Shaun Pryce is in it up to his ears. He's the one who connects Yasmin to Barbara Goodway and he's admitted to frequenting the reservoir. I think we should bring him in.'

'You'll have to see what Fiske says about that.'

Chapter Seventeen

But DCI Fiske had other things to occupy him. In response to the formal complaint from the Skeet family, the Police Complaints Authority team had arrived to begin their investigation and for once, the DCI was happy to let Mariner get on with his job and take the initiative. Thus, when Shaun Pryce arrived at Mrs Paleczcki's the next morning, he found a two-man welcoming committee waiting for him. Half an hour later, Pryce was installed in an interview room while a search warrant was sought and his flat and car turned upside down. Mariner thought he looked even more jittery than the last time they'd met. His actor's mask was beginning to slip.

'I want you to tell me again when, exactly, on Tuesday the third of July you were at the reservoir and exactly what it is you were doing there.'

To settle his nerves, Pryce made a show of a heavy sigh. 'Aren't you lot getting bored with this, too? I went there at about one o'clock. I stayed half an hour. I sunbathed, I smoked a bit of weed. What's the big deal?'

'And you say you were on your own.'

'Yes.' Exasperation was creeping in to his voice.

'You're not always alone though, are you?' Pryce shifted in his chair and for a split second Mariner thought they might have him. 'When was the last time you had a woman down there?'

'I've told you. Weeks ago. They don't like the grass.'

'And who was it, Shaun? Was it Barbara Kincaid?'

'What?' They'd got him. He hadn't seen it coming.

Knox went in for the kill, unleashing the vitriol that should have been directed elsewhere. 'We know, you see, Shaun,' he said, leaning towards Pryce. 'We know that you're the link. We also know that you're a randy little bastard who can't keep his dick in his trousers. You have very eclectic taste, I'll say that for you. Middle-aged housewives to seventeen-year-old schoolgirls. Very inclusive. Were they both threatening to abandon you? Is that what made you mad? Mad enough to kill them? Or is that just part of the turn on for you?'

Pryce was like a rabbit caught in the headlights. 'That's rubbish. I don't know what you're talking about,' he insisted, but the outburst had rattled him.

Knox leaned forward threateningly. 'Are you denying that you knew Barbara Kincaid?'

Pryce hesitated. 'No,' he said, petulantly.

'All right, then. Tell us about her. How did you two meet?'

'I thought she killed herself,' Pryce whined.

Mariner shrugged non-committally.

'So why are you asking these questions?'

'To find out exactly what happened. Just answer the question.'

'I used to do this amateur dramatics thing. She

313

played the piano for rehearsals of *West Side Story*. There was a problem with the electrics one night and I fixed it. Afterwards, in the bar, she came up to me and said her house hadn't ever been rewired and she thought it might be dangerous. She asked me to go and have a look at it. After the run was finished I was resting again so I said I would.'

'When was this?'

'About March time, I suppose.' Around the time that Barbara Kincaid began threatening suicide, thought Mariner.

'Was that the only reason she asked you to go to her house?'

'What do you mean?'

'Did she fancy you?'

'A lot of women do.'

'That must be such a burden,' said Knox sarcastically. 'Was Barbara Kincaid one of them?'

'So you went to the house,' said Mariner. 'Was her husband around?'

'No. It was in the day. He's a teacher. He was at work.'

'That's handy. So what happened?'

'I did the rewiring.'

'That's all?'

'If you must know, she nearly fucking killed me. I was up a stepladder connecting up a ceiling rose and she came up behind me, giving me all the usual crap about her old man being useless in bed. Then she—'

'What?'

'Touched me up.'

'Very delicately put.'

314

'I nearly fell off the bloody ladder and took the light fitting with me.'

'But did you respond? Barbara Kincaid was an attractive woman. And we all know about your famous high sex drive.' Pryce didn't know what to say. 'Or was she too old for you?' said Knox.

'Luckily for me, her old man turned up.'

'So you met Brian Goodway, too. Did you tell him you were a model, or had Barbara already done that?'

'It just came up in conversation, you know.'

'And whose idea was it that you should go and model at the school?'

'I can't remember. His, I think.'

'I bet you jumped at it. All those young girls.'

'It was a modelling job. It's what I do.'

'Did you get paid for it?'

'Why else would I have done it?'

'Mm. Why else would you have chosen to spend your time surrounded by attractive adolescent girls? I can't think. I heard you got pretty friendly with some of them.'

'I like kids.'

'Particularly teenage girls. Was Yasmin Akram one of them?'

'I don't remember. There were a lot of them.'

'You offered to take your clothes off, didn't you?'

'It was one of the kids suggested that. "Show us what's underneath," she said.'

'Who said?'

'Tall, skinny kid. Susan.' Suzanne.

'It was just a laugh.'

'A laugh? These kids were seventeen.'

315

'It was a joke.'

They took a break. Results from the search of Pryce's flat sounded promising so far and they were building a good circumstantial case. Not surprisingly, the items included electrical wires of every gauge imaginable. His car had also yielded a grass-speckled blanket and samples from it could be tested with soil and grass from the flattened area at the reservoir. Condoms found were of the same brand as the used ones that had been picked up.

While they were taking a break, Delrose phoned up to say that Mariner had a visitor; a woman. He expected Colleen and dreaded having to face her. Instead, Anna was waiting for him in reception. Lesser of two evils. But only just.

'Hi,' she said, cheerfully. 'I wondered when I'd see you again. You look terrible.'

'Had a curry that didn't agree with me.' It didn't explain why he couldn't look her in the eye, but if she noticed she made no comment. 'What are you doing here?'

'I tried phoning, but you're a hard man to get hold of. I thought I might stand a better chance of talking to you if I came in person. I've missed you.'

'I've been busy.' Mariner rubbed the back of his neck. 'We're in the middle of something–'

'I know. But I think we need to talk. Can you spare a few minutes?'

'All right.'

They crossed the road and went into the park opposite, where they began a circuit of the

316

boating pond. A couple of little kids with their grandparents were trying in vain to encourage their toy yachts to sail on the smooth expanse of water. Mariner knew how they felt. For days now it had seemed as if the wind had gone out of the sails of their investigation leaving it stale and stagnant as the water around them. Then, today, the first hint of a breeze. He hardly dared hope.

'I just wondered what's going on,' Anna said. 'The other evening you wouldn't stay and now I'm beginning to get the idea that you're avoiding me.'

'It's not that–' Mariner began, too tired for this now.

She moved towards him and made as if to take his arm, but some reflex made him move away, putting a distance between them. Their eyes met and as they exchanged a look he saw the flash of understanding cross her features.

'Just so that you know,' she said, using that phrase of hers that always preceded any straight talking, 'I'd be really hurt to find out that you're shagging someone else, too.'

It cut him to the core. 'I know,' he said helplessly, staring ahead.

She was astute enough to take this as confirmation. 'So you are sleeping with someone else.'

'Not exactly.'

'What the hell does that mean?'

'It means past tense. I slept with someone else, a couple of nights ago.'

'Well, thanks for telling me.' She hadn't been lying. He could hear the pain in her voice. It sliced right through him.

317

'It's not what you think.'

She stopped and turned to face him with the same anger he'd witnessed the first time they'd met. 'So what is it, then?'

'When I couldn't see you. I worked late instead, and afterwards, Millie Khatoon, she's our–'

'I know who she is.'

'Right, well, Millie asked me back to her place for a curry and we ended up getting drunk and having sex. It was terrible sex. Millie would tell you the same thing. We didn't go to bed, we didn't even take our clothes off and it was over in ten minutes. It will never happen again.'

An elderly couple walked by, gazing at them with interest.

'Well, that's all right, then,' Anna said, tightly.

Righteous anger rose in Mariner's chest. 'Oh, and I suppose you and Simon are above all that.'

'Simon?'

'You can't seem to stay away from him. Not that I blame you. He's young, not bad-looking from what I could see–'

'–and apart from me, the most important person in Jamie's life.' Anna rounded on him. 'We're talking about Jamie here, who can't communicate, and for whom consistency is a lifeline. That could explain why I spend so much time with Simon.'

'Even on a Friday night, when you're meant to be having a break from Jamie?'

'Sure, that was more of a social call, but if you hadn't walked away, you would have found out what it was all about.'

'I wasn't invited.'

318

'What, you need a written invitation now? I asked you to stay.'

Mariner gazed out across the pond. 'So what was it about?' Why was it that her questioning of him had sounded entirely reasonable and calm, but he just sounded like a petulant schoolboy?

'Simon has asked me to help with the stall on the day of the festival, so he and Martin had come round to discuss–'

'Martin too? That was a cosy threesome.'

'Actually, it was fun,' she responded, evenly. 'Martin and Simon make a great couple.' She paused to allow that to sink in. 'Simon is gay, Martin is his partner. And if I'd thought that it was in the least bit relevant, I would have told you.'

But even then, when she'd handed it to him on a plate, he couldn't let go. 'That's convenient, isn't it?' he said.

'Oh, fuck off, Tom.' And she turned and walked away from him.

Even if he'd had the energy it would be pointless going after her, he could see that. He would only make things worse. So he went back to the nick and to Shaun Pryce.

They spent all afternoon on Pryce, covering the same ground but not really making any progress. Mariner was distracted and, if anything, Pryce seemed to be gaining control. He was certainly more relaxed than he had been a few hours earlier. In the end they had to let him go. As he stalked up to the office again, Mariner was ready to kill someone. Unfortunately the first person he ran into was Millie, typing at her desk.

'Has the search team come back yet?' he demanded.

'Not yet,' she said glancing up briefly before returning to the report.

Mariner banged his hand down hard on her desk, making everyone in the office turn round. 'So why the hell aren't you out there, chasing them up?' And he strode into his office and slammed the door, leaving Millie staring after him. After a few moments she tentatively went in.

Mariner stood with his back to the room looking out of the window. 'I'm sorry,' he said. 'It's been a long day.'

'Don't let Pryce get to you, sir. If it is him we'll find out in the end.'

Mariner swung round to face her. 'Anna found out about what happened with us.'

'Oh God. How? You don't think I–?'

'I told her.'

'Oh. Good move, sir.'

'I had to. It was gnawing away at me.'

'You have got it bad, haven't you?'

And that was the problem. He had. For the first time in his life Mariner had found a woman he could envisage growing old with. Someone he was finding it hard to imagine being without.

But the deal with Anna had always been no commitment. And now he was in danger of blowing the whole thing sky high.

Mariner's conscience told him that he ought to go over to see his mother again tonight, but after the sort of day he'd had, he couldn't face her. In

320

any case, it was late and by the time he could get there, visiting would be over. Instead, he phoned and spoke to the duty nurse.

'She's fine,' the girl reassured him. 'Though I expect she'll be disappointed not to see you.' I wouldn't count on it, thought Mariner.

Knox had already left and in any case, Mariner didn't feel much like company, so he went home. The evening was warm and sticky again, the air heavy with unresolved tension. Opening up a bottle of home-brew, Mariner went to sit on the bench outside his front door, overlooking the canal. Towards dusk, the sky darkened ominously and thunder rumbled in the distance. A few spots of rain followed, temporarily making the air smell a little fresher, but this time the storm never quite broke.

The next morning he was in the shower, considering their next move with Shaun Pryce, when away in the distance he heard the phone. When he got out there was a message from the hospital on the answering machine, asking him to call back as soon as possible. He hoped it wasn't that they were letting his mother go home early. That was a diversion he could do without today.

'Mr Mariner, I'm afraid your mother has suffered a slight heart attack. You may want to come in.' The voice was calm and unruffled, implying nothing more than a setback, though this would inevitably delay her discharge from the hospital.

On the drive over, Mariner could visualise his mother's frustration as she was wired up to monitors and drips that would further restrict her independence. This had obvious implications for her after-care, too. He'd need to play a more active role, something he didn't relish, but it might mean getting to know each other again, which in turn may present new opportunities too. The nursing sister met him on reception and took him into a side room to explain what was happening. 'I'm sorry, Mr Mariner, we weren't able to resuscitate her.'

For several seconds her words didn't make any sense. Then, one by one, their meaning hit him like a forty-foot wave, almost physically knocking him off-balance.

'She died at just after nine o'clock,' the nurse went on, gently. 'It was very sudden, so it's unlikely that she knew anything about it. She wouldn't have been in any pain.' Her carefully chosen words were designed to offer comfort and consolation. They were words of the kind that had spouted from Mariner's own mouth a hundred times before, when he'd broken bad news to the relatives of crime victims. In all that time it had never occurred to him that one day, he might be on the receiving end. So this was what it was like. A feeling of complete disorientation, as if time had suddenly slowed to nothing.

'Would you like to see her?' the nurse repeated when he failed to respond the first time.

He had to wait a few minutes, while they made her presentable, presumably. But it made no difference. When he went in he didn't see Rose. They hadn't succeeded in making her look as if she was sleeping, as was the desired outcome.

The life in her was gone, leaving only an empty shell. In the past he'd watched families say their last goodbyes, to kiss the cold cheek of their loved ones, but Mariner couldn't bring himself to do that. His mother wasn't there. Why was he so upset? It wasn't as though he would miss his mother's daily presence. They'd hardly seen each other in recent years. And it wasn't that he was suddenly brought face to face with death. Any reminders he might need of his own mortality came regularly at work. Perhaps it was because now he had to accept the possibility that he would never know.

He realised too how much he'd taken her for granted, expecting her to never not be there. He'd always assumed that she'd be one of these women who lived well into her nineties. An afterthought struck him: she'd never meet Anna now.

They were still holding some of his mother's personal effects at the nursing station on the ward so he went to fetch them. 'You've just missed your dad,' said the nurse. 'I think he's gone home.'

Mariner gawped. 'My what?'

Had he been thinking rationally and stopped to consider, Mariner would have recognised the unlikelihood, but suddenly, in a warped kind of way, everything began to make sense. The 'something to tell him', was that his father had reappeared on the scene. It might explain why she was doing up the house, too.

He dashed back to his mother's house, where

323

an old style pushbike was leaning against the wall. That hadn't been there two days ago. He let himself in with the key, his heart pounding in anticipation. 'Hello?'

'Hello. You must be Tom.'

Harry turned out to be a softly spoken widower who had worked for years as an engineer at Potterton's boilers in Coventry and had lost his wife soon after his retirement.

'How long have you known Rose?' Mariner asked.

'About a year. I was planning to move in with her.'

'Were you?' Mariner's surprise was genuine. He was struggling to get his head round the idea that his mother had met another man after all this time. If there had been liaisons over the years Mariner had not been aware of them. As far as he knew, there had been nobody since his father who hadn't stuck around long enough to see his son born. Just like the Akrams with Yasmin, this was where he'd find out how little he knew about his mother.

Harry was flustered now. 'No, it wasn't like that. We were just friends, but I was coming to stay here with her. She'd offered me a room.'

'A room?'

'I'm living in rented accommodation at present but the lease expires at the end of the month and the landlord wants me out, so your mother had said I could have her spare room. It was all above board. We had agreed rent.'

'I see.' Typical of his mother to be adopting waifs and strays, even at her age. As he spoke,

324

Mariner recognised that Harry and his mother had espoused the kind of pragmatic approach to life that is the privilege of the older generation. They'd reached the point where, having taken their share of knocks, they've realised that there's too little time left to waste it arguing about the minutiae. Harry was about to lose his home. Mariner's mother had a spare room. The two things fitted logically together, end of story.

'I'm not a con man,' said Harry, answering the very question that Mariner had moments before dismissed inside his head.

'No.' And you're not my dad.

Harry 'liked to keep busy' as he put it, hence the fresh coat of paint on the house. Mariner's mother had been helping him, but mainly by providing cups of tea, from the sound of it. 'I didn't want her to be up ladders. I don't know why she was.' Harry had come to collect his overalls and brushes. 'I expect you'll want to sell the house and I wouldn't want them to be in the way. No time like the present.'

When Harry had gone, Mariner called the office from his mother's old Bakelite phone and spoke to Fiske.

'I'm very sorry, Tom,' he said, formally. 'Is there anything we can do?'

'No thanks, sir.'

'Police Complaints are still here.' Fiske couldn't resist mentioning it, even though the timing was completely inappropriate. 'They're going through all the paperwork with a fine-tooth comb.'

'That's what they do, sir.'

'Yes. They'll want to talk to you, too.' Fiske paused. 'Tom, I hope–'

'Not really the right moment, sir.'

'Of course. Well, take as much time as you need.'

'Thank you, sir.' I won't be hurrying back on your account. He'd let Fiske squirm. Even if the DCI were vindicated, the fact that there had been an investigation in the first place could blight his career. With any luck, the mud would stick.

The truth was that Mariner was still uneasy about his own part in the fiasco. He should have been more assertive about keeping Ricky's case, and more proactive, both with Ricky and with his mother. Now he'd paid the price for both.

He went to the registry office to record his mother's death. Technically, it had been a sudden death, so there would have to be a post mortem, but it would be routine. The people around her when she died had all been fighting to save her life. Nothing suspicious about that.

Sitting on the hard plastic seat, waiting his turn, it occurred to Mariner that to all intents and purposes he was now an orphan, with very little family to speak of. His mother had a couple of cousins as far as he remembered, but there were no family gatherings when he'd been a kid. It gave him something else in common with Anna, too. She'd lost her parents several years ago, except of course that he didn't really know about the one, and perhaps now never would.

Ironically, if he'd been adopted it would have been simple. These days, there were routes to

326

follow. But not for him. The only way of solving this particular puzzle would be if there was some clue remaining at his mother's house, something she'd hung onto. He thought about the bond between the father of a child and the mother. Ronnie Skeet was a nasty piece of work but it still didn't stop Colleen from letting him back into the house time after time. *'He's the father of my kids,'* she'd said.

Mariner's mother had never given him any reason to doubt that she knew the identity of his father. Was there an unbreakable bond there, too, however tenuous? However effectively she managed to keep him a secret, would there still be some fine strand connecting them? If there was then there would be a trace of it at her house. It was the only place to start. Hours later he was back there.

For the sake of being thorough, he began with all the obvious places, but knowing beforehand that there would be nothing in the bureau in the dining room or in her drawer in the bedroom. It was too accessible. He found all her current paperwork: bank and building society accounts, letters from the last few years. Most of the numbers in her address book were local: friends and contacts made when she moved back up to Leamington. There was nothing from before that time.

Amongst the documents was his birth certificate, but he'd seen that years ago and it gave nothing away. He was officially a bastard. That would amuse some of the crooks he'd put away in the past. She'd kept all his old school reports too, most of them a variation on a 'could try harder' theme. But it was futile. She'd kept a secret for this long. She'd never leave anything around down here that would give it away. Mariner knew where the important stuff was. The past had literally been hanging over his head all the time he'd lived in this house.

When they'd moved in with his grandparents, space was at a premium and, consequently, much of their stuff had vanished up into the loft, and had never, to his knowledge, come down again. Rose had always vehemently discouraged him from going up there on the grounds that he might clumsily put a foot through the fragile floor and into the ceiling of the rooms below, but Mariner suspected the real reason lay deeper than that.

No one had been up there for years, mainly because it was such a production to get up there, involving balancing precariously at the very top of the stepladder before launching off into the narrow aperture. But in adulthood, Mariner had height on his side and the manoeuvre was relatively easy. The loft space was stifling and dirty, everything coated in a layer of black dust. A bare bulb draped over one of the rough timbers provided the minimum amount of light and in the yellow gloom, Mariner could see the enormity of the task: boxes and trunks, rolls of yellowing wallpaper, a collection of old camping equipment that could have belonged to Edmund Hillary, complete with rusting tartan vacuum flasks and heavy canvas groundsheets.

Opening a cardboard carton, he found old crockery and cutlery, including a child's porcelain

328

Peter Rabbit dish that had probably been his. In another, a whole willow-patterned bone-china dinner service. There was a suitcase full of dusty, dun-coloured blankets. Finally, he found what he was looking for in a brown cardboard suitcase with catches that had almost rusted solid. Working them back and forth finally slid them across and the lid flipped open to reveal yellowing paper: letters, cards, newspaper cuttings and photographs. The faded and peeling address label stuck to the inside of the lid had written on it: Rosemary Ellen Mariner, in neat italic ink-penned script. This was his mother's life in London.

She'd been twenty-four when he was born in that other long hot summer of 1959, which left him looking for anything dated 1958–59. Her twenty-first birthday cards were bundled together, as were letters from his grandmother, even a few birth congratulations cards, most from women or couples. There were black-and-white photographs of him as a baby, wrapped in a woollen shawl. There were mementoes from special occasions: tickets from London Zoo, a programme from the Henry Wood Promenade Concert in September 1958: an evening of Sibelius, conducted by Malcolm Sargent.

The only things that might reveal any clues were the letters. He sat on an old crate and strained his eyes to read. The letters were addressed to several different places in London, where his mother had lived an apparently nomadic existence. Mostly, his grandmother described trivial events in Leamington, though occasionally she made reference to things that Rose must have mentioned in her letters home. It was these brief glimpses that Mariner clung to. In the dim light, the curling italic handwriting wasn't easy to decipher and he took his time, anxious not to miss anything.

But he realised as he came to the last, with overwhelming disappointment, that there was nothing to miss. His neck ached and his eyes were sore with the dust and effort. It had gone cooler. When he had emerged back on to the ladder he found out why. It was dark and almost eleven at night. Turning on the landing light, he left a black fingerprint on the switch. He looked as if he'd been up a chimney. He was filthy.

His mother had never gone in for showers so he ran a hot bath and lay in it, soaking. He had a decision to make. He could either waste further endless time and energy trying to uncover something that was probably unattainable, or he could get back to his life. Later, he crawled into the spare room to sleep on it.

Chapter Eighteen

The morning brought with it a firm decision. Mariner locked his mother's house. He'd get on to the estate agent soon and arrange a skip and some visits to a local charity shop. At home he found a message from Anna on the answer phone. It wasn't exactly an olive branch, but carefully handled, it might have the potential to become one. He called her back straight away, half expecting her recorded message. To his surprise she was there, but the conversation didn't go according to plan. 'Where have you been?' Anna asked. 'I've been trying to contact you.'

'My mother's dead.'

'Oh God, Tom, I'm so sorry. What happened?'

'A heart attack, Thursday morning.'

'Why didn't you call me? Are you all right?'

'I'm OK.'

'Do you want me to come over? I can see if Simon could–'

'No!' he snapped. 'It's all right, I'm fine, really.'

'OK, then.'

So the experience hadn't changed him. In an emotional crisis he still couldn't manage sharing his feelings with someone else. It was so long since he'd done it that he'd forgotten how.

It wasn't any less depressing back in the office where, in his absence, nothing much had happened. Fiske was still technically overseeing things but his mind was, understandably, preoccupied with other matters. The team itself seemed to have lost all coherence, too. Mariner recognised that he was still in a state of shock. Tony Knox seemed lower than ever, and recent past history had generated an awkwardness between himself and Millie, all of which was nicely exacerbated by the fact that beyond the initial expression of condolences, suddenly no one quite knew what to say to him.

There had been no progress, either forensic or otherwise, to pin down Shaun Pryce. The grass and soil traces on the blanket in his car were a match with the reservoir, but then Pryce had never denied that he went there. There was a feeling all round that both investigations were beginning to lose momentum as demands on resources continued to be made from elsewhere, and there were mutterings about calling in the murder review team. That and the ominous presence of the PCA was doing little to inspire confidence.

Partly to get out of the building, Mariner went to visit the Akrams, who unusually were both at home. 'You've closed the school?'

'We had to. It was impossible to keep going. We hope to reopen in a few days, but we're in limbo. Until we know who did this to Yasmin we can't get on with our lives. It's like unfinished business.'

'I'm sorry: there's no news, but we're still doing everything we can.'

'Thank you.'

Another uncompromisingly sunny day dawned for Mariner's mother's funeral. He put on one of his lighter suits and perused his collection of dreary ties. Had he been Fiske, he'd have had a whole array of jolly cartoon characters at his disposal, but he wasn't, so in the end he chose a sky/navy stripe.

'Very smart.'

Coming down the stairs, he looked up to see Anna standing in the hallway. She'd let herself in and was waiting by the front door, wearing an elegant floral dress and a wide-brimmed hat.

'I thought you could use some support,' she

said. 'After all, I've had some experience at this stuff.' Over the last few years, death had been a loyal companion, as she'd seen both her parents and her older brother killed. It was Eddie's murder that had brought them together in the first place.

'Thanks, I appreciate it,' said Mariner, truthfully.

She saw him appraising her outfit. 'Would she have approved?'

'She'd have approved whatever you were wearing.'

They spoke little on the drive over to Leamington and he was grateful for that, too. His nerves jangled in anticipation. Not because of the funeral: that he could cope with. But in the days after his mother died, he had placed announcements in both local and national press. At the very least he was hoping to meet someone who would be able to tell him who his father was. And then there was the possibility he hardly dared consider: that his father might turn up in person.

In her will his mother had planned out the ceremony to the last detail: a simple cremation with a couple of pieces of music; 'Ave Maria' and the 'Intermezzo' from Sibelius's Karelia Suite. It had been on the programme of the 1958 Promenade Concert he'd found in the loft and, hearing it now, he couldn't help wondering if the piece had a deeper significance. It was all she'd wanted. Mariner introduced Anna to Harry, who sat beside them at the front of the church, along with Mrs Masud. Turning to look, Mariner saw that the chapel was a respectable two thirds full, a congregation disproportionately made up of women, attributable possibly to his mother's lifelong commitment to the feminist cause. He could tell those who'd known her well: they were the ones dressed for a picnic in the park.

'Anyone else you recognise?' Anna asked him.

'Not a soul.'

There was to be no wake back at the house. His mother had made no stipulation about it in her will, and to Mariner it seemed pointless to invite a group of total strangers to join him in mourning a woman he hardly knew. But he did formally greet people as they left the chapel.

Most of the mourners turned out to be friends of his mother's from Leamington, but then came the encounter that he'd been praying for: a large woman dressed in flowing pink and turquoise, her grey unruly hair loosely pinned back. She smiled. 'You've changed a bit since we last met,' she said. 'I'm Maggie Devlin. I used to sit for you when you were a baby.'

Mariner's heart thumped against his rib cage. 'We're going for a drink,' he said, with astonishing calm. 'Would you like to join us?'

He was in for a disappointment. Maggie had indeed known his mother from her London days, but was as mystified as he was about who his father might be. 'She kept that one close to her chest,' she told him over a gin and tonic in the garden of a nearby pub. 'Rose was a popular girl and nobody was really sure if she knew who the father of her baby was, though I was certain she was seeing someone for quite a while after you were born.'

334

'But she didn't give any clue about who it might be?'

'None. She was good at secrets, your mother. There was just the one day–'

'What?'

'It might be nothing at all.'

'Please.'

'When you were born, Rose was living in a flat in Holborn. I came to see you just after you came home from the hospital, and as I arrived, there was a black car pulling away from the kerb. It caught my attention because it was a big car, especially for round there, like a limousine. It was only afterwards though that I began to wonder if it had anything to do with–'

'Did you get the licence plate?' asked Mariner automatically, before laughing with Maggie at his own stupidity. 'Of course not. Why would you?'

'And I doubt that it would be much help after all these years.'

'No.'

'I'm truly sorry that I can't tell you more. But if I should learn of anything that might help–'

'Thanks.' Mariner gave her his card.

The sun blasting in through the window woke Tony Knox. He had a throbbing headache and a raging thirst again, even though he thought he'd been pretty moderate with the booze last night. He glanced over at the clock. Bugger! Twenty past eleven. He should have been at work hours ago. For a moment he debated whether to pull a sickie, but remembered where Mariner had gone today. It would be good to have something for the

335

boss when he got back. Knox made himself get out of bed and into the shower.

Everyone at Granville Lane was either out or preoccupied, so no one noticed his late arrival. Now he was here he couldn't think of anything purposeful to do. While he considered that, unable to resist the urge, he tucked himself away in a corner of the office and logged on to the old friends website again. But before clicking on to Stephen Lamb's name he checked himself. He'd spent hours staring at that message. It wasn't going to change anything. Before he clicked his way out of the website, a further thought occurred: would Shaun Pryce go for something like this? Of course he would, the self-serving little git. If Pryce was keen to publicise himself, one group he'd really want to know would be old schoolfriends, particularly as he'd enjoyed some modest success. He was bound to want to capitalise on that. And what else might he give away? His exploits with middle-aged housewives? There might be something to learn from Pryce's former classmates, too. He'd not a clue which schools Pryce had attended, of course, but it couldn't be that difficult to find out. His web page had indicated that he was a local lad.

All Knox had to do was systematically work through the secondary schools in the area. Right now, he couldn't think of a better way to keep himself occupied and Fiske off his back for the day. He'd start with Kingsmead and work his way out. Pryce would have left the school either in '87 or '89. For a moment, Knox was tempted to pick up the phone and make his life easier by asking

Shaun Pryce the direct question. He wouldn't need to know what it was about. But then he caught sight of the Complaints officer in the far side of the office, poring over Ricky Skeet's file and decided that he couldn't risk any more aggro. With a weary sigh, he began opening up the message envelopes beside each of the names. The computer was on a 'go slow' so it took for ever.

A pattern amongst the messages quickly emerged. The people who bothered to leave them. all had one thing in common: like Stephen Lamb, they all had shiny, successful lives. Invariably, the message started off with career details: *working as a stockbroker/lawyer/managing director for...* There was a distinct dearth of window cleaners, bin men and unemployed. This was always followed by a description of family life: *married with four children/wife Cordelia, children Dominic (10) and Pandora (8) etc.* Occasionally, someone was bold enough to admit to a second marriage, but even that came across as twice the achievement. Generally speaking, life's failures didn't draw attention to themselves. It was all sickeningly up-beat and did nothing to lift Knox's own blackening mood.

For a little light relief, Knox switched to reading the notice boards where former pupils could post their opinions on anything from their former schooldays. Usually it was the teachers who'd become the subject of perceived injustices and occasional downright victimisation, prompting outpourings of resentment and angst. This was more like it, Knox thought: bitterness to match his own. He was busy marvelling at the human capacity for blame when he almost overlooked a

337

name he'd seen before, more than once, in recent days. Bucking the trend, the attached messages indicated relative popularity. One described in great detail an elaborate April Fools' joke that had been admirably taken. But it was followed by a more cryptic note, posted by someone calling himself 'Stewey': *Goody Goodway: did he jump or was he pushed?* There was one response from a Derrick Farmer: *One of life's eternal mysteries. Gone but sadly missed.*

Knox stared at the screen trying to work out what, if anything, it could mean. The school was another local comprehensive where Goodway must have worked prior to teaching at Kingsmead. Running a search, he found Stewart 'Stewey' Blake on the list of leavers from ten years ago.

For the sake of having achieved something this afternoon, Knox e-mailed him, leaving his mobile number, hoping that 'Stewey' was in the habit of checking his in-box regularly. He waited a few minutes in case there was an instant e-mail reply, but then, unlike Knox, Blake would have better things to do on a sunny Saturday afternoon than spend it hunched over his computer. And it would probably turn out to be nothing. Sensationalism knitted out of a few shreds of circumstantial information: perfect Internet fodder. He looked around the office. Millie was at the Akrams', Charlie Glover out on a call; no one to enjoy a round of speculation with. He needed a drink. There was also no one to see him leave early, so he picked up his jacket and went.

On the way home, of its own volition, Knox's brain began composing his own message for the

338

reunion website: 'Wife has left me because of my womanising, I'm an embarrassment to my kids. Could have made DS or even DI, if I hadn't screwed a senior officer's wife.' What an epitaph.

Slamming shut his front door, the noise reverberated around the emptiness for seconds afterwards. He tried to imagine hearing that same sound every day for the next thirty years, destined to spend the rest of his life alone. He hurled his keys on to the hall table in frustration. What was the point? What was the fucking point?

After a couple of hours, the handful of people who'd come back with them for a drink had drifted away, leaving Mariner and Anna alone at the Coach and Horses. The guest beer was a very pleasing Adnams, and the garden was bathed in early evening sunshine, but Mariner couldn't shake off the gloom that had descended.

'Maybe you just have to accept this as one you can't solve,' said Anna, ever the pragmatist.

'I'll add it to all the others waiting for me back at the station.'

'It's not your fault,' Anna said.

'I can't believe that I'll never know.'

'Does it matter?'

'Right now, it feels like the only important thing, but I suppose that will pass.'

'It has before,' she reminded him. 'And, who knows, when you clear the house you may come across something that you've overlooked.'

Mariner shook his head. 'She was too careful.'

'Why do you think she kept it from you for so long?'

'Who knows? To begin with, I thought it was because of who he was. She liked to give the impression he was somebody important: someone whose reputation might have suffered if it was known that he'd fathered an illegitimate child. In the late 50s a child out of wedlock was still a big deal. But, later, I used to think that maybe she played on that because she thought it would make me feel better to know that he was someone special.'

'So it could have just been a bloke down the street.'

'It might help to explain why we moved away from London in such a hurry.'

'It's a hell of a secret to keep, isn't it? There's no one else you can think of who would know?'

'As Maggie said, Rose deliberately severed links with a lot of her friends when we moved from London. There may be somebody somewhere, but I wouldn't begin to know how to find out.'

'So maybe it's time to start looking forward instead of back.'

Mariner studied his pint for a moment. He had something to say. He just wasn't sure if now was the right time to say it. 'I regret what happened with Millie,' he said at last. 'Really regret it.'

She placed a hand over his. 'I know. And I'm not sure what gave me the right to be so annoyed about it. We've never had that kind of relationship.'

Mariner could almost feel Tony Knox sitting on his shoulder, urging him on. 'I wish we did,' he blurted out.

She wrinkled her nose, as if trying to make

sense of her own feelings. 'Yeah, me too.'

A horde of small children raced by behind them, shrieking with ear-piercing intensity. Mariner swallowed the rest of his pint. 'Let's go home.'

'Your place or mine?'

'Yours. Nobody can reach me there.'

Back at Mariner's house, the phone rang on, unanswered.

When Mariner woke the next morning, Anna was already up. He could hear her moving around and eventually she walked past the bedroom door, already dressed and laden with what looked like an entire jumble sale. It was ten past eight. Mariner propped himself on an elbow and picked up the mug of tea she'd left for him. Anna saw him. 'You all right?' she asked.

'Fine. You?' When she nodded he said: 'Come back to bed.'

She was unsure.

'Half an hour, that's all.'

'And then you'll help me?'

'Yes.'

'It's a deal.'

Standing in the shower a little later, Mariner had a strange feeling. It puzzled him until suddenly he recognised it as contentment. Weird.

'Shall I come with you?' he asked when they'd loaded up her car.

'It's up to you. I'll have to man the stall for a couple of hours,' she warned him. 'I can't do anything about that.'

'I wouldn't want you to.'

341

Bournville Festival was an anachronistic affair dating back to 1902, at a time long before the 'village' had been greedily swallowed up by the suburbs of the spreading city. Although the surroundings had changed, it remained a real village-style event, held on the vast green playing fields fronting the chocolate factory that were for the rest of the year given over to cricket, football or bowls, depending on the season. Alongside the small funfair, exhibition tents, stalls and games had been erected around a small arena, the centre of which was dominated by a traditional maypole wrapped in bright red and yellow ribbons. At the far end of the grounds, an area had been cordoned off for the pyrotechnic display that would end the celebrations late in the evening.

It took several journeys to transfer everything from Anna's car to where the stall was being set up. Here, inevitably, Mariner came face to face with Simon. If he'd expected to be let off lightly with a caricature of a mincing queen he was going to be unlucky. Simon was bronzed, muscular and macho, and Mariner found it hard to believe that what Anna had said was true. He saw her watching him.

'It's not always the ones you expect,' she said.

'No.'

Anna was going to be busy arranging prizes until the festival opened and there were already enough volunteers on hand who seemed to know what they were doing. Mariner felt like a spare part, so he wandered off to see what else was on offer. There were stalls affiliated to every local organisation imaginable. Even the conservation group was represented, he noticed, seeing Eric Dwyer lurking behind a table of soft toys, wooden carved artefacts and the ubiquitous mugs, trying to encourage new recruits to the project.

Even though the festival wouldn't be officially open for another half hour, people were pouring in. At one end of the field was the West Midlands police trailer. Recognising Keith Watson from the OCU, Mariner made for the home security van. In among the advice posters on home security was a display with photographs of Ricky and Yasmin, appealing again for any information anyone might have. Now that the heat was going out of the investigations it was essential to take any opportunities to maintain the profile of the cases and keep the publicity going, but at the same time, even to Mariner, it felt gruesome and out of keeping with the atmosphere of the rest of the event. Unsurprisingly, few people were giving the display much attention. Mariner spent several minutes chatting to Watson before heading towards the exhibitions tent.

Inside the marquee it was bright and oppressive, with the smell of warm canvas on grass that took Mariner back to those childhood camping expeditions. Long trestle tables were covered with pristine white cloths and a series of displays that reflected every creative pastime open to man: everything from home-made cakes, flower arrangements and jam, to prize-winning pumpkins and marrows. There were art competitions for children and adults for which certificates would be awarded later that afternoon for different categories and age groups. The adults' theme was

343

'Reflections of Birmingham' and the one that most appealed to Mariner's taste was literally that: an impressive pen-and-ink sketch of a bank of trees at sunset, mirrored on to what Mariner guessed was somewhere along one of the city's canals. The view was familiar, not dissimilar to the one from his back door.

'Inspector, I didn't know you lived locally.' It was the artist himself who approached Mariner.

'My partner does,' said Mariner, thinking that it was the first time he'd ever referred to Anna that way. 'And I had no idea that you were so gifted. Congratulations, Mr Goodway, it's a superb drawing.'

'Thank you. I'm a bit rusty these days, but suddenly I find myself with some empty evenings to fill. Art can be very therapeutic. Helps to take my mind off things.'

'Of course.' An unwelcome reminder to Mariner that there was still unfinished business. 'Good luck with the competition.'

'Thank you.'

An announcement over the PA system heralded the opening ceremony, and Mariner moved outside again in time for the arrival of the festival queen, attended by her flower girls, all of whom were selected from children born on the Cadbury estate. Mariner was swept along with the crowds towards the main arena where the maypole dancing would begin. Judging by the number of video cameras trained on the dancing, each child had a minimum of two sets of proud parents and grandparents there. Scanning the crowd, Mariner spotted another familiar face. It took him a moment or two to place Andy Pritchard, especially as today his Ranger's uniform had been replaced by jeans and T-shirt.

He was reaching up to position a digital camera and Mariner wondered if he had a daughter among the dancers, though he seemed to remember Pritchard as a single man. Perhaps a niece then, or goddaughter. At that moment, Pritchard glanced up and saw Mariner watching him. Mariner smiled and nodded, but Pritchard didn't reciprocate. Instead, lowering the camera, he turned and began walking away from Mariner, into the crowd. Purely from curiosity, Mariner followed, just to see what he would do, and was interested to note that Pritchard quickened his pace. There were a number of possible explanations. The simplest was that the recognition hadn't been mutual, or perhaps he just didn't feel like talking. Being a policeman could sometimes have that effect on people. Mariner gave it up.

Tired of the crowds, he sought refreshment in the beer tent, but after standing in a motionless queue for ten minutes he abandoned that idea and decided to go and find a pub. Being on the Bournville trust, Quaker and dry, the nearest was going to be a drive away. The incident with Andy Pritchard was niggling at him, too. The more he thought about it, the more he thought Pritchard's behaviour odd. He glanced over to where the Manor Park stall was. Anna was in her element, hidden somewhere behind a heaving mass of people. She wouldn't miss him for an hour or so.

345

Chapter Nineteen

Mariner's first stop was Granville Lane. 'Tony Knox in today?' Mariner asked the duty sergeant.

'He was here earlier, but the miserable sod's done us all a favour and gone home,' was the terse reply.

Up in CID, it didn't take Mariner long to find what he was looking for, though: the information Knox had followed up on the indecent exposures. After plotting the incidents on a map, Knox had rightly identified the pattern as being access to railway stations, but when he looked closely, Mariner found another, more subtle pattern. Each of the attacks had also occurred close to a council park or open space: not on it, but close by. Andy Pritchard used his bike to get around, and what better way of covering bigger distances across the city with a bike than on the train?

Mariner switched on his computer. While he was waiting for it to boot up, he sorted through the phone messages in his in-tray. One was an urgent phone message to contact the forensic service. Mariner called back. Most of the scientists were off for the weekend, but the technician on duty was expecting Mariner's call.

'The gaffer thought you might want to know that we've identified the type of wire that was used to strangle Yasmin Akram. It's a kind of annealed wire, coated with a chemical rust inhibitor.'

346

'Would it have a plastic coating?'

'Wouldn't need it.'

'So not an electrical wire,' said Mariner, disappointed.

'Electrical wire isn't normally exposed like that,' the technician told him. 'It's a fairly soft wire, easily pliable but strong enough to withstand a powerful force.' He sounded as if he was reading from notes.

'Any idea what it would be used for?'

'The clue to that may be in the other substance we found at the joint where the wire had been twisted. In the crook there was a tiny residue of claydium.'

'Which is what?'

'A type of nylon-reinforced clay. Specifically used for modelling. Add that to the wire and I'd say you were looking for someone who's a modelling enthusiast.'

Mariner thought about Pritchard. He could imagine him with his Airfix planes or battalions of model soldiers. Ringing off, he ran a check on Andy Pritchard, but no criminal record appeared and he had no details on the database. Mariner thought about the man. How would he fare with women? Probably not that well. He wasn't particularly good looking, the skin problem had seen to that. Helen Greenwood had mentioned the flasher's complexion. Sunburnt, she'd said. Or could it have been acne? The way he'd looked at Yasmin's partly clothed body had seemed a little off-kilter too. And why had he taken so long to phone it in? What had he been doing in the forty minutes after he found Yasmin's body?

Suddenly, Mariner remembered Croghan's remark about Yasmin's missing underwear. Had it been removed at the time Yasmin was killed or afterwards? Because Pritchard had discovered the body long after Yasmin disappeared, and had no apparent connection with the disappearance, they hadn't thought about checking his alibi. Yasmin's body was discovered in an obscure area of the park. What had prompted Pritchard to even look there? And, most importantly, where had Andy Pritchard been on the afternoon of Tuesday July the third? Mariner wondered what Tony Knox was up to today. He couldn't imagine that it was anything much. Drinking himself into a stupor, probably. The man needed saving from himself.

Mariner rang the doorbell at Knox's house several times and then hammered on the door a couple of times. There was no response. He peered in the window. The place was still a tip. Christ, Knox was hopeless on his own. He went round to the back of the house. The garden was empty and, despite the growing heat, the house still shut up. He peered in through the patio doors and a chill ran through him.

Tony Knox was slumped lifelessly in an armchair. Mariner could see the bottle of spirits on the floor beside him and lying on the sofa within arm's reach, another small, brown bottle. For several moments Mariner's mind raced back over Knox's behaviour during the past few weeks: the mood swings and the pent-up anger, with that unprecedented reluctance to talk about anything, until his recent shame-faced revelation. Putting it all together with the scene before him, it came to one unspeakable conclusion. He banged on the window again. Nothing. Being a policeman the house was like Fort Knox. How appropriate was that? The back door was the flimsiest and, in the end, Mariner smashed the glass to get in. He rushed in on Knox who hadn't moved a muscle. This wasn't good.

'Tony!' Mariner shook him, slapping his cheek with more force than he'd intended. Knox jolted back to life with a start.

'What? What the fuck's going on?' He slurred.

Mariner sat back on his heels, weak with relief. 'Nothing, I thought– Nothing. It doesn't matter.' He'd explain the kitchen window later. His gaze skimmed the brown, stubby beer bottle on the sofa and after a split-second delay, Knox's face cracked into a smile.

'You thought I'd topped myself, didn't you?'

Mariner said nothing.

'I didn't know you cared, boss.'

'Piss off,' said Mariner.

'Listen, if I take that way out it won't be quietly in my own living room. It will be off the roof of the Hyatt with the TV cameras rolling. And you'll be among the first to know. Anyway, where the hell have you been? I've been trying to contact you.'

'I was at Anna's last night.'

Knox raised an eyebrow. 'You talked?'

'We talked.'

'About fucking time. Anyway, I think I've found something.'

'Me, too.'

'Really?' Knox looked disappointed, but he listened patiently while Mariner ran through what he'd got. 'Pritchard sounds like he could be our flasher, but did he kill Yasmin?' he said, when Mariner had finished.

'He had every reason to be in the area. The park is just across the road from the reservoir. And he's definitely a bit odd.'

'It doesn't make him a killer.'

He was right. 'OK, so what have you got?'

'Come and have a look.' Knox took him back up to the little office and on to the "old friends" website.

'Is this to do with Theresa?'

'Not exactly.' He logged back on to the website to show Mariner the original message. Mariner was doubtful. 'It's not much.'

'No. But then I started thinking: what would make a good teacher resign or get the sack?'

'Stealing? Embezzling the school fund?'

'Or having the wrong kind of relationship with the students.'

'Goodway doesn't fit the usual profile. He's got three kids of his own. Happily married man.'

'How happy, though? Barbara Kincaid was pretty scathing to Shaun Pryce about her love life, which might indicate that her husband has other preferences.'

Mariner thought back to his visit to Brian Goodway's home. 'He made some comment about how young and glamorous Barbara *had been* when he met her. I thought then it seemed an odd way of putting it.'

'Maybe "young" is the operative. And if he went off her as she got older, it might have left both of them looking elsewhere for gratification. He gets his from ogling the kids at school–'

'–and along comes Shaun Pryce, for her.'

'He could easily have been lying about his relationship with her. Which makes me wonder about what really happened to Barbara Kincaid?'

'We've no reason to believe she was murdered,' Mariner pointed out.

'It was a sudden, unexplained death.'

'The suicide verdict is unlikely to be challenged. She was taking powerful anti-depressant medication, and her GP at the time has confirmed that she was under a lot of strain.'

'Great cover for Goodway if he's found out that she's having an affair and decided to off her.'

'You've been watching too much crappy TV. Where would Yasmin come into all this?'

'She could have seen Pryce with Barbara Kincaid and grassed on them to Goodway.'

'But it must have all erupted months ago, so why leave it until now to do anything about Yasmin?'

Knox couldn't provide the answer, but luckily for him his phone trilled, temporarily letting him off the hook. He put it to his ear. 'Great. Thanks for getting back to me. Blake,' he hissed, over his hand, before embarking on a series of monosyllabic responses that left Mariner frustratingly in the dark about what they were discussing. Ending the call, Knox was smug and self-satisfied.

'We're on the right track all right,' he said. 'Goodway's departure from St Martin's was

351

sudden and unexpected. No official explanation was given, but rumour had it that he'd invited a sixth former to model privately for him, very privately. One thing led to another, until the kid blew the whistle on him. It didn't go down too well with the parents.'

'Christ.'

'Perhaps, with his wife safely out of the way, Goodway offered Yasmin the same opportunity.'

'And she threatened to tell someone. We need to ask Brian Goodway a few more questions.'

'Let's hope he's at home.'

'He isn't. He's at the Bournville Festival. He may be up for a prize. He's– Christ, the picture.'

'What picture?'

But Mariner shook his head. 'Goodway will be occupied all afternoon. Let's take advantage of that and pay a visit to his house. I just need to do something else first.'

'What about Andy Pritchard?' said Knox.

'I agree with you. Pritchard is small fry. He's up to something, but he can wait.'

Knox waited in the car at Granville Lane while Mariner went in and picked up a Polaroid camera. After that, their first stop was the reservoir, Knox following like an obedient hound at the heels of its master. They walked round to the patch of crushed-down grass that Shaun Pryce frequented and Mariner looked out across the water. It was as he'd thought. Moving in an arc of 180 degrees, he began taking snaps.

'SOCO have already got all this,' said Knox. 'Now might not be the right time to supplement your photo album.'

'Call it a comparative study,' was all that Mariner would say.

From there they went to Brian Goodway's house. The door was answered by a white-haired, elderly lady; Goodway's mother, and as Mariner had hoped, it seemed she was alone in the house.

'Do you think we could come in, Mrs Goodway?' Mariner asked, walking past her before she had time to protest.

'Is this about Barbara?'

'There are just a couple of things we wanted to look at again. We won't take up much of your time,' he assured her.

'Can I make you a cup of tea?'

'That would be lovely,' said Mariner. And keep her out of their hair for a few minutes. The house was three floors of outsized rooms. This might take a while. 'We're looking for the wire and the modelling clay and anything else that might help,' he reminded Knox.

Mrs Goodway was back sooner than he expected, brandishing the same mug he'd been given before: a well-worn version of those on Eric Dwyer's stall.

'Does your son belong to the conservation group?' Mariner asked, wondering if she'd even know.

'He used to, but I don't think he's been for a long time.'

Climbing the stairs, Mariner brushed past pictures hanging on the wall. One in particular stood out. It was almost identical to the one he'd seen this morning in the festival exhibition. At a different time of year, with no leaves on the trees

353

and more rain in the lake, it was an exact copy of the view in Goodway's picture.

'Tony.'

Knox came and peered over his shoulder. 'What have you got?'

'This drawing is almost exactly the same as the pen-and-ink Brian Goodway has entered for the festival competition.'

'So? It's a view.'

Mariner took the Polaroid snaps out of his pocket and held one of them beside the sketch. 'See any similarities?'

'Christ.'

'Strip the trees of their leaves and they're exactly the same. When I came to talk to Goodway after his wife's body was found, he denied even knowing about the reservoir's existence.'

'Maybe he sketched it from a photograph.'

'So who took the photograph? His wife, Shaun Pryce or him? I think Brian Goodway is very familiar with the reservoir. He was probably spying on his wife. Not that it proves anything, naturally.'

Knox shrugged. 'So we keep looking.'

They went from room to room: opening drawers, scrutinising cupboards, searching under furniture, but found nothing.

'Maybe he does all his art work at school,' said Knox.

'There must be something. He told me this afternoon that he paints in his spare time. Where does he do it?' Goodway's mother was hovering in the doorway.

'Does your son have a studio or a workshop where he does his art work?'

354

'Yes, it's up in the roof. You have to open the hatch and pull down the ladder–'

Mariner and Knox were already vaulting the stairs. 'He doesn't really like anyone going up there!' she called after them uncertainly.

'I'll bet he doesn't.'

Though basic, the loft had indeed been converted into a fully equipped artist's studio. Two skylights provided the required natural light. The down side was the lack of evidence that any sculpting went on here: there were only easels and drawing and painting materials; everything strictly two-dimensional. They were not going to find what was used to strangle Yasmin here.

A pile of larger drawings were stacked on end in one corner. Absently, Mariner began to sort through them, unsure of what he was looking for. Until he found it. 'Look at this.'

Knox came and looked over his shoulder. 'Jesus Christ.'

'Actually, Shaun Pryce,' Mariner corrected him. 'This looks like some pretty close-range spying.' The pictures of Pryce were full-length pencil sketches, this time revealing his face, and beautifully drawn. He was also completely naked and in a considerable state of arousal. 'So that's why women throw themselves at him,' remarked Knox.

'And not just women,' added Mariner, as the final piece fell into place. 'We've been barking up the wrong tree altogether.'

A strident female voice rang out from below. 'Who is it, Gran? What's going on?' Chloe Goodway was home for the weekend.

'It's the police,' they heard Mrs Goodway say.

355

'What are they doing here?'

'I'd better go and explain,' said Mariner, starting down the ladder.

But Chloe wasn't in the mood to wait for explanations. 'You shouldn't have let them in, Gran. They can't just come barging–'

'But they're policemen, darling. I expect they're going to help us find out what happened to Mummy.'

'They know what happened to Mum,' Mariner heard as he descended the last flight of stairs. 'I'm going to call Dad.'

'Miss Goodway, if you could just wait!' Mariner took the last stairs two at a time, but he wasn't fast enough.

'Dad? It's Chloe. The police are here. They're up in your studio. What's going on?'

Too late, Mariner snatched the phone from her. 'I really wish you hadn't done that.'

The girl was unrepentant. 'What are you doing here? We haven't seen a search warrant. You have no right–' But Knox was hard on Mariner's heels, and leaving the girl ranting behind them, they ran out to the car and jumped in. As Knox drove at breakneck speed, Mariner called for an area car to come and keep an eye on Goodway's house, then called ahead to Watson to detain Goodway in the exhibition tent at the festival. They arrived, breathless, to find Watson waiting helplessly.

'I missed him. He'd already gone. One of the stewards saw him leave about ten minutes ago.'

'Let's get out a description of him and his car.'

The car was easy. As it turned out, it was still sitting less than five hundred yards from where they stood, left where Brian Goodway had parked it that morning, in front of the row of shops. One of the shop assistants had a girl at the school and had seen Goodway come back to his car and retrieve something from the boot.

'He knows we'd be able to trace the car,' said Mariner. 'But if he's gone on public transport we don't stand a chance.' He looked across at the steady stream of traffic on the ring road. The festival grounds were at the centre of a network served by the railway station at the back of the factory works and a major bus route to the front and sides.

Knox was more optimistic. 'He won't get far. It may take a while, but somebody, somewhere will recognise him.' All they could do was wait, but waiting wasn't Mariner's forte.

'We never found that wire,' said Knox, suddenly. 'Is it worth checking his classroom?'

The school seemed a desolate place without the noisy bustle of hundreds of students. Today, even the caretaker's family had abandoned their house on the site to go to the festival. Parking outside the locked reception area, they walked round to the side of the building and found the door to Brian Goodway's classroom swinging open.

'He must have his own key,' said Knox, but any hope they might have felt was short-lived. The classroom and those around it were completely devoid of life. If he had been here, Goodway had long since gone. The classroom was as much a mess as it had been last time Mariner was here, the forms of half-finished sculptures dotted about.

'He's left us plenty of modelling clay and wire,'

357

said Knox, bagging up samples. 'So why was he here?'

'There's Lily's tan-coloured suit,' said Mariner, seeing the pristine brown overalls hanging on the back of the door. 'Or, at least, the next generation of clean replacements.' It was then that the smell drifted in on the air: the faint, slightly acrid smell of burning. 'Christ. That's what he's here for.'

Following the smell, they ran round to the rear of the building where they found Goodway standing beside the giant pig bins, black smoke billowing from the nearest.

'What are you doing, Brian?'

Goodway reeled round, shocked to see them. 'It's all right, you don't need to tell me,' Mariner continued calmly. 'I know what you're burning, and I know why. Burning won't get rid of all the evidence. Even if the fabric is charred we can still get DNA. We'll still find Ricky Skeet's blood on those overalls, won't we?'

'And you've given us plenty of circumstantial evidence,' added Knox, 'the pictures of Shaun Pryce and the reservoir; the wire you used to strangle Yasmin.' Goodway's eyes widened.

'There might be a way out of this mess, Brian,' Mariner soothed. 'Why don't you tell us all about it?'

Goodway turned away, wringing his hands. 'I've nothing to say to you.'

'Why don't we start with St Martin's,' Mariner said, ignoring him.

Goodway couldn't help himself. 'Nothing happened at St Martin's,' he said.

'So why did you leave in such a hurry? There

358

were rumours. No smoke without fire, eh, Brian. What was the boy's name?'

'Boy?' Knox was totally lost now.

'We were only partly on the right track,' Mariner told him. 'When Stewey Blake said Brian here had approached a sixth former, we both assumed it was a girl, because Brian here is a red-blooded, heterosexual family man. But that's not true, is it, Brian? It wasn't your wife who was having an affair with Shaun Pryce, it was you.'

Brian Goodway sank to the ground, burying his head in his hands. For several minutes he said nothing, then just as Mariner began to approach him, he spoke, his voice hoarse and trembling. 'I realised I was gay years ago,' he said. 'My whole marriage was a sham. I concealed it for years, satisfying myself with the occasional one-night stand. But it got more and more difficult, always feeling that I was living a lie and never being able to just be myself. I knew that eventually I'd have to give in to temptation.'

'Is that why you went to work at the girls' school, so that there couldn't be a repeat of St Martin's?'

'Nothing happened at St Martin's.'

'Only because the kid ratted on you.'

'I'd done nothing improper,' Goodway insisted. 'It was a conversation, a careless gesture, that's all. But I thought working at Kingsmead would be easier. It was. For a while everything was fine, under control. Then when I met Shaun that evening at our house, it was love at first sight. I couldn't get him out of my mind. Inviting him to model at school was just a way of seeing him again. I never dreamed that anything would come of it, especially when I saw him flirting so outrageously with the girls.'

'Afterwards, I took him out for a drink as a kind of thank you and that's when I discovered that he wasn't averse to male company, either. I couldn't believe my good fortune.'

'Pryce is gay?' Knox was incredulous.

'He's still in the closet,' said Mariner. 'Coming out would ruin his chances of being a leading man. You had an affair?' he asked Goodway.

'This time, I thought it was a proper relationship and I knew I'd have to tell Barbara. She'd been suffering from depression for a long time, partly because of the state of our marriage. I thought we'd be able to work out something civilised between us. But when I told her, she was devastated, starting talking about suicide. Then, suddenly, she announced that she was going to tell the children. I couldn't let her do that. Not yet. I wasn't ready. So one night when she went out I followed her. She went down to the reservoir. It was somewhere we used to go together, years ago. I would sketch and she would enjoy the peace and quiet.'

'Not that night, though.'

'I caught up with her on the wooden bridge. I tried to reason with her, but she wouldn't listen. She said that I'd humiliated her and ruined her life and that now she would ruin me. In some strange way I even think she was jealous.'

'She'd made a pass at Pryce. Did you know that?'

Goodway snorted. 'No.'

'So you tipped her into the river.'

'It was an accident. I had her by the shoulders, I was begging her not to tell the children. She just laughed at me. I pushed her–' he frowned '–harder than I thought, the railings gave way and she fell. I went down to help her but knew straight away that she was dead. I was going to drag her out on to the bank and go for help, but then I thought about how it would look. Then I realised that the easiest thing was the drainage tunnel. We'd had a lot of rain and it just carried her down. It was as if it was meant to be.'

'And Yasmin?'

'She was a lovely girl, truly talented. She flirted a little with Shaun but I knew it was harmless.'

'So what, then?'

'She saw us together. Shaun and me. While the weather has been so warm Shaun persuaded me to meet him at the reservoir. I'd introduced him to it when he'd said he needed somewhere private to sunbathe. He talked me into going with him after school. It was exciting.'

'So you were there on that Monday when Yasmin walked past.'

'She'd been to see that boy, Everett, and was taking a shortcut through the reservoir back to the station. The next morning she came to tell me. She said, "You're a queer, aren't you? I saw you with Shaun. It's disgusting." Actually, I think she was quite shocked and upset herself, but she'd come to find out what I'd do to stop her telling anyone. But then I guessed that she was meeting Everett and we came to a tit for tat arrangement:

361

I'd say nothing about Lewis if she would forget Shaun.'

'Cosy,' said Knox.

'I knew it wouldn't last, though. Everett was bound to let her down and then I'd never be able to trust the little bitch to keep her mouth shut. If she let it out I'd be ruined.'

This was what Mariner didn't understand. 'What you and Pryce were doing is hardly illegal. You're both consenting adults.'

'There was my reputation though, the reputation of the school. I'd been lucky at St Martin's. It was the word of a young, impressionable boy against that of, as you put it, a heterosexual family man; the interpretation of a conversation. The head believed me and I was able to resign with dignity and take up another post, my record unblemished. If my sexuality became public knowledge now, all that was bound to be dragged up again. Besides, I have my children and my mother to think of. What would it do to them? I couldn't bear it.'

'So what did you do?'

'I started checking Yasmin's phone during lessons. I don't know what I hoped to find, I suppose knowing she was seeing Everett against her parents' wishes I thought there might be something more incriminating that I could use to buy her silence. When I saw the message from Everett cancelling their meeting at the reservoir, I knew that was my chance.'

'Chance to do what?'

'Talk to her. During the lesson I took her travel pass, and before I left I dropped it on the classroom floor, knowing that she'd have to come back for it and giving me time to get there ahead of her.'

'And what happened?'

'When she got there I was waiting on the bridge. I just wanted to talk to her, but she told me there was nothing to say. Before I knew it she was lying at my feet, dead.'

'Do you always carry sculpting wire around with you?'

'I had it … just in case.'

'In case of what?'

'I don't know.'

'And the brown overalls?' He had no answer.

'And what about Ricky Skeet?'

'I dragged Yasmin down to the drainage tunnel. The water hadn't released but I knew it would within a matter of an hour or so–'

'And take Yasmin down with your wife.'

'But when I climbed back on to the bridge, this boy just rushed at me from nowhere, shouting and screaming that he'd seen what I'd done. He started hitting me with this chunk of brick, but it slipped out of his hand, so I grabbed it and hit him over the head. He fell, but I had to be sure so I hit him again and then I found that I couldn't stop. I kept hitting him over and over.'

'Why didn't you dispose of Ricky's body in the same way as the others?'

'I was going to, but there was so much blood. The stream flows down into the park: I thought someone might see it. And also there would be two bodies in the tunnel already, a third may have caused some kind of blockage that would

363

have drawn attention. I needed to think.'

'So you just dragged him into the long grass and left him?'

'Something made me look up. I thought I saw someone in the window of the nursing home. I needed to get away. I was going to come back later, after dark to move it, but when I came back he had gone. I looked around a bit but there was no sign of him, so then I thought perhaps I hadn't killed him after all.'

'Weren't you worried that he might turn up somewhere and report what he'd seen?'

'Of course I was. I even phoned round the hospitals to ask if an injured boy had been brought in. There hadn't, so there was nothing else I could do.'

Mariner remembered how strung out Goodway had seemed on that first meeting. He must have been beside himself. 'And you didn't know that Yasmin had dropped her phone.'

'No.'

'It must have been a shock when that turned up. If it hadn't been for that, our search would never have switched to the reservoir.'

While they'd been talking, the light had faded fast. In the gloom Mariner moved towards Goodway. 'Come on,' he said. 'Let's get all this down on paper.' But as he moved forward he saw the glint of something in Goodway's hand, the razor thin blade of a craft knife. 'Don't do any-thing–' he began, but before either of them could stop him Goodway drew back the knife and slashed violently at his wrist. Blood sprayed out in a wide, crimson arc as over their heads the first dazzling scatter burst of fireworks lit up the sky.

'Call an ambulance.' Mariner sprang forward and seized the knife, just as Goodway collapsed to the ground, groaning in pain.

Epilogue

DCI Jack Coleman stood surveying the building work going on two hundred feet below him when there was a knock on the door. 'Come.' It was DI Mariner. 'Tom.' Coleman moved forward and the men shook hands.

'Good to see you again, sir,' said Mariner.

'Seems you've done rather well without me these last few weeks: a high profile killer and a potential sex attacker arrested within twenty-four hours of each other.'

'We nearly lost Goodway.'

'But you didn't.'

'No. A dozen stitches and some pretty comprehensive dressings did the job, although I understand they've got him on twenty-four hour suicide watch at Winson Green while he's on remand.'

'And Andy Pritchard?'

'We found dozens of photographs at his place that he must have taken over years, students and young girls around parks in south Birmingham, and we can place him on or near the university campus at the time of each indecent exposure, along with a couple more in other parts of the city.'

'DCI Fiske seems to have left me with a lot to live up to.'

'With all due respect, sir, I'm not sure that Mr Fiske had much to do with either.'

'You got him off the hook with Complaints though, didn't you?'

'I'm sure he's enjoying his refresher course on Risk Assessment. It'll give him lots of opportunity to practise his vocabulary.'

'And Colleen Skeet's happy with that?'

'She's satisfied that we caught Ricky's killer, but I doubt Colleen will ever be happy again.'

'No. I'm sorry about your mother, too, Tom.'

'Yes, sir. Welcome back.'

The publishers hope that this book has given you enjoyable reading. Large Print Books are especially designed to be as easy to see and hold as possible. If you wish a complete list of our books please ask at your local library or write directly to:

Magna Large Print Books
Magna House, Long Preston,
Skipton, North Yorkshire.
BD23 4ND

This Large Print Book for the partially sighted, who cannot read normal print, is published under the auspices of

THE ULVERSCROFT FOUNDATION

NEATH PORT TALBOT LIBRARY
AND INFORMATION SERVICES

1		25		49		73	
2		26		50		74	
3		27		51		75	
4		28		52		76	
5		29		53		77	
6		30		54		78	
7	10/18	31		55		79	
8		32		56		80	
9		33		57		81	
10		34		58		82	
11		35		59		83	
12		36		60		84	
13		37		61		85	
14		38		62	11/14	86	
15		39		63		87	
16		40		64		88	
17		41		65		89	
18		42		66		90	
19		43		67		91	
20		44		68		92	
21		45		69		COMMUNITY SERVICES	
22		46		70			
23		47		71		NPT/111	
24		48		72			